Broken SCARS

J. M. WALKER

Editing: Joanne Thompson
Cover Design and Formatting: Just write. Creations
Photographer: FuriousFotog
Model: Alex Turner

ISBN: 978-1-989782-30-9

THIS BOOK CONTAINS DARK THEMES INCLUDING SEXUAL ASSAULT AND PAST CHILD ABUSE

Dedication

Melinda.
This book is for you.

Thank you

First off, thank you to my readers for your patience. This book has been six years in the making. Lucas Crane has been a side character since my debut novel, Break Me. I didn't know much about him then but now thatI've written his story and knowing that he's finally happy, it's like a sense of peace has washed over me. I wrote this story for NaNoWriMo last year. I lived and breathed this book and wrote it in a month. That's over 90k words in 30 days. And boy has it ever been a ride since.

Joanne Thompson: THANK YOU. Seriously, thank you thank you thankyou. I threw all of my issues, my Alpha/beta notes at you and you helpedme make this story so much better. I can't thank you enough for what you've done but know that I apprcciate you.

Angie, Christina, Jennifer and Melissa: Thank you for reading this story and giving me all of your feedback. I know how hard it can be, reading abook in the raw and providing tips and advice and so on. So I love and appreciate you!

My readers. My Jems. Just everyone! Thank you for being excited for thisstory. I can't wait to take you on this crazy journey. Lucas Crane has definitely earned his right to that happily ever after.

Melinda: You fell in love with Lucas right away. I even sent you the firstfew chapters of his super old story that was a hotmess. AND when I gave up and moved on, you still stood by me and waited patiently for him. I'm SO happy to be able to finally give him to you. Again.

Everyone else: Thank you for reading and for helping me spread theword on this book!!

Playlist

https://open.spotify.com/user/jmwlkr/playlist/4afQC6D4MJo6SYZ Ocx4lbt?si=eHvXutLrT-S7KomvFCQQhg

Prologue

LUCAS

SEARING AGONY RIPPED THROUGH me. My muscles shredded from my bones. Flesh ripped free, tearing and separating as the abuse only worsened.

It felt like I was being torn up by an animal.

My limbs trembled. My skin became damp with sweat.

I tried forcing the evil away, but it only made them hurt me more.

Blue eyes stared back at me. They were filled with pain, pity, and fear. So much damn fear. And then that smell. Those damn delicious roses. The scent was sweet. Almost like honey. They contradicted the atmosphere I was stuck in.

Blonde brows narrowed, those big round eyes pleading for me to stop putting up a fight.

I looked away as the screams shattered through me. As much as I did everything I could to fight off my attacker, my begging only heightened the violence laid upon my body.

"Please." My voice, so young, so innocent. One word was all it took. One syllable was all that was needed to make the pain worsen. I wasn't sure how that was even possible, but it was, and it happened.

"Next."

A sob left me as a new attack was bestowed upon my body. What felt like a lifetime later, the heavy weight on top of me lifted, taking all of my breath with it.

"You did well, Lucas."

The scent of roses suddenly became stronger, making my eyes roll into the back of my head.

"So fucking well."

I turned my head away from the voice. Tears no longer fell down my cheeks. My body no longer hurt. I was numb. Completely and utterly numb.

My mind was broken. I was gone. Far past the point of shattered. My soul, if I even had one anymore, hid and shied away in the corners. The Devil himself would look away at this depravity.

Gentle hands roamed over my body, soothing the ache that had been permanently etched into my soul. Salve was rubbed into my skin. My cuts were bandaged. I was cleaned, fed, and put back in my cage like the rest of them.

Animals. Pets. That's what we were. All because my adoptive parents had an addiction. For hunger. Power. Money. Control. It was all about control. Over people smaller than them. One slap was all it took to force most to their knees. But me? No, I was bigger. It took a lot more than a slap to force me to submit. And I paid for it. I always paid for it.

I vowed from that point on that I would do whatever I could to rid the world of monsters like them.

Even if I died trying.

WIND WHIPPED AROUND ME. I shivered. It was the middle of summer, but Mother Nature decided to play a trick on us and bring fall early. I hated this weather. Give me a beach any day over this. God, what I wouldn't give for a vacation.

Closing my coat tighter around me, I picked up my pace. I only lived a few blocks from the restaurant and thought it would be a good idea to walk. But clearly Mother Nature had other plans for me. I stopped, glanced around me, and realized rather quickly that I was lost. Great. This just made a shitty night even worse. My grandmother was going to kick my ass if I was late and didn't tell her. I couldn't believe this was happening.

So dumb, Lily. So dumb.

No, I wasn't dumb. He was the one who was dumb.

"We're here, having dinner. You don't really need to tell me that we have to talk." But we did. I couldn't continue seeing him. Killian Hayes had been convenient at a time when I was lonely. That was it.

"No." He smiled gently. *"We really need to talk."* His dark eyes flicked back and forth, searching my face. For what, I wasn't sure, but I could sense that he was about to lay a doozy on me.

"I…" He took a deep breath. *"I lo—"*

"Killian Hayes."

Both of us turned to a man coming toward us. He was stocky, with light brown hair and a day's worth of scruff on his strong jaw. He looked to be no older than Killian. *"Sorry to interrupt."* The man smiled down at me before glancing back at Killian. *"But I needed to say hi. It's been way too long."*

I let out a slow breath, thankful for the interruption. My relationship with Killian wasn't going anywhere anyway but this man showing up was clearly a sign. It saved me having to tell Killian that I didn't return his feelings.

"How's it going, Andrew?" Killian mumbled, not taking his eyes off of me.

"Good." Andrew's smile grew. *"How's your wife?"*

My eyes widened. *"You're married?"*

"Lily." Killian reached across the table for my hand.

"I gotta go."

"No, please." Killian shot up from the table. *"Let me explain."*

I had dumped cash on the table to pay for my meal and bolted. I didn't think the relationship was that serious, but I had never anticipated that he'd be married. Fucking, asshole. Killian hadn't been that good in bed anyway. I was more embarrassed than anything.

My grandma had warned me too. She only met him a handful of times but didn't like him. She also thought that he had been hiding something.

Yeah, a wife.

Not that she ever liked any of the guys I dated but this one was different. She warned me, but I didn't listen.

Letting out a frustrated sigh, I pulled my coat tighter around me. I had dressed nice for Killian. Something had been off with him, so I thought wearing something sexy would spark that moment we shared months ago when we bumped into each other at the library. I thought for sure he would have been a good guy. He was FBI after all and we met at the library. I was wrong. So very fucking wrong.

And now I was lost. I wasn't even sure where I was anymore. Not recognizing this part of the city, I breathed a sigh of relief when I saw a sign about a block away.

Crane's Ink.

Alright, I could live with that. Anything was better than being outside. Especially in this area. Hightailing it across the street, I was thankful I reached the door just as the rain started coming down even harder.

The door chimed, indicating my arrival. I pushed it closed, fighting against the wind that had picked up speed.

"Snap" by Slipknot played in the background. It was loud enough that I could feel the bass down to my bones but not too loud where a normal conversation couldn't be carried.

"That's some weather out there," a woman's voice said. "I haven't seen it this bad in quite a while."

A man grunted.

"It's supposed to be summer out." She sighed.

"Alright, you're all done, sweetheart."

My stomach tumbled at the smooth, deep voice. I turned around, finding a large man sitting on a stool beside a bed. A woman was sitting up, holding her shirt against her chest.

"How does it look?" she asked, meeting my gaze.

"Um…" I took a step toward them. "Wow." The tattoo was on her back. It was the image of a tree, partially covered with leaves.

"The leaves falling off the tree mark each month I've been sober," the woman explained.

I counted eight. "That's amazing. It really is beautiful," I murmured in awe.

"I'll clean you up," the man said.

I took a chance and looked at him then.

Even sitting, he was huge. With a buzzed head and an eye patch covering his right eye, he was dangerously beautiful.

Tattoos covered his thick forearms, inching down to the back of his hands. Even the side of his head I could see was tatted up.

His good eye met mine. He frowned, licking along his full bottom lip. He gave me a curt nod before going back to the woman sitting on the bed. He cleaned up the tattoo and placed a bandage on it before tapping her hip. "You're good to go, Lena."

"Thank you," she said, giving him a quick hug.

My stomach twisted. I looked away, not sure about these feelings rushing through me.

"Same time next month?" the man asked.

"Yes. If I make it that long." The woman, Lena, put on her shirt and headed to the counter.

"You say the same thing every month." The man went to the computer sitting on top of the counter. "You'll be fine."

"I'm glad you have faith in me."

"I always have faith in other people," he said. "Fifty."

She pulled out a wallet from her purse and handed him cash.

"Pleasure doing business as always." He winked.

She laughed. "See you later, Lucas." She walked up to me, smiled, and left the tattoo shop.

Lucas. God, even his name was sexy. I fought not to roll my eyes. I really needed to get it together.

"I guess I shouldn't loiter and probably buy something," I finally said, needing to break the unnerving silence.

Lucas grunted, stuffing the cash Lena had given him into an envelope and placed it in what I could only assume was a locked safe in a drawer. Because that's what I would have done.

"Do you sell jewelry?" This conversation was beginning to turn…odd. A man had never affected me the way this one was currently doing.

Lucas's good eye met mine. "You don't have to buy anything." He shut the cash register and came toward me. Crossing his arms under his broad chest, he stood beside me and stared out the window.

The scent of spice wafted into my nose. My core clenched, my palms becoming sweaty at the close contact. He smelled amazing. God, did he ever smell amazing.

"The weather might be like this for the next couple of hours," he said, pulling me from my dirty thoughts. "Is there anyone you want to call to let them know you're safe?"

Was I really safe? This man didn't scare me, but he was huge. He was a beast and I knew with one flick of his wrist, he could break me. A shiver tremored through me at the thought. But there was something in his gentle demeanor with the client that stood out with him. I was curious to find out more about this large man.

My gaze flicked to the clock hanging on the wall. "I'm good." I still had an hour before my grandma expected me home. If I was still at this place, I would call her then.

"Well…"

I looked up at him. "Lily." I stuck my hand out. "Lily Noel."

"It's nice to meet you, Lily Noel." He returned the handshake, slipping his fingers in mine. "Lucas Crane."

My breath caught in my throat. The longer time passed between us, the heavier the air became.

"Hmm…" His lips twitched and that was when I saw them. Scars. They were faint, but I noticed them. His brows narrowed, and he pulled away.

It was on the tip of my tongue to ask what had happened to him, but my grandmother taught me better than that. It would have been rude. Especially when I only just met the guy.

"Did you want a coffee?" Lucas asked, disappearing into another room off to the side and coming back a moment later with two steaming mugs. "It's just black."

"That's perfect." I took the coffee from him. "Thank you."

"You're welcome, Lily Pad."

I laughed. "Lily Pad?"

"It works." He smirked. "Doesn't it?"

"I guess so." My cheeks heated at the nickname. Oh, it worked alright. It worked really well.

(Lucas)

While I made another coffee for us both, I couldn't help but watch her take in my home. Even though this part of the place was my business, my apartment was on the second floor. I had lived here for years, so all of it was home to me.

Lily walked through every inch of the shop, taking in the pictures on the blood red walls.

"All of those images were drawn by me," I told her.

She paused, passing me a quick glance before looking back up at them. "They're beautiful."

I grunted. "Not many people think they're beautiful."

"They don't?" Lily came around the counter and jumped up onto it, swinging her legs back and forth. "Well I think they are."

My heart swelled at her compliment.

She fussed with her light brown curly hair and pulled it on top of her head into a bun. She had a smattering of freckles on her nose and cheeks. Her full red lips were plump. When she was done putting her hair up, she tightened her coat around her. The jacket fell past her knees, but I had a feeling most jackets would. She was a tiny little thing. But curvy. So damn curvy it made my mouth water.

My gaze popped back to her face.

Her bright green eyes met mine. "What?"

"Nothing." I cleared my throat and went back to making the coffee. I lived for the stuff, so I had made sure to have a little coffee area on the back counter. It was accessible whenever I needed a fix.

Once it finished brewing, I poured Lily a mug and handed it to her.

"Thank you, Lucas." She grabbed it from me and brought it up to her mouth. She took a sip, letting out a low moan that shot right to the tip of my dick.

Fuck me. I hadn't had this reaction over a woman in a long time. And when I did, it hadn't been often. I wasn't celibate, but it had been awhile just the same. Sex for an addict could be dangerous and lethal. Especially with the women I came across.

"I feel like I've heard of this place before," Lily said, interrupting the thoughts going through my head.

"Oh?" I leaned against the wall, taking a sip of my own coffee. Black, just like hers. A woman after my own cold, lifeless heart.

"Has this place been in the paper before?"

"Possibly." I shrugged. "I don't read the paper." There was enough shit going on in my head, I didn't need the terrors of the world adding to it.

"I think I've seen it. Not sure." Lily glanced out the window. "It looks like the storm's letting up."

I followed her gaze, noticing the skies clearing. Too bad. "I guess it is."

Lily placed her mug on the counter and jumped to the ground. "I should head home."

"You should." I reached out to push a strand of hair behind her ear that had fallen from the pile on top of her head but thought better of it.

She wrapped her coat tighter around her and headed to the door. "Thank you for the coffee, Lucas."

I nodded once, watching her leave my shop.

Drinking the rest of my coffee, I wondered what the hell had just happened. There was no way I could get caught up with a woman like her. She was innocent. Pure. And something that I did not need at the moment. If ever at all.

Cleaning up our mugs and the coffee station, I put everything away when my phone vibrated in my pocket. Fishing it out, I glanced at the small screen. There was someone at the back door. Checking the time, I was thankful that I had no other appointments for the rest of the night, so I turned off the Open sign and locked the door.

Shutting off the music pumping through the speakers mounted on the walls, I closed shop and headed to the back.

Making sure the security system was set in place and turned on, I went to greet my guest.

Opening the door, I leaned against the frame. "You do know it's rude to show up to someone's house without calling first, right?"

Lena pushed past me. "Whatever."

"What's going on? Is there something wrong with your new ink?" I asked her, closing the door and clicking the lock into place.

"What?" She scowled. "No. Not at all." She pulled off her jacket and placed it on the back of a chair sitting at my dining room table.

I walked back down the hall and waited.

Lena fidgeted. She pulled at her shirt, tucked it into her ripped jeans, pulling it free and repeating the movement.

"Hey." I closed the distance between us and grabbed her hands. "What's wrong? You were fine half an hour ago." I had known Lena for years after she came into my shop strung out on whatever her drug of choice was at the time. I got her clean and then she fell into the bottle.

"I didn't want to say anything earlier when that woman showed up but it's my parents. I love them but God." She blew out a slow breath and then another. "I need a drink."

"No. You don't." I kept her hand in mine and led her to the kitchen. "Have a bottle of water."

"I don't want water, Lucas. I want a drink. Alcohol. Drugs. Sex. Fuck." She pulled her hand free from mine and pushed me back.

"Don't." I gripped her shoulders. "Whatever is going through your head right now, stop it."

Her pupils dilated. "Please."

"No, Lena. We're friends. That's it." She had never made a pass at me before so that was how I knew she was desperate. But I meant what I said. We were just friends.

She pulled away from me, a lonely tear falling down her cheek. "I'm sorry."

"Don't be." I handed her the water before heading to my living room. "Let's watch a movie and talk."

"I hate fucking talking," she grumbled, joining me.

"Would you rather go to a meeting?" I countered. I had been her sponsor for the last two years, but she had been going to AA for the past five. She didn't have a lot of leaves on her tattoo because she kept having relapses. But this year had been different. She had eight tattoos and she was finally determined to get more. She would get there. But not by having sex with me.

"No." Lena sighed, slumping on the couch. She pulled her long black hair free from its elastic. "I'd rather talk to you."

"Tell me what happened." I lifted my knee onto the seat of the couch and gave her my full attention.

"Are we going to watch a movie?" she asked instead of answering me.

I turned on the TV. "There, a movie's on. Now talk to me."

"You know, sponsors aren't supposed to be so damn crabby."

"I'm the only sponsor who doesn't put up with your shit," I threw back at her. "Now talk."

"Fine." She huffed. "My parents are refusing to let me see my daughter."

"They do have full custody, don't they?"

"Yes." Lena picked at the paper wrapper on the water bottle. "I've been good, Lucas. I haven't had a drop since you started my tattoo eight months ago."

"What happened to make them not let you see her?" I knew her parents were controlling but Lena didn't talk about them much, so I didn't know any more than that.

"I showed up with a black eye," she mumbled.

"What?" My hackles rose. "Who the fuck hit you?"

"Who do you think, Lucas? The only man who always hits me." She jumped from the couch. "This was a week ago. I went over to my parents' place earlier tonight, thinking they had gotten over it, but they refused to let me see her because they don't want my daughter to see how much of a fuck up I am." Tears started rolling down her cheeks faster. "I'm trying and I'm failing."

"No." I pushed from the couch and wrapped her in my arms. "You're not failing."

"I just want to see my baby," she sobbed, her voice muffled by my shirt.

"I know, Lena." I held her against me. "I know."

(Lily)

Lucas. Lucas. L-U-C-A-S. Luuuuucas.

I rolled over in bed, covering my head with a pillow, trying to drown out the noise my brain was making.

Tattoos. Eye patch. Tattoos. Muscles. Tattoos. So many tattoos. I kept fantasizing and wondering how many he had. Or how much of him was covered. I never reacted this way to a man before. I usually saw them, decided then and there if I was attracted to them or not, and either went for it or I didn't. But this man…Lucas Crane…was a whole other level of man. One I had never dealt with before and it made me nervous and excited all at the same time.

I sat up, throwing my pillow on the floor. "Seriously, Lily." It wasn't like I had never seen a good-looking man before. No, I had just never seen one that looked quite like…Lucas.

It was pushing midnight but clearly, I couldn't sleep. Only just meeting Lucas a few hours ago, I couldn't get him out of my head. Literally.

Slipping out of bed, I headed out of my room and down the hall. A light in the living room was on. Was my grandma still up at this hour?

When I rounded the corner, I found her in her rocking chair, fast asleep. I smiled to myself, pulled the crocheted blanket off the back of the couch, and laid it on her lap.

Shutting off the lamp, I turned down the volume on the TV and went in search of a snack. Maybe reading the newspaper would help dull my brain enough that I could finally sleep.

Pulling the paper gently out of my grandmother's hand, I went into the kitchen and grabbed a box of chocolate chip cookies off the counter before heading back to my room.

Flicking on the light, I kicked the door closed and jumped onto my bed. "Alright, brain, let's shut you down for the night."

Flipping through page after page of the newspaper, I read every word and stuffed my face with half the box of cookies before I realized it was done. But I was still no closer to being tired than I was an hour ago.

I sighed, rolling over onto my stomach and pulling my laptop from beneath the bed and placed it in front of me.

I checked my social media accounts, email, read all the news sites I could think of, and was still wide awake. What the hell was wrong with me that I couldn't sleep?

Getting an idea, I decided to Google Lucas and his shop. Everything came back clean. Too clean. It was like the guy hadn't existed at all until ten years ago when his shop opened. When I couldn't find anything else, other than a basic website mentioning the services he offered, I dug a little deeper. Something was off, and curiosity got the better of me. I knew there was something else and that it wasn't just a simple tattoo parlor.

Cracking my knuckles, I entered the dark web and searched for him. I eventually came across his tattoo shop. Crane's Ink.

But there was no more information than what he had told me. Which was hardly anything at all.

"Alright, Lucas. Who are you?" After a few minutes, I had hacked into government records that were supposed to be sealed tight. Until I came along of course. But again, nothing was really out of the ordinary. Maybe it was just a simple tattoo parlor.

As soon as I was about to start reading more on him, a message popped up on my computer.

What the hell?

Who is this?

No username or anything? Interesting. I also wasn't stupid though. I logged out of everything, cleaned up my steps and shut down my computer. How could someone know I had hacked in? I had never been caught before.

My heart started racing. God that was a rush.

Putting my computer away before I got into further trouble, I rolled onto my back and stared up at the ceiling. Who the hell was Lucas Crane?

THE SCENT OF COFFEE woke me a few hours later. I must have finally fallen asleep. Rubbing the grit out of my eyes, I sat up. Remembering the unknown person who messaged me last night, I still wondered how they even contacted me. It wasn't like I left a trail. I was smart that way. I wasn't an expert and my hacking skills were hardly something to make a big deal over. But after teaching myself a thing or two about hacking, I knew how not to get caught. Until now.

"Lily, breakfast is ready, girl. Get your lazy ass out here."

I laughed, shaking my head and did as I was told. Making my way to the kitchen, I was greeted by the scent of eggs, bacon, and toast. And coffee. Much needed coffee.

"Hi, Grandma." I kissed her weathered cheek.

"Morning." She handed me a plate. "What time did you get home last night?"

"Just after eight because of the storm." I sat at the table, shoveling a forkful of food into my mouth.

"How was your date?" Grandma asked, placing a mug of coffee in front of me before sitting beside me.

I groaned. "Killian's married."

Grandma's eyes widened. "I was right!" she exclaimed. "I really enjoy being right."

I laughed. "Yeah, you were right."

"So, tell me more."

I took a breath and told her what had happened during my date.

"Did you give him a chance to explain?" she asked, raising a gray eyebrow. "And did you at least take the free meal?"

"I didn't, I paid for my own meal and stormed out of there. I felt like there was something strange about him, but I also thought that if we could get past it, things could have been good." Although, if the date had gone well, I wondered if I still would have ended up at Lucas's tattoo shop. Either way, I was twenty-six and single. Hell, I never even had a serious boyfriend before. I dated, had one-night stands but that was it. Nothing more.

"Well I'm glad he's out of your life, dear. You deserve better than that."

"I know, Grandma." We finished our breakfast in silence. When we were done, I put the plates in the dishwasher and poured myself another coffee.

"Plans for today?" she asked, taking a sip from her mug.

"Nothing really." It was Monday and a day off for me. But I found that I wanted to see Lucas again. Maybe I could get a tattoo or a piercing. Did he do piercings? The thought of him touching me sent a flutter of heat racing over me. I also wanted to know how the hell he found out I was doing research on him. If it was him who messaged me last night anyway. But I wasn't stupid. Everything inside of me told me to be leery. To be careful because if he had his information on the dark web, clearly, he had something to hide. Or he was into illegal shit.

"You met someone." Grandma placed her mug on the table in front of her and sat back.

"I have no idea what you're talking about." My cheeks burned.

"No?" She pointed a finger at me. "You're fidgeting, and your cheeks are flushed. Trust me, I know what that means."

"What does that mean?" I asked, averting her gaze.

"It means that you met someone."

I laughed, rubbing the back of my neck.

"Is he nice?"

"I think so." There was no point in denying it. My grandma was good and knew me well. Too well if you asked me.

"Well, bring him by," she said, picking up the newspaper off the table. "If things go well, let him stay and I'll make my specialty."

"I just met him, Grandma," I reminded her. Although, if I did bring him by and my grandmother liked him, maybe that would help curb my thoughts on if I should trust him or not.

Lily, you just met the guy. Trust isn't even an option at the moment.

I bit back an eye-roll at myself.

Grandma looked at me over the top of the paper and gave me a wink. "Your grandfather didn't like my cooking too much in the beginning. Said it was spicy. Well I showed him a spicy lasagna."

"You made it spicier, didn't you?" I asked, raising an eyebrow.

She gasped. "I would never do such a thing. I'm a good Christian girl."

I snorted, shaking my head.

"Anyway, once you get to know this boy better, bring him by. I'll tell you if he's a keeper or not."

"Alright, Grandma." I leaned down and kissed her cheek. "I will."

(Lucas)

Giggles sounded around me, grating on my every last nerve. I was half tempted to turn up the music to drown out the noise but I didn't think the little girls would appreciate my choice of music. When "A.D.I.D.A.S." by Korn hit the system, the girls stopped giggling. I could feel their judgmental stares burning into the side of my head, but I didn't listen to my music for them.

Go back to your tattoo choices, girls. I had shit to do.

I respected anyone who wanted to get a tattoo. I got it. I had hundreds of them. But when tweens showed up at my shop because they wanted to rebel by getting a tattoo of a butterfly on their tailbone, it annoyed the shit out of me.

Although I shouldn't judge, everyone started somewhere, these girls just irritated me. But I had a feeling it wasn't them. Even though I liked to convince myself otherwise. No, it was a certain woman that I couldn't get out of my head. Add to the fact that I found her snooping around in my shit. She must have been a hacker, since she broke through my firewalls as easily as she did. Or maybe it had been an accident? Nah. No one played around in the dark web because they were bored. I had to up my game. Or I could learn a thing or two from her. I had so many questions, but I also had no idea how to get in contact with her either.

Hacker, Lucas. You are a damn hacker.

Lily had me messed up, I forgot what my skills were. Fucking women.

"I think I want a flower," the one girl told her friend. "Maybe a lily."

My head shot up at that.

"No." The other girl who couldn't have been no older than sixteen, tapped her chin. "How about a rose? Or a skull? A rose coming out of the skull's eye?"

Now that I could do and proudly. The first girl grimaced. Of course she did.

"Um…ew. No. I want something pretty." She looked my way then. "Can you do pretty?" she asked, her eyes raking over me.

"If that's what you want, I can do it." As soon as those words left my mouth, the door chimed, revealing an older woman dressed in a red skirt and jacket suit set. Her blonde hair was perfectly wavy around her tanned and overly made up face.

"Girls, have you decided on something yet?" she asked, her gaze meeting mine. Something flashed in her deep blue eyes. She looked me over, her tongue sliding along her fake pout.

I grunted, shaking my head and went back to my crossword puzzle. Sorry, lady, you definitely don't do it for me.

While I had been with a lot of women and I usually didn't care what they were wearing, I didn't normally go for the fancy prissy women. The ones who were married but had assholes for husbands who would only fuck them to get off. I was all about pleasing my partners. It wasn't just for me. It was for both of us. But this woman? Standing at the door and looking at me like she wanted to break her pussy on my dick? No, thank you.

I went back to my crossword puzzle.

"Girls, either decide what you want to get, or we'll go somewhere else."

A red manicured fingernail came into view. It pushed a wad of cash in front of me. I looked up and was met with lust-filled eyes. Her mouth was plump, a red gloss coating the full lips.

Although women like her didn't do it for me, I was still a guy. A couple pumps of my dick and I could get hard enough to fuck her. There had been a time where I would have taken this woman to the back and made her beg for God to come save her. But that was another life and that would not be happening. Not today. Not tomorrow. No matter how much this woman hinted for it, she wasn't getting my dick.

"Make sure my daughter and her friend get the proper service they deserve." The woman pushed the cash closer, brushing her thumb over my tattooed hand. "Is there a Mrs—?"

"This is too much money." I nodded toward the girls, ignoring her advance. "If they get the tattoos they're wanting, it would be two-hundred for both since they're small." I pulled away from the counter and prepped the nearest tattooing station, the scent of the woman's overpriced perfume following me.

"Fine." She scowled. "Girls, I'll be in the car." The door chimed shortly after that.

I held back a laugh. "Alright, ladies. What'll it be?"

(Lily)

I stood outside Crane's Ink, not really sure why I was there in the first place. Something about meeting Lucas the night before, drew me to him. I was curious and I wanted to know how the hell he could figure out that I had hacked into his personal information. Not that I knew if it was him or not of course, but I needed to be sure. I was off from work today so I might as well put it to good use.

Deciding to get this over with, I entered the shop, the stupid chime on the door announcing my arrival.

Lucas was hunched over a young girl who was lying on her stomach on the bed. She had a pained look on her face while Lucas tattooed whatever it was she wanted on her body.

He lifted his head, looking over his shoulder at me. "Lily."

I swallowed hard as my name dripped off his tongue like honey. "Lucas."

His scarred lips twitched before he went back to work. A few minutes later, he leaned back. "Alright, you're done. I'll clean you up and you can go."

The girl sat up, blowing out a slow breath. "That didn't hurt at all," she said, although her face was pale.

Lucas rolled his eyes.

I snickered.

Once he cleaned her up, she left the shop with her friend, going on and on about their new tattoos and how badass they were.

"What did you tattoo on them? Flowers or butterflies?" I laughed.

"The one wanted a lily." He pulled the gloves off and threw them in a nearby trashcan. "And the other wanted a skull with a rose which I would have gladly done but her friend talked her out of it. So she got a Chinese symbol instead." He shook his head. "I tried telling her the symbol didn't mean what she thought it meant but she wouldn't listen to me. She said Google told her it was right. Yeah, because the internet is always right." He rolled his eyes.

"You knew what it meant?" I asked, shocked that he would even know such a thing.

"Yeah." Lucas stood from the stool and nodded. "What she wanted done didn't actually translate into anything. So she technically just has a bunch of lines on her body." He shrugged. "But who am I to judge?"

"You would think people would educate themselves first," I said, watching him.

"She Googled it. That's enough apparently." He grunted. "I tried telling her. Even her friend told her to listen to me, but she wanted it 'cause it was pretty."

"So, a lily, huh?"

He met my gaze, his mouth pulling up into a smirk. "Yeah."

"I like lilies," I told him.

"So do I." He winked.

I grinned. "Do you now?"

He chuckled coming toward me. "I do."

"They smell good too." I had to tilt my head back to meet his gaze. God, he was tall. So damn tall.

He smirked. "I bet they do."

"I don't think they would taste too good though." My brows narrowed.

A sly grin spread on his face. "I bet I know a lily that would taste good."

My stomach tumbled at the innuendo. "Interesting."

He glanced over my head, a deep frown settling between his dark brows.

I followed his gaze, looking out the window and found a woman sitting in a car, staring our way. "Is she a friend of yours?"

"No." Lucas headed behind the counter. "She's the mom of one of the girls I just tattooed."

"She wanted a little piece of the Lucas action?"

He laughed. "Something like that."

I walked to the counter, finding him working on the same crossword puzzle my grandmother was doing earlier. "You like crosswords?"

"I do." He picked up the pencil laying on the paper. "It's the only reason I get the paper anymore."

"Now that everything's online," I added.

"Exactly."

I leaned over the counter opposite him. "I can give you the answers," I offered, looking up at him then.

"Did you do this one already, Lily Pad?"

My body heated. God, that nickname. "No. My grandma was working on it this morning, but this is the first time I'm seeing it." I tapped the paper. "Eight across is voluptuous."

"What? Oh." He looked down at where my finger was pointing. "I guess it is." He wrote it in. "How did you find me?"

"What do you mean?" I knew what he meant but there was no way I was giving in that easily. I didn't know him. I may have been attracted to him, but I also wasn't stupid.

"Online. You cracked my firewalls. How?"

"Ten down is—"

"Lily," he barked.

I looked up, licking my lips. "What?"

His nostrils flared, his gaze following the swipe of my tongue as it slid across my bottom lip. "Answer the damn question," he demanded, his voice husky.

I leaned back, crossing my arms under my chest. "Ask me nicely."

His jaw clenched. "Lily."

I raised an eyebrow. "Ask me nicely, Lucas."

"Fuck." He inhaled a sharp breath. "How did you crack my firewalls?"

"That's not asking me nicely, but I really have no idea what you're talking about. I don't even know what firewalls are." Although the words leaving my mouth were all a lie, I didn't move my gaze from his.

He chuckled, rubbing the back of his neck. "You're good, Lily Pad. You're really good."

"What?" I batted my eyelashes innocently. "I really have no idea what you're talking about."

"Right." He went back to work on the crossword puzzle. "What are you doing here?" he asked a moment later.

"I came to say hi." I headed back to the door. "It was nice seeing you, Lucas." I didn't wait for him to respond and left the shop. I really had no idea what in the hell I was doing but either way, and maybe I was dumb for it but it was exciting. I enjoyed flirting with him and keeping him on his toes. I had been with countless men only to get hurt in the process. I refused to throw myself at them anymore so instead, I would make Lucas come crawling to me.

I had a feeling that I would eventually tell Lucas that I did in fact use my hacking skills to find out information on him, but I needed to know if I could trust him first.

A black SUV drove past me, slowed, turned around, and came back toward me.

My stomach twisted. Leaning against the wall, I crossed my arms under my chest and pretended to check out my nails.

The vehicle stopped in front of me, the door opening and closing a moment later. "Lily."

I dropped my hand, staring up at Killian. "What do you want?"

"I want to explain," he said, coming toward me.

I scoffed. "I don't want to hear it, Killian. You're married, and you were dating me. There's nothing to explain. It's over."

"Please, Lily," he pleaded. His gaze darted back and forth. "Let me try. I'm sorry. I'm sorry for hurting you. I never meant for that to happen."

I pushed away from the wall and went to walk past him when he stopped in front of me. I frowned. "Killian."

"I swear I didn't." He reached out for me and before I could dodge his touch, he wrapped his arms around me and pulled me against him. "I'm sorry, baby," he mumbled into the crook of my neck.

My heart started racing, my stomach tumbling at the desperation rolling off of him in waves. I tried pushing away from him, but his hold tightened.

"Please let me explain."

"Explain what, Killian? How you're married but still dated me? God, we had sex." Even though I didn't know about his wife, it still didn't make me feel any better.

His shoulders were slumped, bags had formed under his eyes. "I really didn't mean for that to happen."

I met his stare head on, crossing my arms under my chest. "You never meant to be married and fuck me at the same time?"

"What?" He scowled. "No, baby. Please." He cupped my cheek. "I am sorry."

In the beginning, I would have done anything for the attention he was currently giving me. But now, knowing that he was married and never told me, his apologies meant nothing.

I shoved out of his grip, heading back in the direction of Lucas's shop.

"I know where you live, Lily."

I stopped suddenly, glaring at him over my shoulder. "Are you threatening me?"

A dark shadow passed over Killian's face. He blew out a slow breath, rubbing the back of his neck. "Listen, I like you. I like this. I need you."

I laughed. "You sure as hell have a funny way of showing it, Killian." I went to walk away when I found Lucas coming toward us. "Lucas," I whispered.

"You threatening her?" he demanded, grabbing my upper arm and pulling me behind him.

"You need to mind your own business. Lily and I were just talking." Killian stared hard at Lucas, a deep frown settling between his brows.

Lucas peered down at me. "Did he threaten you?"

I looked between them both. Two men who came into my lives at very different times. I sighed. "No. It's fine." Even though it was a threat, I didn't need this man beating the shit out of Killian. Knowing how he was FBI and all, he would get off and Lucas would probably get thrown behind bars. I didn't need that on my conscience.

"Lily," Killian said gently.

"It's over," I told him and started walking away. This time he didn't follow.

"You good, Lily?" Lucas asked, coming up beside me.

"Yeah. Fine and fucking dandy," I mumbled.

"I don't have any appointments until this evening," Lucas said, stopping at the door to his shop. "Did you want to have a coffee? With me?"

"Really?" I asked, wondering what I was getting myself into but liking it just the same.

"Yeah." He rubbed the back of his neck, his cheeks reddening a tinge.

"Okay." I smiled up at him. "I would love to."

Three

LUCAS

WE WALKED BACK TO my shop in a comfortable silence. I wasn't sure who the fucker was that approached Lily but after she left, like a creeper, I watched her walk away and then I saw him. I had memorized his license plate and would search him later that night. Add to the fact that I was sure Lily could find out anything she wanted on the guy as well and we were set. She just wouldn't admit it, but I knew she was good with a computer. Hell, she found me with no issues.

Once we reached my shop, I opened the door for her and locked it up again after she stepped over the threshold. My next appointment wasn't for a few hours and I hardly got any walk-ins during the day so locking the door would hopefully help Lily feel better.

"You don't have to lock the door," Lily said, heading to the coffee machine I kept on the back counter. "He won't be back."

"Who is he?" I asked, joining her.

"Killian Hayes. FBI. Lethal and shady as fuck." She shrugged. "I only slept with him a few times and he's been on my ass ever since. And not in the sexy way either."

A hint of jealousy erupted through me. Well that was something I had never felt before. I barely knew her and if she was as good with computers as I thought she was, there was no way I could trust her. Not yet at least.

"He's a douche canoe but I can't seem to get rid of him." She sighed, pouring two cups of coffee before handing me one. "The sex wasn't even that good."

"I can get rid of him if you want." I took a sip of the steaming liquid, needing to get my mind off of sex and Lily.

"Somehow, I don't think you're kidding," she said, staring at me over the rim of her mug.

"I'm not." I knew people. A lot of people. Most owed me favors anyway after helping them get the information they were looking for.

"As much as I appreciate that, it's been innocent. So far anyway." Lily placed her mug on the counter, jumped up onto it, and continued drinking her coffee. "He will have to cope, because it's over. He'll get a clue soon, I'm sure."

I leaned against the wall, finding that I liked this. Her in my home. Even though she hadn't seen the part I actually lived in yet. But I liked seeing her there. It had been a long time since I'd felt this comfortable with a woman. Even though I wasn't sure I could trust her, I still enjoyed this.

Lily swung her legs back and forth. It reminded me of a child. Carefree and innocent. But something told me that Lily was not innocent. Not at fucking all.

"So, Lucas, tell me about yourself."

I hesitated. "What would you like to know?"

"Hmm…" She placed her mug on the counter beside her. "You probably get asked this all the time but what was your first tattoo?"

I closed the distance between us.

Her breath caught, her eyes widening just a touch.

I lifted my shirt, pointing to a small rose on my hip. "This one."

She looked down. "Really?"

"I got it when I was a kid." The memory of roses invading my childhood, tried slithering into my mind. But I shook my head, forcing that constant nightmare to the back of my mind. "It was ugly at first but once I learned how to tattoo, I fixed it up myself."

"You did?" she asked, her lips parting.

I nodded, pulling my shirt down. Being this close to her, I could see that the freckles on her nose, spread to her cheeks. I could also see a brown speck in her right green eye. It was a tiny flaw in a perfect beauty. My heart picked up speed. A little closer and I could kiss her. A little more and I could have her in my arms and press her up against the wall. A little more and I—

"That's impressive." She jumped off the counter. "I don't have any tattoos or piercings. As much as I like them, I could never figure out what to tattoo on me."

"It's a big decision." I blew out a slow breath, thankful she put some distance between us before I showed her exactly what it was that I wanted to do to her.

Hacker, Lucas. She's a damn hacker.

"Yeah. I guess it is." Something flashed behind her eyes but before I could question it, it disappeared. "Well..." She pulled her phone from her bag. "I should go."

"Do you have plans?" I asked, taking a step toward her until I stood close enough to touch her. Not that it was any of my business, but I found that I wanted to get to know her. To find out what made her tick. What her interests were. How she hacked into my personal information. What made her fucking moan. My dick pushed against the fly of my jeans.

I wanted to trust her.

"Well...no." Her cheeks reddened. "Don't you have appointments coming up?"

In a quick move, I grabbed her wrist.

She gasped, her pupils dilating.

Turning her wrist toward me, I glanced at her phone. "I still have an hour."

"Oh." She licked her lips. "What do you want to do for an hour?"

"Tell me how you found me," I demanded, backing her up until she hit the edge of the counter.

"We're back to that again?"

"Tell me." I pushed my waist against hers.

A breathless gasp escaped her, her eyes fluttering closed.

Yeah, sweet girl. I feel it too. "Tell me, Lily Pad." I pushed into her harder. Knowing she could feel the length of my cock pressing against her lower stomach, I tightened my hold on her wrist. Brushing my thumb along her pulse point, my mouth pulled up at the corner as her heart raced.

"I was curious," she finally said.

"I don't give a shit why, Lily. I want to know how." No one had ever been able to crack my firewalls before.

"I clicked a couple of buttons and hoped for the best." She pulled her hand from my grip and pushed me back until I hit the edge of the other counter. She may have been small but damn she was strong. "And I don't appreciate you manhandling me." Although she said those words, the flush in her cheeks told a different story. "So if you have a question, ask politely or I'll tell my grandma and she'll kick your ass."

I laughed. "Seriously?"

She shrugged, a hint of amusement flashing in her eyes. "It usually works. She's scary."

"I've dealt with a lot of women in my time, but a little old lady is definitely not one of them."

"Well, she may be old but she's definitely not little." Lily giggled. "I'm the short one. Everyone else is tall."

"I like your height." It would be perfect for when she was kneeling in front of me. My dick leaked at that thought.

"Hmm…" Lily placed her hand against my chest. "I couldn't find a lot of information anyway. Just your business, the website that was designed for it, and that's about it. Why would you have that shit on the dark web anyway?"

I shrugged. "I have no reason for any of the shit I put on the dark web. I go there to play, to find people that would pay to have me research shit for them."

Her brows narrowed. "So people contact you if they need something found out and they pay you for it?"

I nodded.

"Huh…" Her gaze dropped to my mouth. "Interesting."

"Lily." My heart thumped. It had been a long time since I'd felt the warm touch of a woman.

"Your heart's racing," she murmured, meeting my gaze.

I pulled her toward me. "So is yours." I gave her wrist a gentle nip. "Careful, Lily Pad. I bite."

Her breath caught. "What if that's what I want?"

I paused. "What?"

She gave her shoulders a small shrug. "What if I like biting, spanking…" She grazed her other hand down my abs. "…whipping."

Fuck. I pushed away from her, blowing out slow and even breaths. "Woman, you can't say shit like that to a man you just met. You don't know me. You don't know what I'm capable of. And there's no way in hell that either of us can trust each other. Not with the shit we are capable of doing with a computer."

"Semantics." She shrugged. "You touched me first. You pushed your hard body up against me, Lucas," she reminded me.

"That was a mistake." I turned away from her and adjusted myself.

"Right." Lily laughed. "I'll see you later, Lucas."

The sound of the door chiming brought my attention around.

Who the hell was she and why the fuck did I just let her leave?

Four

Lily

I DIDN'T NORMALLY GO for walks. You could never be too safe and all but after leaving Lucas's shop and teasing him the way I did, I needed to clear my head. I was comfortable in my own skin and knew my way around a man's body but there was something about him that made me strive for more. He seemed shocked at my words. I liked a little kink with my sex. I wasn't sure if he was shocked because it wasn't his thing, or if he was shocked because it was his thing and he wasn't expecting it to be mine. Either way, I wanted to find out.

But duty called, and I needed to leave. He had appointments anyway.

"Lily."

I spun around and smiled as Toby Hicks walked toward me. He ran the local AA meetings at a nearby church on Tuesdays and Fridays, so I wasn't overly surprised to see him in the area. "Hi, Toby."

"Hi." He held his arms out.

I laughed, running into them. "How are you?"

"Good." He hugged me back. "How are you?"

"Good too."

"How are things going with your man?"

I grimaced, pulling away from him. "It's over. He's married."

"Holy shit." Toby's eyes widened. "Really?"

"Yeah. But I did meet someone new." I smiled up at him. "But I'm taking it slow." Especially after the whole Killian ordeal.

"You deserve happiness, but I don't think you should jump into a relationship so soon." Toby cupped my shoulders, leaning down until he was eye level with me.

"I just met him, Toby." I patted his hand. "I'm not jumping into anything at the moment."

"Good." Toby released me and held out his arm. "Tell me about the new guy."

"His name is Lucas," I said, linking my arm in Toby's. "He's a tattoo artist but that's all I know right now."

"Interesting." Toby scratched his chin. "He's nice I take it?"

"He seems to be. So far anyway."

"Good." He smiled down at me. "But just be careful."

"Always." Toby knew my history with relationships. "I only just met him and I'm not sure if I can trust him yet but…" I shrugged. "You never know."

"Exactly. And trust takes time. You can't know that as soon as you meet someone."

"Oh good." I laughed. "I was starting to think something was wrong with me."

He grinned, shaking his head. "Not at all." We continued walking the rest of the way to Saint Charles Church when he continued, "It took me a long time to trust anyone."

"Really? You?"

His cheeks reddened. "Yes. Oh, Sandra can't make it tonight."

"Is everything alright?" Sandra was his wife and never missed a meeting.

"She has the flu and it's knocked her on her ass. I was going to stay home with her, but she kicked me out. She doesn't want me to get sick either." He released my arm and waved at a passing couple. "But she's on the mend. Slowly of course. But back to my point. It took me a long time to trust her. I had been fucked over by many women, so trust wasn't the first thing I thought of when I met my wife."

"How long did it take you?" I asked, passing him a glance.

"A while. Maybe a year or so. But everyone is different."

I nodded. "True. Well, give Sandra my best." It explained why I only trusted my grandmother these days. Men only wanted one thing and I was sure that Lucas wasn't any different. Although, at this point, neither was I.

"Ready?" Toby asked once we stood outside the church.

"Always." I gave him a small smile and followed him into the old building.

"Hi, my name's Toby and I'm an alcoholic."

My heart gave a start. Every damn time someone got up to the front and stood at that wooden podium, anxiety rushed through me. I feared they had a bad week or a slip up. I always prayed they didn't fall off the wagon, but it happened more often than not.

"My wife is usually here with me, but she has the flu." Toby paused, running a hand through his short blond hair. He pulled at his hoodie and rubbed his neck again. "I almost had a moment this week. Or I did have a moment actually, but I didn't drink. I wanted to. God, I wanted to, but my wife talked me off the ledge. I had a bad day at work. It's not an excuse, I know that, but it's what happened."

I got it. Living day to day with this disease was difficult all on its own. Add the stress of everyday activities in and it made it worse.

While Toby shared his past week with everyone, my phone buzzed in my hand. Glancing around me, I made sure no one heard and discreetly checked it.

Unknown Number: Looks like I found you this time, Lily Pad.

My face broke out into a grin.

Me: What if I said this wasn't Lily and some stranger instead?

I programmed Lucas's number in my phone. I would have fist pumped the air if I wasn't surrounded by people.

Lucas: Send me a picture and I'll be the judge of that.

I bit my bottom lip to keep from laughing.

Me: I'm not alone.

Lucas: Oh? Working?

Me: No. Meeting.

My thumb hovered over the send button. Could I tell him that I went to meetings? I deleted the message and responded with…

Me: No. Just out.

I knew he would have questions after that, but I felt it was a conversation that needed to be said in person and not through texting.

Lucas: I'll let you be then.

Me: No, you're fine. You're keeping me entertained.

Lucas: Bored?

Me: Something like that.

Lucas: You going to stop by tomorrow, making it three days in a row?

Me: Maybe.

Lucas: My next appointment just walked in. I'll see you tomorrow, Lily Pad.

My heart jumped to my throat that he expected me. Looks like I was making it three days in a row.

Me: Have a good night, Lucas.

I put my phone away and thankfully so because Toby was just finishing up his share. Everyone clapped, his face turned red like always while he walked off the stage and came toward me.

"You know, no matter how many shares I do, it never gets easier." He sat down beside me, crossing his arms under his chest.

I laughed, patting his arm gently. "You did fine. Everyone gets nervous."

He grunted and turned to me. "You going to share something?"

I shook my head. "Not this time."

After everyone else went through their shares and personal stories, Toby and I were standing at the cookie station. I poured myself a cup of coffee and took a sip of the heavenly bliss.

"Apparently the meeting on Friday is being moved to the shelter a few blocks from here," Toby explained. "They want to do some work and modernize this place to bring more people in." He excused himself and went back to the front of the room. "All are welcome to attend the two meetings a week at the new place. They've extended the meetings at this location for all days of the week to accommodate the additional members."

"You think that would help?" I asked him when he rejoined me.

He shrugged. "Maybe not but I don't think they're worried about getting more addicts here. They want more people for the church service."

"Ah. Makes sense I guess." I wasn't a churchgoer, but my grandmother used to be. She taught me everything she knew and had me learn by myself as well. She wasn't overly religious but looked for the best in people. I was thankful for that knowing the hell I had put her through.

"Well, I should get home to Sandra. See how she's feeling."

I gave Toby a hug. "Give her my best and I hope to see her at the next meeting."

"Definitely." Toby gave me one of his big smiles that was all teeth and waved to others as he walked out.

I laughed lightly to myself. He was such a good guy. Both he and his wife were two of my favorite people. And my grandma liked them which meant even more to me.

"Hey, Lily."

I waved at my name being called, made small talk, and left the church basement. I wasn't one to usually stick around. I helped clean up every now and again, but I found most nights, I just wanted to listen to everyone share their stories and leave. Quick and easy but a lot of people didn't want that. They wanted to talk. And we did. We talked a lot. But sometimes, I didn't want that. And I also wanted to talk to someone who didn't know about my addiction.

I instantly thought of Lucas. He would probably run away screaming if he knew about my past. Whatever. I didn't live my life for others. Especially a man. Even if he was a beautiful dangerous man at that.

"Lily."

I stiffened, my stomach twisting at the deep voice coming from behind me. I continued walking.

"I know you heard me."

I slowly turned around. "What do you want, Killian?"

His clothes were disheveled, his normally styled hair, unkempt and messy. "I want to explain about my wife."

"There's nothing to explain, Killian. We're over. I don't know how many times I have to tell you that."

"But you need to hear me out." His voice shook. "I need—"

"Listen," I said, my voice firm. "We are over. There is nothing to talk about."

Killian's back stiffened. "I noticed you've been hanging out at Crane's Ink. Are you getting a tattoo?"

"That's none of your business."

"Then what are you doing there?"

I hung out there twice but that still wasn't any of his business. I raised an eyebrow. "Are you stalking me now?"

"No but you should know that Lucas isn't into women like you think. You're going to get hurt."

"Our relationship is over. I don't need to explain myself to you." I spun on my heel and went to walk away when his next words stopped me.

"I looked him up and he's not the man for you, Lily. You deserve so much better. Someone good and pure."

I frowned and kept on walking, thankful that Killian didn't follow me. Lucas wasn't into women like I thought? What the hell did that even mean? I know I affected him when I teased him earlier. I could feel how hard he was, so he was definitely into women no matter what Killian said. So, either he was lying, or he was jealous. Or maybe it was something else altogether.

I continued walking the next few blocks, lost in my head, when I noticed a light in the distance.

Crane's Ink.

Mustering up the courage, I picked up the pace. I know I said I'd see him tomorrow. Would it be too soon to see him again? Would it make me look desperate? Maybe we could have coffee again, or go somewhere to eat. My stomach rumbled at the thought of food.

Once I reached the door to his shop, I pushed it open and saw him tattooing the neck of a large man. His good eye caught mine. He nodded once and went back to what he was working on.

"How many more sessions do you think this will take?" the large man sitting on the bed asked.

"Probably one more. Just need to touch up the color once this heals and then you'll be good to go."

"Good."

I walked around the room, taking in the hand-drawn images on the walls. I came across one I hadn't seen the couple of times I had been at the shop. It was a bouquet of lilies and it was absolutely stunning.

"That's new."

I jumped, finding Lucas standing right behind me. "I didn't hear you."

"Sorry." He gave me a small smirk. "I cleared my throat, but you were in your head."

I glanced around the shop, noticing that we were alone. I looked back up at the image. "It's beautiful."

"Thank you." Lucas came up to my side, crossing his thick arms under his chest. "I don't draw a lot of flowers but I'm always proud of how they turn out when I do."

"You're really talented. I can only draw stick figures." I laughed.

Lucas chuckled with me. "It's definitely a gift I try to put to good use."

"How so?"

He left my side and cleaned up the tattoo station he had been using when I arrived.

"Lucas?" I turned, the air around us suddenly becoming thick with tension.

"Once a month, I have a free-for-all I guess you could call it. People with scars can come and I'll tattoo them for free to try and cover them." Lucas met my gaze. "I've been doing it ever since I opened Crane's Ink. You would know that if you dug a little deeper."

"I would have found that out, but someone interrupted my search," I threw back at him.

A sly smirk spread on his face. "Is that so? So if I wouldn't have caught you, you would have kept going?"

I snorted. "Trust me, Lucas. I don't consider myself a hacker. I get bored sometimes and taught myself how to do basic shit, but I can't create my own firewalls."

"Right, Lily. You must take me for a stupid man." He shook his head.

"I don't give a shit if you believe me or not." I didn't know him; therefore, I didn't trust him. I knew shit. A lot of shit. But he didn't need to know that.

"Well, Lily Pad. Looks like we've hit a crossroad."

"Oh?" I raised an eyebrow. "That's unfortunate."

A laugh boomed through him.

I couldn't help but laugh with him. I turned back to the drawings hanging on the wall, wondering if he could cover my scars.

"Have you ever not been able to cover scars?" I asked, wondering what it would feel like to have his hands on my body.

"I have to use a special kind of ink but yes, sometimes the skin is too sensitive. Or it can be too thick or even too thin and I can't tattoo over it. If that's the case, I'll tattoo around it or include the scar in a tattoo to make it look like it's all together."

I was impressed and had no idea that was even an option.

"So, Lily." He headed to the counter. "Couldn't keep away?"

I laughed. "Don't get all high on yourself, Lucas. I was in the area."

"No one is ever just in the area around here." His gaze popped to mine. "Tell me."

"I'm hungry and wanted to know if you would join me for a late supper," I said all in one breath.

"Really?" he asked. "Why?"

I laughed. "You seem surprised that I would ask you to join me for food."

"I am actually." He rubbed the back of his neck. "Most women don't usually want just food."

"You don't know what I want, Lucas." I shook my head, my cheeks burning as his eye darkened. I cleared my throat. "Doesn't matter. Right now, I just want food."

"Alright, Lily Pad." He gave me a small smile. "I know just the place."

Five

LUCAS

LILY WAS REFRESHING. SHE had the brightest smile. Her big green eyes looked at everything as if she were seeing it for the first time. As I sat across from her in the booth in the nearest Italian restaurant to my shop, I noticed the freckles that adorned her skin in the most delicious way. She was wearing a deep green sweater that accentuated her eyes. The vee dipped low enough that I could see her freckles continued beneath the fabric. My body stirred, my mouth salivated. I had a feeling she didn't realize just how beautiful she was.

"So, Lucas." Lily took a drink of her water. "Come here often?" she asked, waggling her eyebrows.

I chuckled, sitting back in the booth and playing with the napkin wrapped around the silverware. "I do actually. The owner needed some work done on his computer and security system, so I helped him out with that."

"Interesting." She tapped her chin. "How did you find my number?"

"Ah. Yes." I grinned. "I was waiting for you to ask me that."

She shrugged. "I've been distracted."

"Right," I said slowly. "I found you just like you found me."

"I didn't find your phone number," she corrected.

"No, but I'd bet my life savings you could have." I sat forward, reaching across the table and grabbed her wrist. "So tell me, Lily Pad. How did you find me exactly?"

She swallowed, her slender throat working over that movement. "I have my ways."

"Hmm…I'd like to see you in action." I pushed my thumb against her pulse point. "You're good because no one has ever been able to crack through my firewalls before."

"It wasn't hard." Her breath caught, her lips slamming shut.

I laughed, shaking my head. "What if I told you that the information you found was there because I wanted you to find it."

"You're saying that you have layer after layer of firewalls, security, protection…" She attempted to pull her hand from my grip, but my hold only tightened. "…just for fun?"

"I'm saying that I have been waiting for someone to crack it. Not that anyone has ever tried. I'm hardly an interesting person." I pushed my thumb harder against her pulse. "What information did you find?" I already knew, but I wanted to know if she read everything.

"Nothing really." Her pulse skipped a beat.

She was lying.

Pulling her hand from mine, she sat back and crossed her arms under her chest. "Lucas Crane. Aged thirty-three. Both parents are dead. Owns Crane's Ink."

"That's it?" I raised an eyebrow. "That's pretty boring."

She rolled her eyes. "I'm not stupid, Lucas. I know the rest of your records are sealed only because you want them to be."

"I had help in sealing my records," I confessed. "I didn't have a good childhood."

"Well, I'm glad you have them sealed. I'm sure you don't want that information falling into the wrong hands."

"No." I swallowed hard. "I do not."

"So tell me, what's something that's not listed online? Something no one knows?" She licked her full mouth, her gaze dropping to mine. "Tell me a secret."

"Something no one knows?" I thought a moment. Suddenly, a couple walked past our booth, a floral perfume following them.

Pain. Agony. So much damn pain.

"Lucas?"

I jumped, my gaze landing on Lily.

"You good?" she asked, a deep frown settling between her brows.

"Yeah. Sorry." I coughed. "But to answer your question, I have a beautiful woman sitting across from me."

She snorted which was cute as hell. "That's not exciting."

"It is for me," I told her. "I don't have dinner with women often." I scanned the room. That couple from before no longer in sight. But the faint smell of roses lingered. Rubbing the back of my neck, I focused on the present, not letting myself fall into my past.

"No? Why not?" Lily asked, pulling me from my thoughts.

"Because all of the women I have met aren't worth having dinner with." They wanted sex and that was it. So that was all I ever gave them.

"And I am?" Lily asked, her cheeks reddening.

"Yeah." I grinned. "I think you are, Lily Pad."

Her smile widened. "Well, Lucas." She lifted her glass of water, clinking it against mine. "Here's to a new friendship."

I took a sip of my own water. Something told me that this would end up being far more than just friendship.

(Lily)

Something had bothered him tonight. It took me saying his name a couple of times before he heard me. My heart reached out to him. I wanted to hug him, soothe him from his pain but I also had no idea where to start. Lucas was a broken man. It didn't take a rocket scientist to realize that.

He also knew I had cracked into his firewalls and wasn't pissed over it. He probably made them easy to break through just to be funny.

"What made you get into computers?" I asked Lucas once our food had arrived.

"I spent a lot of time alone." He shrugged. "It also kept me out of trouble. Well…at first anyway."

"I did the same. After my parents died, I moved in with my grandmother. I had to switch schools because of that so I had no friends. It was hard, but my computer kept me sane. At first anyway." I winked, using his words.

"I'm sorry to hear about your parents. I never met mine."

I paused in taking a bite of my garlic bread. "You didn't? But you know they died."

"No." Lucas took another sip of his water. "And yes, that's all I know." He stared down at his glass. "Right now, I wish this were a beer."

My stomach twisted. "I know that feeling all too well."

He met my gaze.

Something passed between us at that moment. I wasn't sure what it was, but I found that I liked it. Even though I didn't know him that well and I also wasn't sure how much I could trust him, this was nice. Lucas wasn't like any of the other guys I had met or been with. He could actually carry a conversation without spinning it back to himself or sex. He seemed to actually care what I had to say.

"Do you not drink?" Lucas asked.

"No." How much should I tell him? "I…uh…have an addictive personality. So it's been hard balancing what's right for me and what isn't. Especially when it comes to alcohol."

He nodded. "I get it, Lily Pad. So, what's your day job?"

"Changing the subject?" I asked, smiling.

"I figured this conversation was getting a little heavy." He gave me a lopsided grin which made my stomach flutter.

Clearing my throat, I pushed the noodles around on my plate with my fork. "I'm a receptionist. I actually work at the front desk at my grandmother's retirement home. There hasn't been a lot of hours lately though, so I've been living off of the money my parents left me now that I'm old enough to actually touch it. It's funny though. I call it my grandmother's retirement home, but I don't think she's actually ever stayed there."

"She doesn't live there?"

"No." I laughed. "It's a weird set-up. But she's been volunteering there for years and has made quite a few friends. One of the doctors who no longer works there, thank goodness, put into her head that she was a burden on me and told her that she should move in there. I disagreed of course so we came to a decision to have her spend her time there when I'm not home. She's perfectly capable of taking care of herself but just to be cautious, that's what we decided to do. But sometimes it doesn't always work out that way. She's a stubborn one."

"I bet she is. You're close with her, I imagine?"

"Oh yes. I think you would like her. She's a little…honest." I grinned, shaking my head. "Not many people know how to take her."

"She sounds fun." Lucas smirked.

"She is. She actually mentioned you coming by."

Lucas raised an eyebrow. "You told her about me?"

"Well, not exactly." I sat back, crossing my arms under my chest. "I told her how we met, and she mentioned you coming over." I pointed at him. "I don't know where this is going, but I'd like to see. I have trust issues, but think that you could be worthwhile, to open up a little and try to trust a man again."

"Well, Lily Pad." He gave me a small smile. "I could say the same. Is that why you looked me up? Because you didn't trust me?"

"I wanted to find out more information about you but you're squeaky clean."

"No one is squeaky clean, Lily Pad."

"True."

The air grew thick between us "I play on the computer when I'm bored," I blurted. "Google doesn't cut it for me, so I've ventured into the dark web of all places. There are some unique people on there."

His laugh deepened. "Oh yeah. A guy contacted me once, asking how much I would charge him to tie him up and piss into his mouth." Lucas shuddered. "I'm all for kink but that's too much for me."

"Wow." I grimaced.

"Yeah. I never took him up on his offer."

"I can't imagine why." I giggled.

Lucas's grin grew. He glanced down at my mouth.

I fidgeted in my seat, playing with the hem of my shirt. I wasn't nervous at first but then Lucas would do or say something that made me blush and the butterflies would flutter through my stomach.

"How do you like your food?" he asked, shoveling a forkful of pasta into his mouth.

"It's good." And it really was.

Once we were done eating, I offered to pay for my own meal.

"You don't have to," he told me.

"I know but I want to." I pulled out my wallet and placed some cash on the table between us.

Lucas hesitated but took the bills along with his own and sat them on top of the receipt.

"Well, Lily. That was fun," Lucas said, stuffing his hands in his pockets as we left the restaurant.

"It was." I smiled up at him. We stopped just outside, moving away from the entrance so we weren't blocking it. "Thank you."

"We should do that again," he offered, pushing a strand of loose hair behind my ear.

I shivered at the soft contact, swaying toward him. "We should," I whispered, licking my lips.

His nostrils flared. He leaned down, his mouth mere inches from mine. Just when I thought he was going to kiss me, he placed a soft peck on my cheek instead.

Before I could stop myself, I turned my head, my lips brushing over his.

He stiffened, not pushing for more or less.

I reached out, grabbed onto his shirt and pulled him closer.

His body relaxed at that and he deepened the kiss, moving his hand to the back of my head.

My lips parted, my tongue peeking out to get a taste. A hint. I needed his breath on my lips. But before that could happen, he pulled away.

"Sweet, Lily," he murmured, brushing his thumb over my bottom lip.

"Lucas." I wasn't that sweet. I went to pull him even closer, but he grabbed my hands, stopping me.

"I'll see you later." He kissed my knuckles. "Text me when you get home." He dropped my hands and headed back toward his shop.

I wanted to run after him. To demand to know why he stopped the kiss. To plead for…more? I wasn't even sure but what I did know was that there was something about Lucas Crane that I was drawn to.

Heading home, I couldn't help but touch my lips every so often. His mouth had been soft but firm. Not what I was expecting at all. He was a big guy. I half expected the kiss to be rough and aggressive. And though it wasn't, it made me crave him even more.

When I reached my street, the hairs on the back of my neck rose but I refused to turn around. I knew it was Killian watching me from his black SUV. I wished he would just leave me alone. I didn't care to hear his lame excuses. I would have never pursued a relationship if I'd known he was married. Every time he couldn't make it to one of our dates, I had assumed it was because of his work as an FBI agent. God, I felt stupid, knowing that he was probably with his wife.

As soon as I saw my house, a breath of relief left me. I picked up my pace, the SUV now driving past me. Then when it hit the corner of the street, it made a left turn, and I ran into my house.

Me: I'm home.

Lucas: Good.

I smiled to myself that he had replied instantly, like he was waiting for my text to let him know that I was home safe and sound. I could get used to that sort of treatment.

My grandma took that moment to pop her head out of the kitchen. She frowned. "Everything okay?"

"Yes." It was now. "What are you making at this hour?" I took a deep inhale. Whatever it was, smelled good. Even though I had just finished eating, I could definitely use some dessert.

"I couldn't sleep so I made your favorite." Grandma headed back into the kitchen. "Banana bread with a hint of cinnamon."

I sighed, sitting at the kitchen table. "You know how to make me happy."

She laughed, placing a plate with a fresh piece on top of it. "Did you see that man again?"

"Which one?" I blurted. "I mean…"

Grandma laughed. "The new one you met the other night."

"Oh." I took a bite of the fresh bread. "I did. We had supper together too." I told my grandma all about it. Not that there was a lot to tell but I gave her the details that I knew. I was happy that Lucas seemed to love computers as much as I did. It made me wonder just how much he knew if he could put firewalls up like he did.

I left the part out about him kissing me. Even though it was quick and gentle, something told me to keep that to myself at the moment.

"I have Bridge tonight," Grandma said, cleaning up the dishes and putting the fresh bread away.

"At this hour?" I asked, noting the time on the microwave. It was after nine.

"These people never sleep." She winked.

"You going to kick their asses again?" I asked, helping her.

"Probably." She shrugged. "Not sure yet though. Depends on my mood. I'm feeling a little feisty tonight though, so maybe."

I laughed, shaking my head and kissing her cheek. "Well, have fun. I'm taking the rest of the night off and doing nothing."

"You could call that man. Lucas is it?" she said, waggling her eyebrows.

"Um…no." Although the words left my mouth, calling him might not be such a bad idea.

(Lucas)

"Lucas, you need to give them what they want." That voice. So gentle. So calm. Everything that I was not.

I shook my head, shoving away from the onslaught of my attack.

"Please, Lucas," Mel pleaded, cupping my cheek. The scent of roses wafted into my nose, sending a hot shiver racing down my spine. "You have to take it. If you fight, it'll only hurt more."

I knew that, but I ignored the advice anyway and kicked out.

"Keep fighting me, boy."

Screams tore through me, ripping my throat to shreds. As much as I didn't want to give them the satisfaction, I couldn't help the sounds leaving my mouth. My body ached. My muscles jumped and twitched over my bones. Every inch of me felt like it was on fire.

"You should have listened to me," Mel sobbed.

"Mel," my voice croaked.

"Next," someone shouted.

I fell to the filthy mattress beneath me. As the bed dipped behind me, I could no longer fight off the monsters that had made my life a living hell. All I could do was take it and survive. Although death didn't sound too bad at the moment.

Kill me. Please kill me.

But they wouldn't. No. This was more enjoyable for them.

Our screams. Our cries. Our pleading for it to end.

All of it only made them hurt us more. They enjoyed our submission. They preyed on the weak, forcing us immobile and pleading for mercy.

I laughed. Mercy. Ha!

"Is something funny, boy?"

A sharp pain erupted through my backside. But I didn't make a sound. I could no longer tell what was pain and what wasn't. No sounds left my mouth. No cries. No pleading. Nothing.

I gripped the mattress beneath me and took what I was given.

My eyes shot open, the scent of roses drifting away with the remnants of my dream. Those damn roses were the only thing that kept me going for the longest time. The sweet scent was calming, knowing they represented a safer haven while my body was being torn apart.

My skin was covered in a sheen of cold sweat. But all I could do was lay there. I checked the clock on my nightstand. It was pushing midnight. I wasn't one to go to bed early, but I had grabbed my sketchbook to draw up some new tattoo ideas and must have passed out shortly after.

Sitting up in bed, I rubbed the back of my neck, trying to ease the kink that had taken up permanent residence there since I was a kid.

My past weighed heavily on my shoulders. Every now and again, I would think of her. I wondered if she was able to move on with her life. She would also come into my nightmares from time to time. I hoped she was able to get past the hell we had been through. She had been the only thing that kept me going as a kid. But death still would have been better.

Checking my phone, I saw that I had one missed call from Lily. My body heated remembering the brief kiss we shared. I wanted more but I didn't press her, and I also needed to rein in on that control I felt like I was losing since meeting her only a few days ago.

Opening the text messages, I found the last one between us and typed up a quick text.

Me: Sorry I missed your call.

I put my phone down but it buzzed right away.

Lily Pad: No problem. I was just bored and wanted someone to talk to.

My dick jumped. It was interesting to me that she had chosen me over anyone else.

Instead of texting, I gave her a call.

"Miss me?" she asked, instead of giving me the traditional greeting.

I chuckled. "Always."

She laughed. "It's late. I should let you get some sleep."

"No." My voice came out rough, like I had just gargled with broken glass.

"Everything okay?"

"I…" My chest tightened. "Nightmare."

"Ah. Yes. I've had many of those. They suck. A lot."

"They do." I pushed myself up the bed and leaned against the headboard.

"My parents died in a house fire." Her breath hitched. "I was eight when it happened. I was sleeping. Scariest shit I've ever woken up to and I've woken up in some pretty shitty situations before." She cleared her throat. "Anyway. I have nightmares about fire all the damn time."

"I have nightmares about my childhood." I was not expecting to admit that. "I…uh…anyway, I'm sorry for your loss."

"Thank you but honestly? I love my grandma and know I have a better life because of her. Well…it didn't start out that way, but she has the patience of a saint." Lily sighed. "I really have no idea how she put up with me for this long."

I grunted.

"Anyway, I'm here if you want to talk about your nightmares. We can compare stories." She laughed lightly but there was no humor hidden in her voice.

"Thank you, Lily Pad." Just her telling me about her situation made me feel better. Even though I couldn't give her a lot of my story, hearing her unbiased views helped. It helped a whole fucking lot. She was different than the previous women I had been with. She actually wanted to carry a conversation with me and not just have sex.

"If you could travel anywhere, where would you go?"

I was taken aback by Lily's question. "Although I haven't had the opportunity to see all of the U.S., I'd like to go somewhere exotic like Fiji."

"Oh I would love that! I haven't been to the beach in years."

We spent the rest of the night getting to know one another. It had been a long time since I just spoke to a woman about something other than what they liked in bed. It was a strictly platonic conversation, but I learned a whole lot more about Lily. How she loved to read and do crossword puzzles. I also learned that she hated working out but would do it just so she didn't feel like a 'lump on the couch.' Everything I learned about her, I liked.

We talked about our dreams and adventures that we would someday go on.

Lily wasn't like any other woman I had met before. She was breathtaking and patient. And kind. So damn kind. But I knew there was a layer of sass and seduction beneath her outer shell and I couldn't wait to crack my way through it.

Six

Lily

I HAD KNOWN LUCAS for a few weeks before I got the courage to ask him out again. Even though we had gone out for dinner once and spent every night chatting on the phone since then, something had changed. I found that I was beginning to trust him. Even if it was just small at first. Like when he told me that he was helping a friend make ends meet because she was dealt the short end at life. Or when he told me he'll go to one of the known homeless areas in the city and hand out food, cigarettes, whatever the people needed to get by while they were down on their luck.

Maybe he told me those things so my guard would be lowered. Either way, the more I spoke to him and got to know him, the more I wanted him.

Whatever was passing between us had fast turned into a friendship and I found I liked it. I liked him. His company. Talking to him. When I bumped into him at the grocery store last week while my grandma was with me, there was a quick introduction, but I had ushered her away before she said something that I would end up regretting.

"He's pretty." Grandma waggled her eyebrows.

I shook my head, laughing.

"You definitely need to invite him over now."

A part of me wondered why or maybe I had done something wrong. Maybe he wasn't attracted to me like I was to him.

One Friday afternoon, I had just gotten off work at the nursing home my grandmother played Bridge at and decided to head to his tattoo shop. Once I arrived, I pushed open the door.

"Lucas?" I called out when I saw that no one was there.

A door at the back of the shop opened, revealing him. "Hey." He smiled, coming toward me.

"Have I done something?" I asked, not beating around the bush. "Is it because I hacked into your shit? I promise I haven't done that since, but I really was curious about you. I meant no harm."

"What are you talking about?" He frowned, pausing in his steps.

"We went out for dinner a few weeks ago, we kissed, and nothing's happened since. So either I did something or…"

He came closer, sauntering toward me.

"If you're not attracted to me, that's fine, and if we're just going to be friends, that's fine too but—" I was cut off by a hand in my hair. A hot mouth came down hard on mine. I sighed, taking his tongue deep between my lips.

A soft growl left his chest. He tightened his hold on my hair, tilting my head back even more and deepening the kiss.

Every inch of me came alive. My hands ran up his thick arms to his shoulders. They trailed down his chest to his abs.

"Lucas," I whispered against his mouth. My core clenched. I wanted more. I wanted him. I wanted everything he had to give me. Fuck not knowing if I trusted him or not. Fuck if I'm fresh out of a relationship. I wanted sex. And a lot of it.

All too soon, Lucas broke the kiss.

I whimpered at the loss.

He smirked, cupping my face. "Slow, Lily Pad," he said, his voice husky and thick with arousal.

"But what if I don't want slow?" I asked, breathless. My eyes dropped to his pelvis. "I don't think you really want slow either," I added, noting the large bulge he was sporting behind his jeans.

He released me and took a couple of steps back, putting some distance between us.

"Lucas." I took a step toward him, but he lifted his hand, stopping me.

"I need slow, Lily. I need slow with you." He rubbed his nape, his good eye meeting mine. It was dark. Filled with lust. But he didn't press for more. Even though I wanted him to. God, did I ever want him to.

"Can I ask why at least? Did I do something? Was it because I found out your information? I didn't see anything that wasn't already general knowledge." I was rambling, and I wasn't usually an insecure person but when I had a guy just devour the hell out of my mouth and suddenly stop, it sparked some questions.

"No, I don't give a shit about that anymore. And you definitely haven't done anything. It's just…it's been awhile," was all he said.

"Alright," I mumbled. "If you want slow, then I'll give that to you." Those words left my mouth but even I didn't believe them. But if it was what Lucas wanted, I would listen. For now, anyway.

He nodded. "So, what brings you by?"

"Well…" I hopped up onto the counter, swinging my legs back and forth. "I thought I did something wrong, so here I am."

"You could never do anything wrong, Lily Pad."

"Okay." I thought a moment. "What are you doing tonight?"

"Nothing really." He met my gaze. "Why?"

"Did you want to come over for supper? My grandma has been on me to invite you." She had just asked me again that morning, insisting that I bring my new friend over. The conversation started with me complaining that I liked Lucas, but I hadn't known him for that long and I wasn't sure if I could trust him. She told me the only way to trust someone, was to hang out with him. And if he liked her food, he was a keeper.

"She has?"

I laughed. "Yeah."

"Well…" Lucas grinned. "It's a date." He checked his phone. "I'll be closing up soon anyway."

"Slow night?" I asked. It was only five in the afternoon.

"I always close up early on Friday nights."

"Oh? How come?"

"I don't need the money," he told me. "So I figured instead of killing myself by working long hours, I would give myself a head start to the weekend. My clients understand."

"Makes sense." A part of me wondered why he didn't need the money.

"Ask me," he said, turning to me.

"Ask you what?"

He nodded once. "You have a question. So ask."

"Fine. I know it's rude but I'm a curious person. How come you don't need the money?" God, my grandma would be pissed if she found out I asked a question about someone's financial status.

"People pay me to find out information," he said and that was that.

The tension in the room was thick, so I quickly changed the subject. "Did you need help?" I asked, jumping off the counter.

"No. Thank you though." He locked up the front door and walked past me. "We'll go out the back and take my car."

"Okay." I followed him to the back of the shop and through another door out into a long hallway.

"I live on the second floor," he explained. "This building is old, but all of the electricity and security is brand new."

"Thanks to you right?" I asked.

"Exactly." He gave me a wink.

I wondered what his apartment looked like. Would it be modern and clean? Or rustic and old looking? Maybe manly. Yup, definitely manly.

When we headed outside, we stopped in front of an old black muscle car.

"Wow," I said in awe. "This car is pretty."

Lucas walked around to the driver's side and petted a hand over the hood. "She is."

"Is her name Baby?"

He chuckled. "No."

I grinned that he understood the "Supernatural" reference.

"Maybe I'll call her Lily."

I slid into the passenger seat at the same time Lucas sat in the driver's side. "What, so you can ride her good and hard and not break her?"

He coughed, adjusting himself. "Woman."

"Ah. Come on, baby." I giggled. "You know that's what you want to do. I see the way you look at me."

He shook his head. "You're going to be the death of me."

"Just say the word, Lucas." I wasn't sure where this newfound bravery was coming from, but I liked it. Teasing Lucas was fun. I was waiting for him to snap and give me what I wanted. But until then, I would play.

(Lucas)

She was something else. A breath of fresh air. The light in my darkness. While she sat beside me in my beast of a car, it took everything in me not to reach out and touch her. But I held back. I wasn't sure why. I felt like I had just met my first woman all over again. No. This was different. Lily wasn't like any of the ones I had met already. She was better.

Spending the last few weeks getting to know her had been exhilarating and a turn on all on its own. I knew she wanted me to kiss her again, but I'd meant what I said. I needed slow. I needed to know that whatever this was building between us, would be more than just sex. I didn't do casual hookups anymore. Although I wanted slow with Lily, I didn't want to fuck anyone else and everything in me said that she felt the same way.

Lily gave me her address and while it was about fifteen minutes away, traffic and construction delayed us getting to her place sooner. Which a part of me was thankful for.

"What's wrong?"

"Nothing." I glanced her way before looking back out onto the road. "Why?"

She waved a hand between us. "You seem tense." She reached out, brushing her thumb along my jawline. "And stiff."

The soft touch shot right to the tip of my dick. I gripped the steering wheel. "Lily."

"What?" she said, breathless. "I'm just stating a fact, Lucas."

My body vibrated, my cock pushing against the fly of my jeans. "You're playing a dangerous game."

"Hmm…" Her finger trailed down the length of my neck. "What kind of dangerous game? Will you spank me if I'm a naughty girl? Will you punish me, Lucas? I'm not into that Daddy Dom, baby girl thing but for you, I'm willing to try. Is that it? You want me to call you Daddy?"

My dick leaked. Fuck me.

"Lily," I growled. Blood pumped through me and if I wasn't driving, I would have thrown her into the back seat and made her beg for more.

"What if I want to play this dangerous game you're talking about?" she asked, running her hand down my chest. "What if I want to tease you until you snap and lose control?"

I grabbed her hand, squeezing it until the bones rippled beneath her skin. "Careful, Lily. I bite, and I bite fucking hard. I don't take too well to being teased. If you want something, just say it."

"You know what I want, Lucas." She pulled her hand from mine and slid it down my stomach. "I want you. I want you all over me. I've only known you for a month and we've kissed and talked but that's not enough." She leaned toward me, her hot breath fanning the side of my face. "I want to know what you feel like. If everything is as big as the rest of you." Her hand reached my lap. "Hmm…I think you definitely are as big as the rest of you," she purred, wrapping her fingers around me.

I jumped at the unexpected contact. "Lily."

"Shhh…" She licked along the shell of my ear. "You drive. I'll suck."

"What?" Before I had a chance to stop her, she undid my jeans and pulled out my straining cock.

"Holy hell." Her hand pumped from the base of my cock to the tip. "My fingers can't fit around you, Lucas."

"Lily, what are you—" A groan escaped me when she lowered her mouth down the length of me. "Shit." The car swerved.

She giggled, wrapping her small hand around my balls and licking over the tip of my swollen length. "I can stop."

"Fuck that." I cupped her nape and pushed her back down onto my dick.

She gagged.

"Aww, baby. Is my big dick choking you? You should have thought of that before you started teasing me. Now suck, Lily. And suck fucking hard. Make me come down that slender throat of yours."

She moaned, the suction of her lips gripping me in a vice-like hold.

I kept my hand on the back of her head, forcing her up and down. My cock bumped the back of her throat making her gag, but it only made me thrust up and up. It had been too long. So fucking long since I had a good blow job but this…this was so much more. It was like Lily was sucking the control right out of me. She had the ultimate power and I was putty in her fucking hands.

My balls tightened, my dick swelling in her mouth. A fast release hit me, sending pleasure shooting up my spine. "Fuck me," I breathed.

Lily continued sucking, lapping up every last lost drop I had to give her. When my body calmed, she placed a soft peck on the tip of my dick and sat back in the passenger seat.

"That..." I stuffed my cock away and did up my jeans. "I have no fucking words right now."

She laughed, wiping the corner of her mouth. "Does that tell you what I want, Lucas?"

I grunted. It did. And then some. I was thankful that it was later in the evening and she couldn't see or even feel my scars. And that she definitely couldn't see my tattoo.

If she did, she would have had questions. And I wasn't sure how to answer them or if she would even understand.

Seven

Lily

I WASN'T ONE TO mess around in a car. Especially a moving one. But something told me to test Lucas's limits. He was holding back, and I couldn't figure out why. So when I put his dick in my mouth and he took over, I knew I had won.

My body had heated over the hold he had on my head and I couldn't wait to see how he was in bed. If he wanted slow, I would give him that. But teasing him a little wouldn't hurt.

Every so often, Lucas would look at me.

And I could only grin.

"You're proud of yourself, aren't you?" he asked as we pulled into my driveway and put the car in park.

I shrugged. "I made you come, didn't I? Of course, I'm proud of that."

He blinked. Once. Twice. And then he was on me. He cupped my nape, pulling me toward him then pushed a hand between my legs.

I gasped. "Lucas, we're not—"

"Shut up." He sunk his teeth into my jaw before leaning down to my ear. "Just because your mouth is hot as fuck, doesn't mean you get to call the shots, Lily Pad." His palm cupped my center, pushing and rubbing.

I moaned, a tingle spreading through me. "You were tense. I was trying to help you relax."

"Is that all?" He released me suddenly, rubbing the scruff on his chin. He only shook his head. "We should go before I fuck you in this car."

I glanced in the back seat. "I don't think there's enough room."

"I'd make room." He tapped my hip. "Go. Get out. Before I change my mind."

"So bossy." But I didn't leave the car.

"Lily," he growled, his voice filled with warning.

"Tell me you didn't enjoy it. Tell me you didn't enjoy taking over and forcing your cock down my throat." I grabbed his hand, bringing his fingers up to my mouth. "Tell me, you don't want more."

His nostrils flared. "I enjoyed it. I enjoyed it more than you will ever know. And of course I fucking want more."

I smirked, opening my mouth and taking two of his fingers between my lips. "You tasted good, Lucas."

Something inside of him snapped. It was like an elastic band being stretched too taut. He pushed his fingers against my tongue.

I whimpered, my eyes welling with unshed tears at the delicious but sharp pain.

He pushed me back. "Open your jeans. Now."

With fumbling fingers, I popped open the button and lowered the zipper.

Lucas released my mouth, glancing down at my lap. He brushed the back of his knuckles over the soft spot just above my mound. "I can smell your pussy, sweet girl."

My body leaked even more for him. "I can still taste you on my tongue," I threw back at him.

He grinned, cupping my cheek and crushing his mouth against mine at the same time he shoved his hand into my jeans.

I gasped into his mouth, wrapping my arms around his neck and just…waited.

Lucas trailed kisses down the length of my jaw, pushing his fingers lower and running them over the fabric of my panties. "Nice and wet," he murmured against my throat. "Did having my cock in your mouth turn you on?"

"Yes," I whispered. "I want more."

He chuckled. "You're a greedy little thing, aren't you?"

I grabbed his hand between my legs and pulled it against me. I didn't care that we were in his car. I didn't care that we were in the driveway to my house. I just needed him. That release. That moment between us that we would never get back. "Please."

"Nah, you see, Lily. When you come, I want you to come on my cock. Or face. I haven't decided yet. Maybe I'll watch you make yourself come. Either way, it's not going to be here in the driveway to your grandmother's place." He pulled his hand from my jeans and did them up.

My chest rose and fell, my heart thumping hard against my ribcage. "You're an asshole. At least I made you come."

A booming laugh left him. "Trust me, baby. The wait will be well fucking worth it. And when my fat cock fills this tight little cunt, you'll be thanking me."

"Sorry, Lucas." I patted his cheek. "I don't thank anyone for sex." I kissed him hard on the mouth and sucked his bottom lip between my teeth before giving it a gentle nip.

He jumped, a hard growl leaving him. "Careful, Lily Pad. I'll remember this and bite that tiny little clit of yours until you're squirting all over my fucking face."

I shivered at the thought. "I think that can be arranged."

The side of his mouth turned up, but he only shook his head. Tapping my hip, he kissed my cheek. "Get out."

I laughed, leaving the car, while he did the same and came up behind me.

He wrapped his arms around my shoulders and kissed the side of my neck. "Thank you."

My heart jumped. "For what?"

Without answering, he released me and walked up the sidewalk to my house.

I just stood there. He thanked me. I had never been thanked before. Not for sex. Not for a kiss. And especially not for a blow job. Most of the guys I had been with previously were selfish and only wanted one thing.

Oh God, my feelings for Lucas grew right then.

He stood on the porch, glancing back at me over his shoulder. He crooked a finger.

I only smirked and headed toward him. This was going to be interesting. My grandmother never liked any of the guys I saw. And she had never actually wanted to meet them either. But when it came to Lucas, she had been pleading for me to bring him over.

"Well, it's about time you show up."

My head popped up at my grandma standing in the doorway, staring up at Lucas.

Lucas stuck his hand out.

"It's nice to officially welcome you to my home." She swatted his hand out of the way. "But I don't shake hands." She held her arms out. "Give me a hug."

He chuckled and did as he was told. Which looked funny with the way his big body enveloped hers.

"You smell good." Grandma leaned back, cupping Lucas's face. Her eyes moved back and forth over his.

He cleared his throat, pushing away from her.

I frowned, wondering what that was about.

"Supper is done." Grandma smiled at us and headed into the house.

"I like her," Lucas told me, following her.

"Good." I patted his arm and shut the door behind us.

"Lucas," Grandma called out.

He raised an eyebrow, giving me a look.

"She does her own thing." I shrugged. "I don't even bother questioning her anymore."

He nodded and headed into the kitchen. "Yes, ma'am?"

"First thing, sit." Grandma pointed to a chair at the table. "Second. Don't call me ma'am. My mom was ma'am and she was a bitch."

"Okay." He shifted in his seat. "What would you like me to call you?"

Grandma thought a moment. "I've always liked the name Eleanor."

I laughed. "Her name is Ethel, but I have a feeling she wants you to call her Grandma."

She winked. "You know me too well."

"Alright, Grandma." Lucas smirked. "I like it. I've never had a grandma before."

My heart pained for him.

"Well, sweet boy." She patted his hand. "I'll be the best grandma you've ever had."

"You'd be the only grandma I've ever had," Lucas corrected her.

"Exactly." She went back to the stove and dished up a couple of plates of her delicious beef stew.

I sat beside him, placing my hand on his thigh. "You okay?" I asked softly.

He nodded. "I am." But he wouldn't meet my gaze.

"Lucas." I grabbed his hand, holding it on my lap.

He looked down at me, bringing our joined hands up to his mouth and placing a soft peck on the back of my knuckles. "I'm good, Lily Pad."

But something told me that he wasn't. I knew he had been holding back. I was surprised he had let me take it as far as I did. I could still taste him on my tongue and I found that I wanted to explore every inch of him. To make him feel better because I knew something was wrong or at least…off.

"Alright, Lucas." Grandma placed a plate in front of him. "This is my famous stew. If you don't like it, well…" She grinned. "That's your problem."

"I'm a man." He chuckled. "I don't think I'll have any issues with that." He shoveled a forkful in his mouth. "Holy fu—I mean…" He swallowed. "It's delicious."

Grandma's cheeks reddened. "I'm glad you like it."

My heart warmed. This was something new for me and I found that I liked it. Having him here in our home. Sharing dinner with him. Talking. Spending time together. I could get used to this.

We continued eating in silence. It was nice. Comfortable. Needed.

When we were finished, Lucas cleared the table and started doing the dishes.

"Yup." Grandma pointed at him. "He's a keeper."

Lucas glanced at me over his shoulder. Something flashed in his good eye.

My stomach flipped.

Grandma joined him, drying the dishes while he washed.

I put the rest of the food away, all of us falling into a quick routine.

"So, Lucas." Grandma looked between us both. "Can I ask why you have the eye patch or is that a subject we don't talk about?"

Lucas shifted from foot to foot.

"Grandma," I said gently. I hadn't even asked him about it yet. I figured he would tell me when he was ready.

"I haven't told Lily what happened yet," he said. "No disrespect but I think if anyone should know, it should be her first."

Grandma nodded. "I like that. Okay. I won't ask again."

(Lucas)

"Does it hurt?" Mel asked me.

"Not anymore." I leaned forward, checking out my eye in the bathroom mirror. I had to learn rather quickly how to focus out of one eye. It was odd at first. "Maybe I should get an eye patch."

Mel came up beside me. "I think that would be sexy."

Every now and again, I forgot I actually wore an eye patch. But when someone asked about it, memories came rushing back. It was the same shit, different day with my nightmares. So many damn things triggered them. It was frustrating as hell.

Although I had been asked before if I just wore the eye patch to make me look more like a bad ass. But I was a big fucker. I didn't need an eye patch to make me look lethal.

When Ethel didn't question me anymore about the patch, a breath of relief left me. Lily had never asked about it. I wondered why. She had the patience of a saint because if it were me, I would have demanded answers. I wasn't a patient person. At all. And when it came to her, my self-control was wearing thin.

"Did you want to watch a movie?" Lily asked once the dishes were done and everything was put away.

"Sure," I said, even though I wanted to take her back to my place and return the favor for the delicious blow job she had given me. But as much as I wanted that, I wasn't sure if she could handle me. I wasn't pretty beneath my layer of clothing.

"Well, I'm going to head out. It's Bridge night and I need to kick Beverly's ass." Ethel gave Lily a hug and moved in front of me. "You treat my granddaughter well and there won't be any problems. Understand?"

"Yes. I do." I wrapped an arm around her shoulders and pulled her in for a hug. I never had a family before so when she said to call her Grandma, it made me choke up. So I embraced it with open arms.

Ethel hugged me back. "You need to talk to her," she murmured low enough for only me to hear. She leaned back, cupping my cheek. "You remind me of my husband."

I swallowed hard. "Is that good?"

"Yes." She smiled, her eyes shining. "That's very good." She pulled away. "Have fun. There's fresh apple pie in the fridge."

"Thank you for dinner." I walked her out into the hall.

"Such a gentleman." She patted my arm.

I helped her into her jacket and waited for her to leave before I turned to Lily.

She had a wide smile on her face.

"What?" I asked, raising an eyebrow.

"Nothing." She came toward me. "Nothing at all."

I leaned down and brushed my mouth over hers, which earned me a soft sigh in return. "So…how about that movie?"

Eight

Lily

LUCAS AND I CHOSE a movie. It was some random film that was on TV, but I found I couldn't concentrate on it. He had his arm across my lap and his thumb was brushing back and forth over my ankle. That tiny touch made every nerve ending tingle.

Sitting this close to him, sent a flutter of desire rushing through me. He smelled like spice with a hint of something woodsy. He smelled good. So damn good.

Every inch of me came alive at how close he was sitting. Could he feel it too? This passion bubbling between us?

"Lucas," I whispered, taking a chance and looking up at him.

"Yeah, Lily Pad?" He licked his scarred lips, glancing down at my mouth.

"Hmm…" He placed a soft peck on the corner of my mouth. "What if your grandma comes home?"

"She'll be at Bridge for a while," I said, tilting my head to give him better access to my throat.

"She will, will she?" Lucas lifted his hand.

I linked my fingers with his.

"What do you want, Lily?" he asked, licking along the shell of my ear.

"You," I breathed, running my other hand down his chest.

"What do you want from me?" He pulled me onto his lap.

"More."

"What else?"

"I want to know what you feel like," I said, straddling his waist. "I want to know if you're gentle or rough. Or both. I want to feel you." I placed a soft peck on his lips. "I want…"

"What, Lily?" he asked, his voice coming out gruff. Sliding his hands down my back, he cupped my ass and pulled me flush against him.

"I want to feel you inside me." I rested my hands on the back of the couch, staring down at him and rubbing my pelvis over his.

His jaw clenched, his fingers digging into my hips. "I can feel the heat coming off of you."

"You feel good between my legs, Lucas," I said, breathless. All thoughts of whether I could trust him or not, flew out the damn window when he started moving against me.

He smirked. Running his hands around to my front, he pushed his fingers beneath the hem of my shirt.

My heart jumped to my throat. I grabbed his hands, stopping him.

He raised an eyebrow. "Lily?"

"I…" I swallowed hard, my stomach twisting. I got caught up in the moment and almost forgot about my scars. I knew Lucas wouldn't care about them seeing as he had some of his own, but I had never willingly showed them to anyone before. "I have scars."

"Baby, I can guarantee you that I have more than you ever will." He reached for the hem of my shirt again. "Let me see."

I brushed my thumb over his eye patch. "What about yours?"

"Tit for tat, Lily Pad?" he murmured between clenched teeth.

I nodded, chewing my bottom lip.

"That's a conversation…" His breath caught. "I'm not ready."

"Can I see at least? You don't have to tell me how you got it. Not until you're ready. I just want to see." I continued when he didn't say anything. "You can trust me, Lucas. I'm not like the others."

"Do you trust me?" he asked, tilting his head.

"I…" I hesitated. Did I trust him?

"I'm not like the others, Lily Pad," he said, using my own words.

I nodded. "I trust you."

His body relaxed at that, like he had been waiting for my confession and couldn't move on without it.

Taking a deep breath, he pulled off the eye patch.

(Lucas)

The white film over the iris used to scare people. So instead of walking around with sunglasses on, I eventually got an eye patch. Which seemed to still make people nervous. I couldn't win.

"I think it's sexy," Lily said, brushing her thumb over the jagged scars around my eye.

Something about the way she was looking at me with heat in her gaze, made me snap. In a quick move, I threw her back on the couch and crushed my mouth to hers.

She gasped, taking my tongue deep into her mouth and devouring the hell out of me with that kiss alone.

Hooking my hands around her thighs, I pulled her further beneath me and inched a hand under her shirt. I brushed my fingers over her stomach and that was when I felt them. Bumpy ridges, soft and uneven.

I broke the kiss, staring down at her.

There was a tinge of red in her cheeks, her bright green eyes dark with lust.

"The scars are from the fire that my parents died in," she murmured.

I nodded, covering her mouth with mine again. I didn't need to hear anymore.

Snaking her arms around my neck, she tilted her hips.

I groaned, pushing between her legs. My dick hardened, threatening to explode.

"Lucas," she whispered, arching beneath me.

I took that as my cue and licked up the length of her neck. I sucked and nipped, bit and nibbled until I reached her ear. "I can't wait to fuck this sweet pussy, Lily."

She whimpered.

"And then I'll make you suck my cock and clean me up after." I pushed into her, rubbing against her hot center.

Her chest rose and fell with ragged breath.

"Would you like that, Lily?" I asked, biting the soft skin beneath her ear. "You want to taste yourself on my dick, baby?"

"God, yes." She met my stare head on. "I want to know what you taste when you eat my pussy."

I grinned. Sitting back, I pulled her into my arms.

"Lucas." She threw her head back, undulating against me.

"Mmm…" I cupped her tits, squeezing and massaging them together. Leaning forward, I grazed my teeth over a nipple through the fabric of her shirt.

She gasped, arching into me.

I repeated the movement with her other nipple, a notable shiver trembling through her. "Spend the night with me," I told her. I needed inside her before I fucking exploded.

Lily pushed off of me, smoothing down her shirt and holding her hand out. "Take me to your apartment."

I jumped to my feet.

She laughed.

The sound shot to the tip of my cock. If I died tomorrow, making her laugh would be the best thing I ever did.

Lily locked up the house, sent her grandma a text, which surprised me that her grandma even knew how to use a cell phone, and followed me to my car.

Once both of us were seated in the vehicle, I turned to her. "I need you to tell me that you're sure. It's been awhile for me. A long while and I'm not going to be gentle."

She licked her lips. "Lucas, I've wanted you between my legs from the moment we met."

"Lily," I warned.

She leaned over me, placing a soft peck on my cheek. "I want you to rip me apart. Does that answer your question?"

My cock jumped. Yup. That definitely answered my question.

(Lily)

This was it. In the beginning, I just wanted sex from Lucas. But now that our friendship was building into something more than just physical attraction, it only made sense that this would be our next logical step. I hoped anyway. He was so damn closed off, he made me feel like an open book when in all reality, I had never opened up to anyone. That was a level of trust I never experienced before. Until him.

"Lily." Lucas grabbed my hand, bringing it up to his mouth. "I need you to be sure," he repeated, kissing my fingers.

"I'm sure," I said, breathless.

"It's been awhile for me, Lily Pad. I need you to be ready." He placed our hands in his lap. "I need you to be ready for all of this."

"I've already had you in my mouth." I swallowed hard. "I think my pussy can handle you."

He chuckled.

That chuckle did something funny to my belly. I wasn't sure if it was a warning or not, but I found I couldn't wait for him to not hold back. When he removed the eye patch and showed me what laid beneath it, my chest had ached for him. And then when he threw me back on the couch…it meant something to him. I wasn't sure what, but I needed to know. I needed to understand. I craved it.

Once we arrived back to his place, I slid from the car before he even put it into park.

Lucas killed the engine and did the same.

Both of us paused in our steps, standing only a few feet away from each other.

"Tell me, Lily." His voice was rough, guttural. "Tell me how much you want me."

A sly grin spread on my face. Lifting my shirt just a little, I undid the button of my jeans and lowered the zipper.

His nostrils flared but he didn't move.

Pushing my hand into my pants, I licked my lips. When my fingers came into contact with my center, a whimper escaped me.

Closing the distance between us, he fisted my hair and pulled my head back. "Make yourself come." He covered my hand, helping me rub out that delicious ache.

I moaned. "Lucas."

"That's it, Lily." He leaned his forehead against mine. "Make that cunt gush."

My body leaked at his filthy words, the desire I had for him, coating my inner thighs and panties. Rubbing my index finger over my clit, I cried out at the same time he crushed his mouth to mine. My body shook, chasing that quick release rushing through me.

Lucas pulled my hand from between my legs, lifted me in his arms, and sucked my fingers into his mouth. He groaned, swallowing the essence from my body off of them.

Wrapping my legs around his waist, I reached between us and started unbuckling his belt. "Please. Now. I need you to fuck me now."

Carrying me to the door leading to his apartment, he unlocked it and rushed us inside before slamming me up against it.

Leaning forward, I kissed his chin, his jawline, all the way down to his neck. "You feel so good between my legs."

He shivered, locking the door behind me. "Fuck."

I laughed lightly, tugging the hem of his shirt free from his jeans.

He leaned back, pulling the fabric up and over his head.

My eyes widened. Every inch of him was covered in tattoos. Some black. Some color. But no part of his skin was untouched by ink.

"Look at me."

I met his gaze.

"Tell me you're sure." He gripped my hips, pushing hard between my legs.

"I'm sure." I ran my hands over his thick chest, his muscles rippling and jumping beneath my touch.

"Lily."

"Lucas, if I wasn't sure, I wouldn't be here." I ripped open the fly of his jeans. "Now shut up and fuck me."

"It's been awhile for me. I don't want to hurt you." Something flashed behind his eye. He was hesitating even though the bulge between his legs, indicated how much he wanted me.

Struggling out of his hold, I pushed him back farther down the hall. "I want you, Lucas. I want every inch of you, filling every inch of me." I wasn't normally the dominant type, but something told me that he needed it. At least this once. And I couldn't wait for him to snap and take full control.

In a quick move, Lucas had me thrown over his shoulder. His hand landed against my ass, rubbing the spot soon after. He carried me into his apartment and the next thing I knew, I was thrown onto a bed.

Before I could take a look around me, his mouth was fused to mine. I sighed, running my hands over his hard torso.

Reaching his waist, I slipped my hand inside his jeans and wrapped my fingers around his cock.

Lucas shivered, hooked his fingers into the waist of my jeans and panties, and pulled them down my legs. I kicked them off my feet.

He pushed harder against me, the abrasiveness of his jeans rubbing against my hot, swollen center. He thrust his hips back and forth, brushing against me.

Lucas released my mouth. "I want your cum all over me."

"Oh God." I shivered, squeezing his dick. Cupping his nape with my free hand, I crushed my mouth to his.

The sound of a tin foil wrapper made my heart skip a beat.

He slapped my hand out of the way and pulled his cock free from his jeans. Rolling the rubber down his thick length, he towered over me. He lifted his head, breaking the kiss. "Say it."

"Now."

He shoved forward, thrusting every inch of him inside of me.

I cried out, my back bowing off the bed.

"Fuck me," he growled, sinking his teeth into the side of my neck.

"God, you're so big." I gasped for breath. I knew he had been big just from giving him a blow job, but this was different. I had never felt so damn full in my life.

"Shit, baby. I..." His cock swelled. "I'm sorry. I wasn't expecting you to be so tight."

"Please, Lucas," I panted. "I need you to move."

He leaned his forehead against mine. "I've never felt something so perfect." He gripped my inner thighs, spreading me wide for him and began to move. Thrusting slow and deep, he pushed that pleasure rushing through me into an explosion I had never felt before. He reached that part of me that had never been reached. No matter how many guys I had been with, they couldn't hit it but Lucas? He reached it and made it his. He fucking owned it.

"Your pussy is so damn tight." He cupped my throat, staring down at me. "You're not a virgin, are you?"

I barked a laugh. "No. I've just never been with someone as big as you."

A cocky grin spread on his lips. "You say the sweetest things." He linked his fingers with mine, kissing my knuckles and holding my hands on either side of my head.

I was powerless. Completely and utterly his. With my legs wrapped around his hips and his hands holding mine in a tight grip, all I could do was take what he had to give me.

"So fucking beautiful," he murmured, kissing the side of my neck.

My breath came out in short bursts of air. "Harder," I whispered.

He lifted his head.

"Please, Lucas." I moaned when he pushed forward. "I'm not fragile."

He released my hands, gripped my thighs, and held them down as he powered into me with so much strength, I broke. And I broke fucking hard.

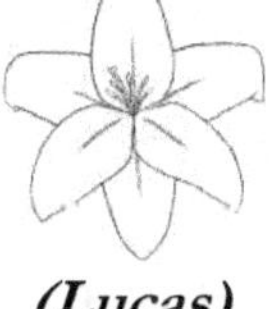

(Lucas)

My body was pulled tight. My wrists and ankles were strapped, and I was spread apart until my muscles bunched.

"Watch," a man said, crouching behind me. "Do you see her?"

I stared up at the ceiling, breathing through the pain coursing through my body. I was naked. Sore. And used. So fucking used up, no wonder the fight was no longer in me.

"I said, watch." The man grabbed my head, lifted it, and forced me to watch the horror before me.

Mel was bent over a bench, her head and hands locked in a wooden contraption. Her cheeks were mottled red, her eyes swollen from tears. I had told her not to cry. I had told her that they only liked it when we showed them how much we hurt. How much we ached. How much we suffered.

She was the one who warned me first, but she didn't listen to her own words.

"Mel." I shook my head. "Stop. Use me. Let her go. Please let her go."

"Why?" the man behind me asked, brushing his fingers down my cheek. "Are you wanting her for yourself? Is that it, Lucas? I know you like that rose perfume she uses. That's why we got you that oil. So every time, it reminds you of her. She is a pretty little thing though. Isn't she?"

I struggled against my binds. "Use me. Fucking use me!"

But they never did. I pinched the bridge of my nose, warding off the impending headache that was trying so damn hard to take control.

A warm body shifted beside me.

A heavy weight lifted off of my shoulders when I remembered where I was and that I was no longer stuck in that basement. I was out of that hell.

While Lily slept beside me, I couldn't help but watch her. Her back rose and fell with each breath she took. The scent of sex permeated through the air. It was bliss. Pure fucking bliss. It had been something I had never felt before. Even after all of the women I had been with, I usually kicked them out after, but the thought never even crossed my mind when it came to Lily. I didn't know why but something about her latched on to my heart and made it hers.

When she told me she trusted me and that I could trust her in return, it sealed the deal for me.

And when she had pleaded for me to go harder, I did but not as hard as I wanted to. I had to rein in that beast, keep him in check before he devoured every inch of her.

"Lucas?"

My gaze shot to hers. She was sitting up, staring down at me.

"Everything okay?"

"You think something's wrong?" I asked. How could she even know?

She nodded.

"Why?" I grabbed her hand, pulling her into my arms.

She curled around me, brushing a thumb over my nipple. "I don't know. Just a feeling I guess."

Interesting. "I'm not sure if anything is wrong exactly." Could I tell her I had another nightmare? "I'm just not used to this," I said instead. It was safer that way.

"Neither am I. I usually leave after." Her cheeks reddened. "Not that I have a lot of one-night stands or anything."

She wouldn't have them again. Not as long as she was with me. Where that thought came from, was beyond me. I cleared my throat. "It's still early."

"Okay." She yawned.

I brushed her hair out of her eyes. She was beautiful. Absolutely breathtaking. And I was the one who put that glow in her cheeks. After I fucked her, I let her be, even though I wanted to keep going for the rest of the night. But I wasn't sure if she could handle me yet.

Resting her cheek on my chest, she let out a heavy sigh.

I ran my hand up and down her back, reveling in the feel of her in my arms and just held on.

Nine

Lily

MY BODY STIRRED. IT had been a few hours since Lucas brought me back to his place. Memories of the night before rushed into my mind. Passion. Ecstasy. And the best damn orgasms I ever had.

Even if nothing came of this, I would forever be grateful to Lucas for showing me what it was like to have a man between my legs who wasn't selfish.

Turning over in bed, I found the spot empty beside me. Sitting up, I ran a hand through my knotted hair before pulling the elastic off my wrist and the mess into a bun on top of my head.

Looking around me, I let out a soft sigh. Our clothes were thrown on the floor, but I was still in my shirt. Lucas hadn't questioned why and thank goodness for that. I knew he had scars of his own and that he wasn't ready to share his story yet, but neither was I.

The door to the room suddenly opened, revealing Lucas. He was dressed in gray sweatpants and a black hoodie. He was holding a tray with two cups and a brown paper bag.

"I have coffee and bagels." He kicked the door closed and came toward me.

My body heated. God, he was beautiful. In a lethal, scary kind of way.

"What?" he asked, tilting his head.

"Just checking you out," I told him.

He chuckled, leaned over, and kissed the top of my head.

I smiled up at him. "How did you sleep?" I asked, bringing the blankets up and around my lap.

"Best sleep I've ever had." He sat beside me, handing me a cup of coffee.

"Same here." I took a sip of the coffee and let out a heavy sigh.

Lucas grinned. "I've never met someone who loves coffee as much as I do."

"I prefer this over anything. If I could live off of it, I would." I laughed. "It's also safer than other stuff."

He only smirked. Reaching into the bag, he pulled out a wrapped package and handed it to me. "I wasn't sure what you like on your bagel, so I got one with just butter on it and another one with plain cream cheese."

"I'll take either. Thank you."

He nodded, handing me one.

I unwrapped it. It was the one with cream cheese and it tasted like heaven.

We ate in a comfortable silence. When we were done, Lucas grabbed the garbage and rose from the bed.

"I guess I should go," I said, glancing at the clock. It was pushing nine in the morning. I had to be at work for one. Not that I wanted to leave Lucas's company anytime soon, but I also didn't want to overstay my welcome.

I stood from the bed which earned me a soft growl. My neck heated. I forgot I was only wearing my shirt.

"Lily."

Not meeting his gaze, I picked up my jeans and panties.

"Look at me."

"I should go," I repeated, ignoring him.

"Lily." Lucas grabbed my hand, pulling me to my feet. He lifted my shirt. "Remember what we said. Trust me."

I met his gaze then.

His gaze dropped to my waist. "Your scars."

"Are horrible," I added, pushing away from him. I had forgotten about them which was a first for me.

"Your scars are beautiful," Lucas said, running his big hand over the scarred flesh of my abdomen.

I wasn't completely scarred but it was just enough that I always kept the lights off when I slept with someone. Until Lucas.

"They mean you're a survivor, Lily."

I pushed my shirt down.

"Take it off."

I frowned. "Why?"

"Because I want to see you."

"Right." I scoffed. "Are you going to show me yours then, Lucas? You told me that I can trust you. Well you can do the same but I don't see you standing there, naked." I raised an eyebrow when he didn't respond. "Didn't think so." I reached for my clothes again when a hoodie fell on the floor in front of me. It was soon followed by pants. I looked up at him, my eyes widening at what stood before me.

Lucas was naked. Completely and utterly naked. He took off his eye patch, throwing it on the floor as well. "Happy?"

I slowly rose to my full height, taking in every inch of his naked body. His flaccid cock jumped under my scrutiny and that was when I noticed the tattoo. All of the tattoos. I knew his torso had been inked but I didn't realize that most of his legs were and also his… "I…you're tattooed. Everywhere." A red octopus sat on his hip, one of its tentacles reaching the tip of his dick.

He turned around.

"Definitely everywhere." Even his ass was covered. I reached out to touch him but thought better of it and pulled my hand back. He was covered in ink. From black and white to color, the intricate designs covered most of his body. But what I also saw, were scars. Ripped and jagged, it looked like he had been whipped. "What happened?"

He turned back around. "Take it off," he said instead of answering my question.

I swallowed hard at the rough demand and pulled the shirt up and over my head before letting it drop to the floor at my feet.

Lucas closed the distance between us, brushing his thumb over my nipple.

I shivered at the soft contact. My scars covered my left side. They went from my hip to just beneath my breast and the side of my stomach. "Would you ever tattoo me?"

"If that's what you want," he said, his voice low. He ran his hands down the scars on the side of my body.

"I think the skin might be too thin," I said, placing my hands on his broad chest.

"Maybe." He licked his lips, staring down at me.

"Will you tell me what happened? I don't need to know now but in time?" I asked, tilting my head back.

Instead of answering, he bent at the waist and placed a soft peck on my mouth.

That was all the answer I needed.

(Lucas)

I was surprised I had shown her my tattoos and scars. Although she had seen most of them the night before, I hadn't revealed all of them to her until this morning. I even took off my eye patch. What the hell was wrong with me? I had never done that for anyone but her. Ever.

After Lily and I had bared all to each other, we took a shower, but we didn't have sex again. As much as I wanted to, something held me back. And she didn't press for more either. I had a feeling that we were too emotionally stripped. Maybe in time, sex would help us through it.

Even though both of us said that we could trust each other, we were still holding back. But we would work through it because there was no way in hell that this was even remotely close to being over.

Once we were finished our shower, I drove Lily home. We spent the car ride in silence. She wasn't like most women I had been with who demanded for me to talk when I didn't want to. Something told me that Lily was just as guarded as I was, and I was determined to crack through her walls.

"I want to see you again," Lily said when I pulled into the driveway of her grandmother's place.

"I want to see you again too," I told her.

"Good." She gave me a soft smile. "Last night…"

I cupped her cheek, placing a soft peck on her mouth. "Was fucking incredible. You are incredible, Lily Pad."

"Thank you," she murmured, kissed my cheek, and slid from my car. "You better call me, Lucas. I know where you live."

I chuckled. "See you later, Lily."

She grinned, shutting the door behind her, and ran up to the small house. She turned, gave me a wave, and disappeared into her home.

Blowing out a slow breath, I pulled out of the driveway as a black SUV drove away. I frowned, remembering that FBI agent Lily had been having problems with. I made a mental note to check him out and ask her more about him.

Pushing that thought to the back of my mind, I drove home. As I was making my way to the tattoo shop, I saw Lena standing at the door. She waved.

I turned on the Open sign and unlocked the door. "Hey. Do we have an appointment today that I forgot about?"

"No." She shook her head, pushing past me.

"What's wrong?" I asked, heading behind the counter.

She started pacing back and forth, rubbing the back of her neck.

"Lena, what gives?" I leaned against the back counter, crossing my arms under my chest.

"I know you can get information." She stopped pacing. "I need you to look something up for me."

"What are you wanting looked up?" I had known her for quite a while, but I didn't research information for just anyone. She and I were friends and I knew she wouldn't go to the authorities on me, but she was also a flight risk.

"My daughter's father." Lena began pacing again. "He has a bunch of shit on me, but I need to have something on him. He wants my parents to keep custody of her. It'll help me when I fight. Please, Lucas. I need to win this fight. I need her in my life. She's the only thing keeping me sober." She came toward me. "Please."

"Don't you have the cops looking into this?" It wasn't that I didn't want to help her. I was retired, and I had to keep my nose clean for fear that I would end up back in jail. I didn't need to go through that shit again.

"Yes, but they're taking for-fucking-ever." Lena rested her hands on top of the counter between us. "I can pay you. Not in money but in anything else." Her dark eyes raked over me.

My jaw clenched. "I think you should leave."

"What?" She laughed. "Are you serious right now?"

"Did I stutter, Lena? We're not having this conversation again. So if that's all you stopped by for, you should leave. Now."

"Lucas." She shook her head, her cheeks reddening. "I need help."

"Not like that you don't. Have a little respect for yourself." I pushed away from the counter as my first client of the day came into the shop. "I have work to do." Ignoring her, I greeted my client and set up the tattooing station. The sound of the bell chiming above the door grated on my nerves. While discussing the tattoo with my customer, I couldn't help but think about Lena and her desperation for information. All she had to do was ask. She didn't have to pay me. Especially not with her body. Although years ago, I probably would have taken it as payment, but it was no longer my thing. And definitely not now after spending the night before with Lily.

The rest of the afternoon went by rather quickly. I had several clients booked for the day. Some with difficult pieces and some with easy ones but no matter what tattoo I was working on, it made the time move fast.

Once all of my appointments were done, I closed up shop and walked the few blocks to the local community center. It had been a routine for the past several years. Tattoo. Eat. Sleep. Meeting. Same shit, different day. And now Lily. Sweet delicious Lily. My body stirred, my thoughts traveling back to the night before. With her snug pussy wrapped around my cock, she was perfect. Everything I needed. And I couldn't wait for more.

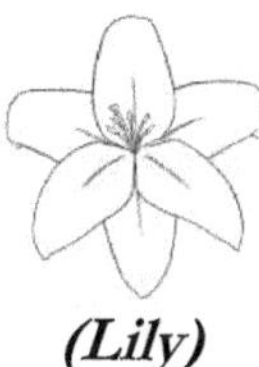

(Lily)

Stepping into the community center, I was greeted by the delicious scent of coffee and cookies. The church was still being renovated and the meetings would be here, now shared with the Narcotics Anonymous group. Since Toby was also a recovering drug addict, it all made sense. I liked this center and what they were known for. In the winter, it was opened up to the homeless, trying to take as many people off of the streets as possible.

"Lily."

I turned and was greeted by Toby. "Hey. How's Sandra feeling?"

"Good." He smiled. "She's here tonight." He looked around him. "Somewhere anyway."

I laughed. "It's weird being here and not at the church."

"I know but the church will be fixed up in a few months and we'll be back there in no time. We have some people in the area helping. They get a free meal out of it and also get paid as well. They're hoping it'll help get some of the homeless off the streets."

"I love that idea." I had recognized some of the people. A lot had come from the church, but some decided to attend meetings at other places instead of going to this one.

"You should come over for dinner sometime soon," Toby suggested.

"I would love—" The hairs on the back of my neck tingled. I looked over my shoulder, finding… "Lucas," I whispered.

He was standing with Sandra. They were talking quietly amongst themselves, but I couldn't help but notice how good he looked. Although I had seen him earlier that morning, he still sent butterflies rushing through my belly. But I wondered what he was doing there.

Lucas glanced over his shoulder, his gaze meeting mine. He licked his lips, turned away, and continued his conversation with Sandra.

"Do you know Lucas?"

I jumped, forgetting I was still standing with Toby. "Uh…"

"Hey, Toby."

My heart jumped as Lucas came up to us.

"Hey." Toby shook his hand. "How was your week?"

"Good. How was yours? Sandra was telling me that she's been sick." Lucas moved closer to me.

"She was but she's better now, thank goodness. She's worse than I am when she's ill." Toby laughed. "Have you two met?"

Lucas stuck his hand out. "Lucas."

"Lily." I smirked, sliding my fingers in his hand.

"Hmm…" Lucas kissed the back of my hand. "It's nice to meet you, Lily."

I laughed, my cheeks heating. "Ass."

Lucas winked.

Toby shook his head. "I'll take that as a yes." He checked his watch. "We're starting," he said, which was his gentle way of saying for us to find a seat.

I sat at one of the empty chairs at the back row.

Lucas sat beside me, placing his arm on the back of my chair. "Care to tell me why you're here, Lily Pad?" he muttered low enough for only me to hear.

"Probably for the same reason you are," I murmured. "We're all addicted to something."

Toby walked to the front of the room, staring out at the crowd. He stood behind the podium, did his usual greeting and asked if anyone wanted to share.

Lucas stood and much to my surprise, walked up to the front.

Toby clapped him on the shoulder and moved off to the side.

"Hi." His good eye burned into me. "I'm Lucas and I'm a drug addict."

My mouth fell open.

"This week hasn't been anything special. The struggles continue daily, but I have met someone, and for the first time since I can remember, I'm excited to see where things will go"

My heart warmed.

"I'm not sure what's going to come of it but it's fun. I know with having an addiction, relationships can be hard but, I'll take it for what it is right at the moment." He rubbed the back of his neck. "It's been almost eight years for me, but not a day goes by where I don't miss it. That delicious high. I realized quickly that I didn't want to submit to it anymore. Especially when it almost killed me."

I shifted in my seat.

Lucas ended his share shortly after that and joined me at the back of the room.

"I had no idea," I said softly.

"I could say the same for you, Lily." He placed his arm on the back of my chair once again and rubbed his thumb back and forth over my shoulder. "Are you going to share?"

I shook my head. "I don't usually."

"How come?"

"Because." I just didn't. Not that I had anything against it, but I was shy in that way when it came to my personal life.

"Lily."

"I don't want to talk about it, Lucas." I crossed my arms under my chest.

"Alright, Lily Pad. I'll take the hint."

I sighed.

The rest of the night was a blur. More people shared their stories. Lucas remained beside me, his big body stiff and rigid. As much as I liked him, I wasn't sure if I could share that part of myself with him. I had already shown him my scars. I appreciated just the same that he showed me his, but it still didn't mean I was ready to share everything with him. And I wasn't sure if I would ever be ready.

Ten

LUCAS

BLOOD COATED MY FINGERTIPS, *dripping off the ends until they fell to the ground in tiny little puddles. I watched the crimson liquid fall.*

Drip. Drip. Drip.

The pain no longer rushed through me. I wasn't sure if that was a good thing or not. Every inch of me was numb. Cuts and scrapes marked my knees and palms. Previous scars were sliced open, forcing them to bleed out onto the ground beneath me.

Sounds of crying slid through me. I covered my ears and squeezed my eyes shut, trying to ignore the begging and pleading for death. It was the only way we could get out of this hell. But it wouldn't work. It never worked.

The cries soon became muffled, followed by gagging.

Bile rose to my throat as the sounds of abuse washed over me.

The cries turned into sobs.

Groans of pleasure made my stomach twist.

"Please." That was Mel.

I couldn't save her. I couldn't save any of them.

No matter how much abuse was laid on us, not many of us died from it. No. If we ever got out of this hell, we would die after. And I couldn't wait.

Death. It was our ultimate savior. But it never came. That would have been the easy way out.

A sharp slice of pain erupted through my arm, followed by a warmth I had come to crave.

My body fell back onto the cold cement beneath me.

The sweet taste of submission slid over my skin, melting beneath it and rushing through my veins.

It was delicious. Sweet. Sweet delicious bliss. And it was mine.

My eyes popped open, landing on the ceiling above me. A sense of loss washed over me once I realized that I was back in my bed and no longer in the nightmares of my childhood. Although for the most part, my childhood sucked, and death would have been better, I missed the high of the drugs that were forced on me.

Rolling over in bed, I reached for my phone and called Lily.

"Yeah," she greeted, her voice husky.

"Lily." My gaze landed on the clock sitting on my nightstand. Shit. It was almost four in the morning. "I'm sorry for calling so late."

"Lucas? That's okay. Is everything alright?"

"No." I pinched the bridge of my nose. "I just needed to hear your voice."

"Oh. Okay. What's wrong?"

"Nightmare," was all I said.

"Ah, yes." She laughed lightly. "You woke me up from mine. So, thank you."

"What happened?" I wasn't sure if she would tell me, but I needed a distraction from the demons of my past.

"I wish we had alcohol for this." She cleared her throat. "I told you my parents died in a fire."

"You did."

"My father was a good man. He just made mistakes and unfortunately, he was an alcoholic. You'd think I would have learned and not followed in his footsteps but ..." She coughed.

"He lit a smoke and passed out. My mom and I were sleeping. The fire took him first. It had been so fast." Her voice wavered.

"Shit, Lily. I'm sorry."

"I woke to my room on fire. God, that pain was nothing I had ever felt before. After that, I moved in with my grandma." She laughed. "I can't believe she never kicked me out. I put her through fucking hell, Lucas."

I grunted. "She loves you."

"Yeah but no one should have to put up with the shit I did." Lily sighed. "Anyway, that's in the past."

"Why do you go to meetings?" I already knew she had an addiction. I just wanted to hear her say it. I wanted to know that I wasn't alone.

"Tit for tat, Lucas."

"Fine." I thought a moment and decided to tell her something not so damn heavy which would lead to her never wanting to see me again. "I grew up in the system. I don't know who my parents were. They died but I was never given their information. When I left the house I grew up in, I spent every day at the library, teaching myself how to use computers. I also read. I read a lot. It was the only time I felt normal. I imagined that I was in those books. That I lived the lives those characters led. I also didn't go to school for computers. I didn't go to MIT or anything."

"But you know just as much as the students there."

"And so do you, don't you, Lily?"

She cleared her throat. "Yeah. I guess."

"It comes naturally for us." I sat up in bed, leaning against the headboard.

"It does. And you still trust me? Even after knowing I hacked in to find your information. That trust is still there?"

"Yeah." My heart jumped. "I do. I know this is fast..."

"We've known each other for over a month now." Lily sighed. "I trust you too, Lucas. I never thought I would find that trust again."

"I get that, Lily Pad."

"I got in trouble a few years back," she said, changing the subject.

I grunted. "Baby, you and me both."

"We should compare stories." She laughed lightly.

"Not over the phone." I wasn't overly paranoid, but I didn't trust that the line wasn't being listened to. I could have called her from a more secure line, but I was desperate and needed to hear her voice when I woke up, so I chose my cell instead.

"Okay, Lucas." She yawned.

"I'll let you get some sleep."

"I work tomorrow but would like to see you after."

My stomach tumbled. "Sounds like a date."

"No. I don't want a date. I want to come over and for you to fuck me into my next life."

I chuckled, my cock lengthening at what she was suggesting. "Sounds even better."

She giggled. "Good night, Lucas."

I grinned. "Good night, Lily."

(Lily)

I hung up the phone, I laid back in bed. I couldn't believe I had told Lucas about the fire. I never told him about my problem and why I went to meetings, but I knew that would come in time. He also wasn't stupid. He probably figured it out already. Talking to him had been easy. Add to the fact he needed to talk to me after having a nightmare, it made me feel even better.

For the next hour or so, I tossed and turned, unable to fall back asleep. Giving up, I quickly took a shower, got dressed, and decided to cook my grandma breakfast.

"Good morning, dear."

"Morning." I held out a plate just as she came to my side.

"This is a nice surprise." She took it and sat at the table. "How's Lucas?"

"He's good." Or I thought he was, but I wasn't so sure after our conversation earlier.

"That's good." Grandma took a bite of her food, swallowed and pointed her fork at me. "I like him, but he has a dark past. Be careful with that, Lily."

"How could you know that?" I asked, placing a mug of coffee in front of her.

"I can sense it." She shook her head. "I've been around long enough to know. All I'm saying is, just be careful. That's all."

"Okay." I frowned, sat across from her, and began to eat.

"Are you two official now?"

"I…I'm not sure." I shrugged. "We're taking it one day at a time. No pressure."

She nodded and went back to eating in silence.

"Do you miss Grandpa?" I asked her, clearing the table of my dirty dishes.

"Every day." She sighed. "I hope you find what I had with him."

"I hope so too." A phone ringing in the distance, jarred through our conversation. "I have to get that." I jogged to my room and answered my cell, wondering who was calling so early. "Hello?"

"Good morning, Lily."

My stomach twisted. "What do you want, Killian?"

"Did you enjoy your date with Lucas Crane?"

I slumped onto the edge of my bed. "Why do you care?"

"He's not good enough for you."

"And you are?" I laughed. "Come on, Killian. You're married. You need to get over it."

"I want to see you. I need to explain"

"Go back to your wife." He was a douchebag. He was a good-looking douchebag, and I fell for it. He no longer did it for me. I had been desperate for a connection, for love and made the stupid choice of dating him.

"Go out with me. Let's talk."

"Why?" I felt like a damn parrot.

"Because I want to see you. I'm sorry for not explaining sooner. I miss you."

"I'm sorry—"

"Before you say no, please just give me a chance to explain."

I couldn't go out with him after being with Lucas. Although we had never made anything official, it wouldn't be right of me.

"I'm seeing Lucas." And I was seeing him later that night.

"We can go as friends then. I just want to see you. To talk"

"Friends. Right." I rolled my eyes. "Come on, Hayes. I know how you work."

"Please, Lily."

Guilt resonated on my shoulders at the desperation in his voice. "Why?"

"I just want to go to dinner. Not a date. Just two friends going out for food. To talk. That's it."

"Will you leave me alone if I say yes?" This was a stupid decision on my part, but I needed him off my ass.

"Yes."

"And you'll keep your hands to yourself?"

"Lily."

"Say it, Killian. Tell me you'll keep your hands to yourself."

"Fine. Yes, I'll keep my hands to myself."

"Good." I stood from the bed. "I'll go out for food with you, to listen to you, but the first time you hit on me or touch me, I'm done. You hear me?"

"Yes," he grumbled. "I hear you."

I shouldn't have agreed to go out with Killian. I wasn't normally this dumb, but he was driving me crazy with his constant badgering and his SUV popping up every time I turned around. I felt sorry for him. But now as I sat at the table in the Italian restaurant with him staring at me like I was his next meal, I suddenly felt dirty. And it was the same Italian restaurant that I had been to with Lucas a few weeks ago. Somehow, I knew that it was intentional.

"One warning, Killian." I took a sip of my water.

"I haven't done anything." He put back the rest of his beer, signaling the waiter over. "Another beer for me and whatever she wants."

"I'm fine with water," I told the waiter. "Thank you."

"You want just water?" Killian sat forward. "Are you sure you don't want a drink?"

"That is a drink," I told him.

"No, I mean like an alcoholic drink."

"Water is good enough for me." My stomach twisted with unease.

"Lily, you never had anything more than water or Coke when we were together. Are you sure you don't want wine? You look like a wine lady. She'll have a glass of your finest red," Killian told the waiter.

"No," I corrected him. "Just water. Please."

The waiter nodded and went back to the bar. The young man glanced at me over his shoulder before looking at Killian. He said something to the bartender. I couldn't read their lips but whatever they were talking about, sent a flutter of nerves racing through me.

"What was that about?" Killian demanded. "I'm trying to show you a good time and you turn down my offer for wine."

"This dinner is not for a good time. You wanted a chance to explain, and I'm giving it to you. I appreciate the offer, but I don't drink, so water is fine." I hated having to explain myself to him.

"Come on, Lily." Killian rolled his eyes. "Everyone drinks."

"Um…that is not true." I knew I shouldn't have agreed to go out with him but a part of me hoped for an apology. My grandmother taught me to be polite and to look for the best in people but clearly, this was not one of those cases. Killian pestering me about my lack of drinking was almost worse than him fucking me when he was married.

"Why don't you drink?" Killian asked as the waiter came back with his beer.

The waiter refilled my water and went to wipe the condensation on the pitcher when he dropped the napkin. He crouched to pick it up. "Lucas is here," he muttered.

My heart jumped.

The waiter stood, walking away and pushing through a double set of doors at the back of the restaurant.

"Everything okay?" Killian asked, now checking his phone.

"Yes." I stood. "I'm just going to use the washroom." Not waiting for him to respond, I headed to where the washrooms were and stopped suddenly.

Lucas was coming toward me. His body was stiff, his back rigid. His strong jaw was clenched tight. And his gaze was zeroed in on me like I was his next victim.

I rushed into the bathroom just as I was tackled from behind. I gasped. My hair was ripped back, some strands pulling free from my scalp. I whimpered.

"I don't like that you're here with another man," Lucas growled, shoving me forward. "We professed our trust in one another this morning, and yet here I find you with another man. Not only that, but a man you used to date."

Before I had a chance to comment, he pushed me into the nearest empty stall. Spinning me around, he slammed me up against the wall.

"Why the fuck are you here with another man?" he demanded, wrapping his hand around my throat.

"I was being polite." I slapped his hand away.

"Polite?" Lucas chuckled, the sound dark and inviting. "Baby, there's nothing polite about this shit. I handed you my trust and this is how you fucking repay me. By going out with your ex."

My back stiffened. "He's an ex because I found out that he's married. There's no going back for me, Lucas. I don't break up marriages."

Lucas released his hold on me, his eye searching my face. "He's married?"

"Yeah." I blew out a slow breath. "I've done a lot of messed up shit but that's a deal breaker for me."

"Why would you agree to go out with him then?" Lucas asked gently, running his finger down the length of my jaw.

"I was being polite. That's the truth. I thought maybe letting him explain, would give him some sort of closure and to get him to stop following me." I shrugged. "I realize now how stupid that sounds, but I promise you, there's nothing there. You can trust me."

Lucas's jaw clicked. "I trust you but I sure as fuck don't trust him."

"I would never expect you to." I stood on tip toes and kissed his cheek. "I don't want him. Only you, Lucas."

(Lucas)

After I had helped the owner of the restaurant with setting up his new security system, I was testing it when I saw Lily and that bastard on camera. I told the young waiter who had been serving them, to let her know that I was there. I was just going to talk to her but when she came down the hall, my alpha instincts took over. Once I found out that fucker was married and there was no way Lily would go back to being with him, I calmed down. For the moment anyway.

"Go back to your little date, Lily Pad," I said, kissing her cheek.

"It's not a date." She shivered.

"You can say it's not a date all you want but he thinks it is." I gave her ass a light tap. "I'll see you after."

She sighed. "Lucas, it's not a date. I told you he was married."

"Tell him that then, Lily."

She went to leave the stall when I grabbed her arm and pulled her back against me.

"Lucas," she whispered. "It's not a date, will never be a date, because as I told you earlier, he's married."

"You need to remind him of that then," I growled, nipping her earlobe.

"I did," she said, turning around and placing her hands on my chest. "I also told him that I would hear him out. Let him explain, and then I would leave."

"Has he explained yet?"

"No."

"There's your answer. He's stalling." I kissed the side of her neck and unlocked the bathroom stall.

"You going to stay here?" she asked me.

"Oh yeah."

She rolled her eyes. "You have nothing to be jealous over. He's not going to do anything."

"You should go," I said, ignoring her. "You don't want him wondering where you are but remember who you're spending the night with."

"Asshole," she muttered and left the bathroom.

I chuckled to myself, took a piss and quickly washed my hands before heading back to the owner's office. Since Lily was here with Killian, I needed to watch and make sure he didn't try anything. Or else I would break his fingers and cut out his tongue. I almost wished he did do something. I needed something to take the edge off. The jealousy coursing through me was new. I wasn't sure how to deal with it, but I knew that no matter what happened tonight, Lily was coming home with me.

Eleven

Lily

WHILE I SAT AT THE table with Killian and ate my meal, I could sense that Lucas was watching us. I enjoyed the jealous side of him. Not that he had any reason to be jealous in the first place though.

Killian was on his third beer when I returned from the washroom, the fifth by the time we were done the meal. His cheeks had a red tinge and his eyes were glassed over. He kept staring at my chest and licking his lips. But at no time did he ever offer to explain anything about his wife.

I bit back an eye-roll. Maybe Lucas had been right.

"I should go," I said, placing my napkin on top of my plate. The meal had been delicious but the company, not so much.

"You haven't had any dessert," Killian said, his voice husky.

"I don't want any dessert," I told him. "Thank you for dinner but I should really get going. My grandmother called me while I was in the bathroom."

He frowned. "You didn't bring your purse with you. How could she call you?"

Shit. "Listen, Killian. You called and invited me here under the pretense that you were going to explain about your wife."

"No." He slapped a hand on the table. "You listen to me, Lily. I was kind and invited you out for dinner when you would have been sitting at home by yourself or worse, holed up with that fucker, Lucas. What do you see in him anyway? Is it the tattoos? The eye patch? Because if that's your thing, I can get tattoos and wear a patch too."

"That has nothing to do with it," I gritted out, grabbing my purse and standing.

"Sit the fuck down," Killian barked.

I took that as my chance and went to walk away when he grabbed my arm.

"Sit. Down," he growled, squeezing my arm.

I winced as the pain from his firm grip spread up my arm.

"Let her go."

I jumped at the deep voice coming from behind me.

"What the hell do you want?" Killian released me, sitting back.

"Come on, Lily." Lucas cupped my nape. "I'll drive you home."

"Thank you for dinner, Killian." I reached into my purse and threw some cash on the table.

"Stay," Killian said, standing.

"No."

"She's my ex-wife."

I looked at him then, my heart panging for the guy who was so damn desperate for more. "I'm sorry that your marriage failed, but that doesn't change anything. I'm with Lucas now."

"Stay. Please," Killian insisted.

"I don't suggest causing a scene." Lucas moved beside me. He towered over Killian by a few inches and was definitely bigger in size.

Killian sat.

I let Lucas walk me out, thankful that Killian didn't cause a scene. "You didn't have to do that, you know."

Lucas shrugged, his hand finding mine. "Did you drive here?"

"No. I walked."

"You did?"

I could feel him looking down at me, but I only stared ahead as we walked hand in hand down the street. "I like walking."

"It's late, Lily."

"It's only eight. And before you tell me how dangerous it is, I already know that. I was actually going to take a taxi to your place but clearly, that's not happening anymore."

"Woman." Lucas pulled me into an alleyway. "Do you know what kind of monsters lurk in the dark around here?"

I laughed lightly, reaching out to touch his strong jaw. "I think the only monster I should be scared of, is standing right in front of me."

"You're going to be the death of me," he grumbled, grabbed my hand, kissed my palm, and pulled me from the alley.

"You like it, Lucas." I laughed. "Admit it."

He only shook his head. "Did you tell your grandmother that you were going to be out again tonight?"

"I did. She was thankful that it is you I'm spending the night with and not Killian. She doesn't like him."

"Neither do I."

I gasped, stopping suddenly and clutching my throat. "You don't? I never would have guessed."

Lucas rolled his eyes. "Women."

I giggled, standing on tiptoes and kissing his cheek. "Take me to your home, Lucas."

"Tell me something about you that no one knows," I said, placing my feet on Lucas's lap.

"Really?" He cupped my shin, turning his body toward me.

"Yeah." I sat forward. "Anything at all."

He tapped his chin. "I have a thing for this woman I only just met a short while ago."

I laughed, gently smacking his arm. "But I already know that. It doesn't count."

"How did you know I was talking about you?" he asked, waggling his eyebrows.

"Because you can't handle me, let alone another woman," I threw back at him.

He chuckled. "True." He thought a moment. "I spent a year in jail."

"Really? For what?" This could be interesting.

"I was…troubled as a teen. Hung out with the wrong people. Got caught." He shrugged. "Your typical shit."

"Ah, yes. The life of a troubled teen." I sighed. "Well if it helps any, I'm an alcoholic," I confessed, getting a feeling that he wanted the subject changed off of him. "Killian questioned tonight why I didn't want a glass of wine. I didn't want to explain it to him." I picked at a random fuzz on Lucas's hoodie. "It's frustrating."

"It can be but that's not something that no one knows, Lily Pad." Lucas pulled me into his arms. "You broke your own rules."

I laughed, running my finger down his jaw. "Fine. I like this guy."

"That's not—"

"Shhh…" I placed my finger against his lips. "I'm not done." I brushed my thumb over his bottom lip. "As I was saying. I like this guy who makes me feel…I don't know, special I guess. I have a hard time trusting people. My grandma is the only person who has never let me down. But I trust you and I've never had a guy become jealous like you were tonight."

"I've never had a reason to be jealous before. Not until you."

"Really?" I tilted my head. "You've never dated a woman who was with another guy who made you jealous? At all?"

"No." Lucas's jaw clenched. "I don't date, Lily Pad. Any time I spent with a woman, ended up in sex. It was all they wanted."

"Well, they're missing out on the best part." My chest pained for him.

"Yeah? And what's that?"

I placed a soft peck on his mouth. "You."

His breath caught. He cupped my nape, deepening the kiss. "You're fucking incredible."

I broke the kiss. "I'm not."

"You keep saying that, but I still don't believe you." Lucas brushed his hands up and down my legs.

"Most of the guys I went out with never cared if I went out to dinner with someone else," I confessed.

"Well, I care, Lily Pad. I don't give a shit if you were out to dinner as just friends. He's a man. So he's competition."

"I'm not attracted to him, even if he is no longer married." Killian was a good-looking guy. Until he opened his mouth.

"But you're attracted to me." Lucas ran his hands back up the sides of my legs and beneath my dress.

"You really have to ask that?" I breathed, pushing to my knees. "I was hoping you would take out your alpha male on me. Maybe let him fuck me in that bathroom stall."

"I was being a gentleman," Lucas said, his voice raspy.

"What if I didn't want you to be a gentleman?" I purred. "What if I wanted to feel you throughout dinner?"

"Fuck." Lucas snapped the sides of my thong.

"Hmm…does that turn you on, Lucas?" I licked down the length of his jaw to his ear. "Knowing that your big dick fills me up to the point, I can feel you after?"

"Lily," he growled. "Take my cock out and drop this cunt on it. Now."

I grinned. "Do you want something, baby?"

"Yes." His fingers dug into the cheeks of my ass. "Lily, I'm not going to repeat myself."

As much as I wanted to listen to him, I sat there and stared at him instead. Something passed between us.

"Lily," he said, his voice rough, his fingers digging into my hips. "Stop staring and give me what I want, baby."

I grinned, unbuckling his belt.

Lucas's nostrils flared. "I need to feel you. Tell me you're on the pill."

"I am." As soon as those two words left my lips, Lucas crushed his mouth to mine.

"I can't say that I've ever had a bath with someone before." I played with the bubbles, leaning against Lucas.

He chuckled, running his thumb back and forth over my nipple. "I can't say that I have either."

"This is nice." Although the tub was small and we had to squeeze into it, it was perfect.

"It is. It's probably the nicest thing I've ever done with a woman before." Lucas pushed me forward, grabbed the cloth off the side of the tub and dunked it in the hot water before running it over my back.

"Really?" I looked at him over my shoulder. "This is nicer than the sex too?"

His gaze popped to mine. His hand paused in its path along my back. "With anyone else, yes. This is nicer. But with you, all of it's nice."

My heart swelled.

"When did you realize you had a drinking problem?"

"When I started putting liquor in my coffee in the morning." I turned back around, taking the hint at the need for the subject change. "But I didn't realize it myself. My grandma said something. I spent months coming home shit-faced. I also spent many nights in the drunk tank because I was too intoxicated to take a taxi."

"Weren't you with your friends?" Lucas asked, running the cloth over the back of my neck.

I scoffed. "I don't have any friends. I've always been a loner. Spent most of my time with my nose stuck in a book."

"Or in front of a computer," Lucas added.

"Yeah." I shrugged, running my finger over a tattoo of a dragon that sat on his calf. "What made you get all of these tattoos?"

"To cover most of my scars. And they're also addicting."

"Well I can't say I've ever been with a guy who has his dick tattooed."

Lucas chuckled. "I was waiting for you to mention it."

I smiled. "I think your octopus likes me."

His laugh got louder. The sound was rich and deep. "I think he does too."

When we finished our bath, I went to get dressed but remembered I only had my dress from my dinner with Killian.

"Here." Lucas handed me a t-shirt and boxers. "These don't fit me anymore. They'll be big but more comfortable than your dress."

"Thank you." I slipped into the white t-shirt and plaid boxers. "Much better." I smoothed my hands down the shirt and looked up, finding Lucas staring at me. "What?"

He cleared his throat, looking away. "Nothing."

"What is it?" I asked, touching his arm.

"I like you in my clothes." He adjusted himself. "A lot actually."

I giggled, sidling up to him. "Really?" I asked, when my stomach rumbled.

"You didn't eat your dinner?" He pinched my chin, tilting my head back.

"I did but I think I worked up an appetite." I patted his chest. "Feed me."

"Yes, ma'am." He saluted me.

I followed Lucas out into the living room. I found that I liked his place. It was small but homey.

"I want to show you something first." He stopped in front of another door at the end of the hallway. "You like reading."

"I do."

He opened the door, turned on the light and motioned for me to enter.

I stepped past him, my eyes widening when they landed on books. So many books. All four walls were lined with floor-to-ceiling bookshelves. A throw rug sat in the middle of the floor with a red beanbag chair on top of it. It was absolutely perfect.

"Oh, Lucas." I smiled up at him. "I wish I had this many books."

He grinned. "Any time you're over, feel free to read whatever you want."

"Thank you." I stood on tiptoes and kissed his cheek.

He stared down at me. Something new passed between us. I wasn't sure what it was but him showing me his library made my heart skip a beat.

Clearing my throat, I stepped back out into the hall as he closed the door behind me.

Without saying a word, he headed to the kitchen.

I curled up on the couch and turned on the TV.

"Alright, Lily. Here's my masterpiece." Lucas sat beside me and handed me a plate with a sandwich on top.

I took it from him and lifted the top slice. "My favorite." I laughed.

"Yeah?" He grinned.

I giggled, kissed his cheek, and took a bite of the peanut butter and jelly sandwich. "Definitely," I said around a mouthful.

He chuckled. "You can never go wrong with a PB and J. Especially when it's strawberry jam."

"I agree. Or cereal," I added.

"Truth." He winked.

While we ate in silence, I found my feelings for Lucas grew with each passing second. I had never felt this comfortable with someone before, let alone a man. And he wasn't just any man. He was Lucas Fucking Crane.

When we were finished eating, Lucas grabbed my plate and brought the dirty dishes to the kitchen. He came back a moment later with two glasses of milk.

"Thank you." I snuggled into his side and took a sip.

"You're welcome, Lily Pad," he said, resting his arm across my lap.

For the rest of the night, we watched movies and talked about nothing important. It was nice. It was needed. It was ours.

Twelve

Lily

I WOKE THE NEXT morning to a loud banging. It jarred through the delicious dream I was having about a large tattooed man who took control of every inch of me. I groaned, grumbling a curse as the banging continued.

"Lucas," I croaked, my voice thick with sleep. After we had used each other good and hard the night before, we passed out on the couch. But now I was regretting that. My muscles were stiff, my mind foggy. "Lucas."

He stirred beneath me.

"Hey." I lifted my head, rubbing my eyes. "I think someone's at your door."

"Fucking hell," he grumbled, pushing out from beneath me. He kissed my head. "Stay here."

I nodded, wrapped the blanket around me, and drifted off.

"I need you," a woman said.

My eyes popped open. Well that woke me up. I sat up, finding a woman standing at the doorway. I frowned. It had been the same woman from when I first met Lucas. He had been working on her tattoo. What the hell did she want and why was she at his apartment?

"Lena, we've been over this. Come to a meeting," he told her.

"Fuck the meetings." She placed her hands on his chest. "Please, Lucas."

I coughed, raising an eyebrow.

Both Lena and Lucas glanced my way. She kept her hands on his bare chest. And his lips pulled up into a smirk.

Looked like he wasn't the only one who got jealous. Didn't matter. She shouldn't be touching him. "Everything okay?" I asked sweetly.

Lucas grabbed her wrists, pushing her back. "Lena, Lily. Lily, Lena. Now, tell me why you're really here."

"You know why I'm here. I need help." She placed her hands on her hips, glaring at me.

I bit back a laugh. Well this was something else that was new for me. I never had to deal with an ex before. I wasn't sure if she and Lucas had ever been a thing but by the way she wouldn't stop touching him and glaring daggers at me, she obviously wanted more. My stomach twisted. She looked to be more his type too. With tattoos and piercings, they would fit perfectly together. The only thing I had marring my skin were scars.

"I'm going to go take a shower," I muttered, rising from the couch.

"Lily, stay," Lucas demanded. "Lena, what the hell are you doing here?"

"Fine." She pursed her lips. "I just need help. That's all. I need to find out what I can on my ex. Please. I'll pay."

"What did I tell you last time? I am not fucking you." Lucas stomped away from her and into the kitchen. He came back a moment later with a mug. "Here." He handed it to her.

She sighed, taking the mug from him and took a sip and then another before letting out another sigh. "I'm sorry." Her cheeks reddened, her dark eyes meeting mine. "I'm not usually like this but…"

"You're desperate," I added for her.

Lucas moved to my side, placing his hand at the small of my back.

She nodded. "My ex is an asshole and my parents are just as bad. You would think they'd be on their daughter's side, but they aren't." Her chin wavered. "I'm such a mess. I need a drink and I need my daughter. She's the only reason I've stayed away from alcohol."

"What information are you wanting to find out?" Now that I understood what was going on, I kind of felt sorry for her.

"I…" Lena looked between us both. "I want to know what kind of shit he's into. I need something on him, so I can get my daughter back."

"Does he have full custody?" I asked.

"No, my parents do but it hasn't helped at all. I still can't see her." Her eyes welled. "Please. I need your help. And I'm sorry for throwing myself at you, Lucas. Clearly, there's something between you two. I'll step back. I just…I'm desperate."

My heart hurt for her. "Is there something we can do?" I asked Lucas.

"I don't do this shit anymore, Lena," Lucas told her. "You know that."

"I know." Her breath hitched. "I just…I need my daughter."

"Will you give us a moment?" I linked my fingers with Lucas's.

She nodded.

"Lucas." I tugged him down the hall to his bedroom. "Is there something we can do for her?"

"No." He turned to walk away but I stopped him.

"If you don't want to help her, let me try."

"It's not that I don't want to help her, Lily." He huffed, rubbing the back of his neck. "I'm trying to be a good boy. If I get caught snooping around, I could end up back in jail."

"Then let me try," I insisted.

"You want to help her after she was hitting on me?" He pinched my chin, tilting my head back. "I saw that jealous fire in you just a moment ago."

"I want to help a daughter get her mom back," I corrected.

He searched my face, grumbled a curse, and pulled away. "Fine."

(Lucas)

Lena and I had been friends for years. That was it. It never amounted to more. I trusted her, but she was desperate and desperate people did stupid things.

"Alright, Lena." Lily sat beside her at the kitchen table. "Give me all of the information you have on your ex and I'll see what I can find out for you."

Lena inhaled a shaky breath. "Thank you. I really mean that."

"I hope so," I murmured.

Lily shot me a look.

I raised an eyebrow, daring her to say something.

She patted Lena's hand. "Do you have a pen and paper?" she asked me.

"Yeah." I found her the items she was looking for and stood off to the side while they discussed Lena's ex. It had come to light that he was semi-powerful in our city. I bit back a scoff. No one was too powerful to not be found. If they had a name, I could find them. I just didn't tell the women that. Truth was, I didn't want to go back to jail. Especially not after finding Lily. I had to be a good little boy for fear that I would get thrown behind bars for the rest of my life.

"Alright," Lily said a half an hour later. "I think this is a good start." She stood, grabbing the pad of paper. "Thank you, Lena."

"No." Lena pulled her in for a hug. "Thank you. And again, I am so sorry."

"Don't be." Lily walked Lena out much to my surprise. "Well, that was fun," Lily said, coming back a moment later.

"You surprise me. Every fucking second I'm with you, Lily Pad, you surprise the hell out of me." I shook my head and headed into the kitchen to make some more coffee.

"Why do you say that?" Lily came up behind me, running her hands up my back. "I just wanted to help her."

I spun on her, grabbing her hands and pushed her back. "You should be careful."

She scoffed, rolling her eyes. Patting my chest, she reached around me and grabbed the mug of coffee I had just poured for her. "Worried for me, baby?" she asked, staring at me over the rim of her mug.

"Woman." I pinched the bridge of my nose. "You don't know the shit Lena said to me."

"She wanted you to fuck her." Lily shrugged. "Who doesn't, Lucas? Look at you."

It was my turn to roll my eyes. Sure, women offered themselves to me quite often, but it didn't mean shit. I had never been interested.

"You're surprised," Lily pointed out. "Aren't you?"

"No. Yes. Fuck. Listen, just be careful. You are way too nice."

She laughed. "Just because I offered to help her, doesn't mean I actually trust her. Also, if I can keep an eye on her, it means I know where she is, and I can make sure she keeps her hands off of you."

"Really." I took the mug from her hands and placed it on the counter behind me. "Why, Lily? Would it make you jealous knowing that she wanted me?"

"Why, yes, Lucas." Lily gripped the hem of my gray sweatpants, pulling me closer. "I think it would. Just like it made you jealous when I went to dinner with Killian."

I swallowed a growl at the mention of that fucker's name.

Lily grinned, leaning her head back. "Still jealous?"

In a quick move, I lifted her in my arms and dropped her on the counter before fisting her hair. Tugging her head back, I licked up the length of her slender throat. "Yes, Lily. I am fucking jealous. But there's a difference. I never fucked Lena. But you fucked Killian. He knows what you feel like. What you smell like. What you taste like."

"He doesn't," Lily breathed, wrapping her legs around my waist.

"He does." I placed a soft bite on the soft spot beneath her ear.

"No. He doesn't because he never tasted me." She pushed me back. "Sex with him was just that, sex. No foreplay. He was an asshole like that."

For whatever reason, that didn't make me feel better.

(Lily)

The mood in Lucas switched as soon as those words left my lips. He lifted me in his arms, crushing his mouth to mine and carried me over to the couch.

"What time do you have to leave?" he asked, his voice husky.

I glanced at the clock on the DVD player. "I have two hours."

"Good." He dropped me on my feet. "Strip and then kneel on the couch. Away from me."

I did as I was told, tossing the clothes to the floor and placing my hands on the back of the couch. My body trembled as I waited for my next instruction.

Lucas brushed his fingers up my spine, placing a soft peck on my shoulder. "Spread your legs."

My skin tingled under his touch. Spreading my knees wide, I stuck my ass out and waited.

He lowered to the floor behind me, pushing his head between my legs.

My eyes widened as I watched him.

He winked and for the next hour, he used me good and hard.

I sighed, my eyes fluttering closed. "Always so damn good."

Lucas chuckled, placing one last kiss on my cheek before pulling me to my feet. He helped me into the boxers and shirt before landing a hard swat on my ass.

"Mine," he whispered, covering my mouth with his.

My heart stuttered.

Oh. Shit.

Thirteen

LUCAS

THE FIRST SLICE OF pleasure erupting through me was unexpected but wanted. It had been a long time since I'd felt something so good. So delicious. So damn tight. The wet pussy sucked me deeper. The moans and gasps for more only made me fuck harder and faster.

But it wasn't enough. I wanted to hurt. To feel that pain I had grown accustomed to ever since I was a kid.

"Hit me," I demanded.

"What?" Wide eyes stared up at me.

"Hit me, whore," I ground out through clenched teeth.

"Fuck you, asshole." The woman pushed away from me. "I don't care how big your dick is. I'm not a whore."

I threw a wad of cash at her. "You are now."

Her cheeks reddened, her eyes glaring into mine. She glanced at the hundred-dollar bills on the bed.

I waited.

It didn't take long for her to cave and get back to bouncing on my dick. Money talked. Although I didn't have a lot of it, I had enough that could get me what I wanted when I wanted it. Women and drugs were no exception.

I shot up in bed, a sheen of sweat coating my skin. The nightmare or the memory rather, rattled through me.

"Lucas?" A gentle hand cupped my shoulder.

I jumped.

"Hey," Lily said gently. "Bad dream?"

I forgot she had come over after work. I grabbed her hand and kissed her knuckles. "I need a glass of water," I said, my throat dry.

She nodded. "Okay."

Pulling free from her gentle touch, I rose from the bed and went out into the kitchen, not bothering to put on any clothes. Grabbing a bottle of water from the fridge, I downed it, threw it in the trash, and grabbed another one.

"Did you want to talk about it?" Lily asked from behind me.

"Not really." I pinched the bridge of my nose, trying to ward off the familiar headache that came with my memories.

Lily had my white t-shirt on and leaned against the doorframe with her arms crossed under her chest. "You sure?"

"It wasn't a dream really. More of a memory. I wasn't...I was an asshole when I was younger." I let out a hard sigh, remembering the shocked look on the woman's face when I threw money at her. "Anyway, it was the first time I had sex with a woman." Or at least the first time where it wasn't out of desperation or forced into it. The women faced my wrath because I had nothing else to give them. But I wanted to give Lily more. I just didn't know how.

"I like you, Lucas."

My heart stuttered. "I like you too, Mel. But not in the way you need."

That was the first time I had hurt her, and it only became worse from there.

"You had a dream about losing your virginity?" Lily asked, pulling me from my thoughts. "Wouldn't that be a good dream?"

I swallowed the bile rising to my throat. "I wasn't a virgin, Lily."

"What?" Her eyes widened a moment later. "Oh. I'm—"

"Don't. Don't say you're sorry. Don't say any of that shit. It's not your fault. It's no one's fault but the adults involved." I shook my head. "Doesn't matter. It's done."

"Clearly it's not done." Lily pushed away from the doorframe and took a tentative step toward me. "Tell me."

"Why, for you to pity me?"

"No." Her head jerked back. "God, Lucas. I just want to know you. That's it."

"You want to know me." My brows narrowed. "You want to know how I was molested as a kid? To tell me how sorry you are for that happening? You want to know that I was forced to do things to other kids…" Bile burned my throat. "It doesn't matter." I pushed away from her.

"Lucas."

"Don't." It wasn't her fault. But the dreams, the fucking memories, were going to destroy me. They had been eating at me ever since I escaped that hell and eventually, I would be consumed by them completely. It was only a matter of when. I couldn't control them. I needed them to stop but I didn't know how. Fuck, I needed a drink. I needed something to mask the demons of my childhood. To get rid of the uninvited guests that had taken up residence in my mind for as long as I could remember.

I stood at the large window overlooking the building beside the shop. The sun was rising over the city. It looked like it was going to be a beautiful day. Too bad my mood didn't match.

"Lucas." Lily came toward me, gently touching my back.

"Lily," I growled, my body tensing.

"Stop." She rested her cheek against my back. "I'm not pitying you. I'm just touching you."

I sighed, thankful that she didn't press for more. Even though I knew she had every right to ask questions, she didn't.

(Lily)

I didn't know what happened to him. After Lucas had blurted about being molested as a kid, he closed up. We had woken up early after he had his nightmare or dream or whatever he wanted to call it and he drove me home. It was on the tip of my tongue to demand answers. To beg to spend the day with him. To make him feel better. But something told me that he needed some time alone. I just hoped he didn't push me away completely.

When we pulled into my driveway, Lucas put the car in park.

I turned to him. "Thank you for last night."

He nodded but didn't meet my gaze.

"Lucas?"

He looked at me then. "What?"

I tapped my mouth.

He leaned over, placing a soft peck on my lips. "Don't be mad at me, Lily. I just...I need...I need time. I want to tell you everything. I need to tell you. I..."

"I know." I cupped his cheek, kissed his forehead, and left the car. Luckily, I made it into the house without being seen by my grandma, so I could quickly change. I was sure she would have questions as to why I was dressed in Lucas's clothes rather than my own.

"Lily," Grandma called out from the kitchen.

I got dressed in sweats and a t-shirt before joining her in the kitchen.

"Did you have a good night?" she asked, placing a mug of coffee in front of me.

"I did. Until this morning anyway." I took a sip of the coffee and let out a sigh. There was still no official title for what Lucas and I were doing but I knew that I didn't want anyone else.

"What do you mean?" She sat across from me.

"I mean…I don't even know what I mean. I like Lucas. I like him a lot. But he's…" I thought a moment. "Troubled I guess is the right word."

"I could actually sense that." Grandma reached across the table and grabbed my hand. "But you like him, and he obviously likes you. That means something. You've known each other for how long now?"

"Nearly three months. Roughly."

"And I have a feeling that whatever's building between you two is only going to continue to grow."

"But I don't know what to do for him." My chest tightened. "I want to help him feel better."

"Maybe you can't. People who come from a troubled past like he has, may never feel better."

Although I understood what she was saying, I still wanted to help him in any way that I could. I wanted to at least help him deal with his past. Whatever that was.

"Just be patient." Grandma patted my hand. "That's all you can do right now."

I nodded but it still didn't make me feel better.

Excusing myself from the table, I headed to my bedroom. The last few weeks had been amazing with Lucas. I learned things about myself I never knew before. I had been with guys. A lot of them in fact, but none of them ever made me feel the way he did. I felt wanted, beautiful, and so damn complete when it came to him that I wanted more. I was addicted to his touch. I craved him. His hands on me. His lips on my skin. His deep voice in my ear, telling me all the dirty things he wanted to do to me.

My skin tingled, the tiny hairs on my body dancing with pleasure the longer I thought of Lucas.

All I knew was that I needed a shower and I needed to take advantage of the ecstasy rushing through me.

The longer I thought of Lucas, the hotter my body burned.

Trudging into the bathroom, I locked the door behind me and stripped completely. Turning on the hot water, I stepped into the shower. I let out a sigh as the liquid rained down over me. My fingers slid down my body, my other hand massaging and kneading my breasts. "God, Lucas," I whispered.

I fell to the floor of the tub, inching my hand between my legs. A soft moan escaped me when I came into contact with my soaked center. Although something had switched between us and I wasn't sure if it was for the better or worse, I still craved him. I needed him in ways I never knew existed before. I needed him all over me. Inside me. In the deepest part of my soul.

I bent over, wishing Lucas were there with me. I imagined his hands on my skin. His mouth on mine. His cock deep inside me while he took us past the point of bliss and into a pool of passion and ecstasy.

Thrusting two fingers inside of me, I rode out the waves of pleasure, his name leaving my lips a moment later on a soft cry. I chewed my bottom lip to keep from crying his name out louder and trembled through my delicious release.

Once my body calmed down, I let out a soft sigh and finished my shower. The release wasn't enough, but it would have to do.

(Lucas)

While I was making myself a cup of coffee, the scent of roses wafted into my nose. I squeezed my eyes shut, savoring the sweet smell. It didn't make sense. It never did. One moment, I hated the smell and the next, I craved it.

Opening my eyes, I glanced around the room, finding one of the other addicts placing a bouquet of roses on their chair. She had a small smile on her face. A man came up to her, pulling her into a hug.

She laughed, wrapping her arms around him. "Thank you for the flowers."

I looked away, not wanting to intrude on their private moment. I gave myself a shake and went back to my cup of coffee.

"Hey, Lucas."

My gaze popped up from the cup I was about to take a sip out of and found Toby coming toward me. "Hey."

"How's it going?" he asked, clapping my shoulder.

"Not too bad." I hadn't seen Lily in a few days but other than that, life was fucking perfect. I bit back a scoff at that.

"You sure?"

I rolled my eyes.

"How's everything else going?"

"What are you asking me, Toby?" I liked the guy but with him being my sponsor, he got a little too personal at times and it drove me crazy. Although, I wasn't always easy to get along with, especially in the beginning, but it still didn't mean I wanted to tell him all of my shit.

"Are you and Lily seeing each other?" He made a coffee for himself and grabbed a cookie from the tray on the table before popping it into his mouth.

"I'm not sure that's any of your business." I wasn't telling him anything more about Lily. He was aware that we knew each other but that was it. And that was all I wanted at the moment. We already had issues with Killian. I didn't need to add another man to the mix. Even though Toby was married, he was still a man and Lily was beautiful. She just didn't know it which made her even more attractive.

"It is my business when both of you are recovering addicts. You can either support one another or drag each other down. I'm your friend but I'm also your sponsor and as your sponsor, I want to know what you could be dealing with."

"I…" I rubbed the back of my neck. "I appreciate that."

"Just be careful is all I'm saying." A dark shadow passed over Toby's face.

My chest tightened. "I will."

"Are you sharing tonight?" he asked, looking out at the crowd gathering.

"Don't I always?" Although I hated talking, telling these people about my life was almost like a cleansing in a way. They didn't know everything, but they knew enough where it felt like some of the weight from my demons had been lifted off my shoulders. It wasn't a lot, but it would have to do. Because if Lily found out everything that had happened to me and what I was forced to do to others, especially to Mel, I wasn't sure if she would be able to handle it.

Fourteen

Lily

AFTER GETTING OFF OF work late because one of my grandmother's friends wanted me to play a game of Bridge with him, I rushed to the church that held the meetings I frequented. But when I reached the door and saw that it was still closed due to renovations, I swallowed a curse and quickly made my way to the center instead. I had been so damn distracted, I forgot to head to the right place.

It was pushing eight at night. The sun was setting over the city. It was later in the summer, so the evening was cooler than usual, but it was warm enough that a light sweater would do.

I should have driven but living in the city, everything was close together, so I didn't think anything of it and walked instead.

Once I rounded the corner, the lights from the center came into view. I picked up my pace. As soon as I walked by an alleyway, I was grabbed from behind.

My heart jumped to my throat, my stomach dropping to the ground beneath me.

I was shoved forward, pushed to the ground and a heavy weight landed on top of me. "Please," I pleaded. "Please stop."

But the person didn't say anything. Their hot breath fanned over the side of my head. The scent of stale alcohol wafted into my nose, forcing bile to my throat.

I struggled beneath them, trying with everything that I was made of to get away from whoever was on top of me. "Stop. I don't have any money."

Hands ripped at my clothes, a heavy fist landed against the side of my face. My head was pulled back and slammed hard into the ground.

Spots danced in my vision, a metallic taste coating my tongue. Agony erupted through my face and my head rang. This was it. I was going to die.

"Please stop," I whimpered.

The person towered over me, the stench of their breath made my stomach churn.

A bang erupted in the distance, followed by a cat screaming. Sirens sounded not too long after that. The person lifted off of me and kicked me hard in the stomach.

I cried out, curling into a ball, pain exploding through my ribs.

They did it again before running down the alleyway.

A sob escaped me. Rising onto shaky arms, I pushed to my feet. My legs wobbled. Every inch of me hurt. I couldn't go home like this.

Lucas.

(Lucas)

After the meeting, I made my way home. It had been close enough to my place that I could always just walk. It was a nice summer night. Not too hot. Not too cold. It was perfect if you asked me. It was my favorite time of year. Even though there were no beaches in the area, I still enjoyed the summer weather.

A sound off in the distance interrupted my thoughts about sand, sun, and water. My hackles rose the closer I got to my car that was parked in the alleyway by my apartment.

A whimper sounded, followed by a soft curse.

I walked around my car, finding a bundled-up heap at the base of my door. "What the hell?"

"Lucas?"

"Lily?" I rushed to her. Her hair was a mess, dirt and debris coated her face. Her clothes were torn. Her nose was off center. She was holding her sweater against it, the material soaked with blood. "What happened?"

Her breath hitched, her eyes shining.

"Alright, Lily Pad. I got you." I picked her up in my arms, cradling her against my chest. Unlocking the door to my apartment, I kicked it closed, relocked it, and carried her inside. Throwing the keys on a table sitting by the wall, I brought her to the bathroom.

When we reached the smaller room, I sat her on the counter and turned on the light. Her light brown curly hair fell in front of her face. It had leaves and sticks in it.

"Look at me," I demanded, my voice rougher than I would have liked.

Bright green eyes met mine.

A growl escaped me. I cupped her cheek.

Her eyes fluttered closed.

"Tell me what happened." Checking her nose, I took the sweater from her when I noticed that the bleeding had stopped.

"I was on my way to a meeting. I stopped off at the church because we were told the renovations would be done but when I got there, I realized that they aren't. I forgot that they were running into problems that delayed them a bit. So I started walking to the center, went past an alleyway and got…I got…" Her chin wobbled. "I was attacked. I don't know by who. I didn't see them."

My vision clouded. "You should go to the hospital."

"No." She shook her head, wincing at the movement. "They're just going to ask me questions that I don't know the answers to and then they'll get the police involved. Like you, I'm trying to be a good girl and stay away from the police. I…"

"Alright, sweet girl. I understand. But you're going to explain that last part to me later."

She nodded. "Okay."

"I have to make a call but let's get this nose taken care of first." I tilted her head back. "If a doctor does this, it'll look prettier."

"I trust you, Lucas," she murmured.

My heart jumped. "Okay, baby. This is going to hurt."

"Just do it." She grabbed onto my waist. "Okay. Go."

"One. Two." Pop.

She screamed, tears rolling down her cheeks.

"I'm sorry." I cupped her face, kissing her forehead. "I'm so fucking sorry." I was going to kill the bastard who attacked her.

"It's fine." She took a breath and then another. "How does it look?"

I stared down at her. Although she was dirty, bloody, and bruised, with her freckles and dark green eyes staring up at me, she was absolutely perfect.

I hurt. God, I hurt everywhere. Even spots that weren't hit or broken by that bastard, hurt.

"How are you feeling?" Lucas asked, wiping a cloth over my cheek.

"I'm sore in spots I didn't even know could be sore."

He gave me a soft smile. "It's adrenaline."

"Oh." I frowned. "How did you know what to do for my nose?"

"I've broken many bones in my life, Lily. I didn't have access to proper medical care at times, so I had to do it all on my own."

"Oh." My chest ached. Everywhere fucking ached. "Thank you."

"You don't have to thank me. I'm just glad you're okay. But I need you to clear the air for me." His dark eye met mine, his jaw clenching. "Did anything else happen?"

"It never got that far. Something spooked him. Or I'm assuming it was a man. They were strong." I touched Lucas's arm. "I wasn't raped."

"Fuck." He leaned his forehead against mine. "Thank God."

"Yes. I've been through a lot of shit in my life but that…" I swallowed hard. "Anyway. I'm sorry if I ruined your night."

"You could never ruin my night." Lucas helped me off the counter and out of my dirty clothes. "I didn't have any plans anyway."

"Oh. Okay." I held onto his hand as he started a bath for me. "I can do this myself."

"Not happening," he bit out, helping me step into the tub.

"Lucas." I cupped his cheek. "Hey."

"I'm having a hard time, Lily. A real fucking hard time. I don't see or hear from you for days and then I come home and find you at my door, broken and fucking beaten." His gaze snapped to mine. "So forgive me for wanting to kill the motherfucker who laid a hand on you."

"I thought…I felt like something was off the last time I saw you. I didn't want to become clingy. I thought maybe you would want me to stay away. I know we started out having trust issues but that's in the past. I do trust you, Lucas. But I…I'm sorry. I just…" I took a deep breath. "I'm new to this."

"So am I. And I trust you too, Lily. I've never had a relationship before. I know I'm new to this." He lowered me into the tub, kneeling on the floor beside me. "But please don't go days again without at least texting me. Alright?"

"Okay. I'm sorry." I leaned over, placing a soft peck on his mouth. "Forgive me?"

He let out a huff. "Yeah, baby. I forgive you. If you weren't broken and bloody, I'd spank your ass for scaring me."

"Give me a few days to heal." I gently patted his cheek. "Then you can do all the spanking you want."

He chuckled, shaking his head. "Lay back."

I did as I was told when a sharp pain screamed through my abdomen. I had been so focused on my nose, that I forgot I had been kicked in the ribs. "Oh God."

"What?" Lucas pushed his fingers against my ribs under my left breast.

I cried out, my eyes welling at the slice of agony erupting through me.

"I think your ribs are broken or at least bruised. Fuck. I'm going to kill him." When Lucas went to pull away, I latched on to his arm.

"No. I need you here with me. Please, Lucas."

"I'm here." He pulled his hand from mine and cupped my cheek instead. "I promise I'm not going anywhere."

"Okay." I blew out a slow breath. "Okay."

After Lucas cleaned me up and helped me into a pair of his boxers and a t-shirt, he led me out into his living room and sat me on the couch. He came back a moment later with two plates and two glasses.

I laughed. "Another peanut butter and jelly sandwich?"

"Only the best for my girl." He kissed my head and sat down beside me. He placed the glasses of milk on the table in front of us.

"Thank you." Although I was in pain, I felt better. He had given me pain meds, rubbed a cream over my skin that would help soothe the ache in my muscles, and fed me. My grandmother was going to lose her shit when she saw me but for now, I would keep what happened tonight just between Lucas and I. I sent her a quick text, letting her know that I was with him and that I was out for the night.

She didn't even hesitate and told me to have fun. God, I loved her.

"I think you should set up a security system at your grandmother's house."

I looked up at Lucas. "You think?"

"Yeah. Something's off with Killian and then you get attacked tonight. I just think it would be best."

I nodded. "I'll get some supplies tomorrow morning and set it up."

"Good." Lucas blew out a slow breath, his big body relaxing. "Good. I need to make that call but I'll be back in just a moment."

"Okay."

He handed me the remote and kissed the top of my head.

I turned on the TV.

Lucas left the living room.

While I ate my sandwich, I couldn't help but wonder what would have happened tonight if my attacker had never been spooked. I shivered at the thought.

"Lily."

I jumped, finding Lucas standing a few feet away.

"Don't think about it. You're safe."

"I...how did you know?" I asked.

"You had a far off look on your face." He sat beside me. "I've been there. I get it. But you're safe. I promise you that you are safe."

"Thank you," I whispered, leaning against him and handed him the remote.

Lucas went through the channels until we came across a comedy. Every so often, we would laugh at something stupid the actors did or said but no conversation fell between us. It didn't need to. It was perfect.

Once I was done my sandwich, I drank my milk and placed the dirty dishes on the table. Laying on my side, I winced through the pain and rested my head on Lucas's lap.

"Sleep, Lily. I got you." Lucas covered me in a blanket, inching his hand beneath it and the shirt I wore. He ran light touches over my throbbing ribs.

"Who did you call?" I asked, laying down.

"Just a friend. I have him looking into shit."

"Okay." I yawned, a thought crossing my mind. I sat up.

"What's wrong?" Lucas asked, a deep frown settling between his brows.

"The person who attacked me was spooked by a noise. It was in the alleyway between two businesses. They might have cameras. It was dark but maybe we can see something."

Lucas's jaw clenched. "I'll work on that. You need to rest."

"But I can help."

"No," he snapped, shoving to his feet.

I pushed off the couch, crying out at the agony tearing through my ribs.

"Shit." Lucas gripped my arms, forcing me back onto the couch. "You need to rest."

"Let me help you. I just…" My body shook. "I don't want to be alone."

"I wasn't going to leave you. I have my friend looking into things but I was going to see if I could find out anything as well." Lucas cupped the back of my neck. "Come with me." He held out his hand.

I slid my fingers in his, letting him help me to my feet.

We walked to a door that stood off to the side, close to the kitchen. I hadn't seen it before now.

"I've never shown anyone this room before, Lily." He brushed his fingers down my cheek. "But I trust you. Don't make me regret this."

"I won't." A shiver rippled down my spine at the threat hidden beneath his words. "Show me, Lucas."

He unlocked the door and pushed it open before pulling me in front of him. Flicking on the light, he cupped my shoulders and moved me farther into the room.

My eyes widened at what lay before me. I knew Lucas was a hacker and had gotten in trouble for it, but I still wasn't expecting to see the four screens staring back at me.

"I do all of my work in here. I have a laptop that I can use when I need to be more mobile. But this has all of the shit we need to find out what we can on Lena's ex and your attacker. If we can see their face."

"I forgot about Lena's ex." God, I had promised her, and I forgot.

"Hey, don't worry about it." He grabbed my hand, pulling me to the chair in front of the desk and sat before tugging me onto his lap. "Do your thing, Lily Pad."

"It's been a long time since I've played with a set up like this," I told him. "I usually just work from my laptop."

"Did you get caught?"

I nodded, chewing my bottom lip and looked away. Running my hand over the sleek keyboard, I bit back a whimper at how shiny it was. How much more advanced this setup was than my lame old laptop.

"Tell me everything that happened." Lucas wrapped an arm around my waist, leaning his chin on my shoulder.

"After the fire, I stayed inside a lot because of my scars. I didn't go out in the summer or wear pretty sundresses or anything like that. I felt like people could see them through my clothes even though I know now that it wasn't possible. But I was a girl who had lost both of her parents, had to move across the country, go to a brand-new school, and all that. I had to leave my friends behind. Although, they weren't good friends because they never tried contacting me." I laughed lightly. "I'm rambling."

"I'm enjoying your rambling." Lucas kissed my shoulder. "Continue."

"Well, my grandma suggested that I go to the library, and so I did. That was when I played with a computer for the first time. Although I couldn't really do much at first. I eventually was able to get my own computer and well…I got caught hacking into my grandmother's lawyer's computer. He was taking more money than he should have when my grandpa died but she didn't have any proof. I got the proof and he was fired, his license suspended, and we also found out that he was involved in money laundering. So it was a win-win for all of us." I shrugged. "God, that was so long ago."

"How did you get in trouble?"

"I was asked how I found out the information and yeah…uh…" My cheeks burned. "My grandma accidently ratted me out. Saying that I found out the information on the 'computer thing.' Her words. It was innocent but I was given community service as punishment. I'm just glad it wasn't any more than that."

"Did you work on your skills so you wouldn't get caught?" Lucas asked, turning on his computer.

"I would never do such a thing. I haven't touched a computer since." I winked.

He chuckled. "Right and I'm your knight in shining armor."

"You are?" I kissed his cheek. "My hero."

He smirked, shaking his head. "Let's do some research."

"Alright." I clicked some keys. "I actually did research on you to make sure you weren't married," I confessed.

"Really?"

"Yeah. Although Killian and I didn't date for long, it still hurt." I coughed when Lucas tensed beneath me. "Anyway, it's done and over with. But that was one of the reasons I tried finding out as much information on you as I could."

"I get it." Lucas kissed the back of my neck. "I promise that I'm not married and have never been married."

"Good." After realizing the cameras between the two buildings where my attack happened, came up with nothing, I went in search of Lena's ex. Hacking into the police records, I searched his name.

Geoffrey MacKan. Even his name sounded douchey.

Half an hour later and we came up with nothing. "He doesn't have a record at all."

"He has to have done something." Lucas slid out from beneath me and started pacing.

"There's not even a speeding ticket." I continued searching. Maybe I missed something. "I can search her parents. Do you know their names?"

Lucas shook his head. "I'll call Lena." He left the room.

I nodded, going back to the computer. There was nothing on her ex.

Lucas came back a moment later. "Here." He handed me a piece of paper with two names on it.

"Okay. Let me work my magic." Although my magic was coming up short it seemed, I was able to find out that Lena's parents weren't as perfect as they led on. "I don't think tax evasion will stop them from having custody of her daughter though."

"There must be something more," Lucas added.

"I'm not sure." I massaged the back of my neck. "I hate not being able to find out anything."

"We'll figure this shit out," Lucas said.

"Yeah."

"Let's take a break. You also need your rest." Lucas held out his hand.

I slid my fingers in his, letting him pull me gently to my feet.

He shut off his computer, walked me out of the room and locked the door behind us. "I need to fix the security on this room," he mumbled.

"I can help you with that. Maybe you should have a fingerprint scanner or something," I suggested.

"See?" He kissed my temple. "This is why I like you."

I laughed, wincing when a sharp pain stabbed me in the ribs. "I need these to heal."

"They will. In time." Lucas went to the kitchen.

I sat on the couch in the living room and pulled the blanket around my legs.

He came back a moment later with two bottles of water. "I'm sure you're wishing it was a beer or something stronger."

"Yeah." I took the bottle from him and removed the cap before taking a long swig of the cool water. "But this will do. It's safer this way I guess."

"I know that feeling." He placed his arm on my lap. "How are you feeling?"

"Just sore but my headache has gone away." I looked up at him. "Thank you for taking care of me."

He nodded once.

Turning to him, I picked at a fuzz on the blanket. "Lucas?"

"Yeah, Lily?"

"Can I ask what happened to your eye or the scars on your mouth or any of the scars you have for that matter?" I cleared my throat. "I know it's not my business, but I just want to know more about you. I know what you've told me already but…"

"My past is not a good one, Lily, and I've spent years trying to forget it." He stood from the couch and headed toward the kitchen. "Are you still hungry?"

I sighed. "No. I'm fine, thank you."

"Alright." He disappeared into the kitchen, not answering any of my questions. I had a feeling that it would be a long while before I got what happened out of him.

If ever at all.

Fifteen

LUCAS

COLD, BLACK EYES STARED down at me. Pain sliced through my lips forcing tears to roll freely down my cheeks, but I didn't cry out. I didn't make a sound. I refused. Because then they would know that they'd won. It was what got me in this situation in the first place. They liked it when we screamed but not when they had company over. It made them look bad. It made them look like they weren't doing their job in taking care of us properly. It made them look like vile human beings if we screamed. Even though the walls in the basement were soundproof, sometimes they brought their guests to the den which was right above where we stayed. And if we tried hard enough, if we screamed loud enough, we could be heard. Maybe not a lot. But some. Enough that it pissed them off and made us regret ever opening our mouths in the first place.

Why didn't anyone ever ask about us?

"You think you're so smart, boy, trying to scream, thinking they will hear you?" The cold eyes glared at me, the voice rough as it slid over my skin.

"Fuck you," I murmured, which came out muffled. I wasn't sure if he understood me but when he pulled his hand back and his fist landed against the side of my face, I clearly thought wrong.

Spitting out the blood that had coated my tongue, I struggled against my binds.

"Sit still." He grabbed my face, his fingers digging into my cheeks. Taking the needle dangling from the string in my lips, he continued sewing my mouth shut. Once he was done, he cut the string with scissors and took a step back. He crossed his arms under his chest and smirked. "Now you can't say any of that shit that always interrupts our production. I really have no idea why I never thought of this before."

"That's because I'm the one who thought of it." She came up beside him, wrapped her arm around his shoulders, and kissed his cheek.

He turned and cupped her face, placing a hard smack on her lips. "You watch too many horror movies."

"But it works." She smirked. "Doesn't it?"

He grinned, covering her mouth with his.

I looked away, but the sound of kissing only became louder and louder. It quickly escalated until they were both panting and gasping for air.

"Are you disgusted by us, boy?" the man demanded. "Is she not good enough to watch? I know you like it when she rubs that rose oil on you."

I swallowed hard, trying to ignore what was happening in front of me.

The sound of skin slapping against skin, followed by moans, slid into my ears. I counted down the days until I could watch them die. Until I could find out their names and make them beg for me to end their lives. It would happen. Maybe not now. Maybe not tomorrow. But I had made it a mission to end them.

"Look at me, boy," the woman demanded.

I looked their way, but I shouldn't have. The man had her bent over the desk, his body slamming into hers. Her eyes were bright with lust and the sounds of pleasure only grew as he fucked her hard and rough.

Something at the corner of my eye, caught my attention.

Mel stood off to the side, hidden in the shadows but I could still see her. She brought her finger up to her mouth. I thought she was telling me to be quiet. It wasn't like I could say anything anyway. But when she stuck her finger in her mouth instead, the tiny hairs on my body rose. Her gaze locked with mine. She brought her hand down to her shorts, reaching beneath the hem and pushing it lower. When she reached that spot between her legs, she chewed her bottom lip.

I shouldn't have been watching but I couldn't help it. I couldn't take my eyes away. She had sucked me into her world, seducing me with the mere touch of her finger. Her gaze fell to my lap, a slow smirk spreading on her face.

I shouldn't have reacted the way I did.

This was wrong on so many levels. My body betrayed me but I couldn't help but watch Mel touch herself.

The man noticed.

I paid for it.

All because of her.

(Lily)

I woke to the spot beside me, empty and cold. I sat up, not sure where Lucas was. Maybe he had gone for a drink of milk. I would do the same if I couldn't sleep.

After our evening of watching movies and pigging out on popcorn, I had fallen asleep on the couch only for Lucas to carry me to his bed. I was still sore from the attack but with him taking care of me, I felt much better than I would have if I had to do it on my own.

Sliding out from beneath the covers, I went to the bathroom. When I was finished, I headed back to bed only to find Lucas huddled on the floor in the corner.

"Oh God." I rushed to him, dropping to my knees in front of him. "Lucas, what's wrong?"

He didn't answer but his big, tattooed body shook and trembled.

I touched his shoulder, his skin cold and clammy.

He jumped, throwing himself in my arms and knocking me over.

"Hey." I wrapped myself around him, holding him against me. "You're fine, Lucas. I got you. It was just a nightmare. I'm here. I'm always here." I murmured those words over and over until he stopped shaking. He didn't release me. He only squeezed me harder. The tight hold he had on my body made me wince as the pain sliced through my ribs, but I didn't care. I was there for him. No matter what.

"Did you want to talk about it?" I asked, running my fingers through the hair at his nape.

He pushed his face into the crook of my neck, his hot breath fanning over me.

"Lucas," I whispered, straddling him.

Although we were wearing clothes, I could still feel every inch of him pushing between my thighs. But this wasn't the right time. I knew that. Even though his body clearly didn't.

"Hey." I leaned back, cupping his face. "As much as I like you between my legs, now's not the right time."

He looked away, kissing my palm.

"Lucas." I placed a soft peck on his scarred lips before standing and holding out my hand.

He placed his fingers in mine, letting me help him to his feet. Although it was dark in the room, I could see the outline of the bulge in his pants because of the lighting of the moon. I shivered. God, he was beautiful. Feral. And all mine.

With his hand in mine, I led him to the bathroom and turned on the water to the tub. "Take off your sweatpants," I told him.

He did, his thick tattooed cock standing proud and pointing toward his belly button.

Clearing my throat, I stripped as well and stepped into the tub.

Lucas did the same, sitting in front of me.

I sat behind him, wrapping my legs around him and pulling him back against me. "Talk to me."

"I hate talking," he muttered, his voice rough with sleep.

"I do too. It seems my grandma has been the only one I've ever talked to until you came along," I said, placing a soft peck on his shoulder.

"I had a nightmare. Or more like a memory." He scrubbed a hand down his face before rubbing the back of his neck. "I didn't have a good childhood. At all."

"You said…you said you were molested." I didn't want to have this conversation and I knew that he didn't either, but I also knew that it could be a form of therapy.

"Yeah, about that." Lucas cleared his throat. "I need to see your face."

I moved out from behind him and sat across from him instead.

He cupped my cheek, blowing out a slow breath. "I was thrown into the system. I was juggled between a few foster families and the final one, adopted me. Maybe they couldn't have any kids of their own, I don't know, but they adopted as many as they could. By the time I was finally able to escape; they had adopted six. I don't know why no one looked for us. Or looked to see that we were okay. I questioned it then and got in trouble. But I can only assume because we were adopted, the case worker deemed them as fit parents."

"Wow." I grabbed the washcloth off the edge of the tub and ran it over his thick bicep.

Lucas cleared his throat again which I had quickly come to realize he did whenever he was nervous.

"Hey, whatever it is you're going to tell me, I won't judge."

Lucas met my gaze then. "My adoptive parents were into child porn and all of us kids were victims of it."

My mouth fell open.

"It went on for as long as I can remember. Although I've tried to forget a lot of it."

"Have you talked to anyone about it?" I asked gently.

"No. Technology then wasn't like it is now. So things took a little longer to be proven and shit."

"Oh, Lucas." I grabbed his hands. "I'm so sorry for what you went through."

He pulled away, leaning against the side of the tub. "I..."

"Lucas?"

"Fuck." He rubbed his neck. "No one knows what happened to us. Except for the people involved."

"Not even the authorities?"

He shook his head. "Not from me anyway. There's only one person who knows but I never actually told him. He just figured it out on his own. So I haven't actually said this out loud. Until now."

"Thank you for trusting me enough to tell me." I grabbed his hands again, thankful he didn't pull away that time.

I linked my fingers between his, running my other hand down his forearm. My palm brushed over bumpy ridges.

"We weren't just raped repeatedly," Lucas muttered. "We were tortured as well."

My chest constricted, my throat working hard over the lump that had suddenly appeared in it. My eyes welled. "I..." My voice cracked.

"Don't, Lily." He cupped the back of my neck, leaning his forehead against mine. "Don't."

"It's like some fucked up horror movie."

"It was worse than that, baby." He kissed my head. "But I'm fine."

"Are you really?" I asked, looking up at him.

"We were forced to do drugs but it's also the reason I continued doing them," he said, ignoring my question. "It helped me forget. My demons are loud. Especially when I'm sleeping or trying to fall asleep. It's like my brain only becomes louder in the silence of the night." He pinched my chin, tilting my head back. "But they've been quieter than usual since I met you."

"Really?" I cupped his shoulders.

"Yeah, Lily Pad." He pulled me into his arms, running his fingers down the center of my torso. "I've never been with someone like you. And I know this is new for both of us, but I like you. I like you a lot."

"I like you too, Lucas." I brushed my hand over the intricate designs on the side of his shaved head.

He smirked. "Can we change the subject now?"

I nodded. "Thank you for telling me what you've told me so far. I imagine it wasn't easy."

"It wasn't but I feel a bit better getting it out. I know there's a lot I haven't said and I want to tell you, but I need time."

"I know." I kissed him softly on the mouth. "I understand that."

"Good." He pulled me flush against him. "I know another way that could make me feel better too."

I smirked against his lips. "What's that?"

Lucas ran his hand down my spine to my ass. His fingers brushed between the cheeks of my rear.

I shivered. "Lucas," I whispered.

"My adoptive parents used to make us watch them having sex. Someone…someone I was forced to…I caught her touching herself." Lucas kissed my shoulder. "I knew it was wrong, but it still turned me on. And I would get whipped for it. He would say that his wife turned me on and he would force me to fuck her when it wasn't them at all that made me hard."

"Lucas." Bile rose to my throat at what he had gone through. "It was…you were watching…" I couldn't wrap my head around what he just revealed to me.

"He would force me to do things—"

"Stop." I silenced Lucas with a kiss. "We can talk more later." It was wrong on so many levels. The depravity of what he had gone through. How someone touched themselves only for Lucas to get in trouble because of it. How hard his cock was between us. Was it me that turned him on or what he had gone through? It wasn't natural. Was it?

"I disgust you," Lucas said, dipping his fingers between my legs.

I whimpered.

"But I also turn you on." His arm wrapped tighter around me. "And it confuses you. Doesn't it?"

"I…" Did it? "I don't know. I don't know what's going on. You're hard and you're talking about your fucked-up childhood and the abuse you went through. I feel sorry for you. I feel so damn sorry but at the same time, I want you to fuck me. What's wrong with us?"

"I'm fucked in the head, Lily." Lucas brushed his index finger over the tight spot at my ass. "I've always been fucked up. And I know you have issues too." He pushed his finger into me, igniting a hard moan from my lips. "You're an alcoholic. You want to be a better person and you try so damn hard to be but there's that tiny bit of darkness still in you," he said, sliding two fingers into my pussy. "You saw me and wanted me that first night. I may be blind in one eye, but I can still tell when a woman wants me to fuck them within an inch of their life."

"Oh, God," I said, riding his hand. "I've never wanted someone like I want you and we just had the heaviest conversation ever and now you're finger fucking me. I can't…this isn't…" I moaned when his hand picked up speed. "This isn't normal."

Lucas bit my chin. "Were we ever normal, Lily?"

"I…I don't…you were dreaming of someone else."

"Not in the way you think. I had no one." Lucas held me tight against him. "I had no one else," he repeated, his deep voice sliding along my skin.

"This isn't right." But it felt so damn good. Even though I was sore, even though Lucas had just confessed to some of the things he had been through, I never wanted him more. I didn't understand this need for him. This feral want. I wanted him to fuck me and rip me apart. I wanted all of him. "I need you."

"That's nice." He sunk his teeth into the side of my neck.

"Please," I whined. "I need you inside me."

"You want my big cock stretching out this tiny little pussy?"

"Yes," I cried out, pushing back into his hand.

Lucas released me, pushing me off of him and stepping out of the tub. He pulled me to my feet and in a quick move, bent me over the bathroom counter. I whimpered, the pain from the attack slicing through my ribs.

"Look at us, Lily." He fisted my hair, forcing me to look at our reflection. "Look at how fucked up we are." He slammed into me at the same time he thrust his thumb into the tight rim of my ass.

I whimpered, slapping my hands against the counter and meeting him thrust for aching thrust.

"Tell me what you see." He covered my breast with his large tattooed hand. "Tell me."

"You. Broken. Tattooed. Beautiful," I said between pants. "Me. No tattoos. But so damn turned on." I caught my gaze, noting the bruises as my eyes glassed over.

Lucas cupped my thigh, pulling my leg out to the side and pushing it up onto the counter to give him better access. "What else?" he demanded, wrapping his hand around my throat. "Tell me, Lily." He pulled me back against him.

"I see us, moving together and making each other feel good."

His eyes met mine in the mirror. One was dark. One was pale. And while he could only see out of one of them, he still looked at me like I was the only thing that existed in his world.

"Come for me, baby." He placed a hand on my upper back, pushing me forward. "Come hard. Squeeze my cock." The harder he thrust, the higher my pleasure soared for him. I had never felt anything like it. This carnal need to mate. This desire for more. This feral want for another human being.

What bothered me, was how he fucked me after giving me some insight into his childhood. I knew I had to talk to him. I just hoped it wouldn't end up in a fight. Because no matter how good he made me feel, this wasn't right. This wasn't right at all.

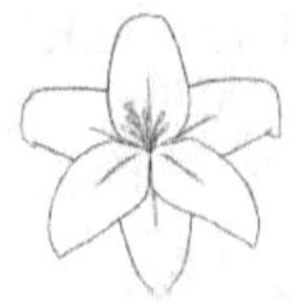

"What's wrong?" Lucas asked me an hour later while we lay in bed.

"Nothing." But I wouldn't meet his gaze. A part of me felt dirty over what we did.

"Talk to me." Lucas tapped my butt. "Lily."

I sighed, rolling over onto my stomach. I winced as the ache in my ribs reminded me of what happened in that dark alley. I cleared my throat, forcing those thoughts to the back of my mind.

"I feel like we shouldn't have had sex after you told me what happened to you. I feel like it turned you on to talk about it. When your dream was about someone else. Your adoptive parents. Your siblings. Whoever it was…And I don't know how that makes me feel. I'm sorry for what happened to you. I really am. But I don't understand the sex part. Help me understand because I really don't want to judge you and I don't want you mad at me and I…I…"

"Hey." Lucas pulled me into his arms. "I'm not mad at you. I don't…" He paused. "I don't know why I needed to fuck you. Maybe it was to make myself feel better. I used to resort to cutting myself, so sex seemed safer than that."

"You did?" I asked, sitting Indian style in front of him.

He sat up, leaning against the headboard before he continued. "I did. I never cut too deep, but I still have some light scars." He pulled the blanket off his lap and pointed at his inner thighs. Faint pink lines marked his skin. They were surrounded by tattoos. "I tried covering them up but only ended up cutting myself more." He shrugged. "I know this doesn't make sense. I get that and I'm sorry for using you."

"No. Don't apologize for that. I'm glad I was able to help you. I just…I guess after you told me that you were forced to watch them, it was almost like you enjoyed it."

"I didn't at first. But my…when I caught her in the shadows, I couldn't…my body…" He cleared his throat.

"Who?" I whispered.

"It doesn't matter."

"Lucas." I cupped his cheek. "Tell me."

"My adoptive sister. Our situation was fucked up, Lily." He leaned his forehead against mine. "I didn't want to watch. I didn't want to react. I knew it wasn't right. I knew it. But I couldn't stop my body from…"

"Reacting," I finished for him.

He nodded.

"So, she touched herself, your adoptive father saw and thought you were reacting to him fucking his wife and you got beaten for it?"

"Yeah," Lucas mumbled. "It happened quite a bit. I would get blamed for shit I didn't do."

"Sounds like…" I caught myself.

"What?" He searched my face. "Tell me."

"I don't want to judge. I had a fucked-up childhood too, but nothing compares to what you went through. Your adoptive sister…I'm just saying that it's not fair what she did. Setting you up like that."

"I know."

"Where you close with her? I mean, as close as can be expected?"

"We helped each other through it," was all he said. "When it first happened, I wasn't sure what was happening to my body at that point. I had barely hit puberty. But my adoptive father definitely didn't like…" Lucas cleared his throat. "Anyway. I was beaten for it and then forced to fuck his wife." He rubbed the back of his neck. "I know a lot. I've been through a lot. But I'll never understand people like them."

"I don't think you're meant to understand them."

"You're probably right." He turned off the light and laid down, pulling me down beside him. "I'm sorry, Lily."

I didn't respond but was thankful when he drifted off to sleep. His breathing became even and for the rest of the night, he was no longer twitchy with the remnants of his nightmares. But I didn't sleep. At all.

Sixteen

LUCAS

THE NIGHTMARE SHOULDN'T HAVE turned me on the way it did but after years of being forced into watching others have sex or touch themselves in this case, I couldn't help the way my body reacted to the thought of it. Lily had said she wouldn't judge but she did. I couldn't blame her. It was fucked up and I couldn't explain it.

While Lily slept beside me, it pushed well into the early morning before she stirred. That was my fault. After taking full advantage of the situation, I fucked her like an animal. Even though she had welcomed it with open arms, I still shouldn't have used her like that. Again, fucked up.

My phone buzzed, indicating an incoming text.

Lena: Has Lily found out anything for me yet?

Me: We're working on it.

Lena: I take it, that's a no?

My jaw clenched.

Me: Stop by the shop tonight.

Lena: Good or bad news?

Me: Neither.

Lena: I thought so.

I sighed, putting my phone back on the nightstand.

"Who was that?" Lily asked, lifting her head. She rubbed her eyes, giving me a soft smile.

"Lena." I pulled out from under Lily and kissed her forehead. "She wanted to know if we'd found anything, so I told her to stop by the shop tonight."

"I hope we can find some more information for her. And…we should probably see if we can find out who attacked me as well."

My chest constricted at that, rage slicing through me. I would find who attacked her. I would find them, and I would kill them myself.

"Lucas?"

I headed to the bathroom. "I need to take a shower."

Turning on the water, I set it to as hot as I could stand it and stepped under the spray. I wasn't sure what was going on. I liked Lily. I liked that I was able to open up to her. But I didn't like that my nightmare turned me on to the point I had to fuck her.

"Fuck," I muttered, dipping my head under the hot spray.

The sound of the bathroom door opening and shutting sent a shiver down my spine. The shower door opened, and Lily stepped in behind me. She placed her hands on my back.

"Last night is bothering you," she said softly.

I nodded.

"Have you thought of talking to a professional?"

I shook my head.

"Okay, well, I'm here. I'll do anything I can to help you. I may not understand it, but I'll help you. I promise, Lucas."

I turned around, grabbing her hands and bringing them up to my mouth. "I don't deserve you, Lily Pad."

Her emerald eyes met mine. "You do, Lucas. You deserve all the happiness in the world after what you've been through."

She didn't even know the half of it.

I turned away, stepping back under the hot water. Although she said the words, I didn't believe her. I had done shit. A lot of shit. Although the people's lives I had ruined deserved it, it didn't make what I did right. Guilt weighed heavily on my shoulders. It was drowning me. Threatening to suffocate me with the air it didn't let me breathe.

"When I was younger, I used my body to get alcohol."

I glanced over my shoulder. "You did what?"

Lily chewed her bottom lip, her cheeks reddening. "You said you don't deserve me. Well I'm not perfect. By any means. At all, Lucas. Before I turned twenty-one, I needed ways to buy alcohol. So I used my body to get it. I just wanted you to know that we all have things we're not proud of."

I stared at her. Her confession was something I never expected to hear from her. "I don't even know what to say."

She shrugged. "I thought I'd share since you seem to think I'm so damn perfect when I'm not."

No, she wasn't. She was human. She'd made mistakes and owned up to them.

"I..." She cleared her throat. "I've destroyed a lot of marriages because of it. I would dress up, pretend I was older than twenty-one too but I had barely turned eighteen at the time. I'm ashamed of what I've done."

"Does your grandma know?"

She nodded. "That's how she got me into AA. Although I have many one-year tokens." She shrugged again. "I'm not perfect, Lucas. But I'm willing to try for you."

My heart jumped. Instead of responding because I had no idea what to say, I cupped her cheek and captured her mouth in a hard kiss.

She sighed, melting into me.

"Thank you, Lily," I murmured against her lips. "Just…thank you."

Seventeen

Lily

IT HAD BEEN A few weeks since Lucas and I confessed some of our history to each other.

We had a hard time finding out any information on Lena's ex. After meeting up with her and relaying that information to her, she ended up breaking down into uncontrollable sobs.

It broke my heart that we weren't able to give her anything other than we would keep trying. But he just wasn't a bad guy. At all. If he was, he was good at covering his tracks, but he was bound to slip up. Whether it be Lucas and I finding out that information or someone else, it was going to happen.

We also set up a security camera at my grandmother's place. I checked the app so often; I was obsessing over it. Lucas would tease me every now and again about it, but he understood. I needed to keep her safe.

Lucas and I had spent every day together since then and although we were growing closer, we never did discuss our past again. I also felt a wall come up between us. Was it even possible to get to know someone and have a wall stopping us from knowing more? I wasn't sure, but it felt like it was happening.

One night, I was laying on my bed, playing on my computer. Lucas was working and while I usually went over to his place, my grandma wanted to have dinner with me. So I stayed home with her instead.

When she left after supper to go play Bridge with her friends, I holed up in my room and tried to find some information on my attacker. We had hacked into the security system, but the cameras were shit and didn't pick anything up. Yet I still checked them frequently. No one had since been attacked in that area from what I could tell. Which was good but frustrating just the same. Clearly, they had set out to get me and only me.

My ribs had healed, and the bruises had faded. I had told my grandmother what happened, and she reacted the way I thought she would. Crying, worrying, and fussing over me. But thankful I was alive and well.

The video chat suddenly appeared on my screen indicating that Lucas was calling me.

I answered, smiling when his handsome face came into view. "Hey."

"Hi, Lily Pad."

My heart warmed at the nickname. "How are you?"

"Not too bad. You?"

"Good. I got a notification on the app that there was movement outside. So I checked and it was just a raccoon. Scared the shit out of me." My cheeks burned at the memory.

"You should have called me."

"It's no big deal, Lucas." My heart swelled that he cared though.

He huffed, shaking his head. "Stubborn woman."

I smiled. "Did you want to come over?" We usually stayed at his place, but I was already changed for the night and just didn't want to go anywhere.

"Not in the mood to go out?"

"Well, I'm not dressed and…yeah."

"Hmm…" He rubbed the scruff on his jaw. "Show me."

I laughed, thankful that the heaviness from just a moment ago, dissipated between us. "Hold on." I slid off the bed and closed my door before clicking the lock into place. Rushing back to my bed, I turned the laptop so it was facing me and took a couple of steps back. "How's this?"

His eyes roamed over me. "Turn around."

I did.

"Bend over."

My body heated. I did as I was told, looking at him over my shoulder.

Lucas smirked, running his fingers along his mouth. "I think you should convince me to come over."

"Oh?" I rose to my full height and turned back around. "I'm in a tank top and panties. This isn't enough to convince you, baby?"

He chuckled, the sound smooth and dark. It sent a ripple of heat over my skin. "No. Convince me, Lily. Show me how much you want me to come over."

Getting an idea, I pulled the chair out from beneath my desk and moved it in front of my bed. I sat, spreading my legs and leaned forward.

"Show me your tits."

I licked my lips, lowering my tank top and cupping my breast.

"So fucking incredible," he growled. "Do you have any toys, Lily Pad? Anything that gets that little pussy nice and hot?"

I grinned, the husk of his voice sliding over every inch of me. I turned, reaching into my dresser and pulled out the Hitachi Magic Wand.

"Oh yeah," Lucas said. "That'll work."

I laughed. "I need to see you too, Lucas."

Lucas pushed his chair back and reached into his gray sweatpants.

"Take it out," I breathed.

"Take what out, Lily Pad?"

"Your cock." I licked my lips. "Your beautiful thick cock." I enunciated each word.

Lucas sat back, pulling his hard length out from beneath the fabric of his pants. "You want this, Lily?" he asked, stroking from base to tip.

"Oh yeah." As much as I wished he was with me, this was exciting. My body heated at the show before me.

"Lily." Lucas stopped stroking. "I'm not seeing you touching that sweet kitty for me."

I almost forgot that I was holding the wand. Sitting back, I placed my feet on the edge of the chair. "You want this, Lucas?" I asked, throwing his own question back at him.

"I want to see it."

I grinned. "Not yet." I turned on the wand, running it down my inner thigh. The vibrations rumbled through me, hitting me square in the clit. Massaging my breast, I pinched my nipple.

"Show me, Lily," he demanded, his hand picking up speed. He licked his palm and went back to stroking.

I shivered, knowing his pre-cum was now on his tongue. God, what I wouldn't give to kiss him. I wondered what it would taste like.

I lowered my top even more.

He groaned.

I smirked.

"Fucking hell." Lucas sat forward.

"Have I convinced you yet?" I asked, my voice husky with need.

"Nah, baby. Keep going. I want to watch that pussy explode. Squirt all over that chair for me, Lily."

I placed the wand on the floor and stood. Lifting the tank top up and over my head, I tossed it to the side and turned before kneeling on the chair.

"Show me," he demanded, his voice rough.

A sense of power washed over me. I could hear the lack of control in his voice. It was rough, thick with lust. Hooking my thumbs into the waistband of my black panties, I lowered them.

"Fuck," he groaned. "More. Show me more."

Holding the back of the chair, I glanced at him over my shoulder. "What do you want to see, baby?"

"Lily." His hand picked up speed.

"Don't come, Lucas," I told him. "Save it for me."

His dark eye met mine, his hand slowing down. "Show. Me."

I stood, lowered my panties and kicked them to the side before kneeling on the chair once again. Spreading my legs, I inched a hand between my thighs and ran it over my soaked center.

"Yeah, baby. That's it. Thrust your fingers into your cunt. I want to hear how wet you are."

God, I loved his rough demands. Inserting two fingers inside me, I shivered, a low moan escaping the back of my throat. My hand picked up speed.

"Use your wand, Lily."

I picked it up off the floor, turned back around and placed my feet on the edge of the chair.

"Use it. Now."

I switched the button to ON. As soon as I pressed the end of the wand against my clit, I cried out. A spark of need exploded inside of me. The vibrations hit a spot I had never felt before. "God. Lucas. I…"

"Don't fucking move it. Come for me, Lily." He stood, stuffing his swollen cock back in his pants. "Do it."

I moved the wand over my clit, my hips undulating against it. "So good. Lucas. I need you. Your cock. All of it. Every inch." My words came out jumbled. I had used the wand before but having him watch me, turned me on more than ever. This had been the hottest and most intense thing I had ever done. "Please come over."

"Oh I am. But you're going to come for me first. I want that cunt sensitive. Come, baby."

"Lucas," I cried out, my pussy clenching and releasing. A gush of liquid left me, but I couldn't stop. The release had been so hard, I couldn't breathe. My eyes slammed shut, his name leaving my lips on a hard scream.

The next time I opened my eyes, Lucas was no longer in the video. My heart jumped, my stomach doing a flip. He was coming over. Although we'd had sex many times, I knew this time was going to be different. Intense. Powerful. Raw.

Knowing my grandma wouldn't be home for a while, I quickly unlocked my door and ran down the hall. I unlocked the main door to the house and rushed back to my bedroom, put my laptop away, and waited.

Ten minutes later and the door to my bedroom slammed open, revealing a disheveled Lucas. He was breathing hard, the bulge in his pants, thick and proud.

He kicked the door closed, ripping his hoodie off his large torso and pulling down his pants.

I stood from the chair at the same time he came toward me. In two long strides, we crashed together. His mouth was fused to mine, his hands in my hair. We fell to my bed in a bundled heap of naked skin. In a rough move, he pushed between my legs and thrust inside of me. He swallowed my scream and pumped hard and deep.

My nails scratched down his hard back before cupping his ass and taking him deeper.

Lucas cupped my thigh, pushing it up and out to the side. While his other hand remained in my hair, he kept a firm hold on my knee.

I was powerless to him as he fucked me within an inch of my being. He pushed into me as deep as my body would allow. I gasped, breaking the kiss and arching beneath him. "Lucas," I sobbed.

He kissed the side of my neck, grabbed my hand, and linked our fingers together.

My heart picked up speed, my breathing becoming labored. "Lucas," I cried out.

He continued to push, his thick length hitting that spot inside of me that only he could ever reach.

My body vibrated, my thighs shaking.

The abrasiveness of his beard scratched at my skin.

Another sob escaped me, my eyes welling at how good he was making me feel. I spread my legs, trying to take him even deeper. I was greedy. Hungry. Ravenous for him. He was so deep inside me, it felt like he was trying to fuck my soul.

Lucas pulled back, his cock sliding out of me. In one smooth thrust, he was back inside me, deeper than before.

I screamed, my back bowing off the bed. A release shattered through me, warm liquid gushing between us.

He growled, nipping the side of my neck. His cock swelled, his own release coating me. It was so damn hard, I could feel the thick cream splashing against the walls of my pussy.

"Fuck," he panted, squeezing my hand.

"Lucas," I whispered, my body shaking.

Once we both calmed down, he pulled out.

I shivered, glancing between us.

His cock dripped.

My pussy clenched at the sight.

"You're a dirty little girl, Lily," he murmured, his voice husky. He pushed the tip of his cock through the wet folds of my pussy, running it over my swollen clit.

I whimpered, jumping at how sensitive I was. "I've never been one to think cocks were pretty or anything but yours…God, it turns me on something fierce."

Lucas chuckled, laying down beside me and pulling the blankets up and over us. He turned me onto my side and slid back inside me.

"I can't," I panted. "No more."

"I'm not fucking you, baby." He kissed my neck, wrapping himself around me. "But I need to be inside you."

My pussy clenched around him.

"Keep doing that and you're going to make me hard again," he snarled into the side of my neck. "And then I will fuck you."

I laughed, pushing my ass into his waist. "I won't complain, Lucas." I yawned.

"Sleep." He covered me with half of his body and pushed my knee up to my chest. "We're going to fall asleep like this and wake up like this."

"Okay," I whispered, my eyes fluttering closed. "I look forward to it."

"Good, sweet girl." He kissed my neck and cupped my breast.

I wasn't sure why he needed to be inside me, but I would take it.

"I've never done that before." I rolled over onto my stomach and linked my fingers in Lucas's. It was pushing three in the morning and we had both woken up, unable to fall back asleep.

"Neither have I." He kissed my hand, resting his other arm behind his head.

"I've always been shy, but you bring out something inside of me," I confessed.

"You? Shy?" He grunted. "That I find hard to believe."

"Hey!" I laughed, smacking him gently. "I've been shy during sex before. There's nothing wrong with that."

"No." He pulled me over him. "There isn't but I can't believe that you've ever been shy."

My laugh hardened. "Why?" I asked, resting my legs across his.

"Because you've never been shy with me is all I'm saying." Lucas leaned on his elbow, running his hand over the scars on my side. He made me forget about them. And I would always be thankful to him for that.

"It's because I'm comfortable with you. And I've never felt this or even done half of the stuff we have with another guy before."

"Good." Lucas met my gaze. "And there's more where that came from too."

"Yeah? Like what?" I asked, waggling my eyebrows.

He chuckled. "Hmm…We could make a video."

"Oh! A sex video. I like it." I kissed his cheek. "We could probably sell it too. Make millions."

His laughter shook through him.

"What? I'm just saying. We look good together. And you're hot as hell. All of these tattoos and muscles. You don't see tattooed cocks often, so I know that could sell our video all on its own."

Lucas raised an eyebrow. "You are too much."

"Just saying. It's an idea. We could call it the 'Lucas and Lily Sex Show.'" I giggled.

"I like the sound of that."

"What? The title?"

"No." He kissed me softly on the mouth. "Your giggle. But The Lucas and Lily Sex Show would only be seen by Lucas and Lily. No one else gets to see us make love."

My heart skipped a beat at the term he used. Something switched between us. I realized then that I was falling for him. And I was falling hard.

Eighteen

LUCAS

MY TONGUE SLID OVER the soft, bumpy ridges. My fingers pushed, hard and deep, into the writhing body beneath me. Gasps and moans slid into my ears. My lips brushed over the dewy skin. The sound of my name caressed my ears. Begging. Pleading. Demanding. So many demands. Some gentle. Some rough.

I ran my nose over the soft crease between Lily's thigh and pussy and took a deep inhale. The sweet scent of her wafted into me, surrounding me with a blanket of bliss.

The sound of a door closing, jarred through the moment.

"Fuck."

I chuckled, kissing Lily's lower belly and rising from the bed. "Until later, Lily Pad."

"I can be quiet," she panted.

"No, you can't." And that was one of the things I liked about her.

"But that was getting so good," she whined, sitting up on her elbows. She licked her lips, her lust-filled eyes meeting mine.

My cock twitched. "Checking me out, baby?" I asked, wrapping my fingers around my dick.

"Oh yeah," she purred.

I shook my head, grinning. She was hungry for it as much as I was but now that her grandma was home, she would have to wait.

"Get dressed. We'll go greet your grandma and then we'll head back to my place. If you want to of course." I got dressed when Lily slid off the bed and came toward me.

"Of course I want to." She ran her hands over my bare chest, stopping me from putting on my hoodie. "Lucas." Her eyes shone. Something was hidden beneath them, and it made my heart stutter.

"Wh—" A soft knock sounded on the door.

Lily jumped back and picked her clothes up off the floor. "Yes?" she called out.

"Just seeing if you're home," her grandmother said from the other side of the door.

"I am. I'll be out in a moment." Lily rummaged through her dresser drawers while I got dressed. She put on a black bra and panty set, followed by ripped blue jeans and a white t-shirt.

As I slipped the hoodie over my head, I felt a small hand cup me over my pants.

"Really?" I asked, lowering the sweatshirt and finding Lily smiling up at me.

"I'm obsessed." She gave me a light squeeze followed by a kiss on the cheek. "I can't help it."

I laughed, smacking her ass.

She let out a squeal, rubbing the spot I just hit. "Asshole."

"You like it, Lily Pad." I grabbed her arm and pulled her flush against me. I smacked her ass again.

She gasped, her pupils dilating.

"Maybe I should see if I can make you come next time by smacking your ass." I kissed the side of her neck. "Or I could smack your pussy." I gave her ear a gentle bite.

She shivered, pushing away from me. "Geeze, Lucas. Give a girl some space." She winked and left her bedroom.

I followed her, shaking my head. I realized then that I could fall for her. Or I was falling for her. I couldn't figure out which. I had closed my heart off so long ago, I wasn't sure how to crack the walls anymore. But I had a feeling that Lily could break the ice my heart was encased in.

I followed Lily down the hall and to the living room.

"Hey, Grandma." Lily kissed the older woman's face. She was sitting on her rocking chair, knitting what looked like a sweater.

"Hi, dears." Grandma smiled at me. "How has your evening been?"

"Oh, you know. Nothing too exciting has happened." Lily sat on the couch, patting the spot beside her. "How was your game night?"

"Good." Grandma winked. "I kicked their asses again. They should really learn not to play with me."

I joined Lily on the couch while they talked about her grandmother's night of playing Bridge.

Lily snuggled into my side, pulling a blanket off the back of the couch and wrapping it over our laps. If we were at my place, I'd have her naked, so I could easily slip back into her tight heat whenever I wanted to. But we weren't so I couldn't. But I could definitely imagine it.

She squirmed beside me. "Stop," she murmured.

I inched a hand beneath the blanket. "Stop what?"

"Stop whatever you're doing."

I chuckled, cupping her inner thigh. "I'm not doing anything."

"You don't have to be doing anything, Lucas." She glanced up at me. "I can sense it." She frowned. "And I have no idea how."

I stared at her. I wasn't sure what she was telling me, but I found that I liked it.

"Oh, Lily. Mrs. Gould told me to tell you that she doesn't need you tomorrow."

"What?" Lily's head whipped around. "That's three shifts this week she's canceled."

"I'm sorry, dear. I just don't think the work is there."

"Come work for me," I blurted.

"What?" Lily glanced up at me, frowning.

"I…" My cheeks burned. "I mean, I'm the only one working at my shop. I have enough business that keeps me busy, but I need someone to book appointments and take payments and all that shi—stuff."

Lily's grandmother laughed. "You don't need to watch what you say around me, Lucas."

"I know." I cleared my throat. "But I will out of respect for you."

She smiled. "I like you."

I chuckled.

"Tell me about this job," Lily said, ignoring us.

"I need help and I trust you." I shrugged. "The offer is there if you want it."

"I…" Lily rose from the couch, shook herself, and headed down the hall.

"Um…" I stood. "Excuse us." I followed Lily. "What's going on?" I asked her as she walked into her room.

"Nothing," she muttered.

"Lily." I closed the door behind me. "Did I freak you out by offering you a job?"

"I…" She sighed, leaning against her dresser. "I don't know. I really don't. I like you, Lucas." She met my gaze then. "I really like you but liking you is scaring me."

"What do you mean?" I wanted to go to her, but something held me back.

"I don't know that either." She looked down at her feet.

I went to her then. Pinching her chin, I forced her to look at me. "Talk to me."

"I'm not used to this. It's always just been for fun. That's what I thought I was getting with you and then this turned into something more." She placed her hand against my chest just over my heart. "I don't want to work for you. I appreciate the job offer. I do. But you being my boss is…weird."

"You wouldn't be working for me." I grabbed her hand and kissed her wrist. "We would work together. I meant what I said. I trust you, Lily. I know we've only known each other for a few months but I like you too. I wouldn't keep fucking you if I didn't."

She bit her bottom lip.

Brushing a thumb over her mouth, I pulled her lip from the onslaught of her teeth. "Lily."

"Lucas," she breathed. "No." She pushed away from me and began pacing. "I can't do this."

"What's going on with you? You didn't seem to complain earlier when I was about to eat your pussy. You also initiated the video sex the other night. You begged me to come over then. You would have kept the doors locked if you didn't actually want me over. And then tonight. Who texted who?" She had sent me dirty text messages followed by a picture of her naked. I couldn't resist so I closed up shop early and drove over.

"Lucas." She stopped pacing. "I'm—"

"If you didn't want anything out of this, you wouldn't have agreed to go on a date with me. We wouldn't keep seeing each other. We wouldn't have spent all this time together. Is that scaring you? Is that what you're telling me?"

"I don't know," she snapped. "Alright?"

"No." I took a step toward her. "That isn't alright. I don't know what you want from me. I've shared my shit with you. I've told you things no one knows. And most of the people who do know, are either dead or have disappeared. But I told you. I told you my childhood." The anger inside of me was rising. I could feel it turning into something I had never felt before.

"You haven't shared everything with me," she threw back at me.

I laughed then. "Are you fucking kidding me right now? So you want every single dirty, dark, and depraved detail? Fine. I'll tell you." I grabbed her arm and pulled her to the chair in front of her desk.

"Lucas, let go." She tried prying my fingers off her, but my grip only tightened.

"Sit." I pushed her onto the chair.

"Lucas." She stood.

"Sit the fuck down," I demanded.

She glared at me but did as she was told. She crossed her arms under her chest, lifting her chin.

My body stirred at her defiance, but I ignored it. "You're complaining because I haven't told you everything."

"I'm not complaining."

"Shut up. Just stop." I placed my hands on the back of her chair and peered down at her. "You want to hear about my childhood. I was raped. Abused. Tortured. All of us were. The sick fucks who were supposed to be taking care of us, made us wish they would kill us instead. I remember one time I had been raped so brutally, I couldn't stop screaming. You want to know what they did to shut me up?"

"Lucas," she said, her voice trembling.

"They sewed my mouth shut." I grabbed her hand, bringing it up to my mouth and ran her fingers over the scars in my lips.

Lily stared up at me with wide eyes.

"But you know what hurt worse than that?"

She looked away.

I grabbed her chin, forcing her to look at me. "I asked you a question."

"No," she whispered. "I don't know what could be worse than that."

"You don't know? I'll tell you." I didn't want to be a dick but her closing up, pissed me off. "When I ripped my mouth open. That hurt worse, Lily."

Her eyes welled.

"So don't get fucking pissed off at me when I don't voluntarily share my story with you." I released her and stepped back, sitting on the edge of her bed. "I'll be lucky if I'm able to have kids. If that's what you want, back out now because I don't know if I could ever give you a baby."

"What?" She shook her head. "No. That's not. God, Lucas, we haven't even gotten that far yet."

"No? Alright then, Lily. If that's not a deal breaker for you, what is because clearly you're pushing yourself away from me and I'd like to fucking know why." I hit my fist against my chest. "Tell me," I shouted.

She jumped. "My grandma's home, asshole."

"I don't give a fuck who the hell is home." I jumped up and in one quick stride, I was on her.

(Lily)

Lucas was losing the control he craved, and it was my fault. When he charged for me and pushed me back, all I could do was stare up at him.

"What the hell do you want from me?" he demanded.

"I want to take this one day at a time. We haven't been together for that long and now you're already talking about kids?" I knew he never mentioned kids because he wanted them with me. He was just testing me.

"You know that's…" He took a deep breath. "I'm losing my patience here, Lily. Either you want to continue this, or you don't. Say the word and I'm either done or bringing you home with me."

God, I wanted that. I wanted to spend the night with him. So why the hell was I fighting this?

"Tell me." His deep growl washed over me. When I didn't answer, he grabbed my hands and lifted me from the chair before throwing me on my bed.

"Lucas." I held up my hands, trying to ward him off.

He grabbed them, spinning me onto my stomach and knelt between my legs. Holding my wrists behind my back, he leaned down to my ear. "Tell me what you want."

"You, Lucas. I only ever just wanted you." This side of him shouldn't have turned me on but it did. Him taking full control.

Him restraining me. Him not letting me move even an inch. Him pushing into me.

"You like this. Me holding your wrists and pinning you down." He smacked his hand across my ass.

I yelped. "Lucas."

He chuckled. "Tell me how you feel. Are you wanting this to end?"

"No," I finally confessed. "But working at your shop…"

"What about it?" He slapped my ass again when I didn't respond. "Lily."

"Working at your shop scares me because if you hurt me, I don't know what I'll do. I'm scared that I'll fall off the wagon." A breath of relief washed over me. I had never expected those words to leave my lips.

Lucas released me.

I rolled over onto my back.

He was staring straight ahead. "You think I'll hurt you."

I sat beside him, cupping his face and turning it toward me. "I don't think you will but if you do…I'm not strong enough for that."

"I have no intentions of hurting you. You also can't live life like that, Lily. You're telling me that you haven't opened yourself up to anyone because you're scared you'll get hurt?"

I shrugged, dropping my hand in my lap and looking away. "People always hurt each other."

"I won't hurt you." He kissed my forehead.

"You can't promise that," I whispered.

He pinched my chin, tilting my head back. "You need to trust me."

How he could be so trusting after what he had been through, was beyond me. His story, the things he had experienced as a child, should have destroyed him. And maybe it did. A part of him anyway. I found I wanted to help him find that piece of him he was missing.

"Come home with me." Lucas kissed the corner of my mouth.

Instead of answering him, I wrapped my arms around him and just held on.

Nineteen

Lily

I WASN'T SURE WHY working with Lucas, freaked me out the way it had. It didn't make sense. He was offering me a job. I should have been grateful but instead, I threw his offer back in his face and made him tell me more of his childhood.

I sighed, staring out the window. A warm hand cupped mine. My heart stuttered. But I didn't look at him.

We drove back to Lucas's place in silence. Our relationship was blooming into something more. Both of us would be stupid to deny it. Maybe that was why it freaked me out. And he couldn't have kids. Or he had assumed he couldn't. I wasn't sure how he knew that or what had happened to him to make it impossible to bear children, but I didn't ask. Did I even want to know?

When we pulled into the alleyway between his shop and the building beside it, he cut the engine. "Look at me."

I met his gaze.

"I'm not sure how you feel. Clearly, you feel something for me or else you wouldn't be here, and you can't say that this is just sex. Even though it's the best fucking sex I've ever had, I know this is something more." He lifted his hand when I opened my mouth to say something. "I'm not proposing to you, Lily. I want to date you. That's it. I'd like to offer you the job as my partner. Not my employee. And before you turn me down again, think about it first." He left the car, slamming the door shut behind him.

I blew out a slow breath and slid from the vehicle, following him into his apartment.

Lucas shut the door behind us and went to lock it when a hard knock sounded on the door a second later. He looked my way.

I shrugged.

He opened the door, revealing Killian. "You have got to be fucking kidding me."

"What do you want?" I demanded, ignoring Lucas.

Killian frowned, pushing past Lucas. "What the hell happened to you?" He cupped my face, earning him a growl.

My ribs no longer hurt but you could still see some of the bruises on my face even though they had faded drastically.

"I fell." I slapped his hand away. "What do—"

"How the fuck do you know where I live?" Lucas demanded.

"I'm a Fed, remember?" Killian searched my face. "I don't believe for one fucking second that you fell." He glanced at Lucas. "Did you fucking hit her?"

Lucas rolled his eyes. "Yeah, 'cause I get off on beating women. It's my thing you know."

I stepped between them and pointed to the door. "I have no idea why you're here or how you got Lucas's address when even I know that you need a good reason to get that information. So if you aren't going to tell us what you want then, get out."

"Lily," Killian said gently. "If he hit you—"

"Get the fuck out and the next time you insult my boyfriend, I'll show you what a true beating looks like." I thrust my arm out again. "Get. Out. Now." He was obviously here for a reason, but I didn't give a shit what that reason was. I didn't want to hear it. I just wanted him gone.

"I'll be seeing you again, Lily." Killian stomped away.

I rushed to the door, slamming it shut and clicking all of the locks into place. "I don't know your security—" I was suddenly picked up off of my feet. "Lucas," I cried.

He threw me over his shoulder and charged for his bedroom.

"What are you doing?" I demanded when he tossed me on his bed.

But instead of answering me, he pulled me to the edge and ripped open my jeans.

I gasped, the button popping off the material and landing on the floor. My whole body turned hot. "Lucas?"

He roughly pulled my jeans off of me and knelt, bringing me closer to the edge of the bed.

"Lucas," I breathed, staring down the length of my body.

He gripped my knees, spreading me open and covering my core with his mouth.

I cried out, my fingers latching on to his head. His hair had grown in some, but he still kept the sides buzzed. "God."

"No," he said against my pussy. "Boyfriend. Say it."

My eyes widened. So that was what this was about? "Lucas."

"Say it," he growled, sucking my clit between his lips and biting down.

I yelped, trying to shove away from him.

In a quick move, he flipped me onto my stomach and bent me over the edge of the bed. His mouth was back on me, his tongue thrusting inside of me. "Say it."

"Boyfriend," I gasped, clutching the blankets. "You're my boyfriend."

He snarled against my center. "Again."

"You're my boyfriend," I cried out, shaking through my unexpected release.

He stood, towering over me and thrust all of his inches inside of me.

I screamed.

"Again. Say it." He fisted my hair, pulled my head back, and sunk his teeth into my neck. "Say it."

"You're my boyfriend." With each thrust, he owned me. I realized then that he was staking his claim. I was his. I belonged to him and having Killian touch me the way he did, brought out this beast inside of him. "More. God, Lucas, give me more."

"You're mine, Lily." His mouth brushed over the shell of my ear.

"Yes." I shivered. "I'm yours."

(Lucas)

I never had something that belonged to me. Until I purchased the building that my shop and apartment were in, I had nothing.

I kissed Lily's neck, inhaling the faint smell of sex. I had used her good and hard. After she told Killian that I was her boyfriend and kicking him out, I snapped. Even though we'd had a fight tonight, hearing her say those words, sparked this newfound awareness inside of me. Was this what I had been looking for all along? I wasn't sure, but I was damn determined to find out.

I kissed her slender throat again.

She stirred, letting out a soft sigh. Her eyes fluttered open.

I had kept a lamp on in the room, so I could see every inch of her. After I had brought her into my bedroom and fucked her good and hard, I didn't let up until she was on the brink of exhaustion.

"I think you broke me," she said, her voice rough with sleep.

I placed a soft peck on her mouth, sliding my tongue between her lips.

She deepened the kiss.

I chuckled. "I must not have broken you that much."

Lily smiled up at me. "Are we good?"

"We are." I brushed my thumb over her bottom lip. "Why wouldn't we be?"

"Well I freaked out tonight and then Killian showed up and…"

"And you said that I'm your boyfriend and I fucked you like a raging animal," I added for her.

"I liked it."

"I know." I leaned on my elbow, running my hand down her torso.

"No." She rolled onto her side. "I liked it a lot. I felt connected to you on a whole other level I have never felt before. With anyone. It's like…" Her cheeks reddened. "It's like you were fucking my soul."

My cock jumped at her words. "I've never been someone's boyfriend before. Am I jealous of Killian? Yes. He had you first. But that's beside the point. You kicking him out tonight was hot as fuck. I've never had someone do that for me either. So, thank you."

"I don't know why Killian was here tonight." She rested her head against my chest. "It's frustrating. He's frustrating. It's like he's causing problems just to cause problems." She sighed, pulling away from me.

"He's an asshole, Lily. Men like that don't need a reason to do anything."

She stood from the bed, revealing her naked, scarred body before me. She was short but curvy. Her pale skin was marred with a few freckles. My favorite one was on the inside of her right thigh.

"Why are you looking at me like that?" she asked, her brows narrowing.

"Because you're beautiful."

She scoffed. "I'm scarred."

"So am I and you seem to think I'm still hot." I shrugged, leaning back against the headboard with my arm behind my head. I bent my knee, letting it fall to the side. The white sheet dipped down below my belly button, resting on top of my cock that was now semi-hard.

Lily's eyes dropped to my crotch, her tongue peeking out to lick along her bottom lip.

I bit back a chuckle.

"You can't do that," she said, her voice husky.

"I'm not doing anything." I ran my hand over my chest and down my hard stomach.

"Lucas." Her nostrils flared.

My dick lengthened. It amazed me that no matter how many times we had sex or how rough we had been, she still always wanted me.

"How many guys did you fuck for booze?" I asked, knowing it would only piss her off. Call me a masochist, but I needed to know everything there was to know about this woman standing only a few feet away.

"Five before I realized that I was good at it." Her gaze popped to mine. "Why?"

"How many more?"

She frowned. "Enough."

"Fine. We'll work with that." I slid my hand beneath the sheet, wrapping my fingers around my dick. "We've already fucked several times tonight but we're going to fuck again."

She came toward me. "Are you going to fuck the guys out of me? You know I've slept with more than just five, Lucas."

"Yeah? Well I've slept with more than just you." My hand stroked from base to tip.

Lily pulled the sheet off of me and straddled my waist. "I want you to forget them."

"And I want you to forget the men you've been with." I sat up, cupping her nape. "Do you think you can help me do that?"

"Yeah." She grabbed my hand from her neck and kissed my palm. "Help me forget, baby."

For the rest of the night, I did.

Twenty

Lily

IT HAD BEEN A few days since I freaked out over Lucas offering me the job at his shop. I wasn't sure if I felt like he had an ulterior motive or what my issue was but by the time the night ended, I was over it.

Six times. Six times we had sex before we passed out. A few days later and I was still sore.

While I was hunched over the counter at Crane's Ink, I couldn't help but laugh at the way Lucas was walking slowly.

Every time he walked by me, he would smack my butt and give me an answer to the crossword puzzle I was working on. Thanks to my grandma, I had become obsessed with them. Although I usually tried to figure them out on my own, doing them with Lucas was fun. I made a mental note to turn it into a sexy game.

"What's that smile for?" Lucas asked, sitting at the tattoo station.

"Just thinking how we could turn crossword puzzles into a sexy game." I tapped the pencil against my chin.

"What? Like strip crossword?"

I laughed. "Something like that."

He chuckled, shaking his head.

The chime on the door dinged.

I looked up from the crossword puzzle and found a large man entering the shop. He had light brown hair, with graying scruff on a strong chiseled jaw. His piercing green eyes met mine. He gave me a small smile and a nod.

"Shephard." Lucas stood, greeting the man and pulling him in for a hug. "How are you?"

"Living the dream," the man I now knew as Shepard said.

Lucas glanced my way. "Lily Noel, Donny Shephard. Shephard, Lily."

I smiled, giving Shephard a tiny wave.

"Since when do you have someone working for you?" Shephard looked between us both.

Lucas only gave me a wink before turning back to his friend. "She's actually working with me. Not for me."

Shephard looked between us, a slow smile spreading on his face. "Interesting." He turned back to Lucas. "Did you get the image I sent you?"

"I did." Lucas sat and showed him his tablet.

"Fuck man." Shephard whistled. "That's perfect."

While they continued chatting about Shepard's tattoo, I went back to work on the crossword puzzle. I had come to learn rather quickly that Lucas didn't book himself a lot of appointments. He liked to keep busy but not so busy that he became overwhelmed.

"I don't want to lose my passion for it."

It made sense. So we spread out his appointments for him. I also had a feeling that he didn't actually need the money.

The door chimed again, revealing Lena.

"Hey." I smiled up at her.

"How's it going?" she asked me.

"Not too bad. You?"

"Good," she said, glancing at Lucas before looking back at me.

He didn't look up when she came in, but he looked our way now. Our eyes locked.

My heart stuttered. God, I loved the way he looked at me.

"So, are you guys official now?" Lena asked, low enough for only me to hear.

"Yeah. I guess we are." I rose to my full height, stretching my arms up and over my head. My muscles twitched. A sharp pain jabbed me in the side. I gasped, rubbing the spot.

"Lily." Lucas shoved to his feet.

"I'm fine." I waved him off. "Do Shephard's tattoo. I'm good." I rolled my eyes when no one moved. "Seriously. I'm fine."

Lucas sat, muttering to Shephard.

"What was that about?" Lena asked a moment later.

"I had…uh…an accident a few weeks back and I'm still a little tender. It depends on how I move. I'm usually good but I think I broke a rib so I'm still healing from that." I didn't want to tell her that I was actually attacked.

"Holy shit, girl." Lena's eyes widened. "Where did this happen?"

"I was walking home." I shook my head. "It's fine. It's done and over with and I'm good."

"Well I'm glad you're okay." Lena blew a strand of hair out of her eyes. "Who's that?" She nodded to Shepard.

"A friend of Lucas's," I told her. "Oh and he's married."

"He is?" Lena frowned. "Too bad. Are you sure?"

"I saw the wedding band and he also hasn't looked our way at all." Even if he wasn't married, he never noticed Lena so clearly, he had no interest.

"Must be nice," Lena muttered. "Anyway, I stopped by to see if you were able to get anything on my ex."

"I told you we didn't," Lucas said.

"Is this her?" Shephard asked.

Lucas nodded.

Shephard nodded to the empty chair by the bed. "Sit," he told Lena.

She hugged her purse tighter but did as she was told.

"Lucas told me that you're trying to get custody of your daughter," Shephard said, while Lucas went back to working on his tattoo.

"I am," Lena murmured.

"I'm a cop and I've been friends with Lucas for years. You can trust me." Shephard looked my way then. "There's still no information on your attack."

My eyes widened. "He's the one you called?" I asked Lucas.

He nodded. "I meant to introduce you two earlier, but we've been kind of busy."

"Well, any friend of Lucas's is a friend of mine." I smiled.

Shephard gave me a curt nod. "Same, kiddo."

"You think you can help me?" Lena asked, chewing her bottom lip.

"I will definitely do my best." Shephard glanced back at the tattoo Lucas was drawing on his inner forearm. "Your ex is too clean. I'm determined to help you get your daughter."

Lena stood from the chair. "Thank you. I appreciate that. I really do." She walked back over to me.

She was supposed to come over a few nights ago but had finally decided to go to a meeting instead. We were both proud of her even though Lucas never said those words exactly.

"I promise we'll do everything we can to help you," I told her. "But we haven't been able to find anything so far. I do suggest continuing your meetings and behaving. I know it's hard. Trust me, I do know that. If I was in your situation, I would probably disagree with me. But it's all you can do because if you aren't patient and do something that could set your parents off, you might never see your daughter again."

"I know." Lena rubbed the back of her neck. "God, I do know this. I just hate not having any control."

Lucas chuckled.

I rolled my eyes. "How about we make a date and we can meet up for coffee and talk about this?"

Lena crossed her arms under her chest. "You're in the program, aren't you?"

I laughed. "What makes you think that?"

"Because you all are obsessed with coffee."

"Not all of us are obsessed with coffee but yes. I'm actually an alcoholic." I shrugged like it was no big deal. I wasn't sure if it was anymore. It wasn't controlling my life at the moment, so I guess it wasn't.

Lena sighed. "Fine. I'll call you." She gave me a quick hug, muttered a goodbye to the guys, thanked them again and left the shop.

Jumping up onto the counter, I continued the crossword puzzle. I finished three of them when a throat cleared.

I looked up, finding Lucas and Shephard staring back at me. "Done already?"

"It's been three hours, Lily." Lucas came around the counter.

"Can you book me in for another session please? I think Shannon wants to get another tattoo as well but I'm not sure yet." Shephard pulled his wallet out of his black leather jacket and handed Lucas a wad of cash.

"I guess I shouldn't argue with you about taking this, should I?" Lucas put it in an envelope and stuffed it into the cash register.

"Nope. I know you're not going to keep the money anyway, but my wife still insists that I give it to you." Shephard's knuckles rapped the counter top. "I should be heading home. It was good seeing you, my man. And it was nice finally meeting you, Lily. I've only heard great things."

"It was nice meeting you too," I told him. "And really? You talked to him about me?" I asked Lucas.

"Of course." He gave me a quick kiss before walking Shephard out of the shop. When he came back inside, he turned off the Open sign and locked up.

"What did he mean that you wouldn't be keeping the money?"

Lucas only winked. He double-checked the door. Satisfied that it was locked, he turned to me. "I stash it away for those in need. Before you say, 'aww, that's so sweet', I'm just paying it forward."

"That is really sweet though."

He shrugged. "I had no one when I was a kid. Shephard saved me and as difficult as I can be, he's never turned on me."

"How did you meet him?" I asked, curious about the older man Lucas was friends with.

"He was one of the cops who raided the place I spent my childhood in. He was just a rookie at the time, ended up going to the wrong address. Thank God for that too." Lucas shuddered. "He's a good guy."

"He sounds like it. Especially if he helped save your life."

"I refuse to let others go through the same shit, so I do what I can. That's why I offer the free tattoos for scars and burns." He finished cleaning up the tattoo station.

My heart warmed for the man who was so big and scary, but kind and gentle all at the same time.

My body heated. Every inch of me came alive knowing that I would have him for the rest of the night. All to myself.

"I can feel you looking at me, Lily Pad." He came toward me and held out his hand.

I took it, letting him help me off the back counter. "I can't help it. You're pretty."

He chuckled, wrapping his big body around me. "I'm not pretty, baby."

I leaned back, cupping his scruffy jaw. "Yeah, Lucas. You are. You're beautiful. Your soul is beautiful. And if no one knows that, then they just haven't been paying attention."

His breath caught. "Lily, I think I'm—"

A loud crash sounded from the back of the place, making us jump apart.

"Shit." He charged for his apartment with me following behind him. Once we reached the door leading to his place, he unlocked it and stepped out into the hall. "Stay here."

"As if." I followed him anyway.

"Lily," he growled, spinning on me.

"I'm safer with you, Lucas." I didn't want to be alone. Especially not after what happened to me in that alley.

"Fine." He turned back around. "Stay close."

He wouldn't have to worry about that. I was right on his heels. One stop from him and I would have bumped into him.

We headed down the hall and once we reached the door leading to his apartment, Lucas let out a curse.

I peered around him, finding the door slightly ajar. My heart started racing. "How the hell did they break in?"

"I have no fucking idea." Lucas pushed it open slowly and entered.

I followed him. "Lucas?"

"Fuck me."

My eyes widened when we reached the living room. His place was trashed. The TV had been knocked over, broken glass surrounded it on the floor. The two bookshelves he had, were now on the ground with books strewn everywhere.

"How come we didn't hear this?" I asked, staring at the mess before me.

"The walls are thick," he said, walking through his living room. "They were obviously quiet until the last second. Probably wanted to make an impression or hoped they would get caught."

"Or they bolted and are fast as hell," I mumbled.

"Stay here. I'm going to make sure we're alone." He trudged through the rest of the apartment, doors opening then slamming closed. "Fuck," he bellowed.

My stomach twisted, my heart jumping in my chest. "What about your room?" I asked when he came back a moment later.

"No one else is here but…" He glanced at the door leading to his computer room. "I swear to fucking…" He blew out a slow breath and headed that way. A hard laugh left him. "This doesn't make sense. There's no way they should have broken in."

I joined him.

Lucas stood inside the room that was now empty.

"Oh God." I clapped a hand over my mouth. "We need to call the cops."

"Fucking hell." He rubbed the back of his neck and pulled his cell from the pocket in his jeans. "Yeah, I'd like to report a break-in."

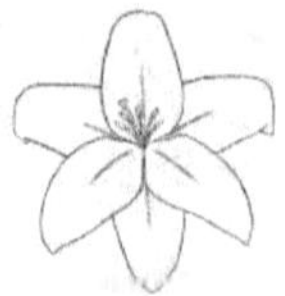

"Have a good night, Officers," I heard Lucas say.

I had started cleaning once I got the go-ahead. The two cops had taken inventory of everything that had been taken. Which was everything in Lucas's computer room. But nothing else had been stolen.

Stuffing the last bit of garbage in the large black bag, I tied the ends and put it with the others.

Lucas went back to his computer room, not giving me a passing glance. I wasn't sure why exactly but that bothered me. I knew he needed his space. That room had been locked up tight and held memories that he wasn't ready to share. It was also proof of a life he used to live to make ends meet.

"I have no idea who the fuck would do this," Lucas said, rejoining me in the living room.

"Any enemies?" I asked, crouching low to lift the bookshelf that had been pushed over.

"Baby, I have a lot of fucking enemies. But none that would go to this length…Actually, I don't even know what they would do to get the information they're looking for." He crouched beside me and we lifted the bookshelf together. I knew he could have lifted it himself, but I was thankful he didn't push me away and let me help him instead.

"What information do you have on those computers?" I asked, picking up book after book and placing them on the shelves.

"Nothing that anyone knows about. It's also the fact that I can get any information I want that usually poses a problem. But anyone who asks me to look for shit for them, I trust. I don't just do it for random strangers off the street."

"But someone who doesn't know that, wouldn't be able to come across it just by turning on your computer. They would have to know where exactly to look for it on your computer."

"That's true." He met my gaze. "But if we were here, who the hell knows what would have happened. Both of us know how to access my computer. I don't give a fuck about me but I sure as hell give…"

"A fuck about me?" I asked, raising an eyebrow.

"Yeah."

I stood on tiptoes and kissed his cheek. "I give a fuck about you too."

He blew out a slow breath. "You always know the right thing to say."

I shrugged. "I'm talented that way."

"You are." He gave me a wink.

We continued to tidy up as best we could. Thankfully, the bookshelves weren't broken but the TV was. Lucas would have to replace it. But he was right, it could have gone down a lot worse. We were still there. Even if we weren't in the same location, we were at the business part of the building. What would have happened… I hugged myself, rubbing my arms.

"Hey." Lucas stepped up behind me. "The place looks great." He wrapped his arms around my middle, placing a soft peck on the side of my neck. "Thank you."

"What if we're here next time?" I turned in his arms. "What if they can't get the information they're looking for and come after you?"

"I'll deal with it when the time comes." Lucas leaned his forehead against mine. "All of my shit is password protected. I've been a good little boy. I use my computers for playing games and doing minor dirty work but nothing that can land me in jail again. I'm not proud of the shit I've done." He pulled away, looking around the room. "Fuck." His fist landed against the wall.

I jumped, rushing to him when he went to do it again. "Hey, that's enough. You're going to hurt yourself." I grabbed his hand, rubbing his knuckles that were now red. "They're just items. You are more important than that shit. We can go to my place for a few days. Lay low until the police are in touch. You left them your cell number?"

"Yeah, they can get in touch with me. I usually work with Shephard and some FBI." He paused. "If Killian has something to do with this..."

"What? Why would he have something do with this?"

"I don't know. I'm grasping at straws here. But he's jealous. Maybe..." Lucas shook his head. "No, that doesn't even make sense."

"You think that fucker is smart enough for this? No. Lucas, he's a dick. I know that, but I can't see him doing this. Hell, he didn't know about you until you and I started seeing each other."

"True but look at what happened during your date with him."

I rolled my eyes and shoved past him. "That was not a date. I told you that. I want you. Only you. Not him. Don't play that jealousy shit with me."

"Baby."

"No." I pointed at him.

Lucas stopped, staring me down.

I shivered at the dark shadow passing over his face at being told what to do. "Listen, you are my boyfriend. Alright? I am in a relationship with you. Not him. I never thought him as serious. He was convenient. But he was a selfish bastard so that was why it was only a few times. Anyway, that doesn't matter. Just...please don't be jealous of him."

"He's a man, Lily. He's competition." Lucas went to the kitchen and came back a moment later with a broom and dustpan. "I'll sweep the alcove. There's a vacuum in the hall closet."

"Fine." Clearly the conversation was over, so I did as he suggested and vacuumed the living room. When we were done, I sat on the couch with my knee crossed over the other.

A plate and a glass of milk came into view.

I sighed but took it and ate the peanut butter and jelly sandwich.

Lucas sat beside me, doing the same.

When we were done, I grabbed the plates and put them in the sink. A hard body came up behind me.

"Lucas." I didn't want to fight with him.

He cupped my shoulders. "I'm sorry. I know I shouldn't be jealous. I trust you."

"I don't want him," I murmured.

Lucas spun me around. "I know." Running his thumb down the length of my jaw, he placed a hard peck on my lips.

I deepened the kiss, latching on to his hoodie. I pulled him tighter against me, taking his breath into my very lungs.

Lucas released my mouth. "I have to call Shephard. He can help me with this. I also need to figure out why they took my computers."

"And we need to figure out who took them. We can go to my place and use my laptop. We can track it from there. And then if we see any activity, we can let the cops know."

"Yeah, we'll let the cops know," he repeated. "Right."

I frowned, placing my hands on my hips. "You are not going after them."

"Like hell I'm not. They took my life, Lily."

"So? They are just computers."

"They are not just computers," Lucas snapped.

I raised an eyebrow.

He blew out a slow breath, rubbing the back of his neck. "Fuck."

"I get that you're pissed but you don't need to yell at me." I crossed my arms under my chest.

"Shit. I'm…" He sighed again. "I hate not having control. My home, the shop and the computers…those are the things I have control of."

"And it's bothering you that these bastards took that control," I added.

"Yeah." Lucas walked out of the kitchen.

"I get you're upset but I don't want you going after them. I will do whatever I can to help you. We can talk to Shephard. But clearly these fuckers were looking for something. They're trying to get something on you. It's not safe. I refuse to lose you."

He headed down the hall to the door of the apartment.

"Lucas." I followed him and smacked his back. "Please. I won't lose you when I've only just found you." I let out a frustrated cry. "Fine. You want to be a dickhead? Go right ahead.

I'm going home with or without you." I shoved past him and left the apartment.

"Don't fucking walk away from me."

"Me?" I spun on him and pushed him back. "You're not talking to me. You're falling into yourself and it's…it's scaring me."

"I'm…" Lucas hesitated, something flashing in his dark eye. "Fine. I won't go after them."

I shook my head, surprised he gave in so quickly. "You won't?"

His jaw clenched. "No."

"Okay." I blew out a breath of relief, my shoulders slumping. I looked around the apartment. It wasn't perfect, but it was better than when we first arrived.

Lucas came up beside me and wrapped his arms around my middle. Pushing his face into the crook of my neck, his mouth brushed over the spot beneath my ear. "I'm sorry for fighting with you."

"I know. I am too." I cupped his arms that were around me. "Tell me what's going on." I turned and placed my hands on his chest.

"I'm fucking terrified that they'll come back, and you'll be with me." Lucas cupped my face. "If something happened to you…"

"Nothing's going to happen." But something already did.

"I came home once to you beaten. If I see that shit again, I'll fucking lose it, Lily Pad."

My chest tightened. "You care about me?"

"Of course I care about you." He turned me completely in his arms and wrapped himself around me.

I leaned my head against his chest, his heart beating hard beneath my ear. "Tell me."

His body stiffened. "I did."

"No." I leaned back. "Tell me more."

"There's nothing to say." He released me and headed back to the front door.

"Lucas." I followed him. "Please. Talk to me."

He spun on me, forcing me back a step. "Talk? You want me to fucking talk? Fine. I'll talk. I'm in love with a woman who drives me fucking crazy. I've told you shit I've never told anyone. At all. And tonight, these bastards who took my computers from me, scare the shit out of me because I don't know if they'll be back. I don't know if they'll turn up when you're with me. And if you are with me and something happened, I would never forgive myself. I would die first before I let something happen to you." He turned back around. "Happy?"

"You're in love with me?" I whispered, taken aback at his confession.

"That's all you got from that?" he asked, looking at me over his shoulder.

"That's the most important part," I told him.

He only stared, something flashing behind his gaze. "Is it?"

I nodded, swallowing hard. "It's never been said to me before. I mean, my grandma tells me it of course but never a man. I…"

Lucas held his hand out.

I took it. We walked out of his apartment in silence.

He locked the place up even though his door had been busted in. "I'm sorry for fighting with you," he said a moment later. "I shouldn't have done that. You're just trying to help and I'm being a dick."

"Don't worry about it," I murmured.

He nodded, kissed the top of my head and led the way to his car.

We drove to my place with our fingers intertwined but no more words were said. He was in love with me. God, I had no idea. It explained everything.

Once we pulled into my drive, I slipped from the vehicle and headed to the house. The lights were turned off, so my grandmother must have been sleeping.

I unlocked the door. "We can go back to your place in the morning, so you can grab some things."

Lucas only grunted.

I shut the door behind him, locked it and headed to my bed room with him following behind me.

When I reached my room, I turned at the same time Lucas crashed into me. Lowering his mouth to mine, he swallowed my gasp.

"Tell me." He released my mouth with a smack. "Say it, Lily."

"I love you too, Lucas," I whispered. And I did. God, did I ever love him.

"I've never had a woman say those words to me before." His hands roamed down my back. "Like you, I've never experienced this. There was someone I cared about but that was it. It was never love. But you have your grandma." He released me and sat on the edge of my bed. "The closest thing I have to family is an old friend. Someone I could rely on when I needed him most. I…" He sighed. "There are others that I would do anything for but with him, he's never asked for my help. Any help I did give him was because I offered." He shrugged. "I don't know. It's different with him." Warmth shone on Lucas's face for the man who clearly had been with him when he needed it most.

"I'd like to meet him," I said softly.

Lucas smiled. "You have."

"Shephard?" I asked and he replied with a nod.

"But you also have us. We're your family, Lucas. That's all that matters." I stepped between his knees and ran my hand through his hair to the back of his head. "I love you, Lucas. God, it feels so good saying those words."

He leaned his forehead against the spot between my breasts, running his hands up my back.

"Do you feel better? After what happened tonight I mean?"

"I feel good enough. I'm still pissed but this pretty little pussy will help me relax later." He reiterated his point by cupping me.

"Definitely later." I giggled, pushing him back and jumped onto the bed beside him. "Now, I don't have the computer set up that you do but I have two laptops and a tablet. The one I play my games on and the other, I do random shit. That's also how I tracked you down and broke through your firewalls that you randomly set up."

"They weren't random, Lily Pad." He laid down beside me. "Show me your computers and tablet. Maybe we can get some of this shit figured out."

I saluted him. "Yes, Sir."

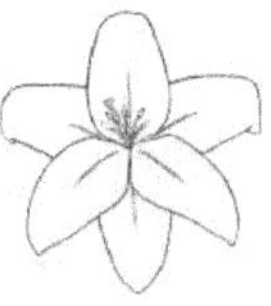

(Lucas)

I loved her. And she loved me. I knew we still had a lot of shit to work through and that we both had demons of our own to battle, but for now, I would soak this up.

Once Lily was seated in front of the computer, I called Shephard.

"Miss me already?" came his deep reply.

I chuckled, sitting beside Lily. "Always. Listen, there's been a situation." I told him about the break in and how they took my computers.

"Shit. Okay. I'm on it. You good though? Lily's safe?"

"Yeah. She is and I'm…dealing." I could use something, anything, to give me that delicious high.

"Lucas," Shephard barked.

Lily glanced at me, a deep frown settling between her brows. She must have heard him.

"I'm here," I mumbled.

"Good. I'll let you go and see what I can find out. And Lucas?"

"Yeah?"

He paused. "Be safe," he finally said. He hung up, leaving me to my own thoughts.

I always liked him. He was the only cop who treated me decently whenever I had to deal with the police. The others felt the need to push their weight around because I was bigger than them.

"You should join the force."

I scoffed. "Unlikely. And besides, you can't have a record to become a cop."

Shephard winked. "What record?"

That had been so long ago, I almost forgot that I was offered a job to be a cop. A cop. Me. Ha.

"You good?" Lily asked softly.

I nodded.

She went back to focusing on the computer in front of her.

While she searched for ways to find the bastards who broke into my apartment, I couldn't help but just watch her. Her index finger was pressed against her mouth. Her elbow was resting on her bent knee. A deep frown sat between her dark brows. Her bright green eyes moved back and forth over the screen as she typed and clicked away. I could probably figure out how to find them myself but giving up this control was exhilarating. So, I let Lily do her thing while I laid on my side and just watched her.

"I can feel you staring at me, you know," she said, an hour later, not meeting my gaze.

"I'm having fun watching you."

She looked at me then. "Yeah? Are you sure it's not driving you crazy that you're not doing this yourself?"

"I don't always need to be in control."

She laughed. "Right. And I'm not an alcoholic."

I ran my hand down her back before moving it beneath her shirt.

She shivered when it came into contact with her skin. A soft sigh escaped her. "I love how you always know when the right moment is to touch me."

"Every moment is the right moment, baby."

She grinned, leaned over, and placed a hard peck on my mouth. Turning around, she laid down and leaned against me before pulling the laptop onto her stomach. "I can't find anything, but I am tracking your computer. They haven't tried using it yet. But I'm going to create a program that will notify us if there's any activity at all. You'll get a notification on your phone and so will I."

My dick stirred. "Fuck, I love you."

She giggled, blowing me a kiss. "They're bound to screw up. I just wish I could figure out who it is."

"They must be good then if you can't figure it out."

She laughed. "I'm not an expert but I like to think I know my way around a computer or two."

"What about who attacked you? Any information on the cameras?"

"They have an old security system. I did contact the owner though and asked him to let me know if he sees anything suspicious. But there's been no other reports of an attack there." Lily tapped her mouth. "Now…" She cleared her throat. "This is just an idea, so don't get mad."

"What?" I asked, my stomach twisting.

"I could talk to Killian—"

"No."

"Lucas."

"What did I say?" I pushed out from behind her and left the bed. There was no way I would let her talk to that fucker. As much as that made me sound like a controlling asshole, I didn't give a shit. She was mine.

"Nothing's going to happen." Lily sat up. "Come with me then. We can talk to him together. We can play Good Cop, Bad Cop." She shrugged. "He might know something."

"Not going to happen." I leaned against her dresser, crossing my arms under my chest.

"You know." She pointed at me. "I love you but you're being a dickhead right now."

"Do I look like I give a shit? I don't trust that bastard."

"Then come with me," she insisted.

"Right." I scoffed. "And he'll definitely tell you everything if I'm there. Come on, Lily. Use your head."

"We're desperate, Lucas. Someone attacked me. I don't think it was random. I've walked down that street before, at night, and nothing has ever happened to me. I know people there. Not everyone but enough. I'm safe. Something was different about that night. You know it too. Killian is up to something. If it's not him, it's someone else. But everything inside of me is saying that it's someone we know."

I looked away, knowing she was right. Hell, I had been feeling it too. But it still didn't mean I wanted to meet up with him.

"Please." Lily came toward me, wrapping her arms around my middle. "Come with me. You can scare him into telling us what he knows."

"What if he doesn't know anything?"

"Well…" She chewed her bottom lip. "Maybe he knows someone who does."

"He already implied that I'm the one who hit you, Lily." That alone was enough to make me hate the guy.

Lily sighed, leaning her head against my chest. "I just want answers. I'm not used to not getting them. I can usually find out all of the shit I want to know on the computer but whoever took your stuff, is good."

"We'll get answers, Lily." I cupped her nape, holding her against me. "I promise." And it was a promise I was sure to keep because I knew that I would do anything and go to any length to find out who attacked my girl.

Twenty-One

Lily

LUCAS NEVER AGREED TO meet with Killian. I wouldn't go by myself. I wasn't stupid. Especially if he did have something to do with my attack. But we needed answers. And he was the only person I could think of that could possibly get the information we were looking for.

Instead of arguing about it further, Lucas and I had put my computers and tablet away and curled up in my bed. Although my bed was smaller than his, it felt good having him in it. His big body was wrapped around mine, his face pressed into the crook of my neck. His hot breath fanned over my skin, his back rising and falling. He had fallen asleep rather quickly. It made me feel good that I could help him with that.

A soft knock sounded on the door.

Slipping out from under Lucas's grasp, I quickly threw on a t-shirt and a pair of shorts and was met by my grandma at the door.

"Morning, dear." She smiled up at me.

"Good morning." I kissed her cheek and closed the door behind me.

"I wasn't sure if you were home. It's early. Did you want me to make some coffee?"

"That would be wonderful. Thank you." I followed her into the kitchen and sat at the table. "I also need to talk to you about something."

"Oh?" She busied herself around the kitchen, making coffee for us. "Everything okay?"

"Well…someone broke into Lucas's apartment last night."

"Oh no!" she exclaimed. "Is he okay?"

"Besides being mad, yes, he's fine. He has a friend, who's a cop, and looking into things. Lucas is actually here," I told her as she placed a mug in front of me.

"I figured that." She sat, taking a sip from her own mug. "I take it things are official now?"

"Yes." My cheeks burned. I laughed lightly. "Anyway, I told him it was okay for him to stay here for a few days. We cleaned up his place as best we could but just in case whoever it was that trashed his place comes back, I don't want him there."

She nodded. "Makes sense. What about work?"

"He actually already called his clients that he had booked and told them a family emergency came up." I shivered at the thought, remembering that his cock had been down my throat while he was on the phone. I had been teasing him and he shut me up by filling my mouth with his dick. It worked.

"Okay. I definitely don't mind if he stays here. It'll be nice having a man around." Grandma waggled her eyebrows.

I laughed.

"That is way too much happy for this time of day," Lucas grumbled, coming into the kitchen. He kissed the top of my head and sat at the chair to my left.

"Someone needs a coffee," Grandma said, pointing at him.

Lucas chuckled, rubbing the back of his neck. "It's been a long night."

"I heard. Did you call the cops?" Grandma poured him a cup of coffee and placed it in front of him on the table.

"Thank you." He took a long sip, letting out a sigh. "I did. Two officers came and took notes on what was missing but I doubt they'll be able to find anything. I called a buddy of mine from another precinct who's also looking into it."

"Why do you say that they won't be able to find anything?" Grandma asked, opening the newspaper to the crossword puzzle.

"Because they only took my computers and I have a feeling that they were after something specific. I just don't know what yet."

"Well, be careful." Grandma smiled up at him, glancing between us both. "You're in love. Aren't you?"

"Uh…" My cheeks burned.

Lucas grabbed my hand, giving it a light squeeze.

Grandma only grinned, shaking her head. "You remind me of my Stanley." She sighed. "Anyway, you're welcome here as long as you need."

"Thank you." Lucas brushed his thumb back and forth over the back of my hand. "I won't overstay my welcome and I'll help out around the house as much as I can."

"Are you a handy man?" Grandma asked, putting on her glasses.

Lucas passed me a glance. "I'm good with my hands, yes."

I coughed. "On that note. I'm going to take a shower."

(Lucas)

"I'm right." Ethel pointed at me. "You're in love with my granddaughter."

"I am." There was no point in denying it. Ethel had been around quite a while. She wasn't stupid.

"I guess I don't really need to give you the standard, 'You hurt my granddaughter and I'll kill you', spiel, do I?"

I chuckled. "You can."

Ethel searched my face. "Something happened to you. A long time ago and you're trying to figure out a way to not let those demons take over your life." She sat forward. "I'm not trying to pry. You don't have to tell me what happened. I don't even want to know. The only thing I care about is my granddaughter."

"I have no plans on hurting her. And yes, I didn't have a good childhood. Hell, I didn't have good teenage years either, but your granddaughter…" I rubbed the back of my neck. "I wasn't even looking for a relationship, but she showed up at my shop out of nowhere and got under my skin."

"She has a way of doing that." Ethel stood and grabbed our mugs before placing them in the sink. "You remind me of my Stanley. I know I keep saying that, but you really do. He was adopted as a baby and his adoptive parents were horrible people. They came from a high-class family, so they thought it would look good to adopt a baby in need." She scowled. "Anyway, it wasn't long after he and I were married that we cut all ties with his parents."

"I can understand that."

Ethel came toward me and placed her hand on my cheek. "You be good to her and she'll do the same. She's had a hard life too, but she doesn't let anyone see it. Her smiles are only on the exterior."

"I will make it my mission to have her smile every day for the rest of our lives. For however long we're together, I'll keep that smile on her face and make it so damn big that she'll feel it down to her bones."

Ethel's eyes shone. She nodded. "Well I'm going to head out."

"At this time?" I asked, raising an eyebrow.

She laughed. "I may be old, but I still have needs." She gave me a wink and left me alone in the kitchen. The sound of the front door shutting a moment later, stirred through me.

Cleaning up the dishes left in the sink, I put them in the drying rack and made my way back to Lily's room. The sound of the shower running sparked a need inside of me. I kicked the bedroom door closed and stripped.

Heading into the bathroom, I inhaled the sweet scent of some type of body wash. Instead of announcing my arrival, I quietly stepped into the shower.

"I was wondering when you would join me." Lily turned around, her jade eyes meeting mine. She gave me a wink, pushing her head under the water and letting it rain down over her.

Before she came out from the under the spray, I cupped her face and crushed my mouth to hers.

She gasped, gripped my arms, and parted my lips with her tongue. That move pulled a growl right from the center of my chest.

Lily giggled. She broke the kiss, licking along her swollen lips.

I smirked, running a hand down the length of her back. "I realized that there's something we haven't done yet." I kissed the corner of her mouth. "Something that I know you would enjoy." My fingers danced along her skin before pushing between the crack of her ass.

She jumped. "I think you're too big for that."

"Nah." I kissed her exposed throat. "I'm never too big for that."

Lily pushed me and spun back around. "I think you're going to have to work me up to your dick. Get some butt plugs or something."

I chuckled. "I fucking love you."

"I'm being serious you know." She glanced at me over her shoulder, her gaze sliding down my naked body. It stopped at my crotch. "Yup. Definitely going to have to work me up."

"You know how to make a guy feel good, Lily Pad."

She shrugged. "I have talents."

I raised an eyebrow. "You do but I'm the only one who gets to experience these talents."

She rolled her eyes, patting my chest. "Yeah, yeah. Now help me wash my hair."

I smacked her ass.

She yelped, glaring at me and rubbing the spot I just hit.

"I'm the only one who gets to make demands." I bent forward and grabbed the shampoo off the shelf. "Isn't that right?"

"You're lucky you're hot." She stuck her tongue out.

A laugh boomed through me.

Her face broke out into a grin. "In all seriousness though, I do like the sound of that."

"You do?" My dick lengthened at that.

"Yeah." She smirked, pointing down at my crotch. "I think Little Lucas likes that idea too."

"Little Lucas?" I turned her around and squeezed some shampoo into my palm. "You don't think it's little when it's deep inside you. And you definitely won't think it's little when it's fucking your ass."

She shrugged. "Semantics."

"Woman."

Her laugh turned into giggles. "Just wash my hair. Pretty please."

"Yes, ma'am." I kissed her shoulder and rubbed my hands together before running them through her hair.

"God, you need to do this all the time." She leaned into me.

"Feels good?" I chuckled.

"Oh yeah." She moaned. "You can go harder. I won't break."

"Fuck," I whispered, my dick now rock-hard and pushing right up against her ass.

"You like that, Lucas?" She reached around her, grabbed onto my dick, and started stroking.

"Fuck, baby. Yeah, I like it. I like all of it." I groaned. God, her hand felt so damn good. I continued washing her hair while she pumped my cock. A shiver trembled through me.

"Mmmm…" Lily pumped hard, stroking from base to tip. "Come on my ass, Lucas."

I wasn't sure how, but my cock grew even harder at those words.

"Do it. Please." She squeezed me. "God, you're so big. You can barely fit in my hand."

"Lily." I wasn't going to last if she kept saying this shit to me.

"So big, baby." She leaned her head back against my chest, stroking me from behind. "Please come."

I gripped her ass, pumping my cock through the cheeks of her rear when my release rocked through me. My cum coated that tight little spot I wanted to fuck. "Lily," I growled, pushing my thumb through my cream and running it over her tiny little asshole.

She moaned. "Put it in me."

Fuck, this woman gave as good as she got. I fisted her hair at the same time as I thrust my thumb inside her.

She whimpered, smacking her hand against the wall of the shower.

"My cum's inside you now, Lily Pad. And I'm going to do what you said." I nipped the side of her neck. "I'm going to stretch this little asshole nice and wide, so it can fit my big dick. I'll make you fucking crave my cock in your ass. I'll fuck you so hard, you'll thank me for it."

She panted. "That's big talk for someone who just came so quickly."

In a quick move, I had her up against the shower with my hand around her neck and my face in hers. "Is that so? You think I'm a two-second man, baby? Is that what this is about? I seem to recall all the times we've fucked, and you've begged me to stop because you couldn't take anymore. What was our longest time? Oh yeah. Six times. It lasted all motherfucking night. So don't throw my fast release in my face."

"Hmm…" She grazed her fingers over my abs. "I like this side of you. Nice and growly. Mean. Grumpy. And still fucking hard." She reiterated her point by grabbing onto my cock.

This woman was officially going to be the death of me.

(Lily)

Kicking my legs back and forth, I tapped the pen against my chin.

"Everest," Lucas said, pointing at the paper.

"Oh! Thank you." I wrote it in the crossword puzzle we had been doing for the last half hour. After our delicious shower, we got dressed and were now laying on my bed.

Lucas had disappeared into the kitchen and came back a moment later with two plates. Both had a sandwich on them.

"What if I don't actually like peanut butter and jelly sandwiches?" I asked him, swallowing the last bite of the sandwich he made me. "And I'm just eating these to be polite."

"Everyone likes PB and J."

"Not everyone. Some are allergic to peanut butter you know."

"I feel sorry for those people." He clutched his chest. "I would die if I was allergic to peanut butter."

I laughed. "So dramatic." I took a sip of my coffee. Lucas could make me these sandwiches forever and I would be happy. Who needed a fancy meal when you had PB and J?

We put our empty plates on the floor and continued working on the crossword puzzle. When we finished, I placed my mug on the floor and grabbed my laptop from under the bed.

Lucas checked his phone.

As soon as both the computer and phone booted up, dings started sounding around us.

Our eyes locked.

"Holy shit." I checked the program I had created to keep track of the usage of Lucas's computer and found almost a hundred attempts at trying to break through his firewalls. "Please tell me that these firewalls are harder to crack into than the ones I did?"

"Of course. That was just a cover-up anyway." He pulled my laptop from me and sat at my desk.

I jumped from the bed and stood behind him. "I wonder what they're wanting to find out."

"I have no idea. Everything that's on them has been given to the respective people already. I don't save anything else ever since getting thrown in jail for something I didn't do."

I laughed. "Right."

"They have no proof, baby." He winked. "Anyway, any pictures I take are on a flash drive."

"Where's the flash drive?"

"Oh shit." Lucas pushed back from the desk and stood.

"What is it?" I smacked his arm. "Lucas, talk to me."

He threw on his hoodie, shoving it down over his head before meeting my gaze. "I think I know what they were looking for."

I WAS NEVER CLUMSY in the things I researched, people I contacted, or the pictures I took. But every now and again, even the best person could make a mistake. This wasn't the case. I never made mistakes. But if I did, I cleaned up my mess and erased my steps before I could get caught. Something told me that this wasn't one of those times and I was going to pay for a mistake I hadn't cleaned up.

"Lucas." Lily pulled on a ripped pair of jeans. "What's going on?" she asked, snapping her bra in place.

"I think there might be something on that flash drive that these people could want."

She raised an eyebrow. "Really? Have they been watching too many movies?"

I shrugged. "I'm not sure but I need to find out."

"Well I'm coming with you. Unless you have the flash drive here."

I clutched my chest. "Now why would I ever do such a thing?"

She rolled her eyes. "Where is it?"

"Have you ever been caught? In all the shit you've done on your computer, have you ever been caught by the police or FBI or worse?"

"Uh…no." She frowned. "Just what I told you after checking into my grandma's lawyer. Other than that, I've never been caught."

"Does your grandma have a computer?" I needed answers and I needed them fast.

"She does. I bought it for her a couple years ago, but she only uses it to play Solitaire."

"Good enough." I headed to her door. "Show me where it is."

Lily threw on a red tank top and followed me out into the hall, leading the way to the back of the house. "This is her sewing and knitting room. Although she doesn't use this room much anymore since she got arthritis in her hands." She stopped in front of a door at the end of the hall and opened it. "Don't mind the mess."

I followed her inside, not surprised that I saw balls of yarn, a sewing machine, and other craft supplies strewn everywhere. "I think it's perfect."

Lily gave me a small smile before pushing some magazines off the table. "I got her a laptop, so she could play her game while watching TV." She flipped open the lid and turned it on.

I sat on the chair and pulled my phone from my pocket. Taking off the back of the case, I pulled out the flash drive before putting the phone back together.

"I never would have guessed."

"Good." I stuck the flash drive into the computer.

"What's on there?" Lily pulled up a stool and sat beside me.

"Just pictures. Most of them are of tattoos I've done or other things I've drawn. I have some clients on here and their kids." I scrolled through the pictures first, thinking I might have accidentally taken one I shouldn't have.

"None of these seem out of the ordinary though."

We went through the rest of the pictures and of course, nothing jumped out at us.

"What else do you have on here?"

I thought a moment. Opening up the files I had stored on the flash drive, I went through each one but again, nothing was worth trashing my home for.

"This doesn't make sense." Lily placed her hand on my shoulder. "I mean, you had a good idea. But nothing seems off."

"I know." I went through the pictures again but got nothing. "There has to be something. These files wouldn't mean anything to someone else. They're mostly contracts with clients who have booked big tattoos or other businesses wanting some graphic designing done. I have lists of names of people I've worked on who come in for my freebie days to get their scars done too. But none of that is so damn important to break into my home for. And the thing is, I don't have a lot of the personal stuff on my computer, only the flash drive."

"You don't put all your eggs in one basket kind of thing?"

"Exactly."

"Could that be it though?"

I looked up at her. "What do you mean?"

"Could you have done some work for someone that's involved in anything illegal? It probably sounds dumb, but you never know anymore."

"No, it's not dumb." I couldn't imagine why anyone would want to know this shit. It was just names of tattoo clients and other graphic designs I had done.

"Did you do any work for a shady company or anything?" Lily took the mouse from my hand and clicked through each picture again.

"No. Not that I know of. They all seemed reputable."

"Of course they would seem reputable. I'm sure they don't flash their dirty work around on neon signs."

"Careful." I gave her hip a pinch.

She jumped, smacking my hand. "I'm serious."

"Yeah, and so am I." But she had a point.

"Lucas, what's this?"

I followed her gaze. "Can you zoom in?"

She did. The image was of a woman standing with a man and a child. The couple was older. There was another younger man with them as well.

"I don't remember taking this picture."

"Does anyone else have access to your phone?" Lily asked.

"No. I was taking a picture of the front of my shop. I didn't even notice these people. I am blind in one eye you know."

Lily snorted. "Please. Your eyesight is fine even though you can only see out of one of them."

"Yeah, well, I still don't remember taking this picture. Zoom out again. All the way."

She did. Now it looked like a normal picture. Crane's Ink was in full view but how the hell had I not seen the couple, child and other man?

"Maybe you took the picture before these guys came into view and never looked at the picture to see how it turned out," Lily suggested.

"Either way, this can't be what those people are looking for. What's it to them? It just looks like a family."

"True." Lily clicked through the rest of the pictures. "This doesn't make sense. That's the only one that's jumped out at me so far and it doesn't look like anything these bastards would want."

"Let me check my files again."

We spent the next couple of hours going through my flash drive. No other pictures stood out. And none of the files seemed to jump out either. But something was wrong. I could feel it in the marrow of my bones. I just couldn't figure out what it was.

"We won't give up." Lily stretched her arms up and over her head before dropping them at her sides. She massaged the back of her neck.

"Thank you for helping me." I squeezed her shoulder, taking over the massage and rubbing out the kink in her neck all because she had been hunched over the desk, trying to help me figure out what the hell was going on.

"I didn't do anything." She kissed me softly on the cheek. "But you're welcome."

"We should head back to my apartment. Maybe we can find something else there. They could have left something behind." I was desperate, but I needed answers. "Hopefully."

"Okay." She patted my hand. "Let's do that."

(Lily)

I knew Lucas was desperate to get answers. When we reached his apartment and entered his home, he went right to the computer room. Even though it had been trashed like the rest of his place, we crouched and searched through each paper that had been strewn on the floor.

"Anything?" I asked, kneeling beside him.

"No. Everything is here. Except for my computers. They didn't take anything else. They could have taken my TV, stereo system..." Lucas rubbed the back of his neck. "Fuck."

"Hey." I placed a hand on his shoulder. "We got this. I'm going to help you find out who did this because clearly the cops aren't doing shit since they consider this a routine robbery."

His jaw clenched. "I hate this...They stole a part of my life and it makes me feel vulnerable." His gaze snapped to mine. "I don't like that shit, Lily."

"I know." I helped him search through the papers before he completely lost it but like he said, nothing was out of the ordinary. Pulling my phone from my back pocket, I checked the program I had created and saw at least fifty more attempts on cracking Lucas's firewalls. "They're determined, I'll give them that," I said, showing Lucas the screen.

He grunted, pushing to his feet. "This was a bad idea."

"No. It was a good idea because it reassured you that there isn't anything here that can help us. If you hadn't checked this place out, you would be wondering and driving yourself crazy." I picked up the papers and placed them in a neat pile on his desk.

"You're too good to me." Lucas kissed the top of my head and left the room.

"Have you heard from Shephard?"

"No, not yet." Lucas grunted. "But he knows shit all about computers. You're the only person I trust who knows anything about them."

"Aww." I grinned. "You trust me, baby?"

He rolled his eyes.

I laughed. "Well…you should call him. See if he's found out anything."

"He said he'd call but okay." Lucas ran a hand over his head before pulling his phone from the pocket in his pants. Holding it up to his ear, he waited. "Shephard, have you heard anything?" He waited. "I know. Okay. Yes, we're both fine. I'm fine." He rolled his eyes. "Alright, thanks, my man." Lucas disconnected the call and shoved the cell back in his pocket. "I love that fucker but he drives me insane sometimes."

I laughed. "I'm assuming he hasn't found anything?"

"Not yet but he said he'd be in touch." Lucas ran a hand through his hair. "He's not part of the precinct here but he's the only one I trust. Some of these local cops are shady as fuck. I didn't want to deal with that."

"I get it." I checked the time on my phone. "I guess maybe we should head to our meetings?" It had been weeks since I had gone. I was surprised Toby hadn't tried contacting me.

"Yeah." Lucas frowned. "I'm surprised Toby hasn't tried contacting us," he said, taking the thought right out of my head.

"He has a lot going on. He's taken on a few more people and I think being a sponsor is weighing on him. I know it would for me." I had been asked a few times to be a sponsor, but I never agreed. I was still battling through my own shit.

"Makes sense. I only sponsor Lena and that's enough for me." Lucas shook his head. "She definitely keeps me on my toes."

"Huh…" I cleared my throat, a sudden urge to hunt the woman down and punch her in the face, taking over.

"What?" He cocked his head. "You're jealous."

"No. Why would I be jealous? She only wants to fuck you. She wants Little Lucas to fill her up and make her scream for her daddy." I stood and headed to his kitchen. "Why would I be jealous over that?"

"Lily." Lucas chuckled. "That was a while ago. She hasn't hinted for anything since. I thought you guys were getting close?"

"We are. Even though it's weird but it doesn't mean…" I pursed my lips, crossing my arms under my chest. "I am not jealous."

His laugh deepened. "Yeah, baby, you are. You have no reason to be jealous. I promise. I don't want her."

"Maybe not but she sure as hell wanted you in the beginning."

"No, she wanted my help. She was desperate," he corrected. "There is no one else for me. Just you."

"Really? What about someone from your past?"

His jaw ticked. "I…fuck. I'm sorry, baby. There is no one." He leaned forward, cupping my cheek. "Do you remember what happened when I found you having dinner with Killian? How jealous I was?"

My chest tightened at the memories. "Yes."

"I wouldn't mind if the roles were reversed." He slid a hand down the length of my spine and cupped my ass.

I slapped my hands against his chest.

"I also wouldn't mind if you forced me up against the wall, dropped to your knees and took me in your mouth." He nipped the side of my neck. "I wouldn't mind if you showed me who I belonged to."

I threw my arms around his neck, arching into him. "Is that what you want? You want to fuck my face all because I'm jealous?"

"No, baby." He bit my earlobe. "I want to fuck your throat."

I pushed him back and dropped to my knees before unbuckling his belt. "Then give it to me good, baby. Let me remind you who you belong to."

His nostrils flared, a wicked grin spreading on his face when his hands gripped the side of my head. "Open wide, Lily."

(Lucas)

Every inch of me hurt. I had never been with a woman who craved sex as much as I did. But I also hadn't been with anyone that I wanted to fuck as much as I wanted to fuck Lily. She gave as good as I did and now we were laying on the couch an hour later, naked, spent, and sore.

"Do you think they'll be back?" Lily asked, lifting her head and resting her chin on her fist. "I mean, we aren't exactly dressed for running away."

"I'm not sure. I guess we should head back to your place but there's nothing else here that they could want. They already took everything."

"Okay." She leaned her cheek on my chest, lazily running her finger over my nipple.

"What is it?" I tapped her ass lightly when she didn't respond.

"I've never been jealous over anyone before." Lily lifted her head. "But knowing Lena wanted you…" She shrugged. "It bothers me."

"Don't let it because you are the only one that I want. Okay?"

"Okay," she repeated.

"I think we're late for the meeting." I noticed that it was now dark out.

"We can go to the late one." Lily placed a kiss on the spot above my heart. "I like this. Being naked with you. It's like we can't hold anything back since we don't have clothing in our way."

"No barriers, baby?" I asked, brushing my thumb along her bottom lip.

"Yeah. Something like that." She gave me a small smile.

She was absolutely breathtaking. I trailed my thumb along her jawline, sliding my hand into the mess of curls falling freely around her face. Her bright green eyes shone. Her full plump mouth parted, a sharp inhale of breath escaping her. "Why are you looking at me like that?" she asked, her voice low and husky.

"You're beautiful." My body grew hard beneath her.

Her cheeks reddened.

"I'm serious," I said, knowing she didn't believe me. "You look at me like I'm the only one who matters in your world. You make me feel things that I've never felt before. Your heart is so damn big, I can feel its warmth every time we touch." I spun us around, so she was laying beneath me. "And this?" I pushed into her. "Is perfect. Every time with you is perfect."

Her cheeks reddened even more. "Lucas."

"Lily." I brushed her hair off her forehead. "I mean it. Everything I say to you, I mean."

Her eyes shone. "God, you know how to make a girl feel good about herself."

I chuckled, placing a soft peck on her mouth. "I don't want you to cry," I murmured, swiping my thumb over a tear that had fallen from the corner of her eye. "I just want you to know how I feel. I don't talk. I never talk. I do my shares at the meetings but even then, it's just basic shit. But I'm trying to talk to you."

"I know," she said, her voice wavering.

"No, baby." I kissed her again. "I want to tell you everything but it's hard for me. It brings me back there and I can't…it fucking scares me. I can't go back there because it'll fuck me up and I don't want that. I don't want you to see that."

"I get it." She ran her hands up and down my back. "Can we do something tomorrow?"

"We can do whatever you want. Just name it."

"Well…" She chewed her bottom lip.

"Tell me."

"I want to go to the beach. After everything that's happened, I just want…I want you. I want to go away with you. We can go to the beach during the day and then dinner at night?"

"You want that?" I asked her, sitting back and pulling her onto my lap. "With me?"

Lily straddled me. "Of course I do. There's no beach near here but there's one a few hours away. Is that okay?"

"Of course."

"Good." She kissed me softly on the mouth. "I love you, Lucas. And I've meant everything I've said to you. I want more. I want you. I want…I want one day at a time with you." She laughed. "God, I'm rambling. I feel nervous."

"Don't feel nervous with me, Lily Pad," I said, my voice firm. "Ever. Do you understand me?"

She nodded. "So…"

I chuckled, leaning in for a kiss.

She grinned, pushing me. "Tell me."

"Yes, Lily." I bit her chin. "I'll take you to the beach and then out for dinner. We can get drunk off of water. We can do all of that. Whatever you want."

She laughed. "I can't wait."

Neither could I.

WE ENDED UP MISSING the meeting the night before and instead returned to my grandmother's house. Toby was bound to kick both of our asses, but he hadn't called. Again. A part of me wondered what that was about.

While Lucas was in the shower, I gathered up some things we would need for our days at the beach on our weekend away. I was excited. Too excited. It had been years since I'd felt the sand between my toes and heard the water crashing against the shore. I didn't care that it was cooler out and that we were probably crazy for going to the beach. I needed this. We needed this.

The water turned off and I couldn't help but imagine Lucas standing in the shower with drops running down the length of his hard body. I shivered. God, get it together, Lily. He was just a man. It wasn't like I hadn't seen one before. But in all fairness, I had never seen anyone that looked like him. At all.

Pushing the dirty thoughts to the back of my mind, I finished packing my bag with a blanket and two towels, and put it at the door near the bag Lucas packed the night before. Not that we would go in the water because I was sure it was probably cold but just in case, I packed them anyway.

Stripping out of my tank top and panties, I rummaged through my underwear drawer for my bikini.

"Hmm…now that is quite the sight."

I laughed, meeting Lucas's gaze in the mirror.

He ran a towel over his head, threw it in the hamper beside my dresser, and slipped the eye patch back onto his head.

"I'm not sure which one to wear." I pulled out a few bathing suits. "Red, black…or…white?"

"White." He stepped up behind me. "Then when it's wet, I can see everything beneath it."

"But then everyone else will see," I reminded him, slipping into the bottoms and pulling them up to my hips.

"Fuck." He brushed his fingers below the cheek of my ass, licking his lips.

"Lucas, you need to stop looking at me like that or we'll never leave." I handed him the strings to the top. "Tie me up?"

He took them from me and did as I asked. With the top securely in place, I continued looking through my drawers for a pair of shorts, a tank top, and a sweater.

"Keep doing that, Lily."

I lifted my head. "Was last night, this morning, and the shower not enough for you?" I laughed.

"Not when you look like that." He cupped himself. "Fuck, baby. I've never had so much sex in my life. You've turned me into an addict."

Our eyes locked in the mirror.

"Don't think about that shit," he bit out, the tension in the air becoming thick.

I cleared my throat, pushing those dark thoughts to the back of my mind. "Can I ask you a question?"

"Depends." He slipped his white t-shirt over his head. "Are you going to ask me about my past?"

"Yes," I said automatically.

He slumped onto the edge of the bed. "Fine. Go ahead."

"How long did it take for you to enjoy sex?"

His gaze snapped to mine. "Not long. Even though I was forced into it at a young age, I'm still human and I'm also a man."

"Did you ever have sex with someone you cared about? Before me I mean?"

Lucas stood, coming toward me. When he was directly in front of me, he gripped my hips and kissed my forehead. "Yeah but it was nothing. And I haven't fucked anyone I've cared about since. Not until you. You're the only woman I want to keep fucking. The only one I want to slip my dick inside and stay there." He kissed the side of my neck. "You make me feel safe," he whispered.

I shivered, snaking my arms around his neck. My nipples pebbled, pushing against the triangles of my bikini top. "You're always safe with me."

Gripping the flesh of my rear, he carried me to the bed and laid me on it before kneeling between my legs.

"We need to go," I whispered, digging my heels into his ass.

Instead of saying anything, he kissed the side of my neck and reached between us. His finger hooked into the crotch of my bathing suit and pulled it to the side at the same time he thrust into me.

I cried out, the burn of his thick cock piercing into my unprepared body spreading over me.

"Take it, Lily," he growled, biting along the length of my throat. "I know this raw pussy likes being used up."

"Yes," I whimpered. The pain sliced through me, my body becoming wet for him.

He grunted. "You're my slutty little masochist, aren't you?"

His words should have offended me but instead, they only made my pussy clench and suck him in deeper.

He chuckled, pushing into me as deeply as my body would allow. He stopped, holding my head in place. My body was pinned to the bed by his powerful strength.

"I love you, Lily Pad." He sucked my bottom lip into his mouth.

"God, I love you too, Lucas." I lifted my head to meet the hard impact of his lips against mine. "Please fuck me."

"No." He leaned his elbows on either side of my head. "The first time I had sex, I was forced to enjoy it." He leaned down, his hot breath scorching my ear. "I came. I came fucking hard."

"Why are you telling me this now?" Anxiety rushed through me.

"Because I need to know."

"Know what?" I asked, my voice shaking.

"That you can handle it." Lucas bit my earlobe.

"What do you mean?" I frowned. "If you're asking me if I can handle you while you're talking about your childhood when you're deep inside me, try me."

Something flashed behind his eye.

"You can't scare me," I added.

"I was twelve when I first fucked a woman."

"I was thirteen when I first felt a dick inside me," I threw back at him. "Are you trying to make me jealous?"

Lucas chuckled. "Baby, you have no reason to be jealous of anyone that I've fucked. You do remember that not all of my encounters were consensual. Right?"

"Then why are you telling me this while fucking me?" I pushed him back and slid out from beneath him. "I love you but you're being a big asshole right now." I stormed into my bathroom, slamming the door shut behind me. God, he was a dick and I had no idea why the hell that just happened.

(Lucas)

I stuffed my aching cock back into my pants and sat on the edge of the bed. Dropping my head in my hands, I let out a deep sigh.

What the hell was wrong with me? Was I deliberately trying to ruin the good that had finally come into my life?

"You're tainted, boy." Manicured nails dug into my cheeks. "You will always be tainted. You won't have any good come to you and if you do?" The woman sneered. "It won't last long. You crave sex. The dark side of it. The sensual side. All of it. You won't be able to find anyone that can keep up and handle that beast inside of you. You're a fucking pervert and my goal is to make you an addict."

And I was. Drugs, alcohol, sex. Coffee was the only thing I allowed myself to have anymore. And sex. But sex always came with a price. Especially now that it involved a woman I was in love with.

Mustering up the courage to talk to Lily, I trudged to the door of her bathroom and gave it a light knock. When she didn't answer, I leaned my forehead against it. "I'm sorry. I'm so fucking sorry. I don't know what came over me. I wasn't trying to make you jealous at all. I have…I have problems. Issues. I don't fucking know anymore. You're the first good thing in my life and I don't know how to take it. I love you, Lily Pad."

The door slowly opened. Lily stared up at me. "Were you wanting angry sex?"

"No. I don't know." I stuffed my hands in the pockets of my gray sweatpants. "I just wanted you."

"You have me. Always." She shoved a finger against my chest. "But you don't need to talk about your past when you're inside me. It's weird and it fucks with my head."

"I know." I cleared my throat. "That was the point."

She raised an eyebrow. "What's that supposed to mean?"

I pushed her farther back into the bathroom and lifted her onto the counter. "I'm not just a drug addict, Lily. I'm addicted to sex as well."

"Am I going to have to worry about you fucking other people?" she asked, leaning back and searching my face.

"What?" I should have expected that. "No. Not at all."

"What if I'm not enough for you? I'm only one person, Lucas. What if I can't give you what you need?"

I opened my mouth to argue, to tell her that she was crazy for thinking that way, but it made sense. She was only one person. The question wasn't whether she was enough for me but rather, if she could handle me and my demons.

I left the bathroom, grabbing the bag Lily had packed for us. "You are enough for me, Lily," I said when I felt her come up behind me. "You have to be enough because I refuse to have it any other way."

"We'll take this one day at a time then, Lucas, but I won't compete with other people."

Bile rose to my throat that she didn't say other women. She knew. Fuck me, she knew.

Dropping the bag to the floor, I grabbed her hand and pulled her to the bed.

"Lucas." She slid her hand from mine. "I'm not fuck—"

"Stop," I snapped.

Her eyes widened.

"I mean…" I blew out a slow breath, trying to gather my thoughts, trying so damn hard to actually speak to her instead of closing up. If we were going to be together and make it through my shit, we had to talk. "First thing." I grabbed her hands, holding them in mine and pulling the strength from her that I needed. "I'm not gay and I'm not bisexual. I have nothing against it but it's not my thing. I'm straight. But I was raped as a kid by both men and women and forced to do things to other kids my age that would make the Devil himself cringe."

Lily looked away.

"No, look at me please. I need you to look at me. I can't get this out if you don't."

She nodded, chewing her bottom lip and met my gaze. "Go on," she whispered.

"I…I don't remember how old I was the first time it happened. I didn't understand until I was older what we were used for. But I remember the pain. It was nothing like I had ever felt before. I…"

"Tell me about the first time you enjoyed it. Where you weren't forced or manipulated into it and you actually wanted to have sex."

My muscles tightened, bunching beneath my skin. "You want to know about that?"

Lily gave me a small smile. "I want to know you, Lucas. All about you. I want to know the man I'm in love with. The good and the bad."

My heart swelled. "I was fifteen. It was one of the other adoptive kids. She was seventeen and counting down the days until she could leave that hell. I had always been big for my age. In…uh…every sense of the word." My mind went back to that time. That dark and dangerous time but she had been the only light in the darkness that had surrounded my life. Until Lily.

"Please, Lucas. I just want to feel something other than pain."

"We'll get in trouble." It wasn't like Mel wasn't beautiful, but I didn't want to get caught and thrown back in the cage.

"I'm almost out of here." Her deep blue eyes shone. "I wish I could take you with me."

"Yeah, like that would ever happen. But I'll get out of here. Eventually." If they didn't kill me first.

"Do you think we'll ever see each other again?" Mel asked me, pushing her blonde bangs out of her eyes.

"I don't know." Honestly, I wasn't sure I wanted to. We had been through a lot. All of us. Together and apart. Seeing her again would be too painful.

"Lucas." Mel shuffled over to me and grabbed my hands. "Please."

I searched her face. "Why me?"

Her eyes fell to my lap before glancing back up at my face. "You know why. I also trust you. I know you wouldn't hurt me. Not like…"

I leaned forward, inhaling the scent of her rose perfume and cupped her face. "I trust you too, Mel."

"Lucas?" Lily frowned.

I coughed, rubbing the back of my neck. "Her name was Mel Huff. We had sex already but never by our own choice. She was leaving soon after that, so she wanted…anyway. It was the first and only time I got any enjoyment out of sex while being locked up in that hell. After that, I fucked any random I could get. And I haven't enjoyed that physical contact until you."

"Where is she now?" Lily asked.

"I don't know. A lot of us didn't make it. It's what our adoptive parents wanted. Less mouths to tell their dirty secrets I guess. I tried looking for her again, but she must have changed her name or gotten married. Or maybe she died. I don't know."

"Did you have feelings for her?"

"I…No. Not the way I have feelings for you." I cupped Lily's cheek. "I cared for her. I'm not going to lie and say I didn't."

"I'm sure all of these old feelings are coming back," Lily said, giving me a small smile.

I dropped my hand to my lap, staring at her. "You're fucking incredible. I'm telling you about the first girl I had sex with and you're acting like we're talking about the weather." Not that I expected her to be jealous, but she was jealous of Lena, so I had assumed she would react the same way when it came to Mel.

"I'm not, really." Lily laughed lightly. "I know I freaked out when it came to Lena, but I guess this is different. You and Mel were together in a dangerous time of both your lives. You only had each other. I know I have nothing to be worried about and that you love me."

"I do." I cupped her face. "I do love you, Lily." I placed a hard peck on her mouth. "I love you more than anything. You've given me so much damn strength, I don't know how I can ever repay you."

"Just love me," she said softly. "That's the only payment I'll ever need."

(Lily)

Hearing about Lucas's first time where it was completely

consensual made me feel…weird. I wasn't sure what it was. Was I jealous? Angry? Annoyed? I wasn't sure but a part of me wondered why I had never heard of this Mel chick before. Another part of me was thankful that she was no longer in Lucas's life. They had been through a lot together. How could I ever compete with that?

Once we left my place, I sat in the passenger seat with Lucas's hand on my inner thigh. I couldn't help but think back to our earlier conversation. He hadn't continued and told me more, but I had so many questions. Was he ever in love with Mel? She was his first technically. Did she mean something to him?

"You're upset," Lucas said awhile later.

"No, I'm not." But I still stared out the window.

"You are. You haven't said anything since we sat in the car. You have questions. So ask me."

"It makes me feel like a jealous nag if I ask," I mumbled.

"I don't give a shit. Ask me anyway."

I sighed, turned toward him, and leaned against the door, keeping his hand in mine. I needed to feel his skin, to feel his touch and the wrath of his power. I needed him. Always him. "Do you think of her often?"

"Not often but enough." His jaw ticked. "I think about what she could be doing. I hope she was able to get past everything. And I also wonder if she was able to move on. We went through a lot together."

I nodded. "Did you love her?"

Lucas's gaze flicked to mine before looking back out at the road ahead of us. "No. It was different with her. We were used the most. She had the perfect body according to them and they got off on that shit. The other kids kept to themselves, but Mel and I had bonded. She was also the first they put me with."

"I don't know what that means."

His gaze flicked to mine. "They made me rape her, Lily."

Bile rose to my throat. "Please tell me they got theirs."

Lucas nodded. "That's how most of us were able to escape. Shephard was actually a rookie at the time. He went to the wrong address after getting a call but he heard screaming. So he followed his gut and investigated. Backup was called and eventually, the FBI showed up. The place had been overrun with Feds. Kids scattered. They probably thought the authorities were going to hurt them just the same. I know that's what I thought. It took a long time for me to trust Shephard."

"He's a good man," I whispered.

"He is." Lucas brought our joined hands up to his mouth. "Whatever you're thinking, whatever you're worried about, I am yours, Lily. And only yours. I've never given myself to anyone like I've given myself to you. You cracked through my cold heart with a mere look. You brought me to my knees with a laugh. And you made this grumpy fucker smile more in the few short months I've known you than in my whole damn life."

My eyes welled, my throat working over the lump suddenly lodged in it. "God, you say the sweetest things sometimes."

"I mean every word." He brushed a hand down my cheek. "I love you, Lily. I've never felt this before. This need for someone else. We may have only known each other for a short time but I feel like I've known you my whole life."

"I feel like that too." I wiped a tear that had escaped and rolled down my cheek.

"Crying for me, baby?"

I laughed, punching him lightly in the arm. "Drive faster, Lucas."

He grinned, giving me a wink.

Bringing my knees up to my chest, I held onto his hand and kissed the scars gracing his knuckles. "Will you tell me what happened to your eye?"

"Uh…" He chuckled, rubbing the scruff on his strong jaw. "I was always big for my age. One kid tried jumping me, I attacked him, but I didn't see the knife. He also thought I was eyeing his girl." He shook his head. "It was a fucked-up situation that I'll never understand. Anyway, he ended up stabbing me in the face. He almost got both eyes, but I was able to fight him off before that happened."

"Wow." I blew out a slow breath. "And here I thought I had a fucked-up childhood." I shook my head.

"I don't want to compare our shit, Lily. We handle things differently, but I like to think my past made me stronger." He shrugged. "That's what I'm hoping for anyway."

Was it possible? What if he saw Mel again? What if Killian tried hitting on me again? I wasn't sure if I was jealous of Mel. Oh, who the hell was I kidding, of course I was jealous of her. She helped Lucas through a terrible time in his life. Because of her, he was able to get through it.

"Did you ever see Mel again?" I asked Lucas.

"No." He pulled his beast of a car into the parking lot of the hotel we were staying at that night, the conversation now done and over with. But because I liked to ask questions, I now couldn't help but wonder what would happen if Mel ever showed up again. And if I could ever compete with her.

Twenty-Four

Lucas

WHEN I PULLED INTO the parking lot of the hotel that was a few hours outside of the city we lived in, I helped Lily get the bags out of the trunk. We walked into the building that had been in a rural part of the small town and I checked us in.

"I put us on the top floor," I told Lily as we walked down the hall to the elevator. The building had twelve floors, but I knew with the view overlooking the vintage town, it would make Lily happy to wake up to the next morning.

"I can't wait to see the sunrise tomorrow morning," she said, smiling up at me.

"I can't wait to put that smile back on your face." I pinched her chin, placing a soft peck on her mouth.

The elevator opened and a woman dressed in a housekeeping uniform rushed past us.

"Excuse me," she muttered, disappearing down the hall we had just come from.

The scent of roses wafted into my nose.

"Rose oil. It gets this dick nice and hard, doesn't it, Lucas?"

My stomach twisted. I shook my head, ridding it of the memory. That was the moment in my life when I was taught that scents could be an aphrodisiac. But there was no way it was her. It was just a coincidence and not one I wanted to experience again any time soon. I had to remind myself that it was nothing like the previous times I smelled it and it was nothing this time around.

"Lucas?" Lily tilted her head. "Everything okay?"

"Yeah." I gave her a small smile, but something still struck me as odd about the housekeeper. I pushed it to the back of my mind and followed Lily into the elevator.

"Are you sure?" Lily asked, placing her hand gently on my arm.

I nodded, grabbed her hand, and kissed her fingertips.

She smiled but it never reached her eyes. Something had changed between us since we woke up in bed together that morning. Revelations had been brought to light and I wasn't sure anymore how to make things right. The questions she asked, I answered completely and honestly but all of these feelings I never thought I had, slid to the forefront of my mind just the same. I never loved Mel. I cared for her enough to not hurt her when the sex between us had been consensual but other than that, I felt nothing.

Once we hit the top floor and headed to our room, I swiped the keycard through the lock and pushed open the door. Letting Lily enter first, I glanced down the hall. A woman now stood at the end of it, but I couldn't make out her features. Everything inside of me said that I knew her. Or that I had once known her. There was no way it was her but that little voice told me it was Mel. It wasn't possible. My nose tingled as the memories of roses rushed through me. It couldn't be.

"Lucas?"

I turned at the sound of Lily's voice. Glancing back down the hall, I saw the woman was gone. I met Lily's gaze.

She stood inside the room, staring at me. Her eyes moved over my face. Something flashed behind them. Pain. Fear. Confusion. She knew. Fuck me, she knew. How she knew was beyond me, but she knew that there was something. Someone. I was being pulled and I had no idea what direction I would end up in.

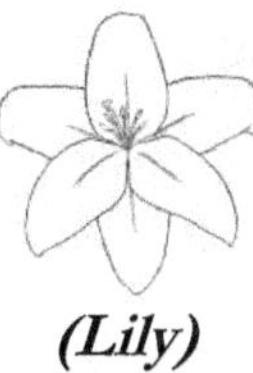

(Lily)

I was jealous of Lena but Mel? I wasn't sure how I felt. Lena and Lucas hadn't slept together but he did sleep with Mel. Or fucked her. Who knows if they even slept? I was obsessing over it and I knew I shouldn't have been. But he seemed off. Ever since he told me about her and now that we were at the hotel, he hardly touched me. He was falling into himself and I didn't know how to get him back.

I wanted to make him forget her but then another part of me was thankful that she had been able to help him through the darkest time of his life. It wasn't fair. It wasn't fair at all.

After putting our bags in the hotel room, we left the building and walked down the street toward the beach. I could smell the salt in the air. I should have been happy. I had been wanting to come to the beach ever since I was a little girl but now all I could think about was Lucas between some other woman's legs. I knew he had been with many women besides me but there was something about this one that bothered me. If he ever saw her again, would she be a problem? Would she try to get him back? I trusted him. I trusted him completely but a past like he had was different. She helped him. And if she showed up again, all of these old feelings could come back and maybe then he would realize that he was meant to be with her and not me.

"Lily." Lucas ran his fingers down my arm before linking our hands. "Stop thinking about her."

"I can't help it when my boyfriend is thinking about her too." I sighed, pulling my hand from his and crossing my arms under my chest. I knew we had issues before this. We had problems talking. We were working on it and he had revealed so much to me this morning, but it was almost like he revealed too much. I wasn't sure how to handle it.

"Lily." Lucas grabbed my upper arm, stopping me and spinning me around. "Stop this. Please."

"I'm not doing anything," I muttered, pulling from his grip and continuing to walk down the sidewalk.

"Lily." Lucas pushed me into an alley until we were out of the public eye. "What's wrong?"

"I don't know," I cried. "Alright? I have no idea. I don't like this feeling. I don't know if I'm jealous. I don't know if I'm envious. I have no fucking idea and it's frustrating because I've never felt this before."

"I shouldn't have said anything, but I wanted to be honest with you." He rubbed the back of his neck. "I want you to know everything about me."

"I want that too." I leaned my forehead against his chest and took a deep breath. He smelled of spice and coffee and it was absolutely delicious. I let out a soft purr.

"Let's go. The sooner we get the beach part done, the sooner we can head back to the hotel and spend an hour or two in bed before dinner."

"I like that idea." I had to push thoughts of Mel to the back of my mind. If I wanted to make this work with Lucas, I would have to get over myself and put on my big girl panties. It wasn't like he knew where she was or anything.

We left the alley hand in hand and made our way to the large beach. It was a cloudier day so the beach wasn't overly packed but there were still quite a few people on it.

Every so often, I caught girls giggling and talking amongst themselves. They would point at us and whisper.

I looked up at Lucas, my body heating. "You can't see it. Can you?"

"See what?" he asked, frowning.

"The girls checking you out. The ladies who are going to be thinking of you when their boyfriends or husbands fuck them tonight." I laughed, tightening my hold on his hand. "You're their fantasy, Lucas."

He grunted. "Yeah. Right."

"Look around us, Lucas." I swiped an arm out in front of me. Men scowled. Women batted their eyelashes. Young girls even shied away but wished Lucas was paying attention to them. Even some of the men stared at him in awe. He was a scary fucker but utterly breathtaking just the same.

"They're probably wondering how this ugly beast got a beauty like you," Lucas grumbled.

I stopped, tugging on his hand and tapping my mouth.

He leaned over, placing a soft peck on my lips.

I cupped his nape, deepened the kiss, and gave the people around us a show. Slipping my tongue between his lips, I sucked the groan from him down deep into my lungs.

"Fuck, Lily." He broke the kiss, brushing his thumb over my swollen mouth. "You're going to pay for that."

I laughed, stood on tiptoes, and kissed his cheek. "I look forward to it."

He shook his head, leading me down the sidewalk.

The onlookers shifted, casting their gazes elsewhere as we walked by them.

Eat your hearts out, girls.

And I would cut any bitch who tried to take him from me. I didn't care who they were or what kind of past they had. Lucas Crane was mine.

Twenty-Five

LUCAS

I WASN'T THE TYPE to pay attention to my looks. I worked out because it helped me with my addiction issues. I didn't work out to look good for anyone but myself. I had scars that made my smiles look more like scowls. Beauty was in the eye of the beholder and all that shit anyway. But Lily made me feel…special. Like I was the only one she saw. Like I was her whole world. And when she kissed me in public, it stirred something feral inside of me. I wasn't sure if she noticed but guys looked at her too. How could they not?

While I laid on my side of the blanket she had spread out for us on the sand, she took off her shorts but left the tank top on. She hid her scars from the world.

"Take off the top," I said gently.

"I'm good." She laid back on the blanket, resting her head on my lap. "This is perfect."

"It is." I wished she would have taken off the tank top, but I got it. A part of me was elated that she let only me see them.

"I can feel you staring, Lucas," she said, bending her knees and crossing one over the other, kicking her foot back and forth.

"You're beautiful. I can't help but stare." I leaned my head on my hand.

"Well you're beautiful too. I can see the ladies looking at you."

I laughed. "They're hiding me from their children."

"Please." Lily snorted. "They're going to go home tonight, fuck their husbands and think of you while doing so."

It was my turn to scoff. "You've said that twice already, but I still don't believe it."

Lily sat up, looking down at me. "Either you're blind in both eyes or you're really modest."

I gave the side of her breast a pinch. "Careful."

She jumped, slapping my hand away. "I mean it, Lucas. Have you seen yourself?" She laid on her stomach, kicking her feet back and forth behind her. "You're sexy as hell."

"Hmm…yeah?" I placed a soft peck on her nose. "Tell me more."

She giggled, a flush of red spreading through her cheeks. "Needing an ego boost, baby?"

I chuckled. Now this I liked and could get used to. "Tell me. What do you see when you look at me? And what do you think others see?"

"Hmm…" She tapped her chin. "I see a beautiful, broken man who tries so damn hard not to wear his heart on his sleeve. I also see a man who loves with every inch of him and cares deeply. I think others see a bad boy. A fantasy."

"Is that what you saw when you first met me, Lily Pad?" The heat between us ignited into a raging inferno. We teased and flirted. Touched and kissed. We were in public, so we couldn't do anything more, but I wanted her riled up. I wanted Lily to fucking explode for me.

"I saw a man who saw me for me. It was like I could feel you reaching into my soul and tickling every fantasy I've ever had."

"Yeah?" My voice came out low and husky. "What else?"

"I…" Her gaze moved past me. She frowned.

I turned, following the direction of where she was looking. "What's wrong?" I asked her, not seeing anything out of the ordinary.

"I don't know. I saw someone watching us."

I sat up, looking around us. My stomach twisted, that familiar feeling from the hotel, hitting me. She was around. She had to be. Or it was someone else from my past. Either way, I wasn't sure I wanted to see them. No matter who it was.

(Lily)

Someone had ruined our moment. I didn't know who it was, but I could feel them watching us. I knew we had issues. Maybe I had jealousy problems but laying on the blanket with Lucas and flirting with him, was fun and refreshing. And now our moods had gone back to the way they were before.

"I think I have sand in places I didn't know sand could reach," I mumbled, shaking out my bathing suit and running it under the water.

Lucas chuckled from behind me. "That's what you get for throwing sand at me."

I feigned a gasp. "I would never do such a thing. It's not my fault that you wouldn't keep your hands off me."

"So you throw sand at me instead?" he asked, raising an eyebrow.

I shrugged. "I had to think fast." I hung my bikini over the edge of the tub. When I stood, I was met with Lucas's dark stare. "What?" I asked, a shiver running down the length of my body.

"You're—" A hard knock sounded at the front door. "Stay here. I'll get it."

"Okay, but first." I tapped my mouth.

He grinned, giving me a quick kiss and leaving the shower.

I finished cleaning off the sand. After I was done, I turned off the hot water and wrapped a towel around my head and body when I heard voices from the other side of the closed door. One was Lucas, and the other was a woman. Unless it was a man with a high-pitched voice. My stomach twisted. No, don't be jealous, Lily. You trust Lucas. He wouldn't do anything to make you think differently.

I slipped into a red dress, smoothed it down my torso and did a little spin back and forth. It was tight, hugging all of my curves, and pushed my ample breasts up even more. It gave me cleavage that would have Lucas begging at my feet and it showcased my ass that I knew he loved. I had every intention of wearing panties, but something told me not to. I was feeling off. With him. With myself. With everything in general. Maybe being completely naked under this sinfully delicious dress, would help. I wasn't sure, but I was willing to try anything.

(Lucas)

"What do you think will happen now?" Mel asked, linking her fingers in mine.

"I'm not sure. I guess once we leave this shithole, we'll both go our own separate ways." I shrugged.

"Is that what you want?" she asked, her bright blue eyes staring up at me.

"Isn't it what you want? You know we can't be together. It's too hard."

Mel released me and stood. She turned her naked body away from me but not before I caught the tears falling down her cheeks.

"Mel," I said gently.

"Don't." She roughly wiped the tears away.

"I'm sorry," I murmured.

"Yeah." She slipped into her black panties. "Me too." She picked up the rest of her clothes and left the room.

Should I have followed her? I was young, so I didn't understand women quite yet, but something told me I should have gone after her. Sure, I felt guilty, but it wasn't like we could spend the rest of our lives together. She was beautiful. She was nice to me when others weren't. She was my safety net while being locked up in this hell but other than that, I didn't feel anything else for her.

I rose from the mattress on the floor and pulled on my ripped jeans and stained white t-shirt. Glancing back at the mattress, shame weighed heavily on my shoulders. I had used her. Even though she had begged for it, I still used her. The faint scent of sex wafted into my nose. It had been the first time I ever fucked a woman and enjoyed it. But she wasn't a woman. She was barely seventeen and I was fifteen. Sure, it was illegal in some states but for us? We were already adults. Wiser beyond our years.

And I had a feeling I'd just lost the one person who could help me through the rest of my time in this fucked up hell I called life.

"Mel," my voice cracked.

She stared up at me, a small smile splaying on her face. "I'm sorry for bothering you but I couldn't go on with my work if I didn't check and see if it was you. I was right. God, Lucas. It's…" She threw her arms around me, snuggling her face into my chest. "It's been way too long. Way too damn long."

I stood there, stock still. My hand was on the doorframe while my other was against the wall. Lily was in the bathroom. If she came out and saw Mel wrapped around me, she would lose her shit and rightfully so. Because I would have done the same thing if the roles were reversed.

"Mel." I tried pushing her off of me, but she only latched on tighter.

"I've missed you. I've missed you so much." She leaned back, staring up at me through unshed tears. Her long blonde hair was pulled back into a high ponytail. Freckles adorned her cheeks. Her lips were painted with a bright red lipstick. The black and gold hotel uniform hugged her small but curvy frame. It had been one thing our adoptive parents loved about her. She was tall, skinny, but her chest was full. She had the perfect body according to them and every other pervert we came across.

"I…" I couldn't speak. I had no idea how the hell she found me. Life was fucked. Absolutely fucked.

"You look good. Still so good." Mel placed a soft peck on my cheek.

The scent of roses wafted into my nose, triggering memories I had forced to the back of my mind long ago.

The door to the bathroom opened.

In a quick move, I pushed Mel out into the hall and shut the door behind me. "What are you doing here?"

"I work here." Mel frowned, swiping her hands out in front of her. "Obviously."

"No, I mean, what are you doing here? In this town?"

"Oh." She frowned. "I wanted a change and to get out of the city. I figured the only way to do that, would be to come here. This town is cute, isn't it?" she asked, a wide grin spreading on her face.

"I don't understand how you're here." It was too much of a coincidence.

"It was meant to be, clearly." Her blue eyes twinkled.

"No." This was too much. It took me back to when I was a kid. We had lived hours from here. How the hell could I end up in the same town that Mel worked at? I spent my whole life trying to get away from those memories, only to run into one while I was taking my girlfriend to the beach. Life was fucking cruel.

"Lucas," Mel said gently. "It's okay."

"No, it's not." I shook my head. "That was you here then. I saw you at the end of the hall. I smelled that damn rose perfume you used to always wear. Why the hell would you still wear it? And you were at the beach. You were following us."

"I still wear that scent because it reminds me of my time with you." Mel grabbed onto my shirt. "I had to make sure it was you, Lucas. I've missed you. I've missed you so damn much."

"Stop," I gritted out through clenched teeth.

"What's wrong? I know you're not alone but this…" She inched her hands beneath my shirt, her fingers grazing over my stomach. "This is right. It's how it should be. Life wouldn't place us back together if it weren't meant to be."

"Don't." I grabbed her hands, pulling them from beneath my shirt. "You can't do this. It's been years, Mel."

"Yeah." She pulled her hands from my grip and wrapped them around my neck. "Years that we have to get back. I'm off in an hour. We can meet up. Like we did a few years ago. God, I miss that."

"Stop." I couldn't do this. As much as I needed her when I was a kid, that was no longer happening. "I'm not—" The door behind me opened. "—single."

"No, you're not." Lily pushed past me and stuck her hand out. "Hi, I'm Lily. Lucas's girlfriend. And you must be Mel."

Mel released me, glancing down at her and back at me. Something flashed behind her eyes. She crossed her arms under her chest, pushing her tits up even higher. Years ago, I was sure that movement would have caused a reaction in me but now, it didn't. A laugh escaped her. "Wow. Well, this is new. It's been awhile but I didn't think it had been that long." She shook her head. "Anyway, it was nice seeing you." She spun around, heading back down the hall.

A hard smack landed on my chest.

I met Lily's gaze. "What?"

She pursed her lips, placing her hands on her hips. "That's her? That's the woman who helped you when you were kids?" She huffed, pushing her way back into the hotel room. "That's Mel?"

"Lily." I slammed the door shut and closed the distance between us. "What's wrong?"

"What's wrong?" she repeated, spinning on me. "That woman is fucking beautiful," she yelled, pushing me. "I was expecting…" She scowled. "Well it wasn't that. She could be wearing a garbage bag and still have men lined up to have their way with her. Hell, I would even sleep with her."

I shook my head. "I have no idea what's going on right now."

Lily pulled the towel off of her head and began running it through her hair. "I can't compete with that."

"Hold the fuck on." I took the towel from her and threw it on the floor before pulling her into my arms. "You don't need to compete with anyone. You are mine. And I am yours. Do you understand me?"

"I suddenly feel very insecure right now and I don't like it." Lily pushed out of my hold and picked up the towel before heading back to the bathroom.

Mel showing up put a damper on our mood but the fact that it made Lily feel insecure about us, pissed me off even more.

SHE WAS BEAUTIFUL. OF course she was beautiful. Mel was supermodel material. Even if it had been years since her and Lucas slept together, I would bet my life savings on it that she was perfect then too. She was tall, long blonde hair pulled back into a tight ponytail. Her mouth had been full and painted a deep red. She was tanned like the sun kissed her skin in the most delicious way. I was being irrational. I knew that but I couldn't help but see in my mind's eye the two of them fucking. My stomach churned.

I had never felt insecure about my curves until now. I was short. Barely five foot three. And I loved food. No matter how much I worked out, the curves would always be there. I had used them to my advantage. Getting men to do whatever it was that I wanted. Having double D's and an ass helped. But now I hated my body. And that pissed me off.

It wasn't fair of me to react the way I did but I couldn't help it. Lucas's and my relationship was new, fresh and I didn't have the best history with men.

"Lily?" A soft knock on the bathroom door forced a sigh from my lips. "Please let me in." The doorknob jiggled. "Please."

My eyes welled. I hated feeling this way. I trusted Lucas. I did. But the way Mel looked at him made me realize that their relationship went past just sex. Even if it was all on her end. She could probably get any man she wanted, too. It didn't matter that he was forced on her. It didn't matter that their relationship was fucked up and they were instructed to fuck other people. God, I couldn't believe I just had that thought run through my head.

"Lily, baby."

As soon as I unlocked the door, Lucas shoved it open and crashed into me.

"Don't ever do that to me again." He pushed his face into the crook of my neck, holding me against him and lifting me off my feet. He ran the scruff of his beard over my cheek. He had let it grow in some and I liked it. I liked it a lot.

I latched on to him, wrapping my arms around his neck and running my fingers through his hair. He let that grow in too. All for me. Everything he did. Was for me.

"Promise me," he pleaded, his lips finding the spot beneath my ear. "Promise me that if you have a problem, you won't run away from me again," he murmured against my throat.

I shivered, turning my head and covering his mouth with mine. The kiss became fast, hot, and desperate. It bordered on toxic, the pleasure snapping between us.

Lucas pushed me onto the bathroom counter, wrapped my legs around his waist, and stepped between my thighs.

He swallowed my sighs. This was ours. This was where we were meant to be. He was mine. I was his. It was broken and tarnished but it was everything that made up us.

I leaned back, taking him with me and pulled his shirt from his pants. Running my hands beneath the fabric, I pushed them up his torso. My fingers grazed over his muscles, finding each bumpy and hard ridge. His body tightened as his tongue dipped farther into my mouth. When my fingers reached the spot above his heart, I reveled in the feel of the powerful muscle beating inside his chest.

Lucas reached between us, brushing his fingers up my inner thigh before reaching the spot that belonged to him. That had only ever belonged to him.

He released my mouth, staring down at me. "I love you, Lily."

"I love you too, Lucas," I whispered. "Please don't ever make me doubt that."

"Never." He placed a hard kiss on my lips. "You're mine. And I'm yours. I don't want anyone else. Only you. Always you."

Lucas kissed the side of my neck, licking and sucking until I was writhing beneath him. The sound of a faint knock on the door to the hotel room crashed through our moment.

"Fuck." His teeth sunk into my skin.

"I…I think someone's at the door," I panted.

Lucas lifted his head, glancing out into the hall before looking back at me. He went to pull away, but I dug my heels into his ass instead.

"Stay, please," I pleaded.

"Are you wanting me to fuck you? You want her to hear?"

I looked away. "I've never felt this before. This jealous need to claim you as mine."

Lucas cupped my nape, pulling my head against his chest. "I love you, Lily Pad. You have no reason to be jealous of her."

I heard his words, but I still didn't believe them. I trusted him but I sure as hell didn't trust her.

"Marry me."

My eyes widened. I leaned back, staring up at him. "Excuse me?"

He gave me a lopsided grin. "You're mine, Lily, and I'm yours. Let me prove it to you."

"So, you're proposing to me?" I coughed, shaking my head and pushing him away from me. "We haven't even been together for six months yet."

"Some people get married in shorter time than that."

I hopped off the counter and sat on the toilet.

Lucas leaned against the doorframe. "I love you, Lily."

"And I love you but marriage? Seriously? Is that the answer?" I finished doing my business, not caring in the least that he had been watching me the whole time because marriage? There was no way that we could get married.

"Why not?" He moved in front of the mirror and fixed his shirt which I now realized was a black dress shirt. He tucked it into black dress pants. God, he looked good enough to eat.

"Are you only proposing marriage because Mel showed up?" I smacked his arm when he didn't respond. "Lucas."

"I don't fucking know, alright?"

I opened my mouth to yell, scream, I wasn't sure anymore but instead, what came out was calm and collected and it made even me nervous. "If we're still together in a year and you want to get married then, I'll say yes. But I need to know if you want to marry me for me or because you're wanting to shove it in her face that you're no longer single."

"Fine." Lucas rolled the sleeves on his shirt up to his elbows.

"Fine? Is that all you have to say?"

He shrugged. "What do you want from me?"

"I want the truth. I want you. I want to go back to before Mel showed up. I just want to be happy. We deserve to be happy, Lucas."

He turned toward me, pinched my chin, and placed a soft peck on my mouth. "I am happy with you, Lily. You're the one who has a problem with Mel showing up."

"Me?" I asked, taken aback. "You can't stand here and tell me that it doesn't spark up some old feelings. I'm not stupid. I may not have gone through what you did but I know that you being stuck in that situation with someone is bound to form an unbreakable bond. What if she wants that again with you?"

He paused. "It doesn't matter," he said a moment later. "I'm with you." He left the bathroom with me hot on his heels.

"It does matter, Lucas. If she feels anything for you, especially…" I swallowed hard. "…if she loves you."

"Loves me?" He spun on me. "Love didn't fucking exist between us. We had no one else so we latched on to each other."

"Exactly, Lucas," I cried. "That's a bond that I could never have with you."

"What the hell are you telling me, Lily?"

"I…" What was I trying to say? "If you…I mean…I'll step aside—"

"Don't you dare finish that fucking sentence." He put on his shoes. "Now finish getting ready. We have dinner reservations." He left the hotel room, slamming the door behind him.

All of the air was sucked from my lungs. A soft sob escaped me. I didn't want to break up with him, but I also didn't want him to stay with me because he felt like he had to either. I had no idea what to do.

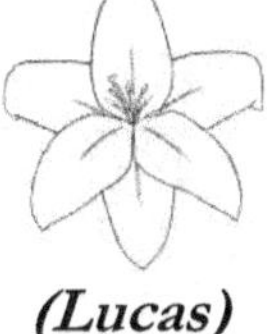

(Lucas)

I was pissed. No, I was fucking enraged. Lily would step aside…fucking please. I wanted her and only her. We had been together for just over four months and she was right. Marriage wouldn't solve anything, but it was a step in the right direction. Or I thought it was anyway. I meant what I said to her. If she would have said yes, I would have driven us to the first courthouse I came across. But she didn't. Because she was the rational one in our relationship.

I was leaning against the wall when Lily appeared in front of me.

"Are we going to have a nice dinner or are you going to have that scowl on your face all night?"

I opened my mouth to say something, but a laugh came out instead. "You drive me crazy, woman."

"Yeah, well, I can say the same about you." She held out her hand.

I took it and pulled her against me in a rough move.

She gasped, slapping her hands against my chest.

"I'm sorry," I said, kissing her softly on the mouth.

"I'm sorry too," she whispered against my lips. "I'm not used to dealing with exes and this is fucking with my head."

"She's not an ex."

"You fucked her. She's an ex something. I have them too, but I didn't continue fucking them."

Thank God for that.

Lily frowned. "You did just have sex with her when you were kids right?"

I cleared my throat but didn't answer.

"Figures," Lily mumbled. "How long ago?"

"We lost touch and ran into each other a few years ago."

Lily blew out a slow breath. "You said—"

"I know what I said. I've seen her once since we were kids. Since we lived in that shithole we called home. I shouldn't have left that out and I'm sorry, but I don't like talking about it." I used Mel to make me feel better and I wasn't proud of that.

"Why didn't you just tell me?" Lily asked, staring up at me with all the hope in the world.

"I was ashamed. My sex life has never been conventional and with her…I don't want to talk about this with the woman I'm currently fucking." I pushed away from Lily, rubbing the back of my neck.

"Fine, I won't ask anymore." Lily came up on my side. "Thank you for telling me though."

I nodded, grabbing her hand.

"We shouldn't have done this." Mel swung her legs over the side of the bed.

"Why not? You show up, we fuck, end of. It's not a big deal."

Her head whipped around. "It's always a big deal with you. With all of you." She huffed, wrapping the white sheet around her tanned skin. "I love you, Lucas."

I laughed.

She glared at me.

"Come on, Mel. You can't seriously love me. What we have is not fucking love. The first time I fucked you, I raped you because I was forced to. I was a kid. I wasn't strong enough to fight them off. And then you still wanted me."

"What the hell are you saying to me?"

"That you're an addict. A nympho. Whatever the fuck you want to call it." I stood from the bed, earning me a small gasp. I always got that reaction and my cock jumped because of it.

"I'm not a sex addict," she whispered.

I spun on her. "No? Lay back on the bed and I'll prove to you that you are."

"Lucas?"

I jumped, my mind taking me back to the present.

Lily frowned. "You good?"

"Yeah." I scrubbed my face. "Sorry. Bad memories. I really don't know why you love me. I used to be such an asshole."

Lily brought my hand up to her mouth. "You're not an asshole to me. And if you were an asshole to her or to any of the other women you slept with, clearly you hadn't found your person yet."

My heart swelled. "You're my person, Lily. You will always be my person."

"Good." She gave me a small smile. "Now feed me."

I chuckled. "Yes, ma'am."

(Lily)

Things still weren't perfect, but they would have to do for now. While Lucas and I sat at the restaurant, I kicked off my heels and placed my feet on his lap.

He smirked, covering them with his big hand and pushing his thumb into the arch of my foot.

I sighed, taking a sip of my water. "Thank you for this."

"You're welcome, Lily Pad." He took a sip of his own water, leaning back in the booth across from me. "Do you feel better?"

"Now that we're not at the hotel where the woman you used to fuck works? Yes, I do."

Lucas rolled his eyes. "That sass is going to earn you a spanking, Lily."

"I look forward to it," I mumbled.

"Now you know how I feel."

My gaze shot to his.

"With Killian." He shrugged. "He doesn't make me feel insecure, but he is competition."

"And how many times do I have to tell you that you have nothing to worry about."

"Yeah." Lucas sat forward. "And how many times have I told you that you have nothing to worry about, Lily? I don't want Mel. No matter what she says or does, she means nothing to me. We were together at a time I needed comfort from a gentle touch. But you've come into my life when I needed it most."

I went to pull my feet from his lap when his grip on them tightened.

"I've spent years going through life only because I had to. Do you know how many times I've overdosed? I should have died but there was a reason I didn't. You are that reason. I realize that now."

My stomach tumbled. "What do you mean?"

"I mean that clearly there was something keeping me here. It's you, Lily. It's always been you."

My eyes welled. I covered my face.

The bench beside me lowered. "I didn't mean to make you cry," Lucas whispered, kissing my head.

"You always say the sweetest things when I need to hear them most and then you make me cry," I sobbed. "I hate you."

Lucas chuckled. "I love you, Lily," he murmured, brushing his mouth along the shell of my ear. "I love you with every inch of me."

"It makes sense though." I reached out to brush the bangs that had grown in some off of his forehead. My fingers ran over the tattoos on the side of his head. "I understand why she would still want you. You would be hard to get over."

"That's never going to happen, baby." He leaned his forehead against mine. "Never."

I hoped he was right.

Twenty-Seven

LUCAS

AFTER WE FINISHED OUR meal in a comfortable silence, I couldn't help but watch Lily. She was absolutely breathtaking. In her tight red dress that hugged every inch of her curves, it fit her perfectly. Her eyes were bright as she took in our surroundings. We couldn't drink but we did have virgin cocktails. Although they were sweeter than what I was used to, I enjoyed the fruity liquid.

"I think I want a Shirley Temple next," Lily said, playing with her napkin. "Or well…I really just want the cherry."

I chuckled. "I'm on it." I signaled the waitress over.

She came over with a wide smile on her face. "What can I get for you?"

"We'll have two Shirley Temples please and can we get a bowl of cherries?"

She looked between Lily and I. "Cherries are for you?" she asked Lily.

Lily giggled. "Yes, I like them a little too much."

The waitress laughed. "I get it. I'll be back with your drinks and cherries in just a moment." She spun on her heal and headed to the bar.

"Thank you." Lily gave me a soft smile.

"Anything for you, Lily Pad." After I had unexpectedly made her cry, I moved back to my side of the booth. We had ordered something light to eat. I wasn't overly hungry, especially after everything that had happened this afternoon. I was hungrier for the woman sitting across from me. But I needed to leave her alone. For a little bit anyway.

A moment later, the waitress came back with our drinks and a bowl of cherries.

We thanked her, and she went back to serving other customers.

"It's funny. I never thought I'd see a man like you drinking a Shirley Temple." Lily laughed, popping a cherry into her mouth.

"What's wrong with Shirley Temples?" I asked, taking a sip of the sweet fruity drink.

"Oh nothing. But you drinking them is kind of odd."

"Why? Because I'm big and tattooed?"

Lily grinned. "Yeah. Something like that."

"I don't give a shit what people think, Lily Pad. You of all people should know that. If I did care, I wouldn't have all of these tattoos." Tattoos were my addiction. They were also safer than the drugs I used to enjoy.

"I like your tattoos," Lily said, winking at me over the rim of her glass.

"Yeah?" I smirked. "And which one is your favorite?"

"Hmm…" She leaned forward, licking her full mouth. "I think my favorite is your octo—"

"Lucas."

Both of us turned at the sound of my name.

Mel was coming up to our table. She was no longer in her work uniform but a formfitting black dress. The vee was deep, showing cleavage that had the men in the restaurant salivating. Her deep blue eyes burned into me.

"You have got to be fucking kidding me," Lily mumbled.

"What do you want, Mel?" I asked her.

"We need to talk." Mel's gaze shot to Lily's. "Alone."

"I'm kind of busy. Can it wait?" Something pressed into the seat of my crotch. "We're on a date," I said, when I realized it was Lily's foot in my lap. Our eyes locked.

Lily's jaw clenched, pushing her foot into me harder. She was making a point.

Duly noted, sweet girl. I know who I belong to.

"I'm sorry, Mel," I said, cupping Lily's foot and pressing my thumb into the arch. "Whatever it is, it's going to have to wait."

"We're in town until tomorrow," Lily told her, rubbing her foot against me.

My dick hardened. This display of ownership did something funny to me.

Mel pressed her full lips together, her cheeks turning a mottled red. "I…I need to talk to you."

"Sit." Lily swiped a hand out in front of her. "Talk, but my boyfriend isn't going anywhere with you." She pushed her foot against me hard.

I jumped, biting back a growl.

Lily raised an eyebrow.

Clearing my throat, I sat back, running my hand up to her calf. "She's right."

"What? Are you his keeper now?" Mel threw back at her.

"No." Lily crossed her arms under her chest. "But I know women like you. Lucas is a big boy and he can do whatever he wants to do. But right now, we're on a date, if you haven't noticed. Obviously, you don't care about that or else you wouldn't be here."

"Pull up a chair, Mel." This was a bad idea. "But Lily's right, I'm not going anywhere."

Mel huffed, spun on her heel, and left the restaurant.

"I'm sorry." I reached across the table for Lily's hand. "I'm so fucking sorry."

"Yeah." Lily linked her fingers in mine. "Me too, Lucas. Me too."

"No, I can't." I refused to give them what they wanted. I couldn't, knowing it would destroy me.

"If you don't, she dies."

I was shoved forward onto my knees. "Please, this isn't right." Not that anything I ever did was right, but this was worse. So much worse than what life had already thrown at me.

"Doesn't matter if it's right or not." The woman leaned down to my ear, running her hand down the length of my spine. "I know you want to. That perfect little dick is getting hard just thinking about it. She's beautiful, Lucas. I know you want to fuck her."

My eyes shot to the mattress.

Mel was restrained, spread open on the bed like a damn starfish.

"No." I didn't want this even though my body thought differently.

"Yes." The woman pushed me.

I fell forward, landing on my hands. "I can't."

"You can and you're going to make us a shit-ton of money too." The woman wrapped her arm around my shoulders, her other hand reaching between my legs. She gripped and pulled, tugged and stroked.

A groan escaped me.

"That's my boy." She kissed my cheek and released me, still pumping her hand up and down my cock. "Get hard, Lucas. So damn hard, she screams when you thrust into her."

I was forced to my feet by two men behind me and shoved onto the mattress.

Mel stared up at me with wide eyes. They were begging, pleading. She was tiny. I was not. I would hurt her. It was what they wanted. I couldn't. There was no way I would fit.

"Do it," the woman demanded. "Now."

I shot out of bed, landing on the floor with a hard 'oomph.' My body ached. My muscles twitched over my bones and vibrated beneath my skin. My lungs burned, the lack of air forcing spots in front of my vision. I gasped for breath I wasn't allowed to have.

So many memories. Nightmares. Evil depraved images rolled around in my head.

The first thrust forced a scream from her lips.

The second thrust earned me a hard cry.

Sex. So much sex.

The third thrust and a groan fell between us.

"Lucas." A gentle hand touched my damp skin. It moved from my shoulder to the back of my neck before pulling me into a gentle embrace.

I jumped, my hips thrusting forward like my dick had a mind of its own.

"Hey."

Lily. I was with Lily.

I looked around us. We were back in the hotel room. We had gone on a date tonight. Mel showed up. Mel. Seeing her had sparked all of these old memories that I had been trying to ignore for most of my adult life. I couldn't do this. I couldn't see her and have things be back to normal instantly.

"Lily," my voice came out rough, my throat dry.

"I'm here," she whispered, wrapping her naked body around mine.

My cock was hard between us. "No." I shoved her off of me, pressing a palm against the thick length and trying to ward off the need I had coursing through me.

Lily's gaze landed on my crotch, her breath hitched. "Who was your dream about?"

A curse left me, my body vibrating at the remnants of my dream.

"Lucas." She knelt in front of me, cupping my face. "Tell me."

"It was a memory. The first time I fuck...I..." I squeezed my eyes shut, shaking my head and thought of anything but sex. But with Lily's naked body so close to mine, I couldn't help but reach out for her. So much sex. Too much. It was a lot. Not enough. It was everything I needed and everything I hated just the same.

"Tell me, Lucas. Tell me about your dream." Lily covered my hand. "You're going to hurt yourself." She pried my fingers off of my dick.

I blew out a slow breath, not realizing I had been squeezing so damn hard. "I was forced to fuck her. Them. All of them. The women wanted it. Got off on it. They made a shit-ton of money. Fuck, I..." I rocked back and forth. I was losing it. I was breaking. I had been doing well until Mel came back into my life. Too many nightmares. Too many demons and I had no fucking idea how to battle them on my own.

"You're not alone." Lily ran her hands over my shoulders. "You're never alone."

I didn't realize I had spoken out loud. "I don't deserve you." I looked up then. "You deserve someone who's not so damn broken."

"I love you, Lucas." She cupped my face. "Your demons, your nightmares, your horrible past, whatever it is, I'll help you through it."

"Why?" I asked her.

She tilted her head, a deep frown settling between her brows. "I love you. That's why."

I believed her but that voice, that annoying little voice told me she was lying and that she would leave me the first chance she got.

"Don't do that, Lucas. Don't doubt my love for you." Lily cupped my face. "We'll meet with Mel later this morning, so you can find out what she wants. Or you can meet with her yourself."

"No. I want you with me." It was safer that way. I didn't trust her. Even though we had been through hell together, I wasn't sure if she would try anything. And with Lily there, she would have to refrain from touching me. Lily was the only one allowed to touch me. Any part of me.

Lily stood, holding out her hand.

I slipped my fingers in hers and let her help me to my feet. We slid into bed, with me wrapped around her. She drifted off rather quickly, but sleep didn't greet me again. Instead, I couldn't help but wonder what the hell Mel had wanted.

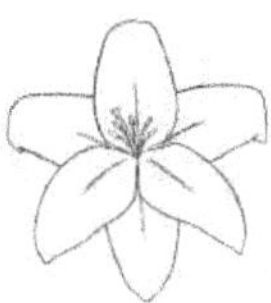

"Come with me," I said the next morning as I put on my jeans and did up the zipper and button.

"I know I said last night that I would go with you, but I thought about it. She won't talk to you if I'm there. It must be important if she interrupted our date over it." Lily placed the hotel menu on the bed in front of her. "I'm going to order room service while you're gone."

"I don't like this." I slipped the white t-shirt over my head and crawled onto the bed.

Lily cupped my face. "I trust you."

"I don't trust her." I pushed my face into the crook of her neck. "Please come with me."

"Are you worried she'll try something?" Lily asked, leaning back.

"I don't know." I kissed her softly on the mouth.

"I trust you, Lucas." Lily brushed her thumb over my mouth. "Now go. Meet with her so we can spend the rest of the day in bed before we have to head home."

"Fine." I huffed, giving her one last kiss.

"Oh, wait." Lily jumped off the bed and went to her pile of clothes on the chair in the corner. She rummaged through it and came back a moment later with a pair of panties. She stuffed them into my jeans pocket. "Come back to me."

I cupped her nape and pulled her in for a deep kiss. "I will always come back to you, Lily. Always."

Releasing her, I left the hotel room before I changed my mind. I needed to find out what Mel wanted and why she would go out of her way to disrupt my date with Lily. I had no way of contacting her, so I headed to the main floor. As soon as I stepped out into the foyer, I saw Mel sitting on one of the couches. She was dressed casually with a magazine on her lap. Her head snapped up.

"Lucas." She stood.

"I wasn't expecting to see you," I told her. "I was going to ask reception how to get in touch with you because clearly, you have something important to say to me that couldn't wait." I walked past her and headed outside, knowing she would follow.

"There's a coffee shop just down the street that we can walk to," Mel said, coming up on my left.

"Fine." I shoved my hands in my pockets, my fingers coming into contact with Lily's panties. My body stirred. Fuck, I loved her.

"I'm sorry for interrupting your date last night," Mel mumbled.

"You're not but nice try."

"Lucas." Mel gently touched my arm.

"Don't." I stopped, glaring down at her. "You want to talk, I'm here but don't you dare fucking touch me."

She flinched like I had slapped her myself. "I'm sorry."

"Stop. You are not sorry. You've never been fucking sorry. So just tell me what the hell it is that you want, Mel."

Her breath hitched. "Bobby died in jail."

Bobby. Fuck, I hadn't heard that name in a long time. He should have been a role model, someone to keep us safe but destroyed our lives instead. "That's what you wanted to tell me? That doesn't sound like a bad thing, Mel." He had been charged after the cops raided their place and his wife got off because she took the stand against her husband.

"No." She sighed. "That's not everything I wanted to talk about."

Once we reached the coffee shop, she pushed open the door and held it open for me.

I grumbled, "Thanks,' and followed her.

We sat at an empty booth, waiting to be served.

"Coffee?" a waitress asked, holding a steaming pot of my favorite addiction.

"Yes, please," I answered.

The woman poured me a cup. "Coffee?" she asked Mel.

"No, thank you. Just an orange juice please," Mel said, not taking her gaze from mine.

I shifted uncomfortably and shoved my hand in my pocket. My thumb brushed over the soft fabric of Lily's panties.

"I'll be back with two menus and your orange juice." The waitress left and came back a moment later with menus and placed a glass of OJ in front of Mel.

"Tell me what's going on," I said once we were alone.

"Well, Bobby died but you don't seem too upset by that."

"Why would I be? Both he and his wife should rot in hell." I leaned back in the booth. "How did he die?"

Mel shrugged. "Heart attack I'm assuming. Carole claimed abuse. Did you know that? She said that she was a victim herself. So that was why she was spared prison. I'm not sure if they said it on the news. I don't watch TV much."

Having this conversation with her, forced these walls up around me. It wasn't safe, the shit from our past that she was bringing up. I knew I had issues. It was why I didn't talk about it. "Do you talk to anyone still?"

"A few people. A couple of the kids died. Overdose, alcoholism, car accidents, your typical shit." Mel shrugged again, running her finger over the rim of the glass.

"There's something else, isn't there?" She wouldn't go through all this trouble just to tell me that our adoptive father died. "What's going on?"

"You love her." Mel's gaze popped to mine. "Lily."

"We're not here to discuss my personal life, Mel."

She laughed lightly, shaking her head. "You've turned into a bit of a dick."

"I wonder why," I grumbled. "Listen, if you're not going to tell me why you needed to meet with me, I should leave."

"I still love you, Lucas. I've always loved you. We were good together. Even when we were forced into it. We…we looked good on camera."

"We were fucking kids, Mel," I growled. It was sick. This wasn't right.

"I want you back," she whispered.

"Don't." Years ago, I probably would have wanted to hear those words but not anymore and especially not now. "I'm with Lily. I love her."

"I know you felt something for me," Mel murmured.

I laughed, scrubbing a hand down my face. "This is unreal. I didn't feel anything for you then and I don't feel anything for you now." I had tried being gentle about it, but she obviously wasn't getting the hint.

"Does she know that we met up a few years ago?" Mel asked, her bright blue eyes meeting mine. She leaned forward, pushing against the table top which enhanced the cleavage in the vee of her shirt. "Does she know how rough you like it? Or how you used to cut yourself? Does she know the things you used to force me to do?" Her tongue swiped along her bottom lip. "I remember the last time and the way you held my head while fucking my throat. It was so hot, Lucas. I need that. I need your control. I need you."

My jaw clenched. "Stop this shit."

"Does she know about our first time and what you were forced to do to me?"

"Stop," I bit out. "Yes, she knows all that shit. She knows everything because I told her. Because that's what people do when they're in a relationship. They talk. They communicate." While it may have taken me awhile to tell Lily everything, I still eventually told her. "I told her about you too because she asked. But she knows that I was never in love with you. She knows that I feel nothing for you."

Mel's eyes welled. "You're lying."

"No. I'm not. Seeing you is bringing up old feelings yes, but it isn't love. It's fear. Pain. Vulnerability. Whatever the hell you want to call it, but I do not love you." It may have been harsh, but Mel needed to hear it. She needed to know that whatever we had, was done. "I wouldn't have fucked you a second time if I wasn't forced into it in the first place."

"Now I know you're lying about that." Mel sat back, crossing her arms under her chest. "You can deny it all you want but you couldn't resist me. None of you could. I remember that last time, even though it was just a few years ago. I remember it like it was yesterday. You felt so good inside me."

"Why the hell are you doing this?"

"Because we are meant to be. I need you, Lucas. No matter what we went through, we were good together."

"And you're fucking proud of that?" I asked, a little too loudly. Other customers at nearby tables turned our way. I cleared my throat. "Listen, Mel," I said, lowering my voice. "We went through hell together, yes, but you need to move on. We both do. Now if you're not going to tell me what's going on, I have to head back to the hotel." When I stood, her next words stopped me.

"I have the videos."

I frowned, looking down at her over my shoulder. "What?"

"The videos," she repeated. "I have them."

"How did you get them?"

"Carole's in a home now."

I frowned. "But that doesn't explain how you got them." None of this was making any sense. At all.

"I was one of the first you know." Mel sat forward, pushing her chest against the edge of the table. "I was also the first girl to be used as well."

"Raped, Mel. You were raped. Not used. Say what fucking happened."

She shrugged. "Semantics." She started running her finger over the rim of the glass. "I haven't watched them yet though. Just a few of you and me. Even though we were kids, we looked good. I can still feel your lips on mine, Lucas."

I sat back in the booth. "What are you going to do with them?" I asked, ignoring her last sentence. As much as I didn't want them, I had to destroy them before they fell into the wrong hands.

"I wanted to give them to you as a reminder of how good we were together."

My brows shot up to my forehead. "Excuse me?"

"We could make a lot of money on these too, Lucas. My mom would like that." Mel's cheeks turned red. "I mean…"

"What the fuck did you just say?" Her mom. No, there was no way. I tried remembering but couldn't. My mind was a blank slate as it tried to protect me from my past.

Mel sighed. "Well I guess there's no use denying it. Carole is my real mother. I don't know where my real father went. Bobby was not him, thank God." She grimaced.

"How did you get the videos?" I asked again.

"Mom left the house to me when she went into the home. I came across them while cleaning. Bobby said he got rid of them all, but he obviously didn't."

I shook my head, unable to believe what I was hearing.

"What home is Carole in?" Tasting my adoptive mother's name on my tongue, forced bile to my throat. I also wanted to be sure that I was far away from that woman as possible.

"Somewhere north of the city. It's a few hours from here. She never got in trouble you know. Just probation. She said Bobby manipulated her." Mel laughed. "She's such a liar. I know she enjoyed that shit just as much as he did." The humor dancing in her eyes quickly left. It was like emotional whiplash with how fast her moods changed. Mel rubbed the back of her neck. "I need you, Lucas. I can't do this without you."

"You don't need me, Mel. You need to talk to someone. Get therapy. But I can't help you."

"Yes, you can." Mel stood from her side of the booth and much to my surprise, sat beside me. "I do need you."

"What are you doing?" I asked, my eyes widening.

Ignoring me, she placed her hand on my leg. "You're the only one who knows what I went through. The only one who can help me heal. I need you." Her gaze dropped to my mouth. "Please, Lucas. Lily doesn't understand people like us. We need sex. A lot of it. It's not our fault either. We were forced into it. We're not meant to settle down with one person."

"But you want me to settle down with you."

"Yes, because I can give you the sex you need. You can do whatever you want to me, Lucas. All of those sick fantasies I know you still have, I'm your willing submissive. You can slap me, hurt me, cut me. I don't care. Lily can't give that to you."

"Mel, you need to stop." I grabbed her hand, preventing it from going higher and removing it from my lap.

"I need you," she whispered, pulling her hand from mine and reaching for my belt.

"What the fuck, Mel? We're in a restaurant." I slapped her hand way.

"That wouldn't have stopped you years ago." She kissed my shoulder. "Is Lily turning you into a prude?" She reached for my belt again, undoing the buckle.

"Stop." I grabbed her hand, careful not to hurt her because I had no fucking idea if she would cause a scene or not. I didn't need that. Not when we were in a public place. My heart started racing. Red flags went off in my head. I should have forced Lily to come with me. But she trusted me. Fuck she trusted me. But hell, I didn't trust myself at the moment. I wouldn't do anything with Mel. I wasn't that type of guy. I loved Lily. I belonged to her and her alone but seeing Mel made this dormant side of me awaken.

"You can feel it too." Mel cupped me over my pants. "I know you can feel it. You're hard right now."

Only because I had a woman back at the hotel who I was going to use to make me feel better. I grabbed Mel's hand, squeezing it to the point a whimper fell from her lips but before I could comprehend what was going on, she kissed me.

Twenty-Eight

LUCAS

BLOOD SEEPED THROUGH MY fingers, running from the cut in my inner thigh thanks to the blade digging into my skin. White hot pain seared through me, forcing a groan from the back of my throat. It was nothing like I had ever felt before. It was fear, pleasure, rage, and pure fucking bliss.

The lingering scent of roses wafted into my nose as the agony took over.

A small hand wrapped around mine, forcing the knife to cut me deeper.

My eyes rolled into the back of my head. "Fuck."

"Lucas."

The mouth against mine was wrong. Familiar. But so damn wrong. I pushed Mel back, breaking the kiss before she could take it further.

"If you know what's good for you, you will get the fuck away from me," I growled.

Her eyes shone but whatever it was she saw on my face forced her to slide from the bench and move back to the spot across from me. Smart girl.

"I'm going to give you one more chance to tell me what the fuck is going on before I go back to my girlfriend and tell her what just happened."

"Lucas," Mel said gently.

"I will be telling her because that's the right thing to do. But you wouldn't know that because you just came on to a guy who is in a damn relationship." My body buzzed, my skin jumping over my muscles. I needed Lily. I needed to explain. I needed…hell, I didn't even know what I needed anymore. But I knew that I needed to get away from this moment.

"If you want the videos, I'll be at the hotel this afternoon." Mel's shoulders slumped, almost like she was admitting defeat.

"I'll be there." I slid from the booth and left the restaurant. I would have to tell Lily about that kiss and everything else. She would be pissed, and I wouldn't blame her. Guilt weighed heavily on my shoulders. If I wasn't with Lily, would I have pushed Mel away? It didn't matter. I couldn't go back to that dark time in my life. Mel brought too many reminders of what I had come from. And I refused to go back to that.

(Lily)

I was curled up on the bed, playing a game on my phone when Lena's number showed up.

"Hey," I answered.

"Hi!"

I pulled the phone away from my ear, laughing. "Someone's excited."

"Yes, oh, Lily. I got to see my daughter."

"That's wonderful!" I sat up. "I'm so happy."

"Thank you! We're taking it slow, but my parents are letting me see her once a month and then we'll work to more visits. It's not a lot but I'll take it. God, will I ever take it."

"I'm so happy for you, Lena. I'm sorry we weren't much help when it came to finding stuff on them or your ex."

"No, girl, don't be sorry." Lena sighed. "It all happened naturally anyway. The sperm donor fucked up. He fucked up bad. He got a speeding ticket. First time in his life and he was being weird about it I guess. Well the cop got suspicious and they ended up finding drugs on him and in the trunk of his car. He will be charged, and it certainly won't look good for his custody battle—he could be declared unfit."

"Well, I'm glad it worked out for you. That's really wonderful news, Lena."

"Thank you for offering to help. You didn't have to when I was hitting on Lucas. I'm sorry for that. I'm so sorry."

My heart jumped. "Don't be. He's hard to resist."

She laughed. "Yeah. But can we meet up soon? I'd love for you both to meet my daughter."

"We can," I said when the door to the hotel room opened. "But I have to go. We'll chat soon."

"Okay. Thank you again, Lily."

We said our goodbyes and I disconnected the call just as Lucas came into the room. His body was stiff. He shut the door behind him and leaned against it.

"Lucas? Are you okay?" I asked, my throat constricting.

He met my gaze. Pushing away from the door, he closed the distance between us and pulled me against him.

I threw my phone on the bed, wrapping my arms around his neck.

With his hands in my hair, he fused his mouth to mine and slipped his tongue between my lips.

I breathed him in, taking him deeper. He tasted of coffee and something sweet. I frowned, pushing him back. "You taste different. And…something else happened, didn't it?" I looked him over. "I know something else happened, but I don't know what."

His shoulders slumped. "What do you mean?"

"I mean that I've been with you long enough to know that you only drink coffee in the morning. Black coffee. So why do you taste sweet?"

He looked away.

"Lucas." I smacked his arm. "Tell me."

His good eye met mine, peering into me, seeing deep inside of me. "Mel kissed me."

I laughed, shoving him back and jumped from the bed. "Of course she did." I started pacing back and forth.

"Lily, that's not all."

I stopped pacing. "Tell me."

"She wants a relationship. With me. She also hit on me. She was mentioning things of our time together. And things I used to be into. Dark things." He shoved his hands in his pockets. "She said you couldn't handle it and that it would disgust you."

"I've enjoyed everything we've done." I frowned. "Why would she say that? What other things are you into?"

"Whenever I cut myself, I wasn't alone." He sat on the edge of the bed. "She helped me."

I leaned against the dresser, rubbing the back of my neck. "Okay…well, you don't do that anymore. What else are you into that we haven't done already?"

"I like it rougher. She tried touching me in the restaurant." He blew out a slow breath. "I'm so fucking sorry. I pushed her away but I'm still sorry, baby."

Bile rose to my throat. This new feeling rushed through me. I didn't know what it was. It was something I had never felt before. It went past jealousy. It even went past possession. "You're mine," I whispered.

"I am," he said. "I am so fucking yours. All of me. Every inch. Every breath. I live and breathe for you."

My eyes welled. "Is she going to be a problem for us?"

"I don't know. You can trust me. Please, baby, trust me. I would never cheat on you but I can't tell you she won't try something again because I don't know." He pulled my panties from his jeans pocket, running his thumb over the black fabric. "She told me she still loves me. She also wants to meet to hand me the videos and pictures that involve me. So I can dispose of them." He looked at me then. "I pushed her away even though she begged for more."

"Brush your teeth," I told him. "I can't kiss you when you taste like her."

He flinched. "Lily."

I lifted my hands, warding him off. "Stop. I'm not…I'm not mad at you. It's not your fault. It's hers. But I need you to brush your teeth."

He nodded, heading into the bathroom.

I slumped onto the edge of the bed before falling to the floor. It seemed that no matter how many steps forward we took, we were forced to take a million back.

Leaning my head against the edge of the bed, I brought my knees up to my chest.

Lucas came out of the bathroom a moment later and sat on the floor in front of me. He pulled my feet out and wrapped my legs around his waist. Running his hands up and down my bare arms, he leaned his forehead against mine.

"I'm sorry," he murmured, the scent of mint wafting into my nose.

I nodded, swallowing past the lump in my throat. "Your body is hard."

"The things she said brought back memories. Of how much I enjoyed being in control. It wasn't about who I fucked but how I fucked." He ran his thumb along my collarbone. "It doesn't make sense. I know that but…" He pulled me closer. "Mel wants to meet up tonight to give me the videos."

"Why?" I grabbed the hem of his t-shirt, inching my hand beneath it.

"She's using it as an excuse to see me again."

"Are you going to meet up with her?" If it were me, I would be destroying those videos. Maybe light them on fire and watch my past life mother fucking burn.

"I should. Then I can have Shephard destroy them." He leaned his forehead against mine. "That part of my life is done and over. But destroying the videos could be therapeutic in a way."

I nodded. "That makes sense."

"Maybe they could help me heal kind of thing. But I need you to come with me."

"Okay."

"Is this it, Lily Pad?" he whispered, cupping my face. "Is this going to break us?"

"I don't know," I croaked. "That depends on you and what you decide."

"I want you, Lily. There is no decision that needs to be made. It's only you. Always you." Instead of saying anything more, Lucas crushed his mouth to mine.

The fact that he no longer tasted like Mel, did something to me. A growl left me, and I pushed him back.

A shocked gasp left him, but it only seemed to make him kiss me harder. It turned frantic, our hands roaming over each other until all I could feel was him. He grew beneath me but never took it further. This was all me. My choice. My control. He was giving it all to me. I wanted to thank him and hurt him at the same time. I wasn't mad that Mel had kissed him. No, I was fucking furious. But not at him.

"I wanted to come back here and fuck you senseless," he whispered against my mouth.

"Why?" I scratched my nails into his chest. "Did the things she say, turn you on?"

"No, but it reminded me of what I used to like." He sunk his teeth into my jaw. "It reminded me of how I used to be."

"Tell me you pushed her away," I whispered. "Tell me again, Lucas."

"I did, Lily." He slid his hands beneath my tank top. "I pushed her away because she wasn't you. I'm yours. Fuck, baby, I belong to you."

I whimpered, a soft sob escaping me. Tears pricked the back of my eyes. "I hate this. I love you. But I'm scared. I'm so damn scared, Lucas." I kissed him, lifting to my knees and shoving him onto his back. "I've never felt this with someone. You completely consume me." I sunk my teeth into his neck. "I want to rip you apart and make you forget that you ever touched her in the first place. I want you to show me how you are. How you truly are. I want your wrath. Your rage as you force your cock inside me." I lifted my head, staring down at him. "What's wrong with me?"

"Nothing." His hands pushed beneath my shorts, cupping my ass. "Nothing is wrong with you. This isn't your fault. It's mine. I'm fucked up. I've been fucked up since I was a kid."

"Normal is boring," I said, my voice wavering.

He gave me a small smirk. "Yeah, baby. It is."

"I just want to move on." I rested my head on his chest, my body shaking. "I want her gone and out of your life. And I want you to stop feeling so damn guilty."

"Lily."

"Don't say that you don't feel guilty because I know you do." I lifted my head that time, placing my hands on his chest and straddling his lap.

His thick erection pushed into me.

I moved my hips back and forth in slow circles.

He swallowed hard, the thick muscles in his neck working over the movement.

"I know you feel guilty that you couldn't stop that shit from happening. And I also know that you feel guilty that she kissed you."

Lucas sat up, pinched my chin, and forced me to look at him. "I do."

"But you shouldn't," I murmured.

"I feel like I cheated on you," he said, his voice cracking.

"No." I wrapped my arms around his shoulders. "That wasn't your fault. She started it."

"Lily."

"Did you like it when she touched you?"

"No." He shook his head. "Not at fucking all."

"Did you want her to continue? Did you not push her away?"

"No, I didn't want her to continue and yes, I pushed her away, but I also wanted to come back here and show you just how rough I can be." He blew out a slow breath. "I don't fucking deserve you."

"Stop. You didn't cheat on me. You didn't." I pushed my face into the crook of his thick neck and held him. We stayed like that for what felt like an eternity. Just holding. Touching. Breathing. I had been with a lot of guys, but nothing ever compared to this. I didn't just love Lucas. I was obsessed with him.

And he was more than my world. He was my very existence.

I HAD GONE WITH Lucas later that afternoon to meet up with Mel, but she actually never showed up. She had delivered a package and kept it with the front desk of the hotel. Maybe she was scared. Either way, I was thankful we didn't have to see her again.

After that, we decided to check out of the hotel right away and head home.

"I can't believe Mel never showed up. Or that she works at the hotel we decided to rent for the weekend," I said, breaking the silence and voicing the questions running through me. "Life is cruel if you ask me."

Lucas grunted, gripping my hand tight in his. "We didn't live anywhere near that town either." He sighed. "But yes, life is cruel. I'll deliver these to Shephard and he'll get rid of them."

"How do you know that those are the videos?"

Lucas's gaze flicked my way before looking back out at the road in front of us. "I don't. But I can't watch them to make sure they are what Mel says they are. So I'll get Shephard to do it."

"God, I wouldn't want that job." I shivered, bile rising to my throat.

"I know, baby. I'd watch them myself, but I know it would just destroy me. I'm man enough to admit that…I'm scared to see them and what they would do to me."

My eyes burned. "I know." It still didn't make sense to me. How could Mel work at a hotel that we decided to spend the weekend at? Did she know Lucas was going to be there? No. I mentally smacked myself. There was no way she could know that.

Once we reached his apartment, we spent the evening cleaning it up and making it livable again. He hadn't said much since we got home.

"Are you hungry?" Lucas asked a few hours later.

"I can always eat." I gave him a small smile. I wasn't curvy for nothing.

He nodded, leaning the broom against the wall and heading into the kitchen. He came back a few minutes later with two plates.

I could never get used to the peanut butter and jelly sandwiches he made me. "I like this," I told him, sitting on the couch and bringing my knees up to my chest.

"Yeah?" He sat beside me.

"Yeah. It's kind of our thing." I took a bite of the sandwich.

"Our thing?" He stretched his legs out in front of him, placing the plate on his lap and bringing the sandwich to his mouth. "I like having a thing."

I laughed lightly. "Me too."

A soft knock sounded on the door, jarring through our comfortable moment.

"Who the hell could that be?" Lucas grumbled, putting his plate on the table in front of us. He headed to the door. "What are you doing here?"

My heart jumped to my throat.

"I was able to find out some information."

A breath of relief left me when I heard Shephard's deep voice.

"What did you find?" Lucas closed the door and locked it up. "I don't have any beer."

"That's fine." Shephard came into the living room. "Hi, Lily."

"Hey." I grabbed up the plates and put them away in the kitchen before joining the guys back in the living room.

"Sorry it's so late. It's been one hell of a day." Shephard knelt on the floor, placing a folder on the table."

"That's fine. I have a favor to ask anyway." Lucas handed him a black duffle bag. "I need you to check what's on these. If they are what I think they are, they need to be destroyed."

Shephard nodded, taking the bag from him. "You have my word."

"Good." Lucas sat on the couch. "So, what's this about?" he asked, reaching out for me.

I sat beside him.

"After you called and told me that Lily was attacked and your apartment was broken into, I did some digging and found out that your computers were actually turned in at the station."

"Who turned them in?" Clearly the person didn't get what they were looking for.

"You didn't hear this from me." Shephard pushed the file closer to Lucas.

"I have no idea what you're talking about," Lucas mumbled, opening the folder.

"Good." Shephard pointed at the folder. "That's—"

"Killian." I gasped, clapping a hand to my mouth at the black and white image of Killian staring up at us from the folder.

"You know him?" Shephard raised an eyebrow.

"Yeah." Lucas shifted beside me. "He has a thing for my girl."

"Interesting." Shephard sat back, pulling one knee to his chest.

"Why do you say that?" I asked as Lucas kept flipping through page after page.

"Because Killian actually got kicked off the bureau about a year ago. He shot a person of interest in a suspected trafficking ring."

"What?" My eyes widened. "He never said that."

"Because he shot someone who may or may not have been involved in a trafficking ring, is beside the point." Shephard pointed at Lucas. "Remember, you more than anyone should know that some people do nice things as a cover up."

Lucas rubbed his nape, rolling his head back onto his shoulders. "I know."

"Why did he get kicked off the force for that?" I asked. "Wouldn't that be a good thing?"

"Sure. If the suspect ended up being guilty. But he unfortunately was in the wrong place at the wrong time." Shephard shook his head. "And it didn't help that Killian was doing illegal searches on his ex-wife's new boyfriend. He was just looking for ways to get fired."

"Who the fuck is this guy?" Lucas grumbled.

"Someone who wanted your computers. I don't have any proof yet, but rumors are that he was trying to find some shit on you. It all makes sense now. If he wants you…" His words trailed off.

"No, this doesn't make sense. We dated but that wasn't for long. That was months ago. He showed up here a few weeks ago but that was the last time I saw him," I explained, not liking where this was going any more than Lucas did.

"Are you sure?" Shephard pulled the file from Lucas and flipped the pages to the back. "Does this look familiar?"

Both of us leaned forward.

"What the fuck are we looking at?" Lucas demanded. "Is that…"

"That's me," I whispered. I took the file from him and looked closer. It was a picture of the alleyway. Even though it had been nighttime, the camera got a clear shot of me on the ground with my attacker on top of me. "How did you get this? We tried finding…"

"You tried hacking into the cameras," Shephard added. "Lucas told me you were good with computers."

"She's better than I am," Lucas said, giving me a small smile.

"I'm really not," I mumbled.

"You are." He kissed my temple. "Be proud. I am."

"Thank you but I wouldn't consider myself a hacker. I just know a thing or two about computers," I told Shephard.

"She's being modest," Lucas said. "Her capabilities far exceed mine."

Shephard grinned. "My boy's in love."

I laughed.

Lucas only shook his head and pulled me in closer to his side.

"Either way." Shephard cleared his throat. "That image was taken and removed from the camera before you could get your hands on it."

"Is this…" My eyes flicked back and forth between the two men staring at me. "It's Killian. Isn't it?"

"It is." Shephard rubbed the back of his neck. "But unfortunately, his face isn't clear enough in that picture. I only know it's him because I overheard him talking to someone else about it. They were planning it. He said something about the girl he's seeing being into someone else. He was jealous. Not in the hot possessive way either." Shephard stood and began pacing back and forth.

"This doesn't make sense. I'm no one important. He could get anyone he wanted. Why me?" I was just a random woman he dated out of convenience. I was no one.

"That's just it." Lucas turned to me. "It's because he can't have you. That's what his issue is."

"But why?" I asked again. "I'm no one special."

"I know I haven't known you for long but the fact that you snatched up Lucas is saying something." Shephard shrugged.

"Uh…really?" I cupped Lucas's shoulder. "Why? Were you unsnatchable or something?"

"That's not a word," Lucas grumbled, his cheeks reddening.

I smiled, placing a soft peck on his cheek. "Either way, this doesn't make sense. At all. If he wouldn't have been spooked, he could have raped me. Or killed me." I forced those images to the back of my mind, not wanting to think about what could have happened.

"It's because you're with Lucas and not him. Some people are like that. They can't have you, so no one can have you. That sort of shit." Shephard pointed at the file. "There's more in there."

Lucas rubbed the back of his neck, flipping through page after page. "This doesn't explain who broke into my apartment and stole…shit."

"What?" I peered over his shoulder. "Is that…"

Shephard nodded, patting himself on the back. "You taught me a thing or two about computers. Remember?"

Lucas grunted. "Yeah but I never expected you to remember half the shit I showed you." He glanced at me. "I was able to get time cut off my sentence for helping this fucker out."

"You can do that?" I asked in awe.

"Probably not but I did it anyway." Shephard sat on the couch beside Lucas. "And you need to elaborate, Lucas. I actually took him under my wing," Shephard explained.

"Really?" I looked between the two men. "You mentioned he saved you."

"Aww." Shephard batted his eyes.

Lucas gagged.

I giggled.

"But in all seriousness…." Shephard paused, letting out a hard sigh. "I was just lucky to be in the right place at the right time."

"That's so fucking true. He helped me when no one else would. He's also the one who made me go to NA in the first place."

"You were in bad form, Lucas." Shephard grimaced. "I don't want to go back to that. Ever."

Lucas grunted. "Neither do I."

"Good." Shephard clapped his shoulder. "Now, enough traveling down memory lane. Your computer got a clear shot of who stole everything. Clearly these guys are amateurs."

"Clearly." Lucas showed me the image.

My eyes widened. "I don't understand. Why?" I asked, staring down at a perfect shot of Killian that Lucas's computer camera took.

"Because Killian is a fucker who is willing to do anything to make ends meet. And luckily, Lucas is smart and had his camera set to record everything standing in front of it." Shephard stood, nodding toward the file in Lucas's hand. "Keep it. I have another one."

"What would Killian need with your computers?" I asked Lucas.

"He probably wanted to see if there was anything on it that can throw me back in jail." Lucas stood, giving Shephard a one-armed hug. "Thank you."

Shephard nodded.

Lucas released him.

"I still don't understand," I said softly.

"I don't understand everything either but I'm working on it. I will find out what's going on. I promise. But I have to ask…" Shephard hesitated. "Did you do any research on Killian?"

"Uh…fuck." Lucas tossed the file on the table. "I meant to, but I was distracted. I must have…" He cleared his throat.

"Well, we'll get this shit sorted. But I'll leave you two alone now. If you need anything, please don't hesitate to contact me. I'll be in touch when I find out anything else." Shephard clapped Lucas's shoulder, grabbed the duffle bag and showed himself out.

When we were alone, Lucas knelt in front of me, taking my hands in his. "Killian is trying to bring me down to get to you. He probably thinks that if he can show that I'm a bad person or whatever, you would leave me."

"Never." I cupped Lucas's face. "You could be the Devil himself but as long as you're good to me, I'd still love you."

"That's a bit extreme," Lucas mumbled.

"Maybe."

"I should have done research on him like I had intended." Lucas rubbed the back of his neck. "I can't believe I forgot to do that shit."

"Hey." I grabbed his hand, kissing his knuckles. "It's okay."

"No, it's not, Lily." He went to pull away, but I only tightened my hold.

"I promise it is. Killian is an asshole and he's looking for something. We'll figure it out. But I don't want you blaming yourself."

"You're too good to me," Lucas mumbled.

"No such thing." I leaned closer, needing to feel him. To touch him. It had felt like so long, I just wanted him to hold me. To tell me that everything was going to be okay. That Killian and Mel would leave us alone. "Lucas," I breathed.

"Yeah?" He licked his lips, inching closer.

"I don't know what to do." His hot breath fanned across my lips. "But I know that right now, I want you."

His nostrils flared, his good eye darkening. "Have me, baby. Have every inch of me. It's yours. All of it." He kissed the corner of my mouth, brushing his lips down the length of my jaw to my ear. "Every last drop, Lily."

I whimpered, my core clenching, but I couldn't move. I couldn't budge. I wanted him to control me. No. I wanted us to control each other. I wanted our love to snap until all we could feel was that raw passion sizzling between us.

"I can smell your pussy." He sunk his teeth into my neck. In a quick move, he pulled me from the couch and onto his lap.

My breath came out in pants. "I can feel how hard you are."

"For you, baby." His mouth roamed down the length of my throat. "Always so fucking hard for you."

"Does it hurt?" I gripped his t-shirt, reaching beneath it to touch his hot skin.

"It does, Lily. It hurts so fucking much."

"I can kiss it better." I bit his shoulder. "I can make that ache go away."

"Nah, baby." He fisted my hair, forced my head back, and stared intently into my eyes. "I want you to make it worse."

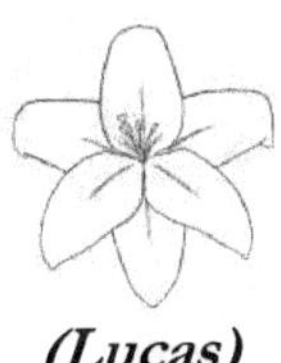

(Lucas)

"Do you know what's going to be done about Killian?" Lily asked later that night. She was on top of my bed, naked, on her stomach with her feet kicking back and forth behind her. She rested her chin in her hands, smiling at me as I got dressed.

"I'll meet with Shephard, make sure he destroyed the videos and also see what I can find out. But I don't want you worrying about it." I placed a soft peck on her mouth. "I have to stop by the shop. I need to email my clients and tell them that I'm back in business."

"Isn't that my job?" she asked, rolling over onto her back.

"It is but if you stay here, naked, it'll motivate me to be quick."

She laughed.

I bent over her, placing a soft kiss on her pretty little clit.

A soft gasp escaped her. "You need to go."

I chuckled. "I'll go and when I come back, we can try this position." I gave her clit one final kiss before placing a peck on her mouth. "Then I can watch my cock fucking your throat."

Her pupils dilated. "God, you say the sweetest things."

"Don't get dressed." I stepped away from her before she distracted me even more. I headed to the door and glanced back at her.

Lily rolled back onto her stomach, her curly light brown hair falling around her face. She gave me a soft smile. The glow in her cheeks was because of me. The marks on her skin? All me. She unleashed something inside of me that I enjoyed, and I couldn't wait to continue exploring it with her.

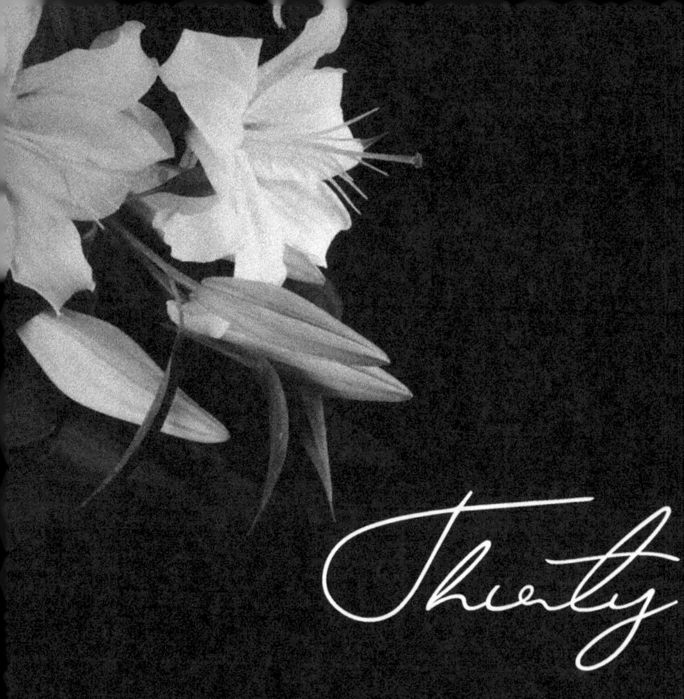

Thirty

LUCAS

WITH MY TOUCH EMBEDDED on Lily's skin and my cum deep inside her, I left her naked on my bed and went to the business part of the building.

When I unlocked the place, I flicked on the lights. A moment of dread washed over me. It was an odd feeling. And one I didn't enjoy either.

I headed to the front. The sun was setting but it was early enough that the street lights weren't on yet. It had been a long fucking day, but the night would end well at least. My face broke out into a grin. I could still feel Lily's touch all over me, smell her, taste her. Hear her.

My body stirred. Clearing my throat, I gave myself a shake and checked my emails. There weren't too many, so I sent off the ones I needed to. I was about to close up when I saw Mel standing at the door.

My stomach twisted.

She gave me a small wave, pointing at the doorknob.

I huffed, going to the door and unlocking it. "What are you doing here?" I demanded, not letting her enter.

"Did you get the package?" she asked, her eyes roaming down the length of me.

"I did and they're going to be destroyed." I went to shut the door when she slapped a hand against it.

"Aren't you going to let me in?"

"No." My jaw clenched so damn hard, a searing pain shot up the side of my face. "You should leave."

"Are you alone?" She looked past me. "Where's your little girlfriend?"

In my bed. Where she belongs. "She's around. What do you want, Mel?"

"To talk." She pushed up against me. "Please, Lucas. I didn't get to see you last night."

"You need to leave," I repeated, stepping away from her. I wasn't sure what she was getting at, but she shouldn't be here.

"Please, Lucas." Mel looked down, her nostrils flaring.

I shifted on my feet, not liking that she was looking at me like I was a piece of meat. I had been fantasizing about Lily, my cock now semi-hard because of it and Mel noticed. Fuck.

"I just want to talk." Her gaze popped back to mine. "I promise."

I searched her face. A moment of pity washed over me, so I stepped back, letting her enter. But I didn't let her near me and headed to the back. "What are you doing here?" I asked again.

"You left abruptly at the coffee shop yesterday morning." Mel followed me. "I wanted to talk to you again. But I didn't want to do it with Lily around."

"What?" I spun on her. "So we could talk about those videos? No thanks."

"It was my childhood too, Lucas." She frowned. "I'm a victim just like you are."

I scoffed. "Right, well, those videos proved that you liked it a lot more than you ever let on."

"Fuck you." She closed the distance between us and shoved me back.

"Stop." I gripped her shoulders, pushing her against the nearest wall. "What the hell do you want?"

"You, Lucas." She reached for me, but I grabbed her hands, pulling them above her head. Her pupils dilated. Shit. She arched against the wall. "So, did you show her that side of you, the side you've been trying to ignore? That delicious side? I remember the first time I helped you cut yourself. Hottest and dirtiest sex I ever had."

My jaw clenched, my stomach twisting over the shit I used to do.

"I want you," she repeated.

"What the fuck is wrong with you? I'm with Lily." I released her roughly and stomped to the back of the shop. I didn't want her following me to the apartment. I had to check inventory anyway, but I hadn't planned on doing that tonight.

"Lucas."

I ignored her and headed into the storage room. The door closed behind me followed by a click. I spun around. "What the hell?"

Mel pulled her dress to her hips. "I know you want me. I can see it on your face, Lucas. I'm not stupid. And neither is Lily. She knows she can't compete with me. I also see that delicious bulge in your pants. Did you fuck her? Did you leave your cum dripping from her soaked pussy?" Mel licked her lips and pulled the dress up and over her head, leaving her naked.

"Put your dress back on." I turned away, averting my eyes.

"Lucas." Mel came up behind me, placing her hands on my back and pressing her body up against me. I could feel the heat coming off of her and smell that damn rose perfume.

"Stop," I said but my voice wasn't as firm as I would have liked.

"Fuck her, Lucas. I know you want it. We all know you want it."

I couldn't do this. I tried shoving Mel off of me, but she only latched on, digging her nails into my skin.

"I know you want me." Mel pushed her hands beneath my shirt, lifted it to my shoulders, and placed kisses on my back.

"Did you tell Lily how you got these scars? How you begged for them and the pain made you come so fucking hard?"

"Stop, please stop." Fuck, I felt like a little boy again. I was trapped with nowhere to go.

"Say it, Lucas. Say that you want me. Say that Lily can never satisfy you like I can." Mel ran her hands over my abs before pushing them into the waist of my sweatpants.

I jumped, taking a couple of steps back until we hit the wall.

Mel gasped, her hand wrapping around my dick.

"Stop," I pleaded.

"Take it, Lucas. Let me show you what you've been missing. Lily can't give this to you. But I can."

Soft hands wrapped around me, stroking, tugging, pulling the pleasure I had never felt before right from my very body. I groaned, arching into the rough touch.

"That's it, Lucas. Take everything you want from me." Hot lips trailed over my chest. "I know you want me. You will always want me."

"More," I pleaded.

Bright blue eyes met mine. "Mama told me you would like it like this." Teeth grazed up the length of my cock, the sweet scent of roses billowing around us.

I hissed, the pain roaring through me. "More."

"That's right, Lucas. My love. I'll give you more. Always more. Always me. Mama wouldn't want it any other way."

"No." I snapped out of it, shaking my head and pushing out of Mel's hold. I backed away from her, palming my erection.

"Lucas, you clearly want me or else you wouldn't be hard right now." She sidled up to me, cupping me over my pants. "Come on, baby." She kissed my chin. "Give it to me like you used to. Fuck me. You can use every inch of my body. It's yours. All of it is yours."

"Stop." My body shook.

Intense pain surrounded me. The agony was hot, brutal but so damn satisfying all at once. I was confused. Turned on. Disgusted with the way I enjoyed it. But I couldn't control it. I couldn't control any of it.

"Take it, Lucas. Mama and Bobby need the money. We look good on camera."

A hot mouth trailed down my stomach to my dick. I had tried so damn hard not to enjoy it. Not to feel any pleasure. But I couldn't stop it.

Lily.

Something in my mind snapped. I could still feel the pleasure coursing through me. It turned hotter. Brighter.

A gagging sound erupted into my ears.

I glanced down, expecting to see Lily when my gaze landed on Mel. My dick was deep in her mouth.

"No." I shoved her off of me, her teeth scraping along my shaft at the rough move. I hissed, the pain slicing into my heart. "You…" I growled. Rage coursed through me. I had never hit a woman before. Not by choice. But this…my hands clenched into fists. "I remember. Fuck, I remember everything. How you used that damn rose perfume to get into my head. How you're still fucking using it. That's why you wear it. I also remember how you seduced me. How you seduced all of us. All because your mom and Bobby put you up to it." I backed up until I hit the shelf, items falling off of it and landing on the floor. I stuffed my cock back into my pants. I needed a shower. I needed to wash her off of me. She wasn't Lily. She wasn't my Lily. But she had me in her mouth. Fuck me. "You knew…you know I'm fucked up. You knew saying that shit would break me. That rose perfume would…" My chest rose and fell. I was on the verge of losing my shit. This was going to break Lily's heart. I was going to lose her. Hell, I didn't deserve her. This was no excuse. It wasn't. "Get out. Get out of my fucking sight."

Mel sauntered toward me. "I remember how you got off watching me. It would make me come even harder when your eyes were on me."

I gripped my shirt, my heart thundering behind the walls of my ribcage.

"It was the only way I could get your beautiful cock inside of me," she went on. "Even though it was just my mouth." She shrugged. "You still taste as good as I remember too. I especially like that pretty little octopus. And what happened when we were kids." She shrugged like it had been no big deal. "You wouldn't have done it any other way. So they made you rape me. But I loved it, Lucas." In a quick move, she stood right in front of me with her hands on my chest. "So good. Best cock I've ever felt. Mama and Bobby loved watching you fuck me." She kissed my chin. "I remember the first time you came inside me. I thought for sure you would have gotten me pregnant. All that cum." She moaned.

"Stop." I shook my head as the memories came rushing back. My mind had tried protecting me but now, I remembered. I remembered it all. I shoved her back. "This isn't right."

"But we have more movies to make." Mel reached up and cupped her breasts, pinching her nipples. "Please, Lucas."

"No." I pushed past her and unlocked the door when a hand slapped against it.

"You're mine, Lucas. You've always been mine. It's why you couldn't have a relationship with anyone. I know it's been me you've wanted this whole time." She cupped me over my pants, pressing her palm into me. "You're still nice and hard too. I told you that you would always want me."

I spun around, forcing her back against the shelves in a rough move. "I'm going to tell you this only once. I love Lily. I belong to her and she belongs to me. I felt guilty because I haven't kept in contact with you but now I don't. You can go fuck yourself, Mel." I shoved away from her and unlocked the door. Throwing it open, I stepped out of the room when I was met with Lily staring back at me.

Her eyes were wide. She glanced past me.

"Hello, Lily. He's all yours now," Mel said from behind me. "We just finished."

I looked over my shoulder, my stomach sinking. Mel was leaning against the table, still completely naked. She wiped a finger over the corner of her mouth.

A sharp inhale forced my head back around.

Lily's cheeks were red, her hands clenched into fists at her sides.

"Lily." I took a step toward her.

She lifted her hand and slapped me. The sting of her palm erupted through me.

"I was wondering where you were. Clearly…" Her chin wobbled. She shook her head and spun on her heel.

"Lily, please wait." I rushed to her, grabbing her arm and stopping her from leaving. "Let me explain."

"Let go of me," she sobbed.

"No, I—"

"Well, it's been fun, Lucas." Mel was finally dressed and headed past us to the door. "Until next time." She glanced at Lily. "Keep him warm for me, okay?"

Lily screamed, diving at her.

I caught her around the middle, holding her back.

Mel only laughed and left the shop.

I placed Lily back on her feet. "Lily, I—"

"Don't." She went to the door, but I stepped in front of her.

"Please let me explain. Whatever you think happened, didn't happen." But something did happen.

"Alright, Lucas." Lily crossed her arms under her chest, leaning against the counter. "Tell me then. Did she touch you?"

I flinched. "Lily, I—"

"Answer the damn question," she snapped. "Did she touch you?"

"Yes," I croaked.

"Where?"

A breath left me on a whoosh. "What?" There was no way she would want to know that.

"Where did she touch you?" Her eyes fell to my waist. "She obviously touched your cock because I can see that hard-on you're sporting. So what did you do? Did you fuck her? Did she give you a hand job? Did she suck your cock?"

I looked away.

She laughed. "God, I'm such an idiot."

"No." I reached for her and before she could jump away from me, I had her in my arms. "I'm sorry. She came in here, begging me but I swear to God I didn't want to do anything. I tried pushing her away. I promise I tried." I rained kisses on Lily's face. "Please, baby. You have to believe me. I didn't know what was happening. I promise I didn't. I…" How the hell could I explain that my body reacted because her touching me brought me back to when I was a kid? And during the memories, she started sucking my cock? It was fucked up and she sure as hell wouldn't believe me because I wouldn't if the roles were reversed. It didn't make sense.

"Stop." Lily struggled against me. "Lucas."

"Please. I can't lose you. Fuck." My chest tightened. "I can't. I refuse."

"You should have thought of that before you let her touch you." Her eyes burned bright with fury. "Before you let her kiss you. Before you let her put your dick in her mouth. Did you fuck her?"

"What?" My eyes widened. "No." I shook my head. "No." I cupped her face. "You're the only one I want. I didn't fuck her. I promise I didn't fuck her."

"But she sucked your cock," she whispered. "Did she make you come? Or no? Is that why you're hard? You didn't come yet? Did you want me to do it for you? Because I can. Is that your thing? Having multiple women?"

"Stop." I shook my head. "Stop with these questions. You know that's not true. I want only you. What happened…what you walked in on…I don't know how to explain it but please let me try. I need to try."

"Did she hint for more?" Lily asked, ignoring me. "I obviously interrupted something. Tell me. You left me alone in your bed after you fucked me. Is that your thing too?"

"No, baby. No." I pulled her away from the door, needing to bring her back to my apartment so I could sit her down and talk to her. To tell her how sorry I was that she had to walk in on that. To prove to her she was the only one that I wanted. She was my life. She was the light in the darkness that shadowed my world since I was a kid. "Please, Lily," my voice cracked. "I need you."

"I can't." A sob escaped Lily. "She was naked. I walked in and she was naked, Lucas. She sucked your cock."

"I…"

"You looked away when I asked. I'm not stupid. She had your cock in her mouth. A part of you that's been mine for the past few months. Or did you have other women too in that time?"

"Fuck no." I fell to her feet, wrapping my arms around her waist. "It's only been you. I'm sorry. She was saying things and it triggered memories. But then I thought of you and I snapped out of it. But she was already…I was already in her…"

"She was sucking you off." Lily's breath hitched. "You cheated on me."

"No." I squeezed her. "I didn't. She forced herself on me." I felt like a little boy again, getting molested and abused repeatedly. Mel was no better than those bastards. "I'm sorry. I didn't want that to happen. I know it doesn't make sense."

"Explain it to me because the images in my head aren't helping. I can only see you two together and it makes me sick. I can see her on her knees."

"I'm sorry. I didn't touch her. But I remember. I need to tell you everything."

"I can't…I can't compete with this. I can't compete with her. Not when she still wants you."

I jumped to my feet. "What are you telling me?" I whispered, brushing my face into the crook of her neck.

"I think…" Her body trembled. "I think we're done."

"No," I yelled, crushing her to me. "I love you."

"Love isn't enough," she cried, pushed away from me, and started pacing back and forth. "Not after what you two have been through together. I see the way she looks at you. Even if what you say is true…even if you didn't want her, your body sure as hell does."

"It's not the same, Lily." I couldn't believe this was happening. After all of this time. After everything we had given each other. "I didn't react to her because I wanted to. I know it doesn't make sense. Fuck, I'll talk to a shrink, so they can explain. I didn't remember everything until now. It's fucked up. I know it is but I…please let me explain."

"Explain?" Lily stopped pacing. "Lucas, there's nothing to explain."

I fell back to my knees, wrapping my arms around her waist. "Please, Lily. I need you. I've been fucking broken until you came along. You've fixed me." My throat burned, tears pricking the back of my eyes. I wasn't an emotional man, but this was far worse than anything I had ever endured. I would take the abuse of my childhood over and over again before dealing with losing Lily.

"I love you, Lucas." Lily crouched in front of me and cupped my face. "But I love you too much to make you stay with me when clearly you still have feelings for her."

"I don't. She's a monster. She's as bad as her real parents, my adoptive parents." I wrapped my body around Lily, squeezing her and holding her tight against me until neither of us could breathe. "It's not the same with her. I had no one else when she was in my life. It's not the same, baby. Fuck, Lily, I can't lose you. I refuse to lose you. I don't feel anything for her. Not anymore."

Tears streamed down Lily's cheeks. "You lost me the moment she came back into your life."

I kissed her face, her tears coating my lips. "Don't say that."

"It's true, Lucas. This shop was closed. Why the hell would you let her in? I know she didn't break in."

"I was being nice." Fuck, I realized how stupid that sounded.

"Being nice?" she repeated.

In that moment I saw her angry stiff shoulders slump in defeat and I knew the next blow was coming.

"Lucas, after all the shit she's put us through already and you were being nice?" Lily shoved to her feet, scrubbing a hand down her face. "I can't do this. I can't be with someone who has feelings for someone else."

"I don't." I fell forward, reaching out for her. "I love you. I love everything about you. I need you. I need your smiles. Your laughs. I need to share my peanut butter and jelly sandwiches with you. I need our coffee dates."

Her sobs hardened. "I...I can't."

My throat closed, my chest tightening at what she was saying to me. "This is it?"

Another sob left her. "I...I think it is."

"No, I refuse to think this is it. I love you, Lily Pad." My body shook.

"And I love you, Lucas, but can you honestly sit here and tell me that you don't want to rekindle things with her?" Her breath hitched. "You two went through hell together. That's a bond that none of us can ignore."

"It's not like it was. I remember now. I remember what happened. My adoptive mom was her real mom. They made her seduce us. It doesn't make sense. I'm not making sense, but I promise if you just hear me out, I can explain everything that I remember."

"I can't." Lily pushed out of my hold.

"Lily," I pleaded. "I can't do this without you."

"I think I should leave. I'm not giving you an ultimatum. I'm not that type of woman so I'm making it easy for you." Lily's voice wavered, her chin wobbling.

Our eyes locked, our souls collided and right there, I felt her pain compound with mine. It left me breathless and unable to continue the fight.

"You will be the only man I'll ever love."

I looked away, the sound of the door shutting a moment later.

Before thinking twice about it, I shoved to my feet and punched my fist through the wall. The bones in my knuckles cracked but the pain slicing through me, only ignited this need, this want for more. The agony turned into a dull roar, reminding me that I was alive and that I was human. A fucked up, broken mess of a human, but a human still the same.

(Lily)

When I had walked in on Lucas and Mel, my world had fallen out from under me. So many thoughts rushed through me. How could he? After all we had shared. I felt that we had finally started to move forward when he threw it all back in my face like I was a piece of shit on the bottom of his shoe. I didn't know a lot about mental health issues. PTSD, or whatever it was Lucas had. Whatever Mel had said to him, triggered memories to the point she was able to suck his cock without his permission?

Bile rose to my throat. I didn't know if that was possible.

Tears fell down my cheeks and I rubbed them away roughly. I wasn't sure if he had feelings for Mel still but what I walked in on didn't prove me wrong either. I was confused. Add to the fact that he never came after me and I was a fucking mess.

Was this it? Was I not worth fighting for? I got my answer when he let me go.

A sob hiccupped through me, forcing more hot tears down my cheeks. I was crushed with the weight of my emotions, defeat resonating on my shoulders.

"Lily."

I stopped suddenly, finding Toby coming toward me.

"We were driving to the center for a meeting, but Sandra noticed you walking. So, I pulled over." He pointed to his car parked across the street. Sandra was sitting in the passenger seat, looking our way. "Is everything okay?"

I glanced back at Toby, shaking my head.

"Lily."

My back stiffened as I heard Lucas coming toward me from behind. "Will you take me home, Toby? Please?"

Toby nodded, glancing over my head. "Are you sure?"

"Yes. Please." I rushed across the street.

"Lily, wait."

I ignored Lucas and ran to the car, jumping into the back seat.

Toby came toward us and sat in the driver's seat. "Home?"

I nodded.

Lucas banged on the window. "Lily, please. I'm sorry. I'm so fucking sorry."

"What did you want us to do?" Sandra asked me gently.

"Just drive," I said, my voice cracking. "Please just drive."

Toby nodded, pulling the car away.

I looked behind us, finding Lucas running after the car. A sob escaped me. I turned back around. "Drive faster. Please driver faster."

Toby did as I said and sped up the car. "He's gone," he said a few minutes later.

I nodded, covering my face. "I'm sorry."

"Did you want to talk about it?" Sandra asked, gently.

"No. I—" My phone rang at that point. I had forgotten I put it in my back pocket. "Hello?"

"Miss Noel?"

My throat dried. "This is her."

"This is Doctor Proulx at the General Hospital. Your grandmother has had a heart attack."

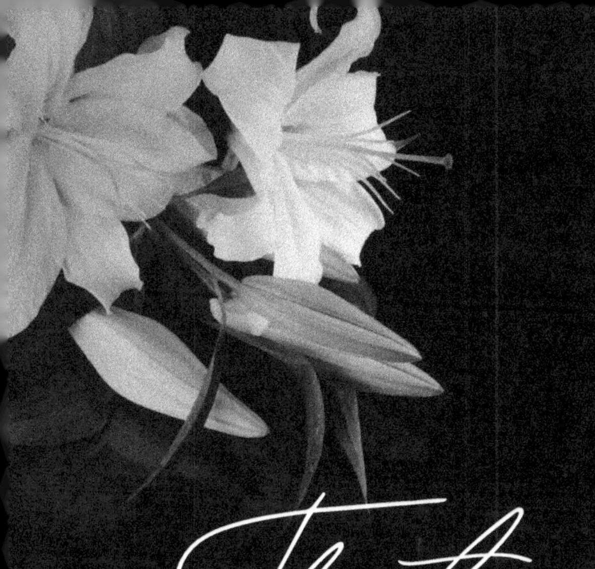

Thirty-One

Lily

"YOU ARE GOING TO stop this shit right now."

My eyes widened at the language leaving my grandmother's mouth. "I—"

"Shut up," she screamed, her face reddening. "Just shut up. I'm sick of seeing you use your body to get that shit. You have a problem. It's not just alcohol to you. It's a damn drug. All these guys that come and go from this place? I'm sick of it. I opened my home to you when your parents died. I took care of you. I was by your side every damn day in that fucking hospital. And for what? All for you to throw it back in my face. Well I'm done. I've been kind, patient. It's time for tough love now, kiddo. What do you say?" Her brows narrowed. "Answer me. Or I'm calling the cops and telling them that you're selling your body. What you are doing could be considered prostitution, and that's illegal in this country."

"You wouldn't," I whispered.

"Try me." Fury rolled off of her in waves.

"I…" I didn't know what to say. What could I say? I fucked up. I fucked up bad.

From that moment on, I hadn't had a drop of alcohol. My grandmother had been right. It wasn't just alcohol to me. I couldn't have a social drink. I had no control when it came down to it. So I stopped drinking altogether. And I had missed it every second since.

"Lily?"

Bone crushing sobs wracked through me. They were so hard, I couldn't control them.

"Hand me her phone."

"Pull over."

I didn't know who was talking. I didn't care. I needed a drink. I needed Lucas. I needed to be happy. I needed us to be happy. I needed Mel and Killian to leave us alone.

Cool air washed over me followed by gentle arms. I didn't know who was touching me. I didn't care but I pulled in the warmth from them and cried. I cried so damn hard, my soul ached.

"Shhh…" The person whispered, rubbing soothing circles on my back.

"Yeah this is Toby. I'm a friend of Lily's. Okay."

"What's going on?" Sandra asked, and I realized then that it was her who was hugging me.

"Her grandma had a heart attack."

"Oh, honey." Sandra hugged me tighter.

"Did you want us to call anyone?" Toby asked.

I sat up, rubbed the tears away, and looked out the window.

Even though I was mad at Lucas, my grandma liked him. We hadn't been together for long, but she meant what she said when she told him that she would take him in as her own.

"Yes," my voice cracked. "Lucas."

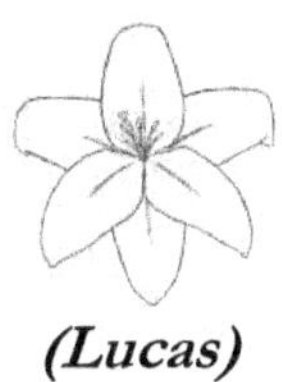

(Lucas)

Pure hard rage rushed through me. It went so deep, I could feel it inside my soul. Seeing Toby drive away with Lily in the back seat forced this newfound fury through me.

"Fuck," I boomed, punching my fist through the wall a second time. The drywall cracked, pieces shattering to the floor.

A phone rang in the distance, but I ignored it and punched another hole in a different part of the wall. Pain screamed up my forearm, my knuckles bleeding the more I punched and the more I punched, the higher my anger rose. It did nothing to curb this agony inside of me.

Lily left me. She fucking left me.

I fell to my knees, falling forward. I didn't know how much time had passed but I didn't care. I needed her. I needed my Lily. My sweet Lily Pad.

A hard sob escaped me, forcing all of the anguish I had felt over the years, tumbling with it. I didn't cry then. Not when my body was being used for another person's pleasure. Not when I was being ripped in half. Not when my mouth was sewn shut. Not when I was whipped and beaten and left for dead. I didn't cry. Not one fucking tear. But now, it hit me like a building had landed hard on my body. I couldn't breathe. My chest felt tight. My lungs felt like they were going to explode from the lack of air I couldn't give them. And why? All because Mel couldn't keep her hands to herself. All because she wanted something she couldn't have. All because both of us were forced into a situation as children that neither of us could control. But I got out. She didn't. Not in her mind anyway. And the fact she still had control over my past, shoved me to my feet and forced me to lift the nearest thing and toss it.

"Lucas!"

I heard my name but didn't know who was calling me. I didn't care. Let them say my name. Let them see how much of a monster I was and that the only way I could be tamed was by having Lily back in my arms.

The beast inside of me was unleashed as I barreled through my living room.

Lifting. Tossing. Destroying.

"Lucas! Calm the fuck down!"

Hands grabbed me but I shoved them off, my fist landing against bone before I could stop myself.

"Fuck!"

"Lucas, I'll fucking Taser you."

Red hot fury danced in my vision. It teased and played, sliding over my skin. It controlled my actions, making me blind with rage.

"Do something!" A woman.

I spun around thinking it was my Lily but when I saw a taller woman, my vision cleared, and I realized that it wasn't her. "Lily," I ground out between clenched teeth.

"Lucas, look at me."

I turned back around, getting in Shephard's face. "What the fuck are you doing here?"

"Are you calm?" he asked, narrowing his brows but taking a step back.

"I asked you a question." My voice was so deep, even I didn't recognize it.

Shephard lifted his hands, warding me off when Sandra stepped between us.

"Lily needs you. Her grandmother is in the hospital. We're going to take you to her," Sandra said in a rush.

"We've been ringing the doorbell over and over. When you didn't answer, I called Shephard to come help." Toby stepped beside his wife.

"How long?" I glanced around the room, trying to find a clock but apparently, I had knocked it off the wall. The living room was trashed like Godzilla himself had barreled through the apartment. The evidence of my rage stared back at me, taunting me.

"It's been almost eight hours, Lucas." Toby placed a gentle hand on my shoulder.

"Eight hours?" I pinched the bridge of my nose. "I lost eight fucking hours." All because I couldn't control my shit and fell into myself. I hadn't realized that much time had passed. "Take me to her but first…" I stepped toward Shephard. "What's going on?"

"Killian." He shoved a file against my chest.

"Tell me." I snatched the file from his hand and tossed it to the floor. "Now."

"It's done. I got a couple of guys from the force to conduct a search, and we raided his place. We found your computers and can have them back to you."

"My computers." I frowned. "I thought they were turned in?"

"They were but Killian had someone on the inside who stole them from evidence to bring them back to him. We also found out that he was one of the kids. One of the other kids who were adopted by the same people who adopted you."

All the blood drained from my face. "What?"

"Let's continue this conversation on the way to the hospital," Toby suggested.

"Move," I barked. "Now."

Toby and Sandra rushed to the door with Shephard and I following.

"Explain," I demanded.

"He had his name changed. He was born as Ronald Olle. He was the main attraction and the one who made them money before you arrived."

"I was there my whole childhood; how does that make any sense?" I asked him. We reached Toby and Sandra's car, slipping into the back seat.

"I guess this was before you hit puberty and you really filled out. I don't know, Lucas. I'm just going by what he said." Shephard glanced at Toby and Sandra.

"I don't give a shit if they know," I bit out. There was no use keeping this to myself any longer. I had spent years doing that and look where it got me. It was about time it came out in the open.

Shephard nodded. "Killian joined the force and moved up to detective, so he could bring down bastards like your adoptive parents, but he had a hidden agenda. He wanted to put you away."

"Me?" I frowned. "What the hell for?" I waited and when Shephard didn't say anything, I laughed. "This has to do with Lily. Doesn't it? Like you said, he can't have her, so no one can."

"It was originally because of Mel. You got both of the girls he wanted." He pulled his phone out from the inner pocket of his jacket and pressed a button.

"He stole both of them from me. Mel and Lily. He deserves to suffer. He deserves to be locked up. So I had Mel play a little game with him." Killian chuckled. "I paid her to seduce him. Although, she probably would have done it for free. But I am a nice guy after all. It's a small world that he just happened to show up at the place she was working at. And get this. It wasn't even the same town we grew up in." Killian's laugh deepened. "He's a fucking mess. The mind's a fragile thing, you know. If you poke it the right way, you can have it doing whatever you want. And she did. And you know what's better? Lily walked in." His laugh deepened. "It'll serve him right for fucking with what's mine."

When the recording ended, Shephard stuffed his phone back into his jacket pocket. "I'm sorry, Lucas."

"Don't." I pinched the bridge of my nose. "I need to see Lily," I said as soon as we pulled up to the hospital.

"Lucas, he'll be dealt with, legally. But he didn't just steal from you. What you went through as kids not only fucked him up, but it took that part of him that had any morals left. We found child porn on his own computers. He was loading them onto yours. He was trying to make it look like you were into that shit, but we caught him in time."

"Fuck. We'll talk later." I slipped from the car. "Thank you for the ride," I told Toby and Sandra and shut the door behind me, not waiting for a response.

I knew Killian was fucked in the head, but I never expected this. This was a twist even I never saw coming. I had to tell Lily but first, I needed to make up for the shit Mel had done to me.

I COULDN'T EAT. I couldn't function. I couldn't do anything. I felt like I had been at the hospital for years when really, it had only been since last night. Or that was how long I thought it was anyway. Maybe it was longer or shorter. I wasn't sure anymore.

"Lily."

My head snapped up, my gaze landing on Lucas. He had his hands shoved in his pockets, his good eye not meeting mine. He looked like a child who had just been scolded.

He wore gray sweatpants with a black hoodie. It was his signature outfit when he wanted to be comfortable. He was dressed casually but still looked lethal and that dangerous part of him stirred something inside of me.

That dark part. That submissive part. That part that needed him.

Jumping from my seat, I had every intention of running to him, but something stopped me. Could I trust him? Mel was a problem. A big problem. If what Lucas said was true, and she had full control over him, triggering memories. Could I compete with that? Could I help him move past that mental break, so it never happened again? And if it did, could I be there for him?

I made a decision. Yes, yes, I could.

I rushed toward him and threw myself in his arms, a sob escaping me.

He hugged me to him, wrapping his arms around me and holding me so damn tight I couldn't breathe but I found that I didn't care. I needed him. This. All of this.

His touch had been embedded on my skin from the very first moment. All of him was pressed up against all of me and it was perfect. It was ours. All of it was ours and no one could take that away from us.

"Lily," he whispered, running his hand over my head. "Fuck I missed you. I missed this. I thought I'd never see you again. I thought we were…I thought…"

I broke out into uncontrollable sobs. My body shook. Everything that had happened since Mel had shown up, came crashing down on me. And then my grandma having a heart attack. I couldn't lose her. I couldn't lose Lucas. I couldn't lose either of them.

"Hey." Lucas lifted me in his arms, carrying me to a nearby chair and placing me on his lap like a child. "Talk to me, baby."

I didn't know what to say. I held him. I held him so damn tight.

Lucas cradled me against him, rocking us back and forth. He ran light circles over my upper back, soothing the pain coursing through me.

"You're freaking me out, Lily Pad." He rained pecks on my face, kissing my tears away.

"My grandma," I said, my voice cracking. "She had a heart attack."

"Shit." Lucas held me against him. "I'm so sorry. Have you talked to the doctors yet?"

"I did last night. I think." I was lost, so damn lost, I didn't know how many hours had passed since I had shown up at the hospital. "What time is it?"

"It's morning. It's been almost eight hours." He gave me a lopsided smile. "Have you seen her?"

"Briefly. She was resting, and I didn't want to bother her or have her to see me cry. I know it's bound to happen. She's getting old. But she's the strongest person I know. This isn't right. The doctors said that it was mild but…"

"I get it." Lucas placed a soft peck on my mouth. "I'm sorry. I'm so fucking sorry. For everything. For the pain I've caused you. No matter what I've been through, losing you hurts the worst."

"You haven't—"

"Don't." He pinched my chin, forcing me to look up at him. "We'll talk about this later." He brushed his thumbs under my eyes.

We sat there and stared at each other. God, I loved him. I loved him so damn much. He had said that I was the light in the darkness that had taken over his life, but the truth was, he was my light too. Every time he walked into the room, my breath caught. My body heated. And my love for him grew.

He looked like he had aged years in a matter of hours. I noticed for the first time that some gray had grown in through his beard. Reaching out, my fingers grazed over his scruff. We weren't that many years apart in age. He was in his early thirties, but the gray was already starting to come through.

"I like this gray," I whispered.

He leaned his forehead against mine, grabbed my hand, and held it tight between us. "I know we have a lot to work through but I'm hoping, I'm praying we can get through this."

"Just hold me, Lucas. Please." I didn't want to talk about everything else at the moment. I moved to the chair beside him and leaned against him.

"Rest, Lily Pad," he murmured in my ear and wrapped his arm around my waist. "I got you. Everything else can wait."

I grabbed his hand, running my thumb over his bruised knuckles. "What happened?"

"I got into a fight with a wall or two," he murmured.

"You did?" I turned, looking up at him. "Who won?"

His gaze flicked down to mine. "I did. I always fucking win, Lily, and I'll spend the rest of my life trying to win you back." His hand cupped my thigh, holding me, squeezing me, giving me the strength I needed to move past this.

"I…" My breath caught in my throat, the words dying on my tongue. I didn't want to be apart from him but the image of Mel naked in his storage room, wouldn't leave my head. Add to the fact he confessed to her sucking his cock. Even if it were true and that he was stuck in his head, it still didn't make it right. It fucked with me. I could still see every inch of her. Her perfect curves. Her full tits. Her slender waist. Everything that I was not. "She's beautiful," I whispered. "I can still see her. And what you confessed…" I swallowed past the hard lump that had taken permanent residence in my throat.

"Fuck." Lucas turned me toward him. "I don't know how to explain that. I don't understand it myself but it's what happened. I'm just being honest with you. But I can tell you that you are beautiful, Lily. You have no reason to be insecure, but I get it. Alright? I do. How do you think I felt when I found out you slept with Killian? There's a lot of shit about him that you don't know but we can discuss it later." He shook his head. "What I'm saying is that I felt…you don't think I have my own insecure moments? I'm fucked up, Lily Pad." He kissed my forehead. "I have scars. I'm sure you've been with other men who are perfect."

"No." I latched on to his hoodie. "None of them compared to you. You are gorgeous, Lucas."

Lucas pinched my chin, tilting my head back to meet his intense stare. "And you are perfect. You don't need to compare yourself to Mel. At all. You're curvy in all the right places. I love the way you feel in my arms. I love the freckles that dance on your skin because the sun kissed your body. I love the deep green of your eyes that darken when you're pissed or turned on. Sometimes both. I love when you chew your bottom lip and it turns red to the point it looks like you're wearing lipstick. I'm sure most women would kill for that."

I laughed lightly.

"I love that tiny brown speckle in your right eye. It's so faint but I can see it. It's a perfect flaw."

"You can see it?" I asked, surprised that he would even notice such a thing.

"I can." He kissed my nose. "I also love how strong you are when I know you struggle. We all struggle. But no matter how hard you have it, you put others before you. You put me before you and I can never repay you for that."

Tears pricked my eyes, my nose burning. "I…"

"I love you, Lily. I will do whatever I can to make this up to you. You have questions and I'll answer them as best I can. We will talk about this, but we need to make sure your grandma is okay first. That's the most important thing right now."

I nodded, throwing my arms around his thick neck. God, I loved him. He pissed me off and drove me crazy, but I loved him. I loved him with every fiber of my very being. I just prayed that our love was enough.

(Lucas)

I wasn't sure if Lily and I were good. I had never been in a relationship before, so I wasn't sure what the signs were. Women were confusing all on their own and add my own fuck up to the mix and I had no idea what the hell was going on.

The doctor came and told Lily that she could see her grandmother. Even though the heart attack had been a mild one, with her age, they wanted to keep her in the hospital under observation for a few days. Much to her dismay.

"Why the hell do I need to stay here? I feel fine."

"Grandma, you know why you have to stay here." Lily patted her grandmother's hand. "I promise that you'll be out soon, but you need to rest and take it easy."

"I play Bridge." Ethel scoffed. "What's easier than that?"

"Is that all you play?" I asked, raising an eyebrow.

Both ladies looked my way.

"I just mean…" I shrugged. "You know."

Ethel laughed. "You can't get the words out? Come on. I've heard you two."

"Grandma." Lily gasped, her cheeks reddening.

A laugh boomed through me. "I have no idea what you're talking about."

"Right. Just because I'm old, doesn't mean shit, Lucas." She pointed at me. "I like sex too there, sweetheart."

"Oh God." Lily covered her face. "I can't believe you two are having this conversation."

I chuckled. "I guess that means you need to take it easy."

"Well, apparently this old ticker can't handle it. This sucks." Ethel sighed. "This sucks a lot."

"Okay, well this got really weird." Lily stood from the bed. "We should go so you can rest."

"Fine." Ethel sat forward. "But I need to know something first." She patted the spot in front of her. "Sit. Both of you."

We did as we were told with Lily on one side and me on the other. Ethel grabbed our hands, bringing them together and held them.

"You two love each other. I see it. God, I can feel it. I know something has happened. I don't need to know what." She looked pointedly at me. "I'm not going to threaten you but when it comes to my granddaughter, she's my life. She's the only family I have left. Whatever happened, I know together, you can work through it." She looked at Lily then.

"I proposed to her," I blurted.

Ethel's gaze popped back to mine.

"But it wasn't the right time," I added.

"You'll know when it is," Ethel said. "Just please don't give up on each other. Lucas, I know you had a hard childhood. I'm not stupid. I can sense it. And while both of you have your own struggles, don't think you have to deal with them by yourselves. You have each other. You have me. That love you have is hard to find, so please don't give up."

My chest tightened.

Lily sniffed, wiping under her eyes. "I love you, Grandma."

"I love you too. Now give this old woman a hug and leave so I can flirt with the hot doctors and get some sleep." She waggled her eyebrows.

Lily giggled and gave her a hug.

"I want a hug from you too, big guy." Ethel held her arms out.

My face burned but I did as I was told.

She gave me a hard squeeze which was strong coming from someone so small. "She loves you. Treat her right and make up for what happened and everything else will fall into place."

I swallowed hard, leaning back.

"Promise me." She cupped my face.

I nodded. "I promise."

(Lily)

"I'm happy to know that she still has her humor," I told Lucas as we walked out of the hospital.

"Me too." He smiled down at me.

"How did you get here?" I asked him, once we stepped out into the cool evening air.

"Toby drove me." Lucas pulled his cell from his pocket. "I'll call a taxi."

A few minutes later, one pulled up in front of us. I gave the driver the address to my place. "You're coming over, right?"

Lucas grabbed my hand. "If you want me to."

I nodded. "Yes, please."

A breath left him, his shoulders relaxing like he had been waiting for me to say those words his whole life.

I held his hand in mine. No words passed between us, but they didn't need to. I wanted to work through everything. I loved

Lucas and while I didn't understand what happened, I was willing to try. For us.

When we pulled up to my house, Lucas paid the driver and we left the car.

We walked hand in hand up to the house when a throat cleared, stopping us in our tracks.

"Fuck," Lucas grumbled.

I slowly turned around, finding Killian coming toward us.

"Well, don't you two look cozy." Killian rubbed the thick scruff on his jaw, his dark eyes flicking between us. "Clearly, you've made up."

"That's none of your fucking business," Lucas threw at him. "How the hell did you get out? Shephard played that little recording for me. Did you pay someone off?"

Killian grinned.

Lucas stepped in front of me. "Why are you doing this?"

"Because I want to watch you break." Killian's face turned red. "I want you to fucking suffer."

"You've lost your fucking mind," Lucas threw at him, his back rigid. "Is that what happened? Were you fucked stupid?"

My heart jumped. "Lucas?"

Killian took a step toward him. "What the hell is that supposed to mean?"

"I know who you are," Lucas told him. "I didn't recognize you at first, Ronny. And I was too damn distracted to do any research on you. You're lucky there. Because if I would have, I'd have found out who you were weeks ago. And then you wouldn't have been able to use Mel."

"I would have found a way and the fucking name is Killian," he snapped, shoving Lucas into me.

I stumbled back a step, grabbing onto Lucas's hoodie.

"You good, Lily Pad?" he asked, not taking his gaze from Killian's.

"Yes." But it didn't mean that I wasn't concerned as to what was about to happen.

"Good." He reached behind him.

I grabbed his hand.

"What do you want, Ronny?"

"Stop calling me that," Killian boomed.

"But it's your name. Or it was. Does Lily know who you are? No. Probably not. Seeing as I haven't had a chance to tell her. So how about we educate her now?" Lucas peered down at me over his shoulder. "Ronald Olle. You know him as Killian Hayes. He's my adopted brother."

My eyes widened.

"Killian, Ronny, whatever the fuck you want to call him, has an issue with me because Mel wanted me and not him. And now you want me."

"And not him," I added.

"He's feeling left out, it seems." Lucas glanced back at Killian whose face was beet red. "Isn't that right?"

"You just wouldn't die. No matter how much I tried getting you in fucking trouble, you took it. You took it all. Whatever they had to give you. You just wouldn't fucking die." Killian's chest rose and fell with ragged breaths. "I hate you. I hate you for coming into our home. It was me. I was the damn star. And then you showed up."

"You're proud of that fact, Killian? We were raped, abused, tortured. We were in fucking movies and you're jealous of me? This isn't about whose dick is bigger. It was about life and fucking death. But I begged to die. I begged repeatedly but they got off on that shit. You know that." Lucas released my hand, taking a step toward Killian. "I tried protecting you. I tried protecting all of you. I didn't want any of that shit to happen."

"You took her from me," Killian yelled, charging for Lucas. "You took her and made her fall in love with you. Mel was mine. She was always mine." He pulled his arm back, slamming his fist against Lucas's face.

I gasped.

Lucas stood stock still, a dark laugh escaping him. "Hit me again, fucker. I never asked for that shit. I never asked for Mel to fall in love with me. I don't want her. You can do whatever you please with that woman. I'm done with that shit."

Although Lucas told Killian that he was done, it only made Killian swing another blow at him. But this time, Lucas caught his fist and forced him to the ground.

Doors slammed shut. Two cops came toward us, their guns drawn.

"Lucas." I rushed to him. "The cops are coming. Lucas, stop."

He released Killian. "You're dead to me."

"Like I give a fuck, asshole." Killian rose to his feet, his dark eyes glaring into me. "I should have fucking killed you in that alley."

My stomach dropped to the ground beneath me.

A growl sounded beside me.

"What have I ever done to you?" I demanded, shoving Killian back. "You're a monster."

"No!" He pointed at Lucas. "He's the monster and you're fucking in love with him. How does that feel, Lily? How does it feel being in love with something that lurks in the fucking shadows? I've seen the shit he did. The kids he forced himself on."

"No." I shoved him again. "He did it to survive. Stop this. Please. You two were in hell together. You should be there for each other."

"Fucking please." Killian turned around and began walking away. "Arrest them."

"What? You can't do this!" I screamed when the two cops charged for Lucas. "Killian. Stop this!"

"Shephard, we need you," I heard Lucas say.

"Killian." But he ignored me and continued walking to his SUV.

"You're not even a fucking Fed anymore you bastard," Lucas yelled. "Do you have them on your payroll?"

Killian glanced at us over his shoulder, a wicked grin spreading on his face. "Keep talking. Your sentence is getting longer by the second."

"Stop!" I ran to him, beating my hands against his chest. "Please stop this."

Killian grabbed my wrists, kicking my feet out from under me and dropped me onto the ground.

I landed hard, the air leaving my lungs on a sharp gasp.

"Let her go!" I heard Lucas bellow.

I couldn't see him. All I could focus on was the cold, soulless eyes staring down at me.

"I should have gotten my fill of you in that alley. I bet you're nice and tight too. I could have broken you in for him. Maybe fuck this sweet little ass too." Killian leaned down to my ear. "I should have ripped you apart and left you for the rats to feast on."

My blood burned through me. Struggling beneath him, I kicked and shoved. I was able to get one hand free and before I thought twice about it, my fist landed against his cheek. Agony screamed up my arm, but I didn't care. I did it again. And again, before he grabbed my wrist.

"Hit me again, Lily. I like it rough." Killian pushed off of me, fisted my hair, and pulled me to my knees.

I screamed as hair ripped free from my head.

"Let her fucking go," Lucas growled.

I saw him then. He was on his knees, his hands handcuffed behind his back.

"Take them." Killian kicked me in the back, shoving me forward.

I cried out.

"They're not worth it. Especially this fucking whore."

One of the cops came toward me.

Before I could run, he grabbed my hands. The sound of a handcuff shackling around my wrists forced tears to my eyes. He tightened them to the point they pinched the skin.

"Get up," the other cop demanded, pushing Lucas.

Lucas stood, coming toward me. "Don't say anything," he whispered. "I called Shephard. He'll help us. But if they ask questions, get a lawyer, baby. Please get a lawyer."

"I will." I leaned forward and placed a quick kiss on his mouth before I was pulled back and shoved into the back seat of the cop car.

Lucas was pushed in beside me, the door slammed shut behind him. "Look at me."

I turned my head toward him.

"You're strong," he murmured. "You hear me?"

I nodded, my heart pounding in my ears.

He leaned his forehead against mine. "Don't say anything."

I nodded again.

The cops sat in the front. We headed to the police station in silence. This wasn't right. This wasn't right at fucking all.

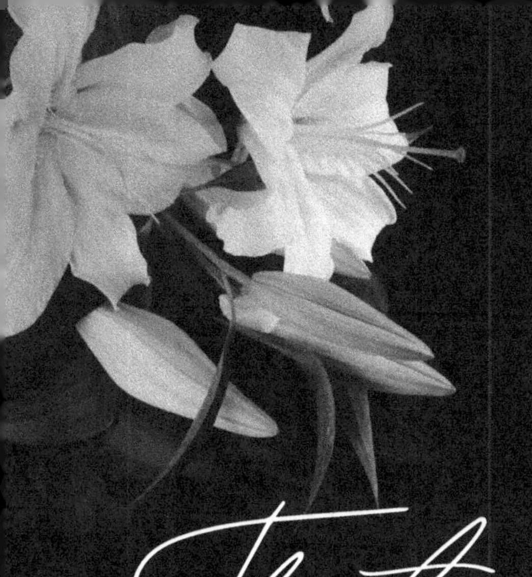

Thirty-Three

LUCAS

AFTER WHAT FELT LIKE years, Lily and I were finally let go. Thanks to Shephard. When I headed outside, I found Lily and him talking quietly between themselves.

She caught my gaze, holding out her arms.

I rushed to her, picking her up and holding her so fucking tight against me. I should have been concerned about breaking her. But I wasn't because I knew that she was strong. She was so damn strong.

"I'm fine," she whispered, wrapping her arms around me. "I'm fine, Lucas."

I placed her gently back on her feet, cupping her face. "Tell me everything," I said to Shephard, keeping my gaze locked on Lily's.

"The cops who arrested you are rookies. They were on break when Killian called them. They didn't know that there was a search warrant out for him. But I was able to have your names cleared and he will be charged."

I glanced up at Shephard then, tugging Lily into my side. "And?"

"I have a tail out on Mel but haven't heard anything yet. So just be careful. Please for the love of God, be careful." He shook his head. "You would think after what you guys have been through, you would stick together."

I grunted. "You would think."

"Let me drive you home." Shephard started walking away.

Lily and I followed.

"Lucas?" Lily said softly.

"Yeah?"

"You okay?" she asked gently.

"Yup." But I wasn't. My body was vibrating. Although neither of us were charged with anything, the fact that Killian had touched her in the first place made me crave his death. My hands clenched into fists. My skin rippled over my bones. My blood was burning through me. I needed a release.

"Shephard?" Lily stopped walking. "I think we should walk home. Lucas needs to burn off some of that rage."

Shephard looked between us two. "Do you want me to follow?"

"No," she answered for us. "But thank you. Thank you for everything." She took a step forward, but I wouldn't let go of her hand. She raised an eyebrow. "Lucas."

"Not letting you go, baby," I ground out. "Not letting you go ever again."

Her breath caught. "Fine." She motioned for Shephard to come toward her.

He did.

I growled.

"Seriously." He chuckled. "I'm not stupid enough to want your girl."

Lily laughed lightly, giving him a one-armed hug. "Thank you for everything. Keep your phone close by. Just in case. But I'm sure we'll be fine."

He nodded. "You good?" he asked me.

"Yup." But I wasn't. Not one fucking bit.

(Lily)

"Look at me." I placed my hands against Lucas's chest. "Hey."

His good eye met mine, his jaw clenching. He tightened his hold on my wrist, running his thumb back and forth over my pulse point.

"We're fine," I reassured him. "I'm fine. I promise."

"He touched you, Lily. That's all I can fucking see. And I'm sure he said vile things to you as well." Lucas wrapped his other arm around my shoulders. "This isn't about me being possessive of you. This is about him threatening your life."

"I know," I whispered, cupping his nape. "But he's gone. I'm fine, baby. I am."

"Fuck." Lucas shivered, leaning his forehead against mine and letting out a slow breath. "I'm losing my shit over here."

"I know that too." I leaned my head back and tapped my mouth.

"I can't, Lily Pad." He tightened his hold on my hand and led us away from the police station, to my grandmother's place.

"You're going to kiss me." I wrapped my hand around his arm. "And I'm going to kiss you back, Lucas. And then we'll talk. We'll have peanut butter and jelly sandwiches and lots of coffee." I tugged his arm when he didn't say anything. "But you will kiss me."

"Fuck, Lily. Of course I'll kiss you but I can't kiss you right now because I'm losing my control. I can't kiss you knowing his hands were on you because I want to kiss you and make you forget that you ever fucked him in the first place. If it wasn't against the law, I'd throw you on the ground and fuck you here until there was nothing left. And then I would expect you to do the same to me. We would own each other and make both of us forget."

I shivered at the thought. "I thought you said it wasn't about you being possessive?"

Lucas grunted. "I lied."

"Alright, Lucas. Take me home so we can wash the police station off of us." And talk. God, did we ever need to talk.

We walked the rest of the way home in silence. It was unnerving in a way. As much as I knew that the sex right now would be explosive, it wouldn't help either of us. So I had to rein in on the control that Lucas was losing.

When we reached my place, I unlocked the door and entered the house.

The door slammed shut behind me.

I jumped, spinning on Lucas.

"Sorry." He blew out a slow breath, rubbing a hand over his head. "I just need a moment."

"Come with me." I held out my hand.

He took it, letting me lead him down the hall and to my bedroom.

"We're going to have a shower." I lifted my hand when he went to speak. "But we're not having sex. Not this second anyway."

His brows narrowed.

"Trust me, as much as I would love it and know that we both need it, we need to talk."

He frowned. "I know but I need you."

"We need to talk," I insisted, heading into the bathroom.

"I can't have a shower with you and not..."

"You can touch me and not fuck me, Lucas." I turned at the same time he crashed into me.

"I need you," he whispered, his rough voice sliding over every inch of me.

"I know," I murmured. "But you need this more. Trust me. Right now, I need…" I stared up at him. "We need this. We need the intimacy of just showering together."

"I don't…" He shivered, his big body shaking. "You're holding back because of Mel. Aren't you?"

"I…" Was I? "No. Not exactly. I need to know that it's just you and me. I need to know that I can trust you again. Please prove to me that I can trust you, Lucas."

He nodded, placing a soft peck on my nose. "I'll give this to you right now, Lily Pad. But come tonight, you say the word and your submission is mine."

My stomach tumbled. Stepping away from him, I stripped.

Lucas's breath caught in his throat, but he took off his clothes as well.

We showered in silence, the evidence of our day washing down the drain. When we were done, Lucas wrapped me in a large towel and lifted me onto the counter. He wrapped a towel around his hips and left the bathroom. He came back a moment later with two bags of ice.

I grabbed one from him. I reached out, taking off his eye patch and pressed the ice pack against his upper cheek.

He grabbed my hand and placed his against my knuckles, stepping between my knees.

I shivered at the cool touch even though having him this close sent a wave of heat rushing through me.

"How bad does it hurt?" he asked, running his thumbs over my knuckles.

I shrugged, flexing my hand. "It's not broken. Just tender."

He nodded. "You did well, Lily Pad. I wasn't expecting you to actually hit him."

"He attacked me. God, after all this time, I had actually hoped it wasn't him. I thought maybe he just had issues. But to actually attack me?" I grimaced, my stomach twisting.

"He's a bastard, Lily."

"I'm sure Killian's face hurts more though." One could hope.

Lucas's face broke out into a grin. "Oh yeah. You got a good hit in. I still can't believe the fucker threw us in jail."

"Same." I removed the pack from his eye. The spot was bruised but it was the only hit Killian could get in before Lucas almost pummeled him into the ground. "If I wouldn't have stopped you, would you have taken it further?"

"You mean, would I have killed him?" Lucas placed the pack on the counter and wrapped his arms around my waist. "Probably, Lily."

I swallowed hard. "Are we…is this…" My breath hitched.

"What are you asking me?" Lucas stared down at me.

I cupped his beautiful scarred face.

"Lily." He pushed his cheek into my palm. "I need to know."

"Ask me," I whispered.

"Are we done? I don't want to be, but I understand. As much as it will hurt, I can't force you to stay with me." He lifted me in his arms, carrying me out of the bathroom. He placed me on my feet before pulling back the covers. "It's been a long night," he said without waiting for me to answer.

Were we done?

I nodded, slipping out of the towel. My cheeks burned when I remembered what I had walked in on. When I told him that I was done. When I realized that I shouldn't be standing naked in front of him, but it was out of habit. "I'm sorry." I crouched to pick up the towel when a gentle but firm hand cupped my own.

"We just had a shower together," he reminded me.

"I know. I just…this feels…"

"It's a habit. Isn't it? Being naked in front of me? Letting me touch you. Hold you. Make love to you. It's all a habit."

I looked up at him and slowly nodded.

"I'm not going to press for anything, Lily. I just want to hold you. That's all. Please let me hold you."

I let him pull me to my feet. I let him cup my face and place a soft peck on my mouth. I pushed back the images of what I had walked in on. I pushed back the idea that it looked like he and Mel had sex even though he was supposed to be with me. They didn't. They didn't have sex. It was what she wanted me to think.

But she did touch him. I pushed back the bile that had suddenly risen to my throat and just felt Lucas's lips against mine.

I felt. I cherished. I owned.

I would conquer this. Whatever this was. Lucas was mine. He had to be. I couldn't have it any other way.

"You said you would explain," I said softly, my voice cracking. "When I walked in on…I wanted to throw up. I've been insecure since she showed up and seeing her with you, naked…" I shook my head. "I've never felt self-conscious of my curves until her."

"Your curves are fucking perfect," Lucas growled. "Don't think they aren't because they are."

"Thank you for saying that but it still doesn't make me feel better."

"I need to explain something to you." He pulled me to the bed, wrapping the blankets around me, shielding my nudity from him. He rubbed his nape, blowing out a slow breath. "I remembered shit from my past. I don't understand the psychology behind it, but my brain blocked some of it out. I've had random blackouts over the years. They don't happen often but when they do, things happen, and I don't remember. I think that might have been why I forgot to do research on Killian." He scowled. "Anyway, my adoptive mom was her real mom."

"You told me that. I should have heard you out. I should have…"

"Don't. Don't blame yourself." He grabbed my hands, holding them tightly in his. "This is all on me. I'm going to be honest with you. You may not like everything I have to say." He brought my hands up to his mouth. "But I need to get this out. I need you to know all of me. Every dirty fucked up detail."

I inhaled a sharp breath. "Tell me."

(Lucas)

"I don't remember any good part of my childhood. From the moment I was born to the moment I escaped, my childhood was fucked up." Lily placed her hand on my forearm. I pulled strength from that touch. "I remember now that my adoptive parents forced me to fuck Mel. She acted like she didn't want it, but I quickly realized that she did. It was fucked up. It was like some sick porn film. I raped her repeatedly. But I wasn't the only one. Other guys my age. Some younger. Some older. Even other girls. They were forced to sodomize her, each other." My stomach twisted. "Our adoptive parents made me watch them fuck each other. Bobby, my adoptive father, forced me to fuck his wife. I was used the most because I had a…my…"

"I understand," Lily said softly.

"I never asked to be this size," I told her. "But I was used the most. Fucked the most. Because I'm big. I…" Memories twisted together. Evil, depraved, vile nightmares that threatened to ruin me. To bring me back to the past.

"We don't have to continue." Lily squeezed my hands.

"No." I blew out a slow breath, turning my body toward her. "I need to get this out. I need you to understand. Hell, I don't even understand but I need to explain what I can, to you. I should have known something was off. She used to wear this rose perfume. It was the only thing I could smell as a kid, it was so strong. It was used against me to the point that it's now a trigger. So when we went to the hotel, I could smell it. I should have known, Lily."

"Roses are popular." She cupped my cheek. "How could you have known?"

"She said she wore it because it reminded her of our time together." I picked at a fuzz on the blanket, my gaze not meeting hers.

"When she showed up at my shop the other night, she said things that brought back horrible memories," I continued. "She smelled like that damn rose perfume and it triggered something to the point I couldn't differentiate present from my past. But something reminded me of you. I heard your name. I don't know how. But your name slid into my mind. And it made me snap out of it. But she had already…she was…fuck, she was sucking me off. I'll never forgive myself for letting it get to that point. I was naïve to think that she could just talk and nothing else would happen." I cupped Lily's face. "I'm sorry. I'm so fucking sorry for breaking your heart. I know it doesn't help but it didn't mean anything. She…"

"Sexually molested you," Lily added.

"Yeah, I guess you could call it that." I leaned my head back against the headboard. "There was a point in my life where I considered becoming celibate. I even considered becoming a man of the Church. I know it doesn't make sense, but I thought maybe if I was a man of the cloth, I wouldn't be tempted to have sex no matter how much I didn't enjoy it as a kid."

"I get that."

"You do?" I asked her.

She nodded. "It's almost like if you were to become a priest or whatever you decided, other people would be less likely to hit on you and things like that as well. They would have more respect for you."

"I know that's not always the case but…yeah."

She gave me a soft smile. "Thank you for telling me."

"Lily? I'm losing my shit over here." I needed to know. "Are you leaving me?" My voice cracked. I hated how desperate I sounded.

"No, Lucas." She threw herself in my arms. "I'm not going anywhere. I still don't understand this mental thing, but I think you have some form of PTSD."

I looked away.

"Hey." She cupped my face, forcing me to look up at her. "It's nothing to be ashamed of. You went through a lot, Lucas. You survived more than most. I may not understand it, but I believe you. I'm sorry for freaking out and not hearing what you had to say."

"No." I leaned my head against her chest. "Don't. Don't you dare fucking apologize. You had every right to freak out. It sounds crazy. I know it does. But that's what happened."

Lily leaned back. "I believe you."

I breathed a heavy sigh of relief. "Thank fucking God."

Later that night, I was holding Lily against me when I clued in that we were still naked. Very naked. My dick twitched beneath her ass. All of the feelings from the past few weeks came rushing back. They were hard. Fast. And they hit me right in the chest. "Lily." I placed a soft peck on her neck. "I need you."

"Lucas," she whispered.

"I need your taste on my tongue." My body vibrated, my hold on her tightening. "Please, Lily. Let me taste you."

She started rocking against me.

"Fuck." I shivered. "Don't tease me." I flipped us so she was laying on the bed beneath me. "Please, baby." I placed a soft peck on the corner of her mouth. "Let me please this sweet little body. Let me show you how much I've missed your creamy cunt on my tongue. I need you. Let me make it up to you. Let me savor you." My voice became lower, my skin rippling over my bones. I had never wanted her so damn much.

Lily cupped my face. "You can wait."

"I don't want to wait." I kissed her palm and slid down the length of her body before sinking my teeth into her hip. "I want to please you. I want to make you explode on my tongue. I want to drink up your sweet sugar. Please. Fuck. I'm begging here."

Her cheeks reddened, her pupils dilating. She was fucking enjoying this. Lifting her hips, she taunted and teased. "How bad do you want it?"

I groaned, the sweetness of her desire wafting into my nose. I glanced down at her shaved pussy. Her clit was peeking through the folds of her center, a drop of cream dripping from her body. "As bad as you, clearly."

She laughed, her cheeks reddening even more. "I love you."

"Fuck, baby," I said, my voice gruff. "I love you too." I kissed her bent knee, trailing my lips down her inner thigh. "I love you so damn much. Everything about you. Everything that makes up you. My sweet girl. My Lily Pad."

"I'm yours," she panted.

A growl escaped me. "I need your pussy."

Her breath caught, her chest rising and falling. She ran a hand over my head, through my hair, and when her fingers brushed the scar of my blind eye, she licked her lips.

"I'm losing my fucking mind," I snarled, giving her inner thigh a sharp bite.

She yelped, her eyes blazing with a heat I had never seen from her before. "Do it. Now."

(Lily)

He covered my pussy in a rough move. It was so hard, I could feel him reaching for my soul. I cried out, latching on to his hair and pulled him forward. I was greedy for him. Although we had been together for quite a while, this was different.

Truths were revealed. Our emotions were raw and stripped. This wasn't us making love. No. This was us claiming each other.

He snarled, shook his head, and shoved his tongue deep inside me.

I whimpered, thrusting up and up.

Lucas groaned, his eyes rolling into the back of his head. He cupped my ass, lifting me and holding me in place.

"God, Lucas," I sobbed, a fast release snapping through me. But it didn't make him stop. I shook. I ached. I trembled. My inner thighs burned. My clit throbbed. It only seemed to make him eat me harder. "I…" A violent scream shattered from my lips as another release rolled through me.

He grunted his approval and flipped me onto my stomach, keeping his mouth on my center.

I pushed back against his face, gripping the blankets beneath me. "Please, Lucas. I can't…"

He released me with a wet smack, landing a hard blow against my ass. His mouth covered my clit, sucking it between his teeth.

A sob escaped me. "Fuck me, Lucas. Please, God, fuck me."

But he didn't. His mouth moved over me. Sucking. Licking. Biting. He covered every inch until I was an aching mess for him.

Spreading my legs wider, I squeezed my eyes shut and waited when something warm and wet moved over the tight little spot between the cheeks of my ass. My eyes popped open, a soft gasp leaving me. His tongue stroked and licked, forcing that pleasure higher and higher. It pushed into me, licking a part that had never been touched by another person before.

"Fuck," I whispered, shaking against him.

Lucas groaned, growled, and snarled. The animalistic sounds leaving him only turned me on even more.

"Lucas," I cried out, a third orgasm trembling through me.

He finally released me, placing a soft peck on my tailbone.

"Please, fuck me," I whined, my body still shaking.

"Nah, baby. I just wanted to eat your pussy." His tongue slid back into that tight little rim. "And your ass."

I shivered. "Fuck me, Lucas. Please. I can't take it anymore."

"I thought we weren't having sex." He towered over me, resting one elbow on the mattress. He placed a soft peck on my shoulder and held my wrists in his other hand.

"Please," I whispered.

He pushed into me, reaching between us and lining his cock up with my soaked center. But much to my surprise, he ran it over the spot between the cheeks of my ass.

I shivered.

"Tell me no, Lily," he murmured, kissing the spot beneath my ear.

"Never," I whispered.

"That's my girl." He chuckled, pushing into me.

My eyes widened, my body heating. "More."

"Fuck, you're a dirty little thing." In a hard move, he thrust all of his cock into me.

I cried out, a sob wracking through me.

"Shhh…" He crooned. "Give it a second."

"I feel so full," I panted.

"My cock's in your ass, Lily." He pulled out and thrust forward. "Of course you feel full."

"God. Harder. Please." I pushed onto all fours and met him thrust for every delicious thrust.

We worked up a rhythm, the sounds of our pleasure erupting through the room.

"You're so damn tight," he groaned, digging his fingers into the cheeks of my ass.

"Lucas," I screamed, a fast release shattering through me.

He grunted, pushing me forward onto my stomach. Slamming his pelvis against my ass, he took everything he wanted and unleashed his powerful wrath on me. He was animalistic in the way he took control. Dominant in the way he forced my hand in the submission he craved.

"Fuck," he growled, sinking his teeth into the back of my neck. His hot breath washed over me. Running his hands up the sides of my body, he linked our hands, holding them above my head and against the mattress. "So good, baby. So fucking good." His cock swelled, spilling his seed deep into my body.

I sighed, taking every last drop and making it mine.

"You okay?" he asked, pulling free from my body.

My heart warmed at the concern in Lucas's voice. "I am." I rolled over onto my back and moved up the bed before leaning against the headboard. "I'm more than okay. I feel you. All through me. I've never felt so…"

"What?"

"Owned."

His cock jumped.

I held my arms out. "Lay with me."

"It's almost four in the morning." Lucas yawned. "Let me clean you up." He went to the bathroom and came back a moment later with a cloth in hand.

"I'm not tired but you can sleep." Truth was, I was wired. Beyond wired in fact.

Lucas knelt on the bed. "I'll hurt you."

"No, you won't. Come here."

"Let me clean you up first." He placed a soft peck on my forehead, dipping the cloth between my legs and brushing it over my properly used center. He dipped it lower.

I gasped, arching into him and spread my legs.

He chuckled. "Like that?"

"Oh yeah." I shivered.

All too soon, he pulled his hand away and disposed of the cloth in the laundry hamper.

"Now will you lay with me?" I asked, reaching my arms out for him again.

He crawled onto the bed and laid on his stomach, his head resting against my chest. I pulled the blankets up and over us, running my hands in soothing circles over his upper back. His breathing evened.

"I got you, Lucas," I whispered. "I'm not going anywhere."

"I love you," he murmured. He shifted, lifting his head and kissing the spot between my breasts. "I don't think I've ever been this relaxed in my life."

"Good." I grabbed the remote control and turned on the TV, flipping through channel after channel until I came across a cheesy romance movie.

Lucas didn't complain about the movie choice. He didn't complain that I wanted to cuddle and hold him against me. He took it and welcomed it with open arms. We still had things to work through, but I just hoped we were finally heading in the right direction.

Thirty-Four

Lily

THE NEXT MORNING, I was taking a shower when the bathroom door opened.

"Lily?"

"Yeah?" I peeked my head out, finding Lucas dressed.

"Shephard wants to meet up for coffee." Lucas cupped my chin and placed a soft peck on my mouth. "I'll see you later?"

"Of course." I smiled up at him.

"Good." He pushed me back, stepping into the shower with me.

"Lucas," I squealed, laughing. "You're going to get wet."

"That's the point." He covered my mouth again, slipping his tongue between my lips.

"You're also going to be late," I said, breathless.

Lucas only shrugged, gave me a wink, and motioned for me to turn around.

I did as I was told, and Lucas took what he wanted from me for the next half hour.

"Now you can go on with your day with my cum deep in your cunt." He placed a hard peck on my mouth.

"Sounds like a good plan to me," I told him.

He chuckled. "I shouldn't be long."

"I'm heading to the hospital to see my grandma," I said, going back to washing my hair. "Hopefully she can get out soon."

"Text me and if you're still there, I'll stop by or you can just come to my place."

"Okay." Could this be it? Could we be moving forward? Could we finally begin to be happy?

"I love you, Lily." He cupped my cheek. "Thank you for not giving up on me." He gave me a final kiss and left the shower.

I smiled to myself, shaking my head at the unexpected tryst. My body heated. Finishing up the shower, I dried myself off and got dressed.

Lucas had left finally. I just hoped Shephard could give him some more answers.

Grabbing a quick coffee for the road, I left the house and made the walk to the hospital. Luckily it was only a few miles away and the weather was nice enough, that I didn't need to take a taxi.

When I arrived, I signed myself in as a visitor at the front desk, and headed to my grandmother's room.

"Can I please go home today?" I heard her ask as I entered.

"We need you for one more night," Dr. Proulx told her. "But I'm thinking you should be able to go home tomorrow."

Grandma sighed, her eyes meeting mine. "Hello, dear."

"Hi, Grandma." I kissed her cheek and sat beside her. "Everything okay?"

"Oh yes. Dr. Proulx just told me that I get to spend another night here. Aren't I lucky?"

I laughed. "You'll be out of here in no time and back to playing Bridge."

She sighed. "Fine."

"I'll leave you two be," Dr. Proulx said, placing the stethoscope around her neck. "But please get your rest, Ethel. You can't go home if you don't."

"Fine," she repeated, crossing her arms under chest. "So how are you doing?" she asked me once the doctor left.

"Not too bad." I smiled for reassurance. Truth was, I was damn near ecstatic. The night before with Lucas had been wonderful. I could still feel him. Every time I moved, I felt him all through me. And we talked. Finally. We talked a lot.

"How are you and Lucas doing?"

My cheeks heated.

She laughed. "That good, huh?"

"Oh, Grandma." I grabbed her hand. "I love him. I love him so damn much. I know we've had our problems. Every relationship does but…" I sighed. "I think we're finally moving past it."

Her smile widened. "That's how I felt about my Stanley. Keep that love, Lily. Keep it, hold onto it, and cherish it forever. It doesn't come around often. Some aren't lucky enough to have it. You do. So keep it."

"Oh I will. There's been some…issues but I think we're moving in the right direction." Or I hoped we were anyway.

"No one ever said relationships were easy. I remember a time when your grandfather went out for coffee with an ex-girlfriend. He was being polite, and they had been friends first anyway, so I thought nothing of it." Grandma snorted. "Well were we wrong. Little did we know that she had a baby and she tried saying it was his."

My eyes widened. "Really?"

Grandma nodded. "But the math didn't add up, so we knew she was lying. Either way, it was stressful."

"I can imagine." My heart swelled, seeing the love in my grandma's eyes that she still had for him. Even though it had been quite a few years since he died, her love for him never dwindled.

"It just proves that you can work through anything. I like Lucas for you and even though he may have a broken past, I see how he looks at you. You are the only one that man looks at."

My cheeks heated. "You think so?"

"Oh, Lily." Grandma patted my hand. "I think everyone sees it."

My face broke out into a grin. "He's supposed to be meeting us here. He had to catch up with an old friend." I didn't go into details. Grandma didn't need added stress. We continued talking about my grandpa and Lucas and how much we loved the men that had come into our lives when we needed them most.

She had been married to my grandpa for years. I wanted that. I wanted it with Lucas. One day. It was all I could ever ask for.

(Lucas)

"Tell me why we're meeting," I said, taking a sip of my coffee.

"Always right to the point." Shephard sat back in his chair, drinking from his own mug. His piercing gray eyes met mine. They were knowing and calculating, but never filled with judgment. It was one of the things I respected about him.

I shrugged. "I have a girl waiting for me."

"Always about the women." He smirked. "I like her."

"So do I. Not that I need your approval or anything," I threw back at him.

He chuckled. "Listen," he said, the humor no longer there. "I wanted to give you an update. Killian will be arraigned on several charges this morning. The judge is not a fan of former officers breaking the law they promised to uphold. He will likely be put away for a long time. And last night's incident, will not be on yours or Lily's records. I know I told you that part already, but I wanted to let you know that I confirmed, and it won't be."

"Good." I blew out a breath of relief. "Lily's a good girl. She doesn't need that black mark on her record because of some jealous fucker."

"True. You don't need that shit on your record either though."

I grunted. "I don't care about my record. I already have one, but I've been a good boy. I've kept my nose clean."

"Either way, it's not on your record."

"Is that all you wanted this meeting for?" I asked, raising an eyebrow and placing my mug on the table between us. We met up at a small café in the nicer part of the city. It wasn't an area I frequented often but the onlookers who stared as they walked past us, made me reconsider visiting more often. Just for shits and giggles.

"Lucas."

The hackles on the back of my neck rose. "What do you want, Mel?" I demanded as she came toward our table.

"I need to talk to you." Her gaze flicked between Shephard and I. "Alone."

"Pull up a chair," Shephard told her.

I shifted in my seat. "I don't think that's a good idea."

Mel grabbed a chair from the table nearest us and pulled it between Shephard and I before sitting down. She fluffed her wavy hair, pursing her full red lips. Her deep blue eyes met mine. "You hurt me."

Guilt resonated on my shoulders, sitting heavy on my body even though she didn't deserve it. I could be an asshole, but this wasn't me. It wasn't how I was wired. "I didn't mean to hurt you," I said gently. "But you forced yourself on me," I said even though we weren't alone. I didn't give a shit anymore who knew my history. "You also almost cost me Lily." I lifted my hand as she went to speak. "No, you're going to listen to me. You need to move on. We haven't seen each other in a few years and then we randomly meet at a hotel."

"Life—"

"Don't you fucking say it was fate because it was not. I love Lily. She's the only one I want. I also found out that Killian is actually Ronny. Did you know about that?" I knew she did, but I had to ask anyway.

Mel looked away.

"Of course you did," I said, playing dumb. "Look, both of us were raised in a fucked-up situation. That wasn't either of our faults. And there was a time where I cared for you. But that time has come and gone. I love Lily. I'm going to spend the rest of my life with her. I'm sorry if you can't get over that but there's nothing more I can do."

Mel met my stare that time, her chin wobbling. Her eyes welled. "Does she know you like I know you?"

My jaw clenched, my teeth grinding to the point a sharp pain sliced up my cheeks. "Doesn't matter how she knows me. You knew me at a different time, but she knows me now. This is the most important time because I'm stronger than what I was. I'm not him. I'm not that boy you fell in love with."

Mel nodded once and stood.

"Stop by the station later." Shephard reached into the inner pocket of his jacket and pulled out a business card. He handed it to her. "I have some questions."

She looked between us both, took the card and walked away.

I frowned, watching her leave.

"Well…that was odd," Shephard mumbled.

"Yeah." I couldn't help but wonder what the point of that conversation was or what Mel got out of it. I was done. With her. With that life before Lily.

"Do you think she'll be back?" Shephard asked, pulling me from my thoughts.

"I don't know." But I had a feeling that it wasn't the last time I would see Mel.

(Lily)

After grabbing a coffee, I got distracted heading back to my grandma's room. I somehow ended up on the main floor, in the emergency entrance section. The signs in this place really needed to be laid out better.

A commotion sounded, pulling me from my thoughts.

"Multiple GSWs," an EMT stated, rushing a man lying on a stretcher toward me. "Patient is Donny Shephard. Aged thirty-eight. Gunshot wound to the stomach."

My heart jumped, my skin breaking out into a cold sweat. "No." I stepped forward. "Shephard."

They rushed the stretcher past me.

"Excuse me." I stopped a nurse. "Is he going to be okay?"

"I don't know, ma'am." The young nurse followed the stretcher behind a set of double doors, taking all of the air in my lungs with them.

Lucas was with Shephard.

I pulled my phone out of my back pocket and dialed him but of course, it went right to voicemail. "Hey, Lucas. Oh God. I'm at the hospital, Shephard was wheeled in on a stretcher. He was shot. Please call me."

I hung up and tried him again, but it kept going to voicemail. I sent him multiple text messages but again, no response.

"Fuck."

That voice. I slowly turned around, a sob escaping me.

Lucas was holding his side, blood seeping between his fingers.

"Oh God, Lucas." I ran to him. "What happened?"

He fell against me. "Mel," he croaked. "She shot…shit…" He wheezed.

"Doctor!" I screamed. "I need a doctor!" We fell to the ground with my hands pressed into his wound.

"Lily," he whispered, his face ashen. "I don't remember her shooting me," he said through clenched teeth. "I was helping Shephard. Fuck, Shephard."

"He was brought it on a stretcher," I reassured Lucas. "He'll be fine. Both of you will be fine."

"Lily." His gaze met mine, forcing my stomach to sink to the ground beneath me. He was scared. It was something I never thought I'd see in him.

"No." I cupped his nape with my free hand, leaning my forehead against his. "Fight for me. Fight, Lucas. You are not giving up." I lifted my hand, the blood rushing out faster than before. A tremor of fear sliced down my spine.

"It's bad, baby," he rasped. "It's really fucking bad."

I nodded, tears streaming down my face. I couldn't say anything else. I couldn't do anything. While Lucas was put on the stretcher, he reached out to me.

"I'm here," I sobbed, holding his hand. "You have to go. They'll fix you. You better come back to me, Lucas. I'm not leaving here without you."

"Fucking right," he bit out through clenched teeth.

"We have to take him," a tall man dressed in green scrubs said.

I nodded, letting go of Lucas.

"Lily!" he yelled. "Lily!"

I fell to my knees as the sounds of Lucas yelling my name pierced through me.

Please God, don't take him from me. Don't take him after everything we had been through. I couldn't lose him. I refused. Not when we were finally making it past all of the shit life had thrown at us. We were strong. He was strong.

Sobs wracked through my body.

"Come back to me," I pleaded. "Please come back to me."

"LILY?"

My head popped up at the sound of my name.

The tall doctor from before smiled down at me. He was young but his dark eyes showed years of dealing with the added stress of the medical field. "Lucas is awake and he's asking for you."

"Oh, thank God." I jumped to my feet, following the doctor out of the waiting room and down a long hall. "Are you sure he's not actually demanding it?"

The doctor chuckled. "You know him well."

"Yeah." My face burned.

"Let's first get you cleaned up." He nodded toward my hands.

I looked down, finding them coated with Lucas's blood. "Oh. I forgot about…"

"It's okay." The doctor stopped in front of a bathroom.

I entered and washed my hands.

"How's he doing?" I asked when I finished.

"He was shot in the side, but the bullet missed vital organs." The doctor led the way down the hall. "He's lost a lot of blood and he'll be here for a few days under observation. But he'll be fine. He's very lucky."

"Oh good." A weight lifted off of my shoulders. "That's really good. But…uh…have you given him any pain meds?"

The doctor stopped, his brows narrowing. "Yes."

"Okay. He just can't have any more than what you've already given him. So, the nurses have to monitor it." It was an uncomfortable subject, but Lucas had been doing well, I didn't want him to have a relapse.

"I understand." He continued walking with me following beside him. "How many years clean?"

"Almost eight." I breathed a sigh of relief that the doctor didn't judge. Battling any form of addiction was hard on our own. Add judgment from others to it and it made it worse.

"That's wonderful. Oh, forgive my manners. I'm Doctor Thompson." The young man stuck out his hand.

"Don't worry about it." I returned the handshake. "I'm sure my boyfriend is giving you a hell of a time as it is."

"He's keeping the nurses on their toes," he said, stopping in front of a door.

"Let me see my girlfriend," Lucas demanded from inside the room.

"Doctor Thompson is going to get her," a woman said.

"Well he needs to get her faster," Lucas shouted.

"Lucas, will you stop trying to pull out your IV. You just woke up. Please just relax."

"I guess I should put him out of his misery," I said, entering the room.

"See?" The nurse rushed to me and pulled me along with her. "She's right here. Please tell me you're his girlfriend," she muttered.

"Yes." My heart stuttered. "I am."

"Thank God. I need a smoke." She rushed out of the room.

"I'll give you two a moment." Doctor Thompson followed the nurse out of the room.

"Lily."

I shivered at the barked command and met Lucas's gaze.

"Come here."

"Ask me nicely," I said, although my voice didn't come out as sure as I would have liked it.

"Woman, get the fuck in my arms." He lifted them for added effect. "Now."

As much as I wanted to fight him just for fun, I needed to feel him instead, so I did as I was told and ran to him.

Much to my surprise, he charged out of the bed and captured me.

"Lucas," I cried, the beeping of the machines going off. "What are you—"

"Shut up." He covered my mouth in a hard kiss, picking me up off my feet.

All too soon the kiss ended but the beeping did not. "Put me down. You just had surgery. You need to rest."

"I need to go home. With you." He held me against him. You would think that I was the one who just gotten shot with how he was keeping me close.

"Lucas." I struggled out of his hold. "Please get back in bed."

"Not letting you go, Lily." He stared down at me. For someone who just had surgery, he looked good. Really good.

I cleared my throat, pushing him back. "You don't have to let me go. You just need to get back into bed, so you don't make these nurses want to retire early."

He grunted, sitting on the bed but keeping his hand locked firm with mine. He pinched the bridge of his nose. "I shouldn't have done that."

I sighed, kissing him softly on the cheek. "No, you shouldn't have."

Two nurses took that moment to enter. They stopped when their gaze landed on us.

"What happened?" the one nurse asked, silencing the machines.

"You ripped out your IV," the other added.

"You took too long to bring me my girl." Lucas shrugged like it was no big deal.

I rolled my eyes, sitting on the edge of the bed beside him, knowing there was no point in trying to argue.

The nurses administered the IV again and cleaned up the cut where he ripped the other one out.

"Now please stay in bed," the younger of the two nurses said. "Or I will strap you to it."

Lucas grunted. "Sorry. The only one strapping me to the bed, is my girl."

"Ignore him," I told the poor nurses. "He's grumpy when he first wakes up."

"I'm Marianne," the older nurse with graying hair told me. "If you need me to shackle him, I will."

I laughed. "I think he'll be fine."

"I am fine," he grumbled. "Just wanted you."

A knowing look passed between the nurses before they quietly left the room.

"You know, you would get out of here faster if you just cooperated," I told him, turning my body toward him and keeping his hand in my lap.

"I hate hospitals," Lucas muttered. He lifted his hand. "It doesn't hurt." He brought my hand up to his mouth. "None of this hurts."

"Did they give you too many meds?" I asked, my heart jumping.

"No. It doesn't hurt because nothing could hurt as much as when I lost you."

My breath hitched. I cupped his face. "You didn't lose me. We were always together. We were just…apart for a little bit."

"It was too fucking long, baby," he bit out through clenched teeth. "Too long."

"I know." My hand slid to his neck, brushing my thumb back and forth over his scruffy jaw. "You got me. You always got me. I never went anywhere."

"I need to go home." He sighed. "I need you with me. I need…"

"I need to know what happened today." I leaned back. "You said you were shot by Mel."

"Yeah." He rubbed the back of his neck. He pulled back the blanket and lifted the hospital gown he was wearing.

My finger brushed over the white bandages on his side. "Have you ever been shot before?"

"No. Stabbed yes. But definitely not shot. I hardly remember it. I was more focused on Shephard." He pulled the gown down. "Have you heard anything about him?"

"He's still in surgery."

My head whipped around, finding two police officers I had never met before, standing just inside the room.

"Who are you?" Lucas asked.

"Are you here to ask him questions?" Although Lucas acted fine, he needed to rest.

"No. We were meeting Shephard for lunch when we got the call. We're here out of support but we wanted to come by and make sure that you were okay too," the one officer said. He was older. Maybe mid-forties, with a strong jaw and piercing blue eyes. He ran a hand through his black hair that had silver peppering the sides.

"How did you know I was here?" Lucas asked him.

"Shephard told us who he was meeting up with first. He's paranoid that way." The officer smiled softly. "But he trusts you. Even though you were a troubled teen when you two became friends, you helped him as well as he helped you. He owes you a debt."

"No." Lucas shook his head. "He just needs to stay alive. That's all I want."

"Can you tell us what happened?" the younger officer asked.

"We were walking back to Shephard's car. He was going to drive me here. I didn't have my car. We walked by an alleyway and Mel approached us. I…" Lucas glanced at me. "I don't remember anything else."

"I'll let you know that we're actually looking for her," the older officer said, a threat hidden beneath his voice. "Well, we'll let you both be. If we hear anything about Shephard before you do, we'll be in touch." The officer handed Lucas his business card. "And please—"

"I'll do the same," Lucas took it.

"Thank you," they both said in unison. They quickly left the room after that, leaving me alone with Lucas.

"There's something else, isn't there?" I asked Lucas.

He released my hand and cupped my inner thigh. "Shephard and I met up for coffee. She showed up. He was nice and let her join us. She was…she accused me of hurting her. I was polite. Because of you. You taught me not to lose my shit, so I kept my cool. Even after everything she's done, I still heard her out. She left. A half hour later, so did we. When she approached us again, she was losing her shit. She was going on about Killian and how I ruined his life. Anyway, she shot Shephard first because he got in her way and then she shot me."

"Do you know where she is?" I couldn't imagine getting to that breaking point.

"No, but I hope they find her." Lucas pinched the bridge of his nose. "She obviously needs help."

"You need rest." I went to move but his hold on me, tightened.

"I don't fucking think so," he snapped.

"There's not enough room on this bed for both of us and you need to rest. I'll be right in this chair." I slid off the bed, grabbed the chair, and placed it as close to his bed as I could. "See? We can still hold hands." I linked my fingers in his, placing a kiss on the back of his knuckles.

"I don't like this. I don't like taking one step forward only to take a million fucking back."

"I guess it's how life works." I shrugged. "I don't know, Lucas. I'm just happy that you're alive because it could have been worse. It could have been so much worse."

"I know." He stared at me.

"What?" I asked, fidgeting under his scrutiny.

"Marry me."

I barked a laugh. "What?"

"Marry me," he repeated, his voice firm.

"You can't be serious, Lucas. We…I…really?" He had proposed once and that was out of desperation but this…this was something else.

"I love you, Lily." He tugged my hand, pulling me back to my feet.

I sat on the edge of the bed again, facing him. "I love you too, Lucas, but is marriage really the answer?"

"Why not? I realized today that life is too fucking short. I could have died. There have been many times I should have died but I didn't. I used to take that for granted. I don't want to take it for granted anymore."

"What are you saying?" I murmured.

"I'm saying that I want to marry you and live every day to its fullest." He pulled me closer, cupping my cheek. "Marry me, Lily. Be my wife and make me the happiest fucking man on this planet."

My heart swelled.

"Actually." He leaned back. "Marry me. Right now. Right here."

"What?" My eyes widened. "How?"

"There's a chapel here. I'm sure the person working it is ordained. So what do you say?"

"I…" I searched his face. After everything we had been through and especially today, I realized that I couldn't live without him. "Yes. Yes, I'll marry you."

He grinned, pulling me into his arms, and wrapping himself around me.

I giggled, placing soft pecks on his mouth. "I can't believe we're going to do this."

"I need you to be my wife, Lily. I've never…fuck, I've never felt this way about someone. Or anything for that matter. It's love but so much more."

"I know," I whispered. "I feel it too."

"Yeah?" He pinched my chin, forcing my head back to meet his dark stare.

"I do, Lucas. I love you to the deepest part of me. It's past my soul. It's my being. You are inside me. Everywhere. And this love I feel for you goes beyond that."

"Fuck." A soft growl left him. "I love you."

(Lucas)

I was desperate for her. To make her my wife. To have her in my home. I wanted her things taking over my apartment. I wasn't sure if I could have kids, but I wanted to try. With her.

"How do we do this? Doesn't it take a little bit to get a marriage license?" Lily asked, leaning against me. Although I should have been in pain, I found that I wasn't. I wasn't sure if it was because of all the shit I had been through as a kid or what, but the only pain I felt was not having Lily bouncing on my—

"Lucas?" She looked up at me. "Did you hear me?"

I squirmed. "Yup."

"What's wrong?"

"Nothing." I kissed her head. The nurses and doctor had been good and let Lily stay with me. It was usually family only or spouses, but she was mine and would be my wife. I just needed to figure out who to ask and how to make it happen before I lost my shit even more.

"Are you sure?" She frowned. "We can wait."

"No," I snapped. "I mean." I cleared my throat. "I need you. I need this. I need to make you my wife. We can get the marriage license. I'll pay. I'll give them all of my fucking money if needed but I need to go home. To our home. I just..." I was losing it. Being holed up in the hospital didn't help either.

"Okay." She stood from the bed and backed away before I could catch her.

"Lily," I growled.

She giggled, leaning over the bed and placing a chaste kiss on my lips. "Let me find our priest, baby."

I shivered. I wasn't a submissive man by any means but one look from her, I would drop to my knees and say, 'Yes, Mistress. As you please, Mistress.'

Lily raised an eyebrow.

"You better get that priest while I talk to the doctor. Find out when I can leave before I fuck you right here and make you beg for them to come save you."

"Geeze, Lucas." She coughed, her cheeks reddening. "Save that promise for later. Oh. Before I forget." She reached under the blanket and slid her hands beneath the hospital gown. When she came into contact with my cock, I jumped. Her soft hand wrapped around my dick, gave it a couple of pumps and forced a groan right from the back of my throat. "I think it's going to be you who does the begging, baby." She released me and sauntered away with a sway in her hips.

I ran a hand over my head, breathing out a slow breath and palming the raging erection I was now sporting.

Holy fucking hell.

Thirty-Six

Lily

I NEEDED TO BE his wife. I was wondering at first if I was making the right choice but with the feral look in Lucas's eyes, I knew it was right. To feel this wanted, needed, owned, had never been something I thought I would need, but I realized that I did need it. And so did he. We were two broken souls who came together at a time when we weren't even looking for it.

"Lily?"

I spun around on my heel. "Grandma." A nurse was pushing her in a wheelchair. I ran to her. "How are you feeling?"

"Much better." She held her arms out.

I enveloped her in a hug, holding her as tight as I could without hurting her. "That's good. I'm so glad."

"They're actually letting me go today but I was told that you were here. Is everything okay?"

"Oh yes. Much better. Lucas was shot but he's fine." I fell to her feet, holding her hands.

"Oh God. I'm glad he's okay." She cupped my cheek. "Are you okay?"

"I am. I really am. Listen, there's something that I want to talk to you about." I stood just as Dr. Thompson joined us.

"Sorry to interrupt but I have news on Shephard. Lucas was asking about him. The surgery went well and he's resting. You can see him in about an hour."

"Oh, thank you. Lucas will be happy to hear that." My cheeks heated when I remembered what I was doing out in the hall in the first place. "This is going to be an odd question but is there a priest who works at the chapel here?"

My grandma gasped but I ignored her.

"There is." Dr. Thompson narrowed his brows. "Father Metcalf is here quite often."

"Do you think I could talk to him?" I wrung my hands in front of me. "Please?"

"Of course." A twinkle flashed in his eyes. "You two planning something before Lucas leaves the hospital?"

"Maybe." I glanced down at my grandma. "Only if my grandma approves."

"Hell fucking yes," she yelled, fist pumping the air. "I mean." She cleared her throat, folding her hands in her lap. "I approve."

Laughter erupted around us.

"You go get the priest," Grandma told me. "I'm going to have a chat with your fiancé."

(Lucas)

No matter how long I had to stay in the hospital, I wasn't leaving it until I made Lily my wife.

"Lucas?"

I sat on the edge of the bed. "Yeah." I had just finished getting dressed in green scrubs since my clothes were cut off and taken away for evidence.

A nurse rolled Ethel around the corner in a wheelchair.

"What are you doing in that?" I teased, nodding toward her.

She rolled her eyes. "Doctor's orders. Don't get me started."

I chuckled.

"How are you feeling?" she asked. "I heard you've had quite the adventure. When did all this happen?"

"Uh…yesterday?" Time was lost on me. I wasn't able to leave the hospital yet, but I was thankful they at least let me put on clothes other than the hospital gown. Even if it was just a pair of green scrubs. Although every time I had gone for a piss, the nurses would giggle. Women. Yes, I had tattoos. Everywhere. What could I say? The ink was addicting.

"Thank you," Ethel told the nurse as she wheeled her closer to my bed.

The nurse glanced at me, her cheeks reddening. She quickly spun around, bumping into a cop. She muttered a sorry and left the room.

"I heard you had that effect on women," the cop told me.

I shrugged. "I have no idea what you're talking about." Either way, I didn't care.

The cop chuckled. "First thing, I'm Officer Masters. I just wanted to let you know that we found Melanie Huff."

A breath of relief escaped me. "And?"

"She is being detained. Charged with two counts of attempted murder. The judge will likely throw the book at her.

He doesn't take too kindly to trying to kill a cop. We've actually been looking at her for a while."

"You have?" I shook my head. "Why?"

"We've arrested her a few times for prostitution, but she has behaved lately." The officer shrugged. "Anyway, I know you need your rest. I just wanted to stop by to tell you that."

"Did you see Shephard?" I asked him, hopeful that my friend was awake.

"I saw him first actually. He's doing well and wants you to come see him as soon as you're able."

"Thank you."

The cop nodded and tipped his hat to Ethel. "Ma'am." He turned and headed out of the room.

"Does that make you feel better?" Ethel asked once we were alone.

"I'm glad Shephard's doing well but Mel…I just hope she gets the help she needs." That familiar guilt still sat on my shoulders but only because I felt like I should have been able to do something for her. For all of them.

"Hey." Ethel wheeled her chair closer to me and grabbed my hand. "Whatever happened, it's not your fault. Do not take responsibility for what she did. Or for what happened in your past. It's not your fault. Do you hear me?"

I nodded. "I hear you but—"

"No, listen to me. I know my granddaughter and she loves you. She loves you for you. She doesn't care what you came from. Make her see that you don't care either."

"I don't. I swear that I don't. I only care about this, about now, and about a future with her. I want to make her happy." I looked up just as Lily entered the room with a priest following beside her. "I want to make you happy," I told her. As soon as she said yes to marrying me, I had used my phone to get things underway when it came to the marriage license.

Lily's eyes shone. She rushed to me and cupped my face. "I want that. I want you. I want to make you happy too."

"You do." I stared up at her and tapped my mouth.

She grinned, placing a hard peck on my lips. "I also like this look," she whispered in my ear. "You need to keep these scrubs."

A sly grin spread on my face. "I can make that happen."

(Lily)

"I love you, Lily. And while this may be unconventional, I could marry you in the middle of the desert and it would be perfect."

My eyes welled as Lucas's sweet words whispered over me.

He kissed my hands, my fingertips. My palms.

"I mean it. You're perfect. Everything about you. From your lips to your hair to your curves to your smile. Everything. I know we've had our problems and we both come from dark, dangerous pasts but together, we can heal. Together we are strong."

I nodded, swallowing over the hard lump that lodged its way in my throat. "God, you say the sweetest things sometimes."

He chuckled, bringing our hands up and linked our fingers together. "I love you, Lily Pad, and I promise to spend the rest of my life, doing everything I can to make you happy."

A sniff sounded from somewhere in the room but all I could focus on was the man standing in front of me. Although he was in scrubs and I was in leggings, a tank top, and a sweater, it was perfect. This was so damn perfect.

"I can't wait to grow old with you, Lucas. You came into my life when I didn't know I needed it. I wasn't even looking for you and yet, there you were."

His lips pulled up at the corners, giving me that sexy as hell grin of his.

"As unusual as you think this is, it's actually not."

Both of us turned to Father Metcalf. He only smiled. "Trust me." He glanced over his shoulder. "Isn't that right?"

Dr. Thompson chuckled. "Yeah, we've seen at least one or two marriages happen here."

I laughed.

Lucas pulled me into his arms. "Can you do your magic please and make this woman my wife?"

My body heated as a part of Lucas pushed between us. If we were alone, I would have said something, but we weren't. So instead, I just held him tight, leaning my head against his chest.

"I definitely can." Father Metcalf smiled. "We got the marriage license, so we can make sure this is official."

"You got it that quickly?" I asked.

"Your fiancé here did." Father Metcalf grinned.

I looked up at Lucas. "How?"

He only winked.

"I know you don't have rings, is that right?" Father Metcalf asked.

"Not here, no."

"What?" I leaned back, staring up at Lucas. "You have rings?"

"I do." Lucas pinched my chin. "I'll give them to you later."

"Them?" I whispered. I couldn't believe this. He really had rings already?

Lucas winked, turning back to Father Metcalf. "Please, Father."

Father Metcalf's smiled widened. "Of course."

(Lily)

"I now pronounce you husband and wife."

"Lucas." I leaned back on the hospital bed. "We're married."

"We are. And we're going to go home and I'm going to make love to my wife. Over and over again." He slammed the cupboard door shut. "Are you ready for that, Lily? Are you ready for what I want to do to you? For all the times I want to come inside you?"

I shivered at the thought. He was finally coming home tonight. We had been married for almost a week, but it felt like he had been in the hospital for longer. He had seen Shephard who was doing well and would be out of the hospital in a few more days. I was glad.

Doctor Thompson had told us to take it slow, but I knew the man I was married to. He didn't want slow.

"Yes," I told him. "I'm ready for that and more."

He closed the distance between us, placing a hard peck on my mouth. "If it wasn't frowned upon, I'd take you to the bathroom and—"

"Shut up and kiss me so we can leave, and you can take care of all of those promises."

A wicked grin spread on his face. He cupped my cheek.

I leaned into his palm, covering his hand with mine.

"I love you, Lily," he said, all joking aside.

"And I love you, Lucas." My heart swelled. "Now, let's go home."

A HOT MOUTH CAPTURED mine in a hard, bruising kiss. Hands roamed through my hair, tugging me forward until a tongue was so deep in my mouth, I could feel it down to my soul.

As soon as we stepped out of the taxi, Lucas was on me. He pushed me up against the door leading to his apartment. His cock strained behind the green scrubs, pressing into my lower belly.

Lucas fisted my hair, cupped my jaw with his other hand, and held my head in place as he devoured my mouth.

I reached inside his pants, wrapping my hand around his thick length, bringing that part of him I had begun to crave, to life.

He snarled, fucking his tongue deeper between my lips.

I moaned, latching on to his dick. My thumb brushed over the slit, sliding over the pre-cum that was leaking from his body. I shivered, knowing how much he wanted me. Although he just had surgery a week ago, he was released from the hospital. He had been like a caged animal and now that he was free, I was his ultimate prey.

The sound of clinking erupted into my ears.

I pulled away from him long enough to see him fumbling to unlock the door. As soon as it pushed open behind me, I attacked his mouth.

He growled, pushing me backward into his apartment. We stumbled into his home. Lucas kicked the door closed, cupped the back of my head, and slid his tongue against mine.

With my hand firmly around his cock, I stroked and pulled, forcing him to shiver against me. I reached lower, cupping his heavy balls.

"Fuck," he groaned, biting my bottom lip gently.

I whimpered, the sharp pain shooting right to my clit.

His hands roamed up the sides of my body.

Lucas slammed me up against the wall, ripping my shirt in half.

I gasped, arching against him, my body becoming wetter for him.

He released my mouth, trailing hot kisses to the side of my throat. His big hands cupped my breasts over my bra, pushing them together. He kissed down to my collarbone before covering a nipple. His teeth grazed over the sharp peak.

I panted, pulling my hand free from his pants. Running my fingers through his hair, I pulled off his eye patch before tossing it to the floor.

He stared up at me, lowering the cups of my bra and flicking his tongue back and forth over a budding peak. Closing his mouth around a nipple, he sucked it between his teeth. Pleasure shot through me, heating every inch of my skin.

Lucas ran his hands from my waist to my ass, pulling my leggings down my hips. He kissed his way up to my mouth.

I moaned, snaking my arms around his neck and pulling him hard against me.

With some maneuvering, I pulled the leggings and panties down one leg.

Without giving me a chance to process what was going on, his hand was between my legs.

I gasped, my back bowing away from the wall.

But he didn't let up. While he pleased my lower body, his tongue continued to fuck my mouth. His fingers thrust in and out of me, the sounds of how wet he was making me, erupting through the hall.

I broke the kiss, gasping for air. "Lucas."

He cupped my chin and covered my mouth with his, stealing my very breath.

I grabbed his hand that was between my legs and pushed it against me, undulating my hips back and forth.

That only made him kiss me harder. No words left him. No demands. No dirty talk. He spoke to me through his touch and touch alone.

Lifting my one leg, I curled it around his waist, opening me up to him. I cried out, the pleasure erupting through me faster than I had ever felt before.

He grunted his approval, his fingers fucking me harder and faster.

My hands roamed down his chest to the waist of his green scrubs but before I could reach for what I wanted most, he slapped my hands away.

I whimpered, reaching for him again.

Lucas grabbed my hands, holding both of my wrists and pulling my arms up and over my head. A breathless gasp escaped me, my body dripping even more for him.

He chuckled against my mouth, deepening the kiss.

I was completely restrained by him. My legs shook. My thighs burned. My heel dug into his ass. The scruff of his beard that had grown in more, scratched at my cheeks. Lucas utterly consumed me. My breathing became labored. An electric current rushed through me.

Lucas slid his fingers from my body and slowly pushed another into me.

I moaned, all thoughts lost to him.

He finally broke the kiss, staring down at me. "Come hard for me."

"Fuck me. Please, Lucas." I undulated my hips back and forth.

"Why? What do you want?" He released my wrists and cupped my jaw. "Tell me."

"I want you inside me," I whispered, licking my lips at the large bulge in his scrubs. "I want your cum dripping from me."

"Hmmm…those are dirty words for someone who just got married." He kissed my cheek.

"Make me yours, baby." I cupped his nape, placing a kiss on his neck. "Make me hurt."

"Fuck, Lily." He pulled his hand from my body and lifted me.

"Take me here. Please, Lucas." I cupped him over his pants. "I can't wait anymore."

"Put me in you, Lily." He sunk his teeth into the side of my neck. "Show me how much of a slut you are for it."

I reached a hand inside his pants and grabbed onto him in a rough move.

He shouted out, slapping his hands against the wall on either side of my head. "Now. Damn it."

"Tell me more, Lucas," I purred, licking along the length of his jaw.

Lucas spread my legs even more, cupping my inner thighs and squeezing his fingers into them. "Do it now."

I pulled his cock free from the confines of his pants and released it at the same time as he thrust forward. I gasped, arching into his deep thrusts. He hit that part that had always been for him. Every single time he reached it, I shattered. He pulled back, rutting into me like an animal.

"Come," he demanded, breathing hard against my neck.

"Make me, Lucas. Make me come all over this big cock."

"Fuck I love you." He pushed my leg out to the side, spreading me open even more. I wasn't flexible, and this was surely going to hurt tomorrow but at this point in time, I didn't care. About anything.

"Come, Mrs. Crane," he purred against my throat. "Come for your husband."

I grinned, holding onto his shoulder. "Harder."

"That's my girl." He leaned back, staring down at me. "Come for me."

A tremor of pleasure erupted through me. I moaned, circling my hips against him and taking every inch he had to give me. "Faster. Please. Faster. Give it to me. All of it."

His hips powered forward and back. Sweat coated his brow. His gaze was hard and focused. "Fuck, Lily. I'm losing it over here."

I licked two fingers and ran them across my clit.

"That's it, baby. Fuck, I love watching you touch yourself." Lucas leaned his forehead against mine, his cock swelling inside of me. "Shit, Lily."

An explosion of pleasure slammed into me. I cried out.

Lucas covered my mouth with his, his own release following mine.

I swallowed his shout of ecstasy, our cries of pleasure mixing as one.

"Fuck me." He shivered, releasing my mouth.

"Don't," I said, stopping him from pulling out. I looked down between our joined bodies, a hot shiver rippling down my spine.

"Nice and creamy, baby," he said, pulling out and wiping the head of his cock over my clit, his cum now all over my pussy. He thrusted back into me slowly. "You're mine, Lily. You've always been mine and now you smell like me."

I reached between us and swiped a finger over the cum on my clit and stuck my finger in my mouth. "I taste like you too," I whispered.

His nostrils flared. He pushed into me hard, going as deep as my body would allow.

My mouth fell open.

He kept pushing and pushing.

"Oh…" A blinding light danced in my vision as a hard release crashed through me. It was so damn intense that I couldn't utter a sound.

"I'm in the deepest part of your soul." He kissed the spot beneath my ear. "Can you feel that? That's me fucking your being."

"Holy," I gasped. "Shit."

He chuckled, pulling free from my body. The tattoo of the octopus tentacle glistened. "You like my tattoo?"

"Uh…I think we've established just how much I like your tattoo."

Lucas grinned, placing me gently on my feet. "That's a thing you know."

"Oh, I know it's a thing. I never thought it would be my thing, but I've seen some super sexy graphics with women and tentacles and what those tentacles are doing to them and…" My cheeks burned.

"You're a dirty girl, Mrs. Crane." Lucas lifted me in his arms, carrying me through the apartment.

"I'm your dirty girl, Mr. Crane." God, I still couldn't believe we were married.

Once we reached the bedroom, he placed me on the bed and took off his clothes. He opened the drawer of his nightstand and pulled out two small black velvet boxes.

"Lucas," I said on a gasp. "Is that…"

"I got these a few days before I was shot. Maybe a week before? I can't remember. I wasn't thinking straight, and I thought that maybe if I proposed to you officially that you would say yes, and everything would be fine. I know that's not the case now that my head is clearer. I'm sorry for assuming."

"No. Don't be sorry." I slid off the bed and reached for one of the boxes but pulled my hand back. "Should we get dressed or something?"

He chuckled, lowering to one knee. He opened one of the boxes. "Lily, will you continue being my wife?"

I laughed, falling to my knees and placing a hard kiss on his mouth. "Yes, Lucas. For the rest of eternity, I will continue being your wife."

He grinned, placing the gold wedding band along with a single solitaire diamond in behind it.

"Wow. This thing is bigger than my face."

A laugh boomed through him. He kissed my cheek. "It's all yours, baby."

"My turn." I held out my hand. "Pretty please."

He placed the box in my hand. I opened it, another gold band staring up at me. It was identical to mine but thicker.

"I know most brides help pick out the rings, but I saw these and—"

"They're perfect, Lucas. I promise." I took out the ring and placed the box on the floor. "I know people are usually dressed—"

In a quick move, Lucas pulled me into his arms.

I gasped.

He wrapped a hand around his cock, pumped twice, and thrust back inside of me.

I moaned. "I wasn't done yet."

"I don't give a fuck." He nipped the side of my neck. "I want to be inside you when you claim me as yours."

"God." My pussy clenched around him at his words. "I love you." I slid the ring onto his finger, earning me a hard growl.

We linked fingers, taking the next few hours to consummate our marriage. Officially.

"I guess we have to move your stuff in here now," Lucas told me later that night.

"Yeah." I kissed him hard on the mouth. "But that can wait. I need you back inside me."

"Again? You're not tired? Or sore?"

"Never."

"Good. I wasn't going to give you a choice." He flipped me onto my stomach and sunk his teeth into my shoulder blade.

I giggled. "Do what you want, my husband."

"Fuck, I like the sound of that."

"Me too," I breathed.

"I'm going to spend the rest of the night making love to my wife."

"Yeah?" I cupped his cheek when he kissed my shoulder.

"Yeah, baby," he said, his voice husky.

"Good, because I need you, Lucas. Always and forever."

"You have me, Lily Pad. Always. Forever. For fucking eternity. I'm yours. Only yours."

My breath hitched. This was it. This was ours. This was us. It took so long to get here that I would never take our happiness for granted ever again.

Lucas was right when he said that we came into each other's lives when we needed it most. I wasn't sure how, but I didn't just love this man. I lived and breathed him. Our souls connected. Our beings intertwined. We fought hard, but we loved even harder.

He was mine. And I was his.

And this was ours.

Epilogue

I DIDN'T WANT TO be here. I hated hospitals. I hated anything having to do with medical shit. And now I was stuck having to talk about my feelings.

With Lily's hand firmly in mine, I waited for what felt like years before a large man approached us. His smile was warm and friendly, but his eyes were determined and focused. He was a man of business. A large man. He was still smaller than I was, but I also wasn't stupid. I wouldn't mess with him.

"Mr. and Mrs. Crane?" he asked, stopping just in front of us.

"Yes," both of us answered at the same time.

"I'm Dr. Santos but please, call me Matteo." He stuck his hand out.

We stood.

Lily returned his handshake first.

"It's nice to meet you," Matteo said, gearing his attention to me and sticking out his hand again.

"I don't mean to be rude." I shook his hand. "But I don't want to be here."

"I understand that." His grip on my hand tightened. "But I promise, I will not judge. Whatever you have to tell me, stays with me and me only. Also, if you don't want to be here, you can leave at any time."

"Lucas," Lily said gently. "Give it a chance. Just one chance. For me."

My jaw clenched. "Fine."

(Lily)

I held Lucas's hand while he talked to Matteo who in turn would nod every so often. He wrote things down in his notepad. He commented when needed and asked questions where necessary but other than that, Lucas did most of the talking.

"You feel guilty," Matteo pointed out, rubbing the graying black scruff on his tanned jaw. His dark eyes flicked to mine before glancing back at my husband.

"I do. I wish I could have saved them. I'm not sure if it was because I was the biggest of us all, even though I wasn't the oldest. I just wish I could have done more. I felt like it was my job." Lucas shifted beside me. "Honestly, I think I would have relapsed already if it hadn't been for meeting Lily."

"Really?" My head whipped around.

"Yeah." He gave me a small smile. "I thought I was doing well even though I continued having nightmares. And then you came along and brought this light into the darkness of my life I never knew I needed. I was walking through shadows since I was a boy until you came along. Until you strode into Crane's Ink and strutted around like you owned the damn place."

I laughed, wiping a lonely tear that had fallen down my cheek.

"This woman has helped me," Lucas told Matteo. "Because of her, I haven't died with a needle sticking out of my arm."

"I understand that." Matteo crossed his ankle over his opposite knee. "I'm going to tell you a story. I know it's unconventional, but I've never been known to do things the right way."

"Okay..." Lucas released my hand and cupped my knee.

"I met my wife when I was going through a rough time. She had been through hell as well and we helped each other. We didn't resort to drugs or alcohol but for us, we were addicted to sex. I'll be honest with you. I'm a sadist and knowing my wife could give me what I needed, helped us both. It has helped me more than I have ever told her. Now we've been married for almost fifteen years with two beautiful children and we couldn't be happier. Relationships are hard." He pointed at us. "But the question is, do you want to put in the work? Are you willing to do whatever it takes to make each other happy? You have PTSD, Lucas. Severe PTSD. Especially after telling me about those things Mel had said to you that triggered memories. The mind can be fragile. Especially if broken. And unfortunately for you, it is. But I can see the growth already. I didn't know you when all of this was going down, but I can see now how far you've come. And obviously, Lily has helped you through all of this."

"I'm going to help him through his future too," I added. "I lost my parents to a fire. That's why I started drinking. And I have scars. I thought they were ugly, but Lucas made me realize that I'm a survivor as well."

"Looks like meeting me is good for both of you," Matteo said, giving me a wink.

I giggled, my cheeks heating.

Lucas coughed, tightening his grip on my knee.

I bit back an eye-roll. I couldn't help it. Matteo was good looking. If you liked them older that is.

"You talk about your sexual desires like they're nothing," Lucas interjected. "You're not ashamed of them?"

"No." Matteo stood from the chair and headed to his desk. "I've learned over the years that with the right person, as long as it's safe and consensual, it's okay to like the darker side of sex. Just do your research, take lessons from a trained professional, whatever the case may be, and you'll be just fine."

Lucas was dominant, but our sex life wasn't overly kinky. Not yet anyway.

"And with what you've been through, using sex as an out like you did before meeting Lily, makes sense," Matteo added.

"Right." Lucas closed up after that, not offering further information about his past. Matteo had his work cut out for him, but I knew that with time, Lucas would tell him everything and it would help him heal. Or at least make him feel better.

An hour later and Matteo was walking us out of his office. "So, was it that bad?"

Lucas grunted, and I couldn't help but smile.

"No," he grumbled. "Thank you." He squeezed my hand, holding it tight. I realized then that he hadn't let me go since we arrived at Matteo's office.

"Of course. It's my job." Matteo rubbed the back of his neck. "Can I ask you a question? And this is coming from a parent."

"Uh…sure." Lucas stiffened.

"I need to know. Did they get theirs? Your adoptive parents."

"Yeah." Lucas relaxed. "They all did." He had told Matteo about Killian, or Ronny as he was known as a kid, and Mel also.

"Good." Matteo nodded, blowing out a slow breath. "Same time, next week?"

I looked up at Lucas then.

"Yeah, I think I need it." Lucas shifted, giving his shoulders a small shrug.

"I'll be here, Lucas. For as long as you need." Matteo clapped him on the shoulder, gave me a small smile, and headed back into his office.

"How do you feel?" I asked Lucas.

"Emotionally raw." He pinched my chin, placing a soft peck on my mouth. "Let's go home, Lily Pad."

(Lucas)

"Alright, Lily Pad." I pulled off the glove. "I'm done."

She sat up from the bed, swinging her legs over the edge.

It had been several hours since we went to see Dr. Santos for the first time. Once we arrived home, I had told her I wanted to give her a tattoo. She never even hesitated.

Lily looked down at the side of her stomach, her breath hitching. She looked at her reflection in the floor length mirror. Rising from the bed, she walked over to the mirror, checking out the phoenix I had tattooed on her. It was a mixture of oranges, yellows, and reds. The bird rose from the fire that was lightly tattooed on her scars.

"It's…" Her eyes shone, her chin wobbling.

"Baby." I walked up behind her. "I didn't mean to make you cry."

"It's beautiful," she whispered, wiping away a tear that had fallen down her cheek. "God, it's beautiful. Lucas, you're so damn talented."

My cheeks burned at the compliment. "Thank you."

"I mean it. I…" She sighed. "I feel like you're branded on my soul."

My body stirred at that. "I am." I wrapped my arm around her, resting my chin on her shoulder. "You're mine, Lily. We didn't travel through hell together for nothing."

Her jade eyes met mine in the mirror. "I want your name on me."

My cock jumped. "What?"

She turned in my arms, pushing me back until I hit the edge of the bed. "I know you've said that it's a cardinal rule not to tattoo a name on someone, but I need it. I'm yours. You're mine. Like you said, we wouldn't have traveled through hell together if this wasn't meant to be. If we weren't meant to last and stay together forever. Please, Lucas."

I thought about it for a moment. My name on her skin. My name in her flesh. It would be a permanent reminder that she was, in fact, mine.

"Okay. I'll do it."

Her face lit up.

"But, on one condition." I prepped the tattoo gun.

"What condition is that?"

"I want you to tattoo your name on me," I told her, pulling on another pair of rubber gloves.

"What?" She laughed. "You can't be serious. I don't know anything about tattooing. And I'm not an artist."

"You don't need to be." I handed her a piece of paper. "Write down your name."

She hesitated, chewing her bottom lip.

"Lily." I put the pen in her hand. "Do it."

She wrote down her name and I did the same.

After I got the tattoo designs prepared, I chuckled at the deep frown set between her brows. "You have nothing to worry about. You should have seen some of my original tattoos. They were worse than what you can do. Trust me. And all you're tattooing, is your name. There's no shading, no color. Just your name." I sat on the bed, straddling it and turned Lily toward me. "I need your name on my skin just like you need mine on yours."

She took a deep breath. "Okay."

"Where do you want my name?" I asked her.

"Right here." She tapped the spot above her heart.

I smiled, placing a soft peck on her nose. "I'm your heart, baby?"

"Yeah," she whispered.

I chuckled lightly.

An hour later, my name was marked in her skin. I never thought this would happen. It was usually against the rules to put a name on someone, knowing that relationships might not always work out. But this was different. This was needed. For both of us.

"Where do you want my name, Lucas?" Lily asked, her beautiful eyes meeting mine.

"On my right wrist." I handed her the tattoo gun. "So every time I jerk off, I see your name."

Lily coughed, a laugh escaping her. "Way to kill the mood."

"Me? You're the one who always makes everything about sex," I reminded her.

She gasped. "Who me? I'm innocent." She batted her eyelashes.

"Right," I said slowly. "Hurry up and tattoo me, Lily Pad. The sooner it heals, the sooner I can test it out."

"Geeze, Lucas." Her cheeks reddened. "But you don't need my name on your wrist to jerk off."

"No." I kissed her hard on the mouth. "I don't. But it's a nice added touch."

She giggled, shaking her head. "Alright, baby. Tell me what to do."

Sometime later

"Hello." I took a deep breath, ignoring the eyes staring back at me. "My name is Lily Crane and I'm an alcoholic."

"Hello, Lily."

I gripped the sides of the podium, taking another deep breath. And another. "I've been sober for…God, almost ten years."

A round of clapping erupted through the room. But the person who mattered most, sat in the front row, a huge grin spreading on his face.

I smiled back. "I couldn't do it without my husband. Being with him has given me the strength I needed to overcome this disease. There have been so many times where I wanted a drink. But I'm sure we've all been there." My thumb brushed over a crack in the wood. "I've never shared before. I don't really know why. I know you all wouldn't judge me. I just…I felt like my shares weren't important enough. Maybe? I don't know. But I do know that without the support of my husband and grandma, I would have relapsed already. This week has been extra hard. It's been a year since she died." My chest tightened. "She died happy though. She was almost eighty. But God, I miss her." My eyes welled, that familiar burn, tingling the back of my nose. "I know she wouldn't want me to give up. So...yeah. That's all."

Another round of clapping erupted through my ears.

I quickly left the stage and joined the empty chair beside Lucas.

"I'm proud of you, Lily Pad." He kissed my temple. "So fucking proud of you."

"Thank you." My heart swelled. "Thank you for everything and for standing by me, even when it was hard and I was difficult."

He cupped my face.

Wrapping my hand around his wrist, I brushed my thumb over the tattoo of my name. My body heated, remembering how it turned him on to have my name branded in his skin.

The meeting ended shortly after that. Lucas had come to mine for support and I went with him to his for the same. Sometimes our meetings intertwined but usually, they remained separate.

"Thank you for being by me when I was difficult too," Lucas said once everyone was rounding up the chairs. He kissed me softly on the mouth. "I meant what I said when I married you three years ago." He placed a hand on my swollen belly. "Through thick and thin. Through the good and the bad. I would walk through hell, as long as I have you by my side."

I sniffed, tears rolling freely down my cheeks.

"I mean it, Lily Pad." He hugged an arm around me, pulling me against him.

"God, I love you." I leaned back, tapping my mouth.

He smirked, placing a hard kiss on my lips.

"Lily."

My head snapped around, finding Lena coming toward us. "Lena." I rushed to her and threw my arms around her.

She laughed, hugging me back.

"It's been awhile." She released me, smiling at us both. "I see it's been a long while." She pointed at my belly.

I sighed, cupping my stomach.

"Oh." Her brows narrowed. "I got that envelope."

Lucas shrugged, his face going impassive. "I have no idea what you're talking about."

She scoffed. "Right."

I bit back a giggle. Lucas had been saving money for her and her daughter ever since Lena started going to him for tattoos. He said it was the least he could do after all the business she had brought in for him.

I fell in love with him even more at that point.

"How are you doing? Lily told me you got your daughter back and you have full custody now." Lucas cupped the back of my neck.

It took Lena quite a while to get custody of her daughter, but she told me during our last phone conversation a few weeks ago, that her parents said her daughter needed to be with her mom. I was so happy for her.

"I do." Lena's smile widened. "I started going to meetings too. This is my first time at this one. I've been going to the one closer to my place since I moved."

"I'm proud of you, Lena." Lucas nodded as Toby and Sandra came toward us.

"Thank you." Lena's cheeks reddened. "I have to go but I just wanted to say hi in person and thank you both for everything."

We gave her a hug, happy she was now making a better life for herself and her daughter.

I turned to Sandra, holding my arms out.

She laughed, closed the distance between us, and returned my hug.

"I am so happy to see you both," she said, squeezing me. She leaned back, cupping my stomach. "How's the little one?"

"Good." My heart swelled. I still couldn't believe I was growing a human inside of me.

"It's been too long," Sandra said. "How's everything else? You guys good?"

I laughed at the onslaught of questions.

Toby grinned, shaking his head. "Don't mind her. She's missed you guys."

"Yes," I said as Lucas came up behind me. "We're good."

He clapped Toby on the back, pulling him into a one-armed hug. "We are very good."

"I'm glad." Toby returned his embrace, smiling down at me. "You two deserve it."

"We do." Lucas leaned down and kissed my cheek. "Don't we?"

I cupped his face and kissed him softly on the mouth. "Yes." I was glad that he finally realized it. He deserved all the happiness life had to give him. He deserved it and more.

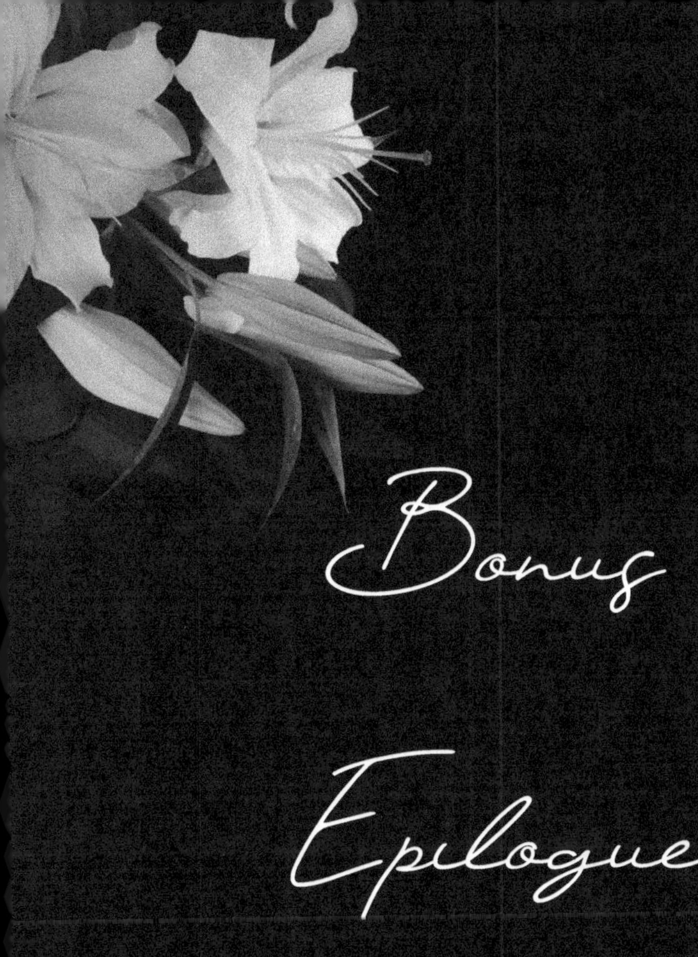

Bonus Epilogue

LUCAS

LILY WAS DUE WITH our first child anytime now. It had been a few hard months for her with morning sickness and all, but she never complained. At all. Even when she should have.

After the brutal abuse I had endured as a kid, I didn't think I could have kids. Not that I ever got checked out for it. I had just assumed.

While Lily slept soundlessly on her side, I pulled the covers off of her and lifted her tank top to just below her breasts.

Cupping her stomach, I waited for that familiar kick. When it happened, I smiled.

"Daddy's here," I whispered, leaning down and placing a soft peck on her stomach. A flutter erupted beneath my hand again. My smile grew. "Daddy is always here," I added. "I will give you and your mommy the best life you could ever have. You won't have to want for anything." Leaning over Lily, I grabbed the tub of coconut cream off the nightstand. Twisting off the cap, I dipped two fingers into the sweet-smelling lotion and began rubbing it into her skin. "I hope you have a big heart like your mommy and a fierceness like her too. I can't wait to tell you all the stories of how we met." The clean version anyway. "I will love you. I will cherish you. I will make it my mission to keep a smile on your face."

Lily stirred. "What are you doing?" she asked, her voice thick with sleep.

"I couldn't sleep." I still had nightmares, but they weren't as bad as before. I had been seeing Matteo on a weekly basis for the past few years. It helped. It helped more than I could ever understand. "So, I'm talking to our daughter."

"Okay," Lily whispered, a soft smile splaying on her face. "I think she likes it in there."

I chuckled, laying on my stomach and resting my head just beneath Lily's breasts. "It's nice and warm. She's safe."

"She'll be safe out here too," Lily murmured, running her fingers through my hair. "I promise."

I knew we would have issues. Especially if she looked anything like her mother. But I would worry about that when the time came. Right now, I would take this. I would hold it and cherish it. These girls were mine. All fucking mine. And I would never take them for granted. Lily and I had come too far for that.

(Lily)

"Are you done?"

I smiled up at my husband. "I am," I said as I wrote, The End. It was the next morning after Lucas had woken me up by the sweet words he was saying to our daughter.

"And you're really not going to publish this?" Lucas asked, sitting down beside me on the bed.

"No. It's ours. I feel like it's almost too personal to be published." I shrugged. We had talked about changing the names in our story so that I could publish it, but I decided against it. I had never been a writer but after everything that had happened to us, I had this itch. And it wouldn't go away until I scratched it by writing this book.

"I just can't believe it's done," I said, closing the laptop. "I mean, it's been quite a few years since I started it."

"It opened old wounds, baby." Lucas kissed my cheek and placed my laptop on the nightstand. "It makes sense why it took so long to write it."

"True." I tapped my mouth.

He grinned, placing a hard smack on my lips. "Thank you," he said against my mouth.

"For what?" I pulled back. "I haven't done anything."

"You have." He cupped my cheek. "You didn't give up on me. You did things that most women would have run away screaming from. I just want you to know that I appreciate you not giving up on us."

"I love you, Lucas. Remember that." We thankfully hadn't heard from Mel or Killian after they were sentenced to the maximum penalty for their crimes. Shephard, already close with Lucas, became a close friend to me as well. After getting shot, he retired from the police force and focused on his family. He wanted to watch his kids grow up and spend more time with his wife. "Besides, it's not that big of a deal."

Our problems were no more and were just the typical ones a married couple had. And we were due to have our daughter any day now. Twenty-four more hours and she would be overdue. She was already stubborn like her father.

Lucas pulled me from the bed and grabbed the hem of my shirt. "It is a big deal. You could have left me, and you didn't."

"I left you for a few hours," I corrected, lifting my arms up. "But you could have left me too."

"Never." He pulled my shirt up and over my head before lowering to his knees. "You had every right to walk away."

"It doesn't matter." I ran my fingers through his hair. I liked that he had grown it in some but still kept the sides shaved. "Those were the longest hours of my life. Being away from you. Not touching you."

"Not kissing you," he added, placing a soft peck on my stomach. He pulled my shorts and panties down my legs, leaving me completely naked for him. "Not talking to you."

"You never told me what you did for those hours that I was gone." I sat on the edge of the bed. "I know you lost it and punched the wall a few times. But did you do anything else?"

"No."

"You didn't?"

He shook his head. "I didn't. Not me personally anyway. Toby and Shephard ended up cleaning up my place while I was with you. They're too good to me."

"You deserve it," I told him. "You deserve all of it and more."

"I lost it, Lily," Lucas continued. "I was ready to give up. To stop fighting. And I took my rage out on my apartment."

"I'm sorry," I whispered, holding out my hand. My wedding set sparkled in the dim lighting of the room. "This is permanent, Lucas."

"It is." He covered my hand, bringing it up to his mouth. "It's forever, baby."

My heart jumped.

"I think I scared Toby and Shephard during those twenty-four hours too." He chuckled as the memories rushed back.

"I'm glad they were determined to help you. To help us."

"Me too." He kissed the spot above my belly button. "I was determined to win you back. I fucked up. I know that. Even though I didn't start it, I didn't stop it as fast as I should have. Doesn't matter if I was stuck in my head and I was on the verge of a mental breakdown." He rolled his eyes at that. Matteo had been trying to get him to stop making fun of himself over it and to take it seriously, but Lucas always said that it still wasn't an excuse.

"I'm lucky to have you," he continued. "I'm so damn lucky and I promise to never take you for granted again."

"I love you, Lucas." A flutter erupted through my belly. I laughed, grabbing his hand and placing it on my swollen stomach. "She loves you too."

Lucas grinned, his eyes shining. He started wearing his eye patch less and less when we were at home. He placed a kiss on my stomach. "I can't...I still can't believe I got you pregnant. I thought for sure it was impossible."

"Nothing's impossible, baby," I whispered. "Not when it comes to us."

"That's so fucking true." He kissed my shoulder. "I also never thought that you could look even more beautiful but seeing you swollen with my daughter is a beauty all on its own."

I laughed, laying back on the bed. "You like that, Daddy?"

"Do not call me that," he growled.

I laughed harder. "You only hate when I call you that because it turns you on."

"Yeah, because our daughter is going to call me it and it'll be weird." He lightly tapped my hip. "So stop."

I saluted him. "Yes." I winked. "Daddy."

"Lily," he said, his voice filled with warning.

"No more." I tapped my mouth. "Promise."

"Good girl." He placed a hard kiss on my lips. He moved up the length of the bed, pulling me into his arms, and grabbing the remote off the nightstand. Turning on the TV, we ended up watching an old black and white zombie film.

I snuggled into Lucas's side, thinking over what the past several years had been like for us.

Pain. Love. Passion. Intense ecstasy. Heartache. So much heartache. My grandmother would be proud of how far we had come.

I placed a hand on my stomach, feeling our daughter move beneath my touch. Ettie. Our sweet Ettie. She would be named Ethel after my grandma but Ettie for short, knowing my grandmother wouldn't want her having such an old name.

"I love you, Lily." Lucas covered my hand that was on my belly. "And I love our daughter. More than either of you could ever know or understand."

My heart swelled with even more love for this man beside me. While we had problems, difficulties, whatever you wanted to call them, our love was strong. In the end, it conquered everything we had been through.

Both of us were scarred and broken in our own way, but our love was the bind that put our pieces back together again.

Because of that, we could move on, we could grow, and we could become a little less shattered.

A little less scarred.

And a little less broken.

THE END

Bonus Scene

LUCAS

I STARED DOWN AT the tiny little bundle. While Lily fed our daughter, I couldn't help but watch. She was perfect. Both of them were perfect. Ettie was almost two months old. Two months. I couldn't believe I had a hand in creating something so damn…perfect.

"You're staring," Lily said, smiling up at me.

"I can't help it." I brushed a hand over Ettie's tiny little head while she nursed. "She's perfect. You are perfect."

Lily's eyes shone. "I'm not but thank you. I still can't believe we created her." She looked back down at Ettie. "It's funny because I never really wanted kids. Or I never thought about it anyway and then now…God, I wouldn't change this for the world. For anything."

A knock sounded at the door interrupting our little happy moment.

A glance passed between Lily and I.

"Who could that be?" she asked, standing from the couch.

"I have no idea." We didn't get visitors often. And if we did, it was usually Toby and Sandra, Shephard and his wife, or Lena and her daughter. That was about it. And they always called or texted first now that we had Ettie. "Stay here." I had learned not to be so damn paranoid but with everything that had happened when Lily and I first got together, one could never be too safe.

Heading to the door, I checked the security camera on my phone but didn't recognize the person standing on the other side. Unlocking the door, I opened it, finding an older woman. She was short. Probably a few inches taller than Lily and she was round and plump with wrinkles sitting at the corners of her eyes.

Her dark eyes stared up at me, her mouth falling open on a soft gasp. "It's you."

I frowned. "Excuse me?"

"God, you look so much like him," she continued. "All this time. Finally, after all this time." Her eyes shone, a tear falling down her cheek. Before I knew what was happening, she threw her arms around my middle.

"Uh…" I stiffened. "I'm sorry but…who are you?"

"Oh." The woman released me, taking a step back. "Forgive me." She wiped her cheeks. "It's been so long. I just…"

"Lucas?" Lily came up beside me. "Everything okay? I put Ettie in her bassinet. Oh…hi."

"Ettie," the woman whispered. "You have a daughter? I have a granddaughter."

Alarms started going off in my head. My stomach dropped. "What the fuck did you just say?"

The woman flinched, shaking her head. "I'm sorry. I…God, this is so hard. I've spent years looking for you. Thirty…" She frowned. "More than thirty years…"

"Lucas," Lily whispered.

I grabbed her hand, holding it tight in mine for fear that I would start freaking out. A ball was about to drop. I knew it. I could feel it. This woman. Something about her was familiar.

"Lucas," the woman said, chewing her bottom lip. "I'm…I'm your mother."

"Where are my parents?"

Bobby sneered. "They never wanted you. Why do you think you're here?"

My eyes burned. I had never thought about my parents before. Especially since I was told they were dead but that part of me, that tiny part, held onto the hope that they were looking for me.

"I..." My chest tightened. I took a step back. "You're dead. You're supposed to be dead." That was what Bobby and Carole told me. I believed them. God, I believed them.

Lily stepped in front of me, keeping her hand in mine. "You need to explain before I kick you out on your ass for upsetting my husband."

"I..." The woman took a deep breath. "I had you when I was young. Just a girl. I was barely fifteen. Your father left me after that. He ended up in jail and died a few years into his sentence. I was a drug addict. Addicted to everything. I didn't have a chance of keeping you. But I wanted you. God, did I want you. Once I became clean, I searched for you, but because you were adopted, your records were sealed shut and your last name was changed. I couldn't find you. I'm so sorry. I'm sorry." Tears rolled freely down her cheeks.

"Did you want to come in?" Lily asked, her voice thick.

The woman nodded.

"Okay." Lily released my hand, leading the way into the living room with the woman following behind her. All of the air was sucked from my lungs the farther Lily got away from me.

I closed the door, locking it up tight and leaning against it. This couldn't be happening. After all of these years. After more than thirty fucking years. And now she showed up?

"Excuse me for a moment," Lily told her. She came back down the hall toward me. "I don't know what's going on right now but whatever it is, I'm here. Alright? Don't close up on me again. After all we've been through. After all of the work you've put in. After—"

In a quick move, I wrapped my arms around her and pulled her against me.

She sighed, returning my embrace. "We'll figure this shit out, Lucas. We will."

I released her, grabbing hold of her hand.

Lily brought it up to her mouth, kissing my scarred knuckles. "Ready?"

No. I swallowed hard but nodded anyway.

She turned, keeping her hand locked in mine and led me to the couch. She sat, pulling me down beside her. "You need to explain."

The woman nodded. "My name is Lucy Crane," she said softly.

My heart jumped.

"I named you after me because you were the best thing I ever did. Even though I was so damn young. You were the best part of my broken life. I was just a kid. I know that's no excuse. God, I know that. But it's the truth."

"How did you find me?" I asked, my voice rough like I had gargled with shards of glass.

"I saw your face in the paper. You were standing in front of your business. It was the tenth anniversary of your shop. It was highlighting the fact that you cover scars and burns for people."

"I thought I got rid of that picture," I mumbled. I hated being the center of attention even though Shephard had insisted the picture be taken. Recognition was not the reason behind why I did what I did.

"That's where I remember you from," Lily blurted. "I knew you looked familiar when I first met you, but it slipped my mind as to where I'd seen you before."

"But why now?" I turned back to the woman, the stranger, the one person I had begged for ever since I was a damn kid. "If you saw my face in the paper, you could have shown up sooner. My information was listed with that picture. I don't understand why you waited so long." I had no intention of being rude but none of this made sense.

"I tried." Lucy, fucking hell, wrung her hands in her lap. "I've been trying to get clean, so I could come see you."

"How long ago did you see that picture?" I asked, not sure how I felt about us having something in common.

"A few years ago," she murmured. "After I saw it, I made a vow to get clean."

"How long?" I stood from the couch and began pacing.

"Ever since I saw your picture. So…five years."

"Five years." I blew out a slow breath. "You saw my picture five years ago and you're only just showing up now? What do you want? Is it money?"

"What?" Lucy's eyes widened. "No. Not at all."

"Then why the fuck are you here?" I shouted.

Ettie started crying.

"Shit." I rubbed the back of my neck.

"I got it." Lily rushed off to our bedroom to take care of our daughter while I stared down the woman who let me go.

"I know you're mad," Lucy said softly.

"No." I shook my head. "I'm not mad. I'm far past being mad."

"I didn't come here expecting us to be one big happy family. I came here to let you know that I found you. I don't expect a relationship with you. I just wanted you to know that…I'm here."

"You should have stayed away. It was better before you showed up because right now, I'm confused. The fact that my mother is sitting across from me after all of these years is fucking with my head. I spent my childhood, begging, praying for you to come find me and take me away from the hell I was placed in. But you never came. The things I went through…" Bile rose to my throat, my stomach churning. Matteo was going to have a field day with this information at our next appointment.

"You had it hard," Lucy said.

I laughed. "Lady, you have no fucking idea."

She nodded. "I'm sorry. I know it doesn't help but it's true. I see that you're happy though. Whatever it was you went through, you survived it." She stood from the couch.

"I just wanted you," I blurted. "Even though I was told you died, I still prayed for you to come find me. For you to come save me." My voice cracked. I suddenly felt like a little boy.

"I know." She came toward me. "I'm sorry, Lucas." Once she stood right in front of me, she placed her hand tentatively on my chest right above my heart. "You look like him."

"Is that good or bad?" I mumbled.

She gave me a soft smile. "That's good. I loved him. Even though I was young, I still loved him. But he was older, your typical bad boy, and he made some stupid decisions which cost him his life."

"I'm sorry," I murmured.

"Don't be." Lucy stared up at me, her dark-colored eyes bright and shining with unshed tears. "I'm sorry for everything you went through. I'm sorry I wasn't there to protect you like I should have. I'm sorry for not being the mother you deserve. I- I'm…" Her breath hitched.

"I…" I swallowed hard, covering her hand that was still on my chest. "I've spent my whole life missing something. And then my wife, Lily, showed up and that was when I realized it was her, I had been missing."

"I'm glad. I'm really glad." Lucy wiped under her eye.

"But I…" I didn't know this woman. Hell, I didn't even trust her. But… "Do you have proof?"

"That you're mine?" Lucy chewed her bottom lip. She pulled two pictures out of the pocket of her jeans. "I've aged quite a bit. But I was able to sneak in a picture before you were taken from me. And this…" She handed me the other picture. "Was your father."

I took the images from her and glanced down at them. The picture of the man staring up at me was like I was looking in the mirror. Although he didn't have as many tattoos as I did, his eyes mirrored my own. But was this proof enough? The second image was of Lucy as a girl, sitting in a hospital bed, staring down at a baby in her arms. The baby looked like Ettie. My daughter. My breath caught.

"I know it's not enough proof. We can get a DNA test. Whatever you need." Lucy placed her hand on my arm. "I just wanted you to know that I'm here. I know it's over thirty years later, but I promise, I'm here. Even if you want nothing to do with me, I'll always be here."

I looked between her, the pictures, and back to her.

The hairs on the back of my neck tingled. I glanced up, finding Lily standing at the entrance to the hall leading to our bedroom. She was wiping under her eyes, smiling softly at me. She nodded gently.

That was all the encouragement I needed.

I pulled Lucy closer, much to her surprise, and wrapped my arms around her.

She gasped, a sob breaking free.

My eyes burned, my throat working hard over the lump lodged in it.

"Lucas," she whispered.

But I didn't answer. I couldn't. My mother was now in my arms. I didn't need a DNA test. I didn't need any further explanations. I needed my mother. My mom.

"I'm so sorry, my sweet boy," she said, her voice muffled by my shirt. "I'm sorry for everything."

I held her against me, not knowing what to say.

"I don't expect you to forgive me." Lucy stepped out of my embrace. "I don't expect that at all."

"Would you like to stay for a coffee?" I asked, my voice thick.

Her eyes welled. "I would love to."

"Lucas?" Lily came up to me when Lucy moved to the couch.

I cupped Lily's face, bending down for a kiss.

"You good?" she asked against my mouth.

"I don't know," I told her. "But I know she's not lying. I don't know how I know that, but I just do. Can I forget?" I glanced at Lucy who was staring our way. "No, but I am willing to forgive. Maybe not now. Maybe not tomorrow. But some day."

"Thank you," she said softly.

"No." I wrapped an arm around Lily's shoulders. "Thank my wife." Because of Lily, I was able to open up my heart and break down the walls surrounding it. It would take time. I knew it would. But I would give Lucy, my mom, a chance. Even if it was more than thirty years later.

Lily sat on the couch beside Lucy. They talked quietly amongst themselves while I excused myself to make all of us coffee.

When I reached the kitchen, a breath left me. A weight I didn't know was there, lifted free from my shoulders.

I always craved having a family. A mom. A dad. A wife. A child.

My mother.

My mom.

She was here. She was sitting in my home.

I never had a family before.

Now, I had a wife. I had a daughter. And I also had a mom.

Although Lily and I were still battling the demons of our past, together, we were strong enough to face them. We were strong enough to heal. To love. To be happy.

And to conquer.

# About

J.M. Walker is an Amazon bestselling author who also hit USA Today with Wanted: An Outlaw Anthology. She loves all things books, pigs and
lip gloss. She is happily married to the man who inspires all of her Heroes and continues to make her weak in the knees every single day.

"Above all, be the HEROINE of your own life..." ~ Nora Ephron

Stalk Me!

https://linktr.ee/authorjmwalker